H. Leighton Dickson

DRAGON

OF

SAND & STORM

The Autobiography of a Goddess

A *Dragons of Solunas* Novel

H. Leighton Dickson

For Luna.
May you fly.
May you soar.

CONTENTS

ACKNOWLEDGMENTS

Once again, all thanks to my writing peeps,
the Laughing Foxes, for keeping each other
sane during these last years.
Or at least, for sharing in the
madness.

All thanks for my crazy family, for the same reasons.
Your patience is as deep and wide as
the sands of Gifah.

And finally, for you, dear reader. If not for you, I
would have given up long ago.

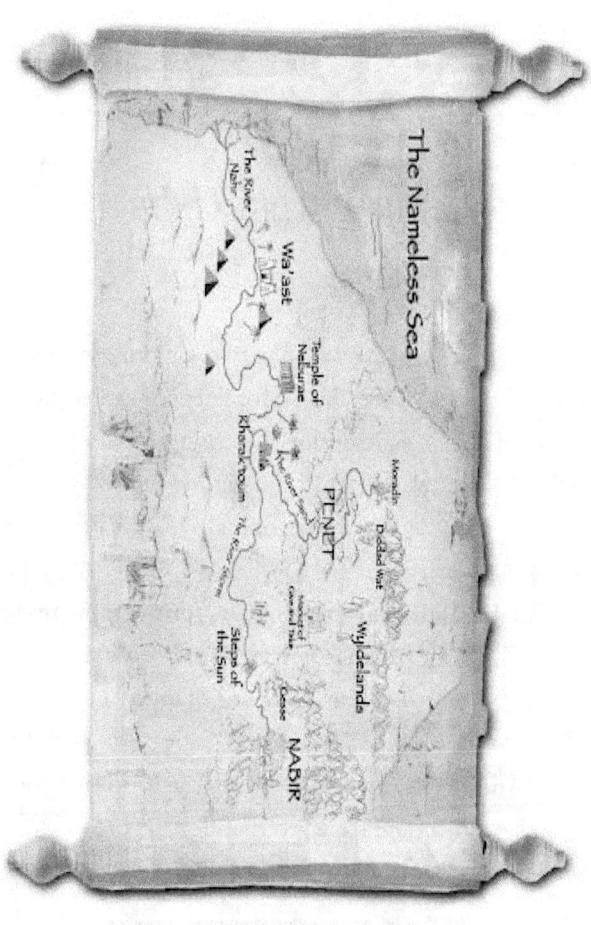

The Nameless Sea

The River Nabir

Wa'ast

Temple of Nekurae

Kharak'room

PENET

Mooralin

Dodkad Wat

Wyldelands

Steps of the Sun

NABIR

GIFAH

1

SAND

*"The Sand and the Storm made the Mighty River Nahr,
And the Mighty River Nahr made me."*

That is a saying taught to the Reed people when they are young, but I think it works for dragons as well. For creatures of the sky, it is surprising how much of our lives are spent in the water. But perhaps more significantly, how much of our blood is spilled in the sand.

I suppose this makes sense. We are forged on a Wheel of Elements – of sand, water, sun, and need. We are also created to thirst for fire, as this is our heritage and our birthright, given us by the great god Rath'nahr. The skies are our reward, our respite and refuge, for all the other elements have teeth. If we survive them, we are milled to shine like gold.

I am Anekh Sun, daughter of Selis Anekh, dragon goddess of the sun. I was not born with this name, however, and it was because of the Wheel that I became her. Proud, strong, fierce, and good, Protectress of the House of Bey, symbol of the Ophar and the sun-rich land of Gifah. This Wheel of sand and sky began to forge me even before I was born, when my world was confined to the walls of a shell, and the golden scales that shaped my destiny.

All was gold then, liquid gold that flowed past my eyes and lapped my lids with the rhythm of my heart. Molten gold forming wing and tail, shaping claw and scale. Coiled and curled and occasionally turned, my world was bound in a leathery shell, where I slept and grew and dreamed. Sometimes, my dreams turned to those of fire, but those dreams were fleeting. For the most part, I was content to drift and dream, certain this world was big enough for me until one day, I heard something outside the shell.

I had never heard anything before, and this sound woke me from my golden dreams into a new and urgent world of need. I remember flexing my spines and stretching my neck, but I was blocked by the smooth, strong wall of the shell. In darkness, I gnawed at the shell's lining with tiny front teeth. I scratched at it with needle-like claws. The lining sheered away but the leather was not moved. I listened again for the sound, but there was only silence. I wondered if I had imagined it, for dragons are creatures of reckless imagination, and I felt the urge to drift back to dreams when I heard it again. I nudged the shell with the pick of my beak. It caught and tore and, to my utter surprise, my nose pushed through.

For the very first time, air filled my nostrils and I lay still for several long moments. I had never thought about breathing. But now, I filled my chest, marveling in the sensation of ribs moving in and out, in and out. I raised my wing, pushed a claw through the hole, and forced my beak further. The shell split apart then, and my cheeks slid out between the leather into a wall of dark sand. The sound trilled again. I pushed with my back legs, reached with my front and slowly, weakly, I dragged myself out. The leather slid across my fledgling body and with each scrape of my tiny claws, the sand crumbled beneath. I tunnelled up, claw over claw, digging towards the warmth. I was dimly aware of other shells breaking beneath me, but I was focused on the scrape and the sound and the sand.

Scrape, sound, sand. My entire world then was the scrape, the sound, and the sand. In the Wheel of the Elements, sand was my first spoke. I recall blinking for the first time, grateful for double lids that swept grit from my eyes. This breathing was difficult too, as the soil pressed upon me, spilling down with each swipe of my wings.

Beneath me, I could feel the struggles as other shells cracked, and other hatchlings began this same climb. They pushed upwards but caused the sand to crumble and shift. More than once, I tumbled back down to begin again. And so, I called out, a warble of pathos and tiny dragon beauty, and waited for the sound to return.

Suddenly, the world above me thundered as great claws dug into the earth. They sheared huge amounts away with each swipe, and my eyes were blinded as light beamed down in a hazy wave. I blinked again and again only to see a vast set of teeth bearing down to meet me.

Before I knew it, I was swept up in a mouthful of sand, pressed between a ridged roof and a tongue. A blast of hot breath forced silt out between the teeth, and I realized that there were four others, wriggling, chirping, and struggling beside me. Then, our great cage began to move, up and down, side to side. I peered between the fangs, seeing a plateau of gold sand and blue sky, and a ribbon of green weaving through the dunes. My first smell of water was a sweet contrast to hot breath, and my chest thudded like a tiny drum at the sight of the river that would draw the line of my life in the sand. The glorious, relentless, mercurial River Nahr.

The banks of the river were lined with palms and when we stopped, the teeth leaned down to spit us into a sandy hollow. Our five shapes tumbled together, all legs and tails and dewy-wet wings, and I fought my way out from the jumble of them. I needed to see. I needed to know. For months, my world had been dreams and gold. Now, there was sun, there was sand, there was water, and there was the great trilling teeth that I later called my mother.

She was a small drakina, green and young, and I watched with wonder as she swung her fine head, plucking rushes from the riverbank and placing them carefully over us to block the sun. The rushes slid and she rearranged them clumsily but with great patience. I remember how it was something that she had to repeat many times a day, and I wondered if she was inexperienced in the ways of nesting. It was not a good place for a nest, I would later learn, for it was exposed to both predators and the elements. Perhaps we were her first clutch. Perhaps, there were no better options here along the banks of the Nahr. Still, it was home for the first few weeks of this new and wondrous life, and I would not have been who I am today without it.

I shared the nest with four other hatchlings – two silvers, a green, and a blue. I was the only drakina, and I fought hard to get my share of the fish that my mother would regurgitate from her morning forays down the river. She would open her great mouth and we would madly scramble over each other for bits of flesh and scale. For the first weeks, we stayed deep in the nest, growing in strength and size. My brothers were restless, constantly snapping and biting at each other in mock battles. All except the green. The green was never a strong hatchling. I wasn't surprised when he didn't stir one morning, didn't mourn when our mother removed his dry body from the nest. I think she ate him. The sands of Gifah are harsh and the Wheel is relentless. Best he be gone early than endure a life of hardship caught under the spokes.

A similar fate met my blue brother. One day, I was watching the Sons of Sobeth hunt for wraiths and wyrms in the reeds. Called sobethi, the Sons of Sobeth are very much like dragons, but they have no wings, and they make their home in the waters of the Nahr. It was both exhilarating and frightening to watch them in the rushes, their neck spines flat, only their eyes visible from the surface. Their patience was limitless, their speed deceiving. Many a wyrm disappeared in a splash of tooth and jaw.

So, my brother. As I've said, the young drakes were restless and playful, and they bullied me incessantly with nips and scratches and 'accidental' bumps. One day, I was watching sobethi on the banks of the Nahr when the whirlwind of silver and blue rolled my way. But this time, I was ready. As the blue bumbled into me, I swung my head and spat a wad of acid that caught him in one eye. He lurched backwards, wings flapping, and he tumbled down the high bank, tip over tail, through the reeds to splash into the dark rushing flow of the river.

I flattened into the sand and peered over the edge, expecting the worst. To my surprise, he bobbed up, shaking his small head, and spitting water from his nostrils. He cocked his beak one way, then the other. Soon, he settled onto the waves and floated, wings folded across his back. His tail swayed smoothly behind, making the same wavy patterns in the surface of the water the way our tails do in the sand. He did not see the eyes moving towards him. He did not heed my chirps of warning. The river splashed once and he was gone, crushed by the Wheel in the jaws of Sobeth and leaving a trail of bubbles in his wake.

The silvers gave me a wide berth after that.

That left my two brothers and me. We were growing and hungry, so our days were spent foraging for food. We chased sandwyrms along the palm roots and flushed pic-beetles out of the scrub. We dug for and found scorpioch eggs, delighting in the sting as they went down our throats. But we needed more, so our mother spent less time at the nest, and more time away in search of food. Each night, she would return, cover us with her wing and raise her dragon voice to sing to the stars. It was plaintive and lonely and oh, so beautiful, and we would join her, warbling in fledgling harmony. Her heartbeat was the drum of my early life.

During the hot afternoons, we'd stay down in the sand, and ventured out only in the cool of morning or evening. I enjoyed perching at the edge the riverbank, waving my thin wings in the river breeze, and dreaming of the day they would carry me on the winds like my mother. Sometimes the silvers would join me, other times I was alone. I didn't mind either way. The river was hypnotic and the smells from it filled my nights with dreams. I imagined what it would be like to catch a fish in my talons, to bite down and feel it squish between my teeth. Dragons are many things, but hunters first. It is said we were made by the god Rath'nahr to pull his skyboat, the Sun, but our bodies were created to slay, not pull. I understood that even at this age. While a dragon may be worshipped, she may never be truly tamed.

And ah, the river. The river, the mighty Nahr. Giver of life and broker of dreams. I have spanned its fearsome length, from delta mouth to mountain source, from Penet in the north to Nabir in the east. I have fished in its waters; I have hunted its banks. I have loved and I have lost in the spokes of this river, the Sand and the Storm. I have watched the river people as they warred with each other, their towns turning to ash under a rain of fire, their homes swept downstream to feed Aketh, Sobeth and Haffih, dragon gods of floods, death, and water. And yet, I have seen these same towns rebuilt, for the reed people are as resilient as the rushes that grow along the water's edge.

I remember the first time I saw the reed people. It was early evening, and the sun was almost finished her daily flight across the heavens, painting the sky a shimmering gold. At first, there was simply a dark shape on the Nahr, and I wondered if it was a very large sobethi, weaving its way through the waters. But as it came closer, I realized it was not a sobethi at all, but rather, a nest made of woven rushes that hung together far better than our nest ever did. A single white wing captured the breeze and I saw creatures dipping poles into and out of the water. Instinctively, I tucked myself into the sand.

To me, they looked like river reeds. Lean, and graceful, moving about on reedy legs and passing things to and fro with reedy arms. Their noises carried over the water too – barks and mumbles and laughs, not the chirps and trills of dragons. I breathed their scent as they passed – smoke and oil and hemp and salt. Pressed into the sand, I watched the nest-boat sail past, fascinated at the thought that this world held far more than what I had known. It was then that my brothers decided to join me on the bank, tumbling and wrestling and setting the great Wheel of our destiny into motion.

Because the reed creatures on the nest-boat saw us.

I had been good, tucked into the sand and hidden with all my gold. I was always good, but my brothers, with their squabbles and flashing silver, were never good. This time, they were unmistakable. The reed creatures pointed and shouted, and my chest threatened to burst with fear. For their part, my brothers froze at the sight, eyes fixed on the nest-boat, and I was terrified that our lives would end, there and then. But the boat continued its slow journey downriver, soon becoming a speck in the glimmering surface of the Nahr.

Believe me, my dreams were vivid that night.

I never saw the nest-boat the next day, nor the day after that, and I'm certain it would have become little more than a memory had not the Wheel sent us another challenge by way of our mother.

She had found a new hunting ground and began to bring back strange new kills, ones with flaxen pelts and tender meat. They smelled very much of the reed creatures, and some of them had bells tied around their thin necks. I didn't think much of it then. We were hungry and growing and innocent. We played with the bells for days until they sank deep in the drifting sand, and then, she'd bring us another.

One evening, as I perched on the riverbank, waving my wings, and watching the wyrms hunt pic-beetles among the reeds, a shadow crossed the sun above me. I glanced up to see my mother, spinning in wild circles above the dunes. She had a flaxen carcass in her talons, and the smell of it wafted down, mixing with the tang of blood and reed creatures. She was dragging one wing as she descended, and I scrambled towards the nest, diving in on top of my brothers just as she landed, shattering the roof with her neck, and sending the sticks raining down on us.

After a long moment, I peered up, expecting to see the green leather of her wing stretched out across us. It wasn't, but I stayed. She had not called us up, and I always listened for her. I obeyed. I was good.

It has taken me a lifetime to learn a very different lesson.

Regardless, my brothers scrambled over me to the surface, eager to see what she had brought home. Slowly, I followed, my claws sinking into the sand, unwilling to rise above it. I peered over the ridge to see my brothers tugging at the new carcass, tearing at its flanks, and gnawing at its spindly legs. Again, there was a cord around its neck with a bell attached. I knew this creature had belonged to the reed people and I knew that my mother had fallen upon the Wheel for hunting it.

I crawled over to her. She lay, eyes glazed, jaws parted, blood collecting in the hollows of her teeth. Strange sticks protruded from her neck and belly and flank. I bit into one, feeling the wood splinter beneath my teeth. Her breath rattled so I released it, smacking my beak at the taste on my tongue. As my brothers gorged themselves, I curled up under her jaw, feeling her pulse drum weakly along my spine. At some point, my brothers crawled back into the nest, but I stayed, sharing my feeble warmth as the golden sun fled the skies, pursued into the horizon by her suitors, the moons.

I had never seen the night sky before then. It was cold and vast and dark and bright at the same time.

Creatures called to each other across the dunes. Scorpiochs scurried and sand beetles dug. The waves of the river laughed softly against the rushes. The brother moons danced overhead, one wide, the other a sliver. They looked like eyes watching me from above and I wondered if they were the eyes of Rath'nahr or some other god. At some point, I slept, waking only when the sky spun gold from the stars.

My mother did not see it. Her eyes were covered with sand.

I lowered my head across my wings, a strange ache tightening my throat. I didn't know what came next. I didn't know anything at all.

When my brothers awoke, they scrambled out, biting and chittering as usual. They returned to the carcass, ate their fill for the morning and tugged at the thread that bound the bell. Finally, one silver lumbered towards me, nudging at our mother with his sharp, shiny beak. Nothing. The second joined us and trilled at her. Nothing. He folded his silver wings and sat on his haunches, head cocked first one way, then the other. He trilled again. It was a plaintive sound picked up by the first, and together, they repeated it over and over again, warbling up and down in dissonant harmonies. It was heartbreaking and sad, and I was moved to join them. Soon, our juvenile voices echoed down the Nahr in fledgling dragonsong. Our mother had been young and alone, and the Wheel was relentless and cruel. We wove a story for her that still echoes in the Great Halls of the Sky.

Day became night, night became day, and despair became detachment as the Wheel began to turn us to sand. At some point, the reed people came in their nest-boat from the Nahr, trudging up the banks and through the palms to find us. I remember the squeals of my brothers as they were gathered up and shoved into baskets. I remember hands around my own neck, prying me from my mother's body even as my claws strained to stay. I remember a chain clasped around my leg, and a bolt of twine binding my wings so I could not move. And the last thing I remember, before my own basket swallowed the sky, was the sight of my mother buried by sand, and the spokes of the Wheel on my back.

2

THE HOUSE OF SEB

I was told the Great God Rath'nahr created the reed people while sitting one day on the banks of the river Nahr. The other gods had abandoned him, and he was lonely, so he wept, and his tears spilled onto the rushes. From them, the first men formed, stepping out of the waters and vowing to serve him forever. I believed it. They looked like the dried reeds that my mother would use to build our roof – thin and tanned, with nobs and branches, limbs and ribs. But I suppose they are like fresh reeds as well. They are strong, lean, easily bent but impossible to break. There are as many of them as grains of sand in the desert. If you pull one out, others take its place. Still, the Wheel rolls over them as well as dragons, and I ache almost as much for them as my own kind. Even now, I will protect them with my life.

I spent several days on the nest-boat in a basket made of reeds, captive of a people made from the tears of a god. Several times, they opened the lid to drop in pieces of fish, but I was beyond hunger and thirst. I was a dragon, born in sand and forged by need, and I needed my mother more than fish. I could hear my brothers in baskets nearby, had no doubt that they devoured the morsels dropped to them. I wasn't resentful. It was their way to eat and wrestle and live, taking what the Wheel would give them and when. It's all that can be expected of a dragon, really. Our spirit rises and sets like the sun in the sky, or like the brother moons who pursue her.

Finally, the nest-boat came to rest, and the basket was lifted from its perch. I felt my stomach lurch as it swayed, pieces of rotting fish sticking to the sides like scales. I could hear the barking of voices and the crunch of feet on wood, then sand, then stone. The world grew still, the lid was removed, and a hand reached in for me.

I snapped my teeth but once again, the hand grasped my neck and pulled me, twisting and spitting, from the basket. My wings were still bound and I'm sure I looked like a wyrm, thin and pathetic like they are.

This man was lean. His hips were draped in rough linen and a collar of gold circled his throat. He pulled me close and slipped his fingers into my mouth to pry the gums from my back teeth. It was awkward, and I wrapped my tail around his arm for balance.

"You have removed none of her scales for seket?"

"None, Master Seb. We know her value."

"Any sign of sythstone?"

"None, Master Seb. We checked the dead drakina too. No sign."

"Good. You couldn't pay me to take her if that were the case."

I gagged at his fingers, bit him again. My teeth did nothing. I was pathetic, a wyrm.

"Do you know why, Kida?" the man asked.

Another reed person stepped into view. Smaller, thinner, with a smooth head and large eyes.

"Sythstone creates fire, and fire is the spear of the gods," she said. "Once a dragon has tasted fire, she is dangerous and can never be trusted."

"Once she has tasted fire, she is having you for dinner." He flashed his teeth, then looked back at the first man. "Unbind her. I need to see her wings."

The man released his grip on my neck and moved his hand to my feet, catching them as if he knew how to hold a young dragon, as if he did this every day. The first reed reached forward with a blade and suddenly, my wings were free. I battered and beat, but after so long bound against my back, they were trembling as if newborn. He pulled at them, stretching the leather, and testing the bones. I nipped at his hands again, tightened my tail on his arm.

He bared his teeth once again. I bared mine and hissed.

"Magnificent," he said, and he turned. "Kida, what do you make of the new drakinet."

"She's beautiful, sebbah," she said. "A gift from the goddess."

Her eyes round and very dark, sparkling with life.

"The Ophar will be pleased," he said. "We'll have wine tonight, I think."

He fastened two links of gold chain around my legs and passed me over to the one called Kida. She, too, held me as if experienced, and I snapped her fingers. But then, she did a most unusual thing. She lifted the other hand and laid it on the crest of my head, pressing down with a strong yet gentle touch. I froze mid-chomp as the hand trailed down my neck, smoothing the baby soft spines into place. She repeated this action, pressing and smoothing, pressing and smoothing, and I didn't know what to do. I should have bitten harder, torn the skin, drawn blood, but I didn't know what to think. At some point, the man called Seb turned away, and I softened my teeth, content just to hold the finger of this strange, young river person.

"You are a good omen," said the girl, drawing me close to her face, studying me with those great eyes. "A sign from Selis Anekh of the Sun."

She ran her hand across the ridge of my eyes now and I believe I closed them. I may have trilled. I was young and tired, after all. Her voice was like the lapping of the Nahr.

"Little daughter of Anekh," she continued. "It will go well for our house if the Ophar chooses you."

I released my grip on her finger to look up at her. She smiled and I wished to fall into the dark, soft, sparkling world that was her eyes. It was the first wish I had ever made. Dragons are made of need, not wishes, but this felt like dragonsong, sweet and strong and sad like home.

Seb returned.

"Take her to the drakmet," he said, fixing a length of fine chain to the links at my feet. He clipped them to a band of gold at the girl's wrist. "The harness room has been emptied and filled with straw. Don't let her in with the others. Her scales are too perfect."

"I won't, sebbah."

"And don't feed her. She can't bond with you."

"One piece of wyrm?"

"Water only. We have three days until the ceremony. She's thin but she won't die."

And the tall man was gone, leaving me with the girl, chains of gold on my legs, and an ache in my belly.

"I'm sorry, little daughter of Anekh," said the girl called Kida. "But the Ophar has commissioned a gift for the new courtyard, and if you are chosen, the House of Seb will be restored to glory."

She moved her hand again, and this time, I stretched my chin into it, eager to feel the sensation along my jaw and throat. She ran her hand down my neck, gently picking sticky bits of dried fish and basket from my scales.

"But I'll be with you until the Ophar's son has learned how to raise a dragon," Kida continued. "With him, I think that will take a very long time. Besides, one piece of wyrm can't hurt."

She clutched me to her chest then, and I could hear her heart, strong and sure. It reminded me of my mother, so I tucked my face under her arm and stilled my trembling limbs. She gave me a squeeze and walked out into the sun-soaked streets of Wa'ast, Royal City of the Ophar, Scepter of the Gods and Ruler of the Golden Land of Gifah.

Those next days went by quickly, and I learned about where I was and what was expected. Dragons are quick learners, (I quicker and keener than most) and I revelled in my time in the drakmet, or dragon nursery. It was a low building with mud brick walls, straw floors, and small windows high up. There were other dragons in the drakmet - greens, blues, greys, and browns, but no silvers like my brothers, and certainly no golds. Most were larger than me. I almost forgot how large my mother had been, how she'd carried us in her teeth and rode the breath of the wind. I still ached for her, and in truth, I missed my brothers too.

I learned that Kida was a vaskar, or dragon handler. She had been at Seb's drakmet since she was very young and had worked hard to learn these skills. There were other vaskars in the drakmet, but I never saw them. I wondered if they each had a dragon of their own.

Every morning began with a bath in shakhet milk. I could barely sleep at night because of the joy that was shakhet milk. Kida would roll out of the straw, slip me a piece of wyrm, and carry me to a basin filled to the brim. It was the same temperature as the air, and I would leap from her arms into the deep white where I would splash and float and preen. She would rub the milk across the thin film of my wings, work it into the scales of my neck, and along the length of my whipping tail. I would gladly have spent entire days swimming and diving in glorious white. Besides, I would gulp great mouthfuls until my belly was full, and I had to admit it went down nicely after the wyrm.

I'm certain the sebbah suspected, but he never said.

Then, after the bath, came inspection. I wasn't sure what they were inspecting, but the sebbah and his reeds would spend hours measuring my teeth, my claws, my wingspan. They made sketches with chalk and paprush; they wrote figures on tablets of slate. It was then that I think I learned as much of Kida's people as they learned about me. They were not like dragons. They were not colourful like us, no greens or blues or silvers or golds. Rather, they were many shades of the same hue. Some were tall, others not, some thin, others round. They were smoother than dragons, though, with barely a scale or spine to be found. I wondered if they bathed in shakhet milk too. I wouldn't blame them. It was wonderful.

For three nights, I sat in her arms by the glow of the braziers, as Seb regaled his fellow reeds with stories of Sobeth, A'Toth, and Othorys, Naret and Harathor and, of course, Rath'nahr, the father of them all. According to legend, Rath'nahr crossed the heavens each day in a chariot pulled by Selis Anekh, Dragon of the Sun. Each night, he was pursued by his brother Syth in a skyboat pulled by twins Amok and Khamet, the dragon moons of the world. Seb spoke about the history of Gifah and the Ophar's court, of how dragons turned the tide for the House of Bey so long ago, and how there would always be a Great Gold, or the dynasty would fall to another house. He also talked about the dangers of something called sythstone. Wild dragons would eat it and breathe fire like the wind. It made my teeth ache to hear of dragons eating such a thing, but the heat in my belly told another story entirely. Those nights, my dreams were filled of gods, suns, moons, and fire.

Each night, I slept curled in Kida's arms, safe and warm and sung to sleep by the drumming of her heart. I could hear the other young dragons in another room in the drakmet. I wondered if they had a vaskar to keep them warm, or if they only had each other. I often thought of my brothers and hoped that, wherever they were, they were together, wrestling and bumping and living as only they could.

On the end of the third day, Kida dimmed the oil lamp and lay down on a bed of straw. She pulled me with her, and I stretched out on her chest. She stroked my head and neck, smoothing the baby soft spines and studying me with her great, dark eyes.

"Tomorrow, everything will change," she said. "I wish it wouldn't, but I know it'll be good. You'll do well, my Anekh Sun. You are too perfect for the Ophar to refuse."

I didn't know what she meant, but I loved the sound of her voice. It lulled me to sleep every night, along with the sound of her heart.

"I remember when my *mitra* died, and my *bappa* took me upriver to Wa'ast for the very first time. I was very young, and scared, but he knew the sebbah was a good man and that I'd have a good home here as a vaskar. So, I know it'll be…"

She gathered me into her arms, tucked me under her chin.

"…it will be the same for you. You'll see. You'll have all the wyrm you could ever want, and you'll grow strong and proud and safe…"

She trembled and I lifted my head. Water spilled like little rivers from her eyes, and I dabbed her cheeks with my tongue.

Salt.

"You have a destiny, dear Anekh. One day, you'll be the Great Gold of Gifah. They will worship you because you took a journey upriver like I did. I'm happy here, and I know you'll be happy in the palace, but still, sometimes I miss my *mitra,* and I miss my *ba*, and I know I'll miss you…"

Her voice caught and she hugged me tightly. I let her, not understanding the ways of the reeds, but I took her thumb in my teeth, gently and with great comfort, content to hold her in the way of dragons. I slept soundly that night, but truth be told, I'm not sure she did.

The next morning, my bath was different with scented oils and ikarat petals added to the milk. I was dried with the softest of towels and was taken from the drakmet into the blinding light of midday. The sun burned my tender eyes and scorched my fledgling scales. I was grateful to have Kida carrying me, for I'm convinced I would have curled up in a charred coil if left to myself.

Through my blinks, I could see white walls and towering columns and pillars painted with the most magnificent of patterns. Tall, green palms wavered in the heat. Colourful awnings flapped in the breeze. Reed people rushed past us, talking, laughing, shouting, singing. Finally, we slipped under a high stone lintel into a room that smelled of spice, and coolness fell like the night.

I was immediately surrounded by a dune of people.

They poured fragrant oil on my head, and I closed my eyes, feeling it trickle along the ridges of my skull. I purred as many hands worked it into my skin, smoothed it across the delicate leather of my wings. They dried me with linen cloths and placed several trays of colour around me. One woman reached for my feet, and I snapped at her. Kida caught my beak in her hands.

"No, Anekh," she said. "You must let them. It's for all of us."

And she leaned forward, bringing her forehead to mine, her eyes becoming larger than anything in the world. I fell into them blindly, trusting my young life to her, only glancing briefly as women painted my talons with liquid gold. I cocked my head, now fascinated, as they stroked the colour across each wing claw, swept gold across the long talons of my feet. Kida held my beak, and I did not struggle. I did not even blink as delicate brushes drew lines in liquid kohl around my eyes. They painted my wings with the colours of dragons – blue and green and red and brown. Symbols whisked into my scales with brushes of hair and rush. They slid golden anklets around my thin legs, draped fine chains across my claws. Finally, they held up a collar of hammered gold with jewels of blue, green and red, and fastened it around my throat with a click.

Kida released my beak and they all stood back to admire me.

"Beautiful," said one.

"A gift," said another.

"She'd be worth a palace in seket," said another.

"No," said the first. "She needs each and every scale to be perfect. Seb will have us flogged if even one is missing."

They all murmured at that.

With my painted wings wide, I hissed at them all.

"She has a temper," grinned a third.

"Just like the Ophar's son."

"Or the Ophar's wife."

"She scares me," said the first.

And they laughed.

I've never understood laughter. I suppose it's not something dragons do. It never fails to take me by surprise, and I never know if it is a sound of happiness or fury. Perhaps, it's a bit of both. Reed people are almost as complex as dragons in that regard.

A shadow fell across me, and all the women stepped back as the sebbah passed between them. His eyes were painted too, and he wore a wide golden collar around his neck. I wondered if he were trying to look like a dragon. If so, I have to say he had not succeeded.

He studied me with his painted eyes.

"Well done. Well done," he said. "But she's young and may not be enough. We have stiff competition with the House of Thah."

Kida looked up at him.

"They have two silver drakes," he said.

He caught my painted feet in his hands and held me high to study the designs on my wings, the gold on my claws, the kohl at my eyes. I lashed my tail and bit his thumbs in protest. My teeth were tiny but surely deadly.

He smiled.

"But she's dramatic, I must say. This may increase our odds." He glanced sharply at Kida. "Have you fed her?"

Kida looked down.

"She drinks the milk from her baths every morning."

"But no wyrm?"

"No, sebbah. Only milk."

I would gnaw the flesh from his thumb. It would be bone before he knew.

"Good. She'll be hungry and angry. Selis Anekh of the Sun should be a drakina of heat." He grinned again. "Anekh Sun, Eye of Fire, Wing of Fury. We may stand a chance."

"And if not?"

"Seket. She's young and her scales may be small, but the temple will pay well for a gold and Gifah needs the Weeping. It's late this year."

He turned and two men approached, carrying a golden case on long carven poles. A Wheel was engraved on its lid, and entwined in the Wheel, dragons. They laid it across the table, slid the heavy lid aside with a thud. The sebbah stepped forward.

"Well, little Anekh Sun, it's time for the goddess to choose your path. Temple sacrifice, or life forever in the Ophar's courts."

He folded my wings and lowered me into the case. I
struggled in his grip and bleated a cry for Kida, my
world, my girl that was strong as a dragon, but the lid
slid over me, and the world fell black as a dreamless
night.

3

THE OPHAR'S COURT

It didn't take long for me to realize that there was a spoke of shadow on the Wheel of the Elements, since most of the changes in my life occurred in the dark. The sand pit where I was hatched. The basket of reeds on the nest-boat. This chest of gold. All dark, all confining, all portents of upheaval and change.

I stayed very small in this case of gold as it bumped along, carried by men with poles. We finally came to a stop, and I wondered if they were planning to leave me here to die in the dark, covered in paint and smelling of spice.

Soon, I heard muffled speech and the sound of many voices. Finally, the lid slid off and light spilled into the darkness. I sprang from the case, praying my untried wings would take me up and away from this horrible cage.

My teeth rattled at the yank of a chain and my feet were pulled down, held fast to the wrist of the man known as Seb.

There was silence for a brief moment, then suddenly, the room erupted in cheers.

I flapped and hissed, snapping at Seb's fingers, bleating my most furious bleats. I wanted out, I wanted away. I wanted Kida and my baths and my brothers and my mother and the marvelous, terrible waters of the Nahr. The cheering deafened me and terrified me, and the room blurred as I tried to take it in. We were in a court with high pillars and beams of painted wood. Palm branches waved and oil lamps flickered, and the smell of dragon was very strong. The House of Seb stood in a row behind us, but behind them were more people than I had ever seen, but I was alone among them, and I could understand why the god Rath'nahr wept.

A man stepped forward and the room fell silent once more.

"The riches of Gifah are pleasing to the Ophar," said the man. "And the choice will be difficult. The House of Seb will present our final offering before the majesty of Rath'nahr."

I saw Kida, pleading with her great, round eyes. I would have fallen into those eyes had Seb not spread his arms wide, pulling me out to the side like the balance of a scale.

"You honour us, wise Josiat, esteemed vizier of the court," said Seb, turning. "And to our divine son of the gods, blessings from the House of Seb."

He bowed. I flapped in vain against it. There was a murmur in the crowd.

He straightened and turned in a slow circle, arms outstretched and taking me with him. I saw rows of men with cases of wine and rows of women with chests of jewels. There was furniture and ornaments and vases and silks all around as offerings and gifts. As we spun, I could have sworn I saw the flash of golden dragonscale beyond in the outer courtyard. But it was only a flash, for Seb turned to face the front once more.

"Selis Anekh, Goddess Dragon of the Sun," he said, his voice loud and ringing. "Rises at dawn to serve her celestial master, Rath'nahr. From one horizon to the next, she crosses the heavens, pulling his fiery skyboat and giving light to all the people of Gifah."

He paused, and for some reason, my heart hammered in my chest. In front of us all, a man in white linen sat upon a seat made of gold, next to a woman as painted as I. On their left, stood a young woman; on their right, a young man. Behind them all, a man with hair the colour of the sun.

Seb smiled.

"Today, most honoured Ophar, I present to you Anekh Sun, glorious daughter of Selis Anekh. Like her mother the goddess, she is perfect in every way, and she is a humble gift from the House of Seb to the Most Royal, Most Revered, and Most Divine House of Bey."

The man in white linen rose from his seat.

I hissed at them both, beat my wings against Seb's arm. I bit his thumb, and he flicked my beak and lights popped behind my eyes.

The man stepped forward, the young man and woman flanking him like the moons. The painted woman stayed back, however, watching everything with quick, dark eyes.

"A golden drakina," said the man. "A gift from the goddess, herself."

Like Seb, his lids were thickly lined with the colour of slate. Unlike Seb, his scalp was covered in a tall headdress of green and gold, and he carried a staff of hammered bronze.

"She is Anekh Sun, Eye of Wisdom, Wing of Grace," said Seb. "Raised in our very own drakmet. She will be your very own Winged Sun, elegant and proud, fiery yet bonded fully to the House of Bey."

He bowed slightly once again, and I was forced to bow with him, his fingers tight over my feet and talons. I beat my wings at the offence.

"If the Most Royal Prince Beyat wishes to meet her—"

"What about the Most Royal Princess Shesset?"

Seb straightened, and both he and the man called the Ophar turned. The young woman stepped forward. She was different than Kida, with small eyes instead of large, high cheekbones instead of round, and a wide smiling mouth. To me, she looked polished and sharp, like a spear.

"What if the daughter of the Ophar wishes to meet the daughter of the goddess?"

"Shesset," hissed the painted woman. "Know your place."

"Don't be a fool, Shesset," said the young man. He wore white linen at his hips, a blue sash across his chest, and a wide circlet of gold at his throat. "A dragon is a king's symbol. And you will never be king."

"I'm first born, Beyat, and I can rule if father chooses." She glanced around at the crowd and grinned. Her eyes glinted like steel. "And at least, the people will know my beard is false."

There was laughter from the court of reeds.

"Shesset," said the Ophar. "Don't provoke your brother on the Day of Dedication."

"He wants the throne. I want the dragon."

"The drakina is mine by right," growled Beyat. "As is the throne."

"And you…" The Ophar turned to him. "Don't claim the throne while your father still sits on it."

The young woman grinned. The young man glowered and stepped back. The painted woman laid a hand upon his arm and the sun-headed man leaned in to whisper in his ear.

So much to take in. So much to see. I knew nothing of this world, these people. I wanted my vaskar to take me home.

I looked to Kida, called to her. Her eyes flashed. She shook her head. I called again and Seb yanked the chain at my feet. I snapped again at Seb's wrists, wishing I were a sobethi. I would leave nothing but bubbles and blood. He flicked my beak again, and I sat back, folding my painted wings until the stars stilled their dance behind my eyes.

"Anekh Sun calls for her mother," he said quickly. "The goddess will be honoured if you choose her daughter."

"She is a marvelous gift, husband," said the painted woman, and the Ophar held out his hand. She took it, sliding gracefully to his side.

"You are correct, Nefheru, best of wives and goddess of women." He turned to the crowd. "These are all marvelous gifts! I will be sorely tested to choose."

"The gifts are not done yet, Majesty," said the vizier, and all eyes turned. "The House of Thah wishes to present."

"The House of Thah is late," said Seb. "And therefore, has renounced its right to present."

"The House of Seb denies an offering to our Most Royal Ophar and his Court?"

The crowd moved aside as row of reeds pushed through. Vaskars, from the looks of them. Two men stepped forward.

"May the great god Rath'nahr smile upon the House of Bey by day," said one.

"And may the twin moons of Syth light his dreams by night," said the other.

Two silver cases were brought forward, carried by reeds on long silver poles. Both cases were placed with a single thunk on the smooth marble floor.

"Behold," cried the man, arms wide. "The children of the moons, Amok and Khamet, gifts from the House of Thah!"

The cases were flung open, and two drakes leapt up, streaking like arrows towards the high ceiling. Like me, they snapped down at the end of their chains, and they called to each other in shrill, metallic squeals.

My heart leapt to my throat. I felt the heat boil onto my tongue.

My brothers!

I called to them, struggled with wing and tail and neck and teeth but Seb had my feet firmly clasped in his hand, links of gold chain wrapped tightly around his wrist. Likewise, they sprang towards me but were restrained by the reeds from the House of Thah.

My brothers were alive. They were alive! My chest would surely burst.

The Ophar stepped forward.

"Two silvers and a gold," he said softly, stroking his beard. "The Heavens above us rejoice."

"Both in one season, oh great king," said the vizier. "You have found favour with the gods."

"The House of Bey was born with the favour of the gods," growled Beyat.

"There is a saying in Remus," purred the sun-headed man. "That there must be a Great Gold in the House of Bey, or it will fall."

"That is the saying, yes, Adriam," said the Ophar. He did not look at them, kept his gaze fixed on my brothers. "But we still have Netjeh, and there are so many wonderful gifts."

"Netjeh is almost dead," Beyat hissed. "He hasn't moved in years."

"You know nothing of dragons," said the girl, Shesset.

"Go back to your maps and your beads."

"Husband," said the painted woman, Nefheru. "Son of the gods and light of my eyes, tell the court you accept the golden drakina for your son, and for the House of Bey."

The Ophar looked at her, then at his daughter and then his son. He looked at the vizier and the long row of supplicants with their cases and gifts. Finally, he looked at my brothers then at me, and stepped away from his wife. He raised his staff above the ground, brought it down once, twice, three times.

"Gentle people of the God's Court," he said. "The House of Bey has ruled the Golden Land forever, and our pleasure is your profit. Today, you have made us proud with your offerings. Your generosity has made it impossible to choose which best honours the land of Gifah and the new court of Ruby Whispers. Will it be the jewelled headdress from the House of Seknethut, or the illuminated paprush scroll from the House of Rajet? Will it be the urn of black wine from the growers of Thenes or the cloak of rassa pelt from the Emperor of Remus?"

"It is the honour of Remus, oh Glory of the Gods," said the sun-headed man. Adriam, the Ophar had called him.

The Ophar turned back to the crowds.

"Or will it be a dragon?"

He looked at my brothers, who flapped and hissed. He looked at me. I cocked my head at him, blinked slowly, the kohl weighing down my lids. He smiled.

"It is true that Netjeh is old," he said. "And as dragons age, they turn to stone, then to sand. And a Great Gold must be in the House of Bey, or the House shall surely fall…"

I was tired and the paint on my scales was caking. I turned to nibble a flake of blue. Seb tugged the chain and I snapped at him. The Ophar laughed and raised his hands.

"You have made me proud today, People of the Gods!" he announced. "So today, I will make you all proud. I accept all of your gifts."

There was a murmur from the audience behind me.

"What?" asked Beyat.

"Majesty," said the vizier. "Such a thing has not been done."

"And yet, I have just done it." He stepped forward. "Nefheru, you are my second wife and mother of my son, but you are the ruler of my heart. I gift you the jewelled headdress. Wear it in honour of the House of Seknethut."

She lowered her eyes but did not smile.

He turned to his son.

"Beyat, Son of the Ophar and Spear of Gifah, I gift you the children of the moons, Khamet and Amok. Royal silver drakes for the Second Seed of the Kingdom."

I watched Beyat's hands curl into fists. I knew what it meant. I had claws of my own.

"Majesty," bleated the vizier. "Your son—"

"Is second born, brilliant yet impulsive. He must learn to control himself, much like these young drakes, and perhaps under the guidance of his tutor from Remus, one day he will. Shesset, however…"

He turned to her, and she straightened like a spear.

"She is the Glory of the House of Bey, destined to rule in my stead when Rath'nahr calls me to the Fields of Ever Spring. Clever, strategic, and loyal. Her mother died giving her life, and I dedicated her then to the goddess Neburanna and to Selis Anekh, dragon of the Sun. It is only natural, then, that the daughter of Selis Anekh should be hers."

Her eyes beamed like shafts of light.

"What?" snapped Beyat. "No, I don't accept this."

"It is the word of the Ophar," said the Ophar.

"It's wrong," growled the young man. "To rule is my right."

"No one is ruling yet," said the Ophar.

"Perhaps no one is ruling at all."

He whirled, snatched my brothers from their vaskars and stormed from the Ophar's court, the sun-headed man trotting after him. My heart ached at the sight of my brothers, shrieking and flapping until they disappeared from the court. Still, I called after them, spread my wings and beat the air.

"He is fire," said Nefheru. "Perhaps the moons will soothe him."

"Fire is the root of Gifah," said the Ophar. "It makes us gods."

"The moons call the Nahr," said the girl, Shesset. "And the Nahr gives us life."

"You will be a wise ruler, Daughter of Glory."

"Is the drakina truly mine?"

"As much as Netjeh is mine," he said. "As much as any man may own a dragon."

"Then, may I ask one more thing of the House of Seb?"

He stepped aside, spread wide his hands.

"You are the light of my eyes," he said to her. "Anything you ask, I give."

She smiled and turned to the House of Seb, folded her hands behind her back.

"Master Seb," she said. "I am stubborn and proud like my father, and I like to get my way. But also, like my father, I know that there is much that I do not know, and that will make me a good ruler one day. In light of this, I ask you to add one thing to your generous gift today."

"Anything, Daughter of Glory," said Seb.

"Give me a tribute," she said. "A servant from your worthy House. Bond her to me now and forever, to teach me the ways of dragons."

He gaped at her.

"Surely, the House of Bey has royal vaskars?"

"Surely, we do." She grinned. "But I do not want a royal vaskar. I want her."

And she pointed to Kida. My Kida. My heart. My reed. I unfurled my wings at the sight of her and trilled.

"See?" said Shesset. "The goddess has chosen."

"Husband, no," said Nefheru. "The girl isn't even Gifahn. Why bring a stranger into our house?"

The Ophar turned to Seb.

39

"The girl is clearly not of Gifah," he said. "Did you buy her in Karadoum?"

"No, most glorious son of Rath'nahr," said Seb. "Her father is an honourable man, a trader who brings me fledglings and fish. He bonded her to me to work as vaskar after her mother died."

Seb glanced at my reed, then at the Ophar.

"It was said her mother was Lamoan."

"An ancient people," said Shesset.

"Once," said Nefheru. "Lamos is no more than traders and thieves."

"One day, people may say the same of Gifah," said the Ophar. "I approve this tribute."

Seb nodded and Kida stepped forward, hands folded carefully in front of her. She did not look up.

"Welcome to the Ophar's Court, not-royal vaskar," said the princess.

Kida said nothing as Seb passed me over, and I can say that it was with great joy that I sprang onto her wrist. I snapped at the air once, vindicated, before scooting sideways to fold myself into the crook of her arm. Home.

"She knows you," said the princess.

Kida smiled shyly.

"She likes to be carried."

"Like a baby. What is your name?"

"Kida, princess. It's the Lamoan word for destiny."

"Destiny," said Shesset. "It is destiny, then, that I choose a Lamoan vaskar for my Great Gold. It is a crown and portent. I will unite all the kingdoms of the God's Land, one day."

She turned to the Ophar, bent her knees slightly.

"Thank you, esteemed father of Gifah – and of me – for the drakina and the vaskar."

A reed rushed in from an outer court, dropped to his knees before the Ophar.

"A boat from Thenes," he said. "The Weeping has begun!"

A cry went up from the crowd.

"The gods have smiled on your choice, oh wise Ophar," sang the vizier. "The Nahr rises to bless you and the land of Gifah."

I didn't know what this meant. I was young, and the Wheel rolled on.

Still smiling, the Ophar leaned into his daughter.

"Learn what you can," he said. "And do it quickly. I fear the fire is spreading and Netjeh is too old to catch it."

She nodded and turned her back to the great crowd of reeds. Kida moved to follow, slowing only for a brief moment to glance over her shoulder at the House of Seb. She lingered too long, I thought, and I butted her chin with my beak. She turned back and that was the last I ever saw of Seb and the House that bore his name.

4

THE HOUSE OF BEY

Dragons are not good at counting.

There is one thing, two things, three things and four things. Even five things we can count, but then there is more up to ten. More than ten things become ten and. Ten and two. Ten and ten. Ten and ten and ten, like so. I think for reeds, counting is simple but for dragons, it is esoteric, a puzzle created for confusion. an arcane construct of numbers and the significance of amount. Reeds even count time and put great weight on its passing. Not so, dragons. We are as we are, when we are, whether we be under Selis Anekh, or under the cool, indifferent eyes of the moons. So, I don't how many days it was after I joined the House of Bey before I saved the life of the princess. It wasn't many, to be sure. Maybe ten. Maybe less.

It was the time of the Weeping, when the Nahr rose with floodwaters from the Rivers Sand and Storm. Josiat, the vizier, told stories of the Weeping, how it was the Nahr remembering the tears of Rath'nahr and blessing his people with silt-rich waters for their farms and orchards. I liked Josiat. He didn't know dragons, but he reminded me of Seb and my first days in the drakmet. I'm not sure he approved of Kida, however. She was not a Royal vaskar, and he often questioned her regarding my health, temperament, and training. He also spent much of his time overseeing the siblings' education. The mornings, he spent with Beyat, but Adriam was the prince's primary tutor now, sent as a diplomatic courtesy from a land called Remus across the Nameless Sea. I'm not sure what Beyat learned from either of them, but then again, I spent little time in the prince's company, nor the company of my brothers. That made me sad, and I would remember the times when they would wrestle and bump, and I would snap them away. I regretted those days, now, but with all the distractions of palace life, I found it easy to push such memories out of my mind.

The princess' room was large, bright, and high on a second level of the palace. It was open on one end with a wide, pillared terrace that overlooked the Court of the Great Gold. Near the terrace, I had a clay nest filled with strips of linen and irawat petals. Kida, however, slept on a divan at the foot of the royal bed, so most nights, I slept with her, tucked snug within her arms and dreaming under the drum of her heart. Breakfast was wyrm and fish. Dinner was shakhet lam and sweet cakes, and I drank all the milk I wanted from the pool in which we bathed. I loved that pool. If I'd thought that my small tub of shakhet milk in the drakmet was blissful, I can tell you that it was nothing compared to Shesset's pool. Every morning, it was filled with milk, lily petals, scented oil, and me.

I can't even begin to describe the jewels I wore. A wide collar of hammered gold, encrusted with rubies and lapis, amber and crystal. I was bejewelled with leg bracelets on a fine chain, and rings on the talons of my feet. All the jewels were colours of dragons – red, green, blue and gold. No silver, never silver. I never stopped to wonder why, although in retrospect, I should have.

Most mornings, we trained in the Court of the Painted Palm, a wide stone yard with pillars that held up a colourful roof. The princess was relentlessly curious about dragons and our care, so Kida shared everything she knew. She showed Shesset the proper ways to hold me, how to keep the arm steady when I would perch on a wrist, how to stand razor straight when I would balance on her shoulders and spread wide my wings like a crown. She showed her how to stroke my head and neck, going with the spines and flattening them with the slightest of pressure. And best of all, how to scratch the buds of my horns as they pushed through the scales in their bloodless advance.

I learned many commands in Kida's Lamoan tongue during those days. *Luf* meant catch, and I became proficient at snatching tossed strips of wyrm with one snap of my beak. *Tat* meant bring, and I learned how to retrieve objects and willingly let them go. *Paret* meant perch on the tip of a pole, although why I needed to learn this escapes me to this day. I learned *kevet* – to flex my growing spines in preparation for filing; *koht* – to remain still for the kohl that daily lined my eyes; *psat* – to balance on Shesset's shoulders behind her head, arching my neck and holding my wings wide for hours at a time to maximize their regal effect. I was also taught *teer*, the command to fly, but truth be told, I never flew. My wings were only for show, painted every morning with stories of Rath'nahr, Selis Anekh, and the gods of Gifah. In fact, my wings were so heavy with paint, that the *psat* required all of my energy to keep them extended and still.

The afternoons, however, were spent with Josiat. The princess was clever with numbers and maps, strategies and histories, and she was eager to learn his many lessons. She also learned philosophy, religion, engineering and measures. She debated with Josiat in governance and spent hours learning how to use her voice to bend others to her will. Shesset was skilled in music and dance, in combat and with weapons. In fact, she kept a bow and set of golden arrows above her bed and would sometimes shoot at pots, urns and palms in her room. Her ladies-in-waiting didn't like this, and neither did the servants. She would laugh and pretend it was her brother and riddle the makeshift targets with arrows. I often wondered if she would slay him one day. Blood, it seemed, was both priceless and plentiful in Gifah.

For the most part, however, the lessons were tedious so I would nap, groom my spines, or stare out the balcony for a glimpse of Netjeh, the Ophar's golden drake. He slept beneath the stones in the Court of the Great Gold.

According to Josiat, Netjeh had been with the House of Bey for generations. He was so old that he couldn't move, and the palace builders were constructing his tomb around him. In fact, it was almost finished, and I knew that soon, they'd slide the stones to close him in. Called a per ameht, it was a massive four-sided structure that was wide at the base and narrowed to a point high above the ground. It was made of mud bricks that were larger than men, and they used ropes and pulleys, scaffolds and logs to roll the bricks and slide them in place with dozens of workers. Sometimes, I could see Netjeh's large head inside the per ameht and would study him as the princess poured over her afternoon lessons.

He never opened his eyes. He never twitched a lip. I never saw him move, and if it hadn't been for the fact that his breath was hotter than the sun, I would have thought him a statue like so many others that adorned the palace. The Ophar had been right. Netjeh was slowly, steadily, turning to stone.

I wondered how long he'd been here, how long he'd been sleeping. It wasn't difficult to imagine why he slept, for it would take so much food to keep a drake his size active. Sleep was the only way for him to live, and somehow, I knew he could stay alive like this forever. At some point, his soul would sink beneath the sand and cross the UnderRiver that flowed beneath the world. From there, his spirit would be weighed by the goddess Maeth and he'd fly to the Fields of Ever Spring. According to Josiat, reeds and dragons live with the gods forever in those glorious fields.

I wondered if I might live to be as large as Netjeh, and what it would feel like to sleep the days away as if they were little more than blinks. I also wondered if my mother would have reached this size one day had she not stolen flocks for us. The last memory I had of her was her downed shape and the dunes that worked to consume her. Perhaps the wind would carve a per ameht out of her bones one day. I hoped she'd find good hunting now in the Fields of Ever Spring.

Netjeh was not the only dragon in the Court of the Great Gold, however. Very young dragons flew through all the palace courtyards, squawking and singing and darting through the palms on their brightly coloured wings. Called flutterbys by the ladies of the Court, they would soar above me, entreating me to join them. Part of me wanted to, but they were only flutterbys, not Great Golds. Great Golds were royal dragons and the pride of the great houses. Shesset often said how I would be worshipped one day, so I could not entertain thoughts of play. I certainly never flew. My wings were too perfect, Kida said, my scales worth a thousand dragons. I was carried all over the palace, either in Kida's arms or on Shesset's shoulder, into and out of every room without ever needing to use my wings. In fact, like my early life on the banks of the River Nahr, I would perch on the bannister, feet chained to the posts, and fan my glorious wings in the evening breeze. Down below, reeds would stop and marvel at my beauty. They would wave and call me goddess, and some would bow or toss sweet figs up for me to catch.

My new life was opulent and sweet, and the air smelled of incense, oil and the rising Nahr. But the Wheel never stops rolling, from sand pit to riverbank, drakmet to shakhet pool, so on one of those mornings of this new and wonderous life, everything changed once again, setting my wing on the path of destiny.

The princess' ladies came in, as they did every morning, with her linens and her gold. This time, the Ophar's wife, Nefheru, came with them. I was Shesset's dragon, so I had little contact with the Ophar or his painted wife. But dragons are skilled at smelling strife, and I smelled it in her. She was a quiet woman, but her eyes danced with fire, like an overfilled oil lamp close to tipping. I knew nothing of reeds and their hatchlings, but clearly, she preferred Beyat over Shesset. Despite her plea for me on that first day, I often felt that she would be happier to see my golden scales pinned to a wall alongside the trophies or sold as seket in the healing markets.

So. That morning.

I was playing in the shakhet pool, paddling and diving and snapping up all the irawet petals as they filled and sank. Shesset sat on the edge of the pool while they fussed over the many intricate braids in her hair. When Nefheru entered the room, she brought a scent with her that made me stop my splashing. It was a bone of memory from long ago, so I rose to the surface of the pool and floated there a moment, head cocked, breathing it in.

"I have your dedication dress," said Nefheru. "Your father has commissioned it from the House of Thenet'kan."

"Show me," said Shesset.

She rose from the bath, and her ladies rushed to her with towels of fine cotton. Kida knelt at the edge of the pool, called me over.

The scent was there, skittering around my memory, but the petals and oils were so strong.

"Anekh? Come."

Nefheru waved a hand and the women held up two bolts of fabric, one a milk-white silk shift, and the other netted sheath with gold threads.

"It has been generations since there has been a dedication like this, with dragons like these," said Nefheru.

"Anekh," Kida repeated, and she tapped her fingers on the side of the pool. "Come here."

I ignored her and opened my beak, tasting the air with my tongue.

Shesset held her arms out as a shift was slid over her head. It was the colour of irawat flowers, delicate and ethereal.

Another woman stepped forward with the netting, and golden beads sparkled in the morning light.

Shesset reached out to touch the beads.

"Exquisite beadwork," she said.

"A rare and intricate process, I'm told," said Nefheru.

Shesset frowned.

"These are not beads."

"Scorpioch eggs," said Nefheru.

"What?"

"In amber," said Nefheru. "Completely harmless. As I said, a rare and intricate process."

Scorpioch eggs. I remembered digging for them in the sand of the riverbank, crunching them in my fledgling teeth. I also remembered the barbs and the stinging. I hopped up onto the pool's edge and growled, low in my throat.

"Anekh," said Kida. "No, come here."

The princess turned her head.

"What's wrong with her?"

"That drakina is spoiled," said Nefheru. "That makes her dangerous."

"Like me," said Shesset. "Spoiled and dangerous."

"You should skin her and sell her scales. Seket is a sought-after cure for many ailments."

"She's a Great Gold of Gifah," said Shesset. "Symbol of the Ruling House."

"A Great Gold of Gifah, swimming in a pool of milk?" Nefheru mocked. "She's not your pet."

"And you're not my mother."

"Anekh, come," said Kida.

And they raised the netted shift over the princess' head.

For all their strengths, the reeds have many flaws. Smell is one of them. Hearing is another. Dragon hearing is impeccable, and I heard the sound I'd heard during my days digging in the sand on the banks of the Nahr.

I launched from the edge of the pool, talons extended, virgin wings beating furiously towards the princess. The women shrieked and dropped the netted sheath to the floor. I landed on it, clawing the threads, and snapping at the beads. Kida lunged forward, grabbed my tail, and hauled me backwards. She gathered me tightly in her arms, but I thrashed and flailed and tried to break free.

"I told you!" cried the painted woman. "She's dangerous!"

"Why did she do that?" cried Shesset. "Why?"

"I don't know," said Kida. "She's never done anything like that before!"

This was bad, very bad. I had to get the netting and the scorpioch eggs woven within its threads. I struggled in Kida's grip, hissing and snapping and needing to get to it. Bad. Bad. Bad. It was all I could think.

"I'm telling your father," said Nefheru. "He'll send her to the temple at once. They'll skin her for seket before the moons rise!"

"Princess," said one of the women, and she pointed at the netting. It was moving.

Slowly, Shesset stepped over to it. She peered down before springing away.

"Gods in the heavens," she snapped. "Get it out of here. Now!"

Kida moved forward, hugging me tightly, despite my squirming. I could get it if only she'd let me free.

"They're hatching," she said, and she released me.

I sprang from her arms onto the netting, snapping at the beads woven between the golden threads. Smaller

than my scales, there were tens and tens of tiny
hatchlings, their clear shells rendering them almost
invisible amidst the flashing of the beads. But I could
see them, and I could eat them. They popped against my
teeth, crunching and stinging, but I gobbled them down,
nonetheless.

"Bald Scorpiochs," said Kida. "One sting is fatal."

"I said, get it out of here," growled Shesset.

The ladies moved forward with towels and urns. One
of the women threw a blanket across the netting, and,
gingerly, she bundled it into an urn. One of the tiny
scorpiochs dropped out, ticking as it scurried across the
polished tile. I pounced, catching it under my talon and
tossing it into the air. Proudly, I swallowed it whole.

Shesset narrowed her dagger eyes at the painted
woman.

"You brought this to me."

"It was your father's request," Nefheru said. "A
commission from the House of Thenet'kan."

"A dress made of Bald Scorpioch eggs?"

"I'm sure there was a mistake."

"A dress made of live Bald Scorpioch eggs is a
mistake?"

Nefheru lowered her eyes.

"I was told the beading process is complex," she said.
"The eggs are dipped in liquid amber just before
hatching. Clearly there has been an issue with the setting
of the glass."

"Clearly," said Shesset.

"The House of Thenet'kan will be erased from the royal warrant."

Nefheru glanced at the ladies.

"Scrub this floor and make sure there are no eggs left anywhere. Gifah will not lose her only princess due to a scorpioch sting."

And she looked back at me.

"Regardless, your dragon has dealt with it."

"Yes," said Shesset. "She's saved my life."

"We will need to commission another dress," said Neferhu and she smiled. "By tomorrow, before the Dedication at the Temple of Neburanna."

"Perhaps I will wear one of yours," said Shesset. "Bring me your finest dress."

Nefheru's fire eyes flashed, but she bent at the knees.

"Of course, my princess."

And she turned on her heel and left the room, taking most of the air with her.

"Anekh, come," called Kida, and, this time, I willingly obeyed, my claws tapping as I pranced across the floor. I sprang into her arms and the princess moved to her side.

Scorpioch shells were stuck to my teeth, and I snapped my beak to rid myself of them.

"She *did* save me," Shesset said, and she stroked the baby-soft spines on my head. I purred at the touch. She rarely touched me. But now, she studied me with shining eyes, and I could almost see the Wheel of Elements spinning behind them.

"And she may have just saved Gifah," she said quietly. "This was no market mistake, no beading accident."

"The Goddess has protected you," said Kida. "It's an omen."

"She's the omen," said Shesset.

Shesset stopped stroking so I nipped her, catching her thumb in my tiny teeth. She gasped.

"Don't worry," said Kida, "She does that. She's not biting, just holding."

"Daughter of Selis Anekh," said Shesset. "She will light the path to my destiny."

The ladies in waiting returned to the room. One held up a brush, dripping with blue and red and gold.

"It is time for her wings, princess," she said.

"Her wings can wait."

And I closed my eyes, content to let them pet me a while longer before the paint. I'm grateful I didn't know that it would be the last time for tens and tens and tens of days, that I would be content.

5

THE TEMPLE OF NEBURANNA

The next morning, we joined the Ophar, Nefheru, Josiat, and a large entourage in the Court of the Painted Palm. The prince and his tutor were there too, with my brothers, Amok and Khamet, one perched on each royal shoulder. I trilled at them, eagerly flapped my wings. Their heads snapped in my direction, but they did not trill. They did not flap. Instead, they watched me with unwavering stares. Their beaks were bound so they could not open, and their feet were chained together with silver rings.

Kida reached up to comfort me, but the sight of them in that moment haunts me even to this day.

We were led in procession through many courtyards to the royal embankment on the river. There, a huge nest-boat made of wood, ebony and gold awaited us. It was only my second time on a nest-boat, and I learned that it was called a barge. It had two linen wings that caught the wind and a striped canopy that provided

shade. Twenty reeds rowed against the currents, their
long oars splashing into and out of the river like the
beating of a dragon's heart. We moved through the
waters like Sobeth himself and I saw many of his sons
hiding along the Nahr's high banks. They watched us
with hungry eyes.

Still, I had to admit that I was happy to be back on
the river.

Within hours, we pulled up to a stone embankment,
where we were met by dozens of reeds. I took my place
on the shoulder of the princess, and as a group, we were
ushered beneath the lintel and into a vast inner court. My
heart leapt to see flutterbys swooping between the
pillars. A little blue with gold stripes swept down to me,
twittering as he streaked past. I sang to him, and he
returned, circling and singing until Kida chased him off.
I did steal another glance at my brothers, perched like
epaulets on the shoulders of the young prince. He
walked at a respectful distance behind his parents, but
his eyes were daggers. I suspected Shesset looked much
the same, but, from my vantage point, I couldn't see.

While the Wheel turned dragons to stone, it seemed
to turn reeds into knives.

Soon, the procession ground to a halt and a priest met
us, arms wide.

"Welcome, oh esteemed Thutmen'nahr II, son of the
gods Rath'nahr and Thutmen'nahr I. You are the
Heavenly King, Ophar of the House of Bey, and Glory

of the God's Land of Gifah. Welcome to the Temple of Neburanna, Sister-wife of Rath'nahr and Goddess of Life and Dragons."

He turned.

"Welcome, Nefheru, Beloved wife of the Ophar and ideal of all women. Welcome, Shesset-Isset of House Bey, Light of the Heavens and Daughter of Neburanna, sister-wife of Rath'nahr and lover of the Most High God. Welcome, Beyat-Rath of House Bey, Son of Othorys and Spear of the World. Your presence honours us all."

And he bowed low to the ground, but not long.

"And welcome to you too, Adriam of Bangarden, emissary of Remus and trusted advisor to the House of Bey."

Adriam smiled like a sobethi. Many teeth flashing in the sun.

"I am Tetterhu Toht, High Priest of the Temple of the Veterneht. I welcome you in the name of Neburanna, Goddess of all Dragons."

The priest bowed again.

"Today, on this Day of Dedication, we join with you to celebrate the goddess, Neburanna, in the ways of the gods, with games, food, and sacrifice. Our dragons will delight the Royal Family, even as they honour Neburanna in spirit, in flesh and in blood. But first, permit me to indulge you in a tour of the Divine Drakmet."

A Divine Drakmet! Back at the palace, I delighted to watch the flutterbys from Shesset's terrace – they would dance before me, sweeping and soaring over the Ophar's courts, but I'd never set claw in the Royal Drakmet, so I was unfamiliar with how the little ones were kept. I'd often wondered if it was like Seb's, with low roofs and much straw. Surely, a Divine Drakmet would be more wonderous still.

It was the first of many disappointments. The buildings were very much like Seb's, long and low, with walls of clay and roofs of red tile, small windows, and straw floors. But, unlike Seb's drakmet, there were no common rooms for the young. Instead, they were walled off into tiny pockets, each containing its own dragon. The first building housed dragons as young or younger than I, and the windows were open so they could come and go as they pleased. Through the mesh screens, we could see them sleeping, playing, nibbling on bones from other, larger animals. My little blue and gold friend was there, and he leapt to the screen, running his small beak up and down the mesh. I leaned to greet him, but Shesset flicked my tail with her finger.

"Remember your place, Anekh," said the princess. "They're beneath you."

I resumed to my position. Still, my heart was heavy as the little blue and gold clung to the mesh, trilling as we passed.

We moved on to the second stable that housed dragons between one to two years of age. They were roughly the size of a full-grown reed, wings bound, and noses pierced with rings of hooped gold. But I sat forward when I noticed a very strange thing.

"What is that?" asked Shesset, and she pointed to one of the stalls. "Why are they missing their tails?"

Beyat snorted, but the priest, Tetterhu Toht, turned to address her as he walked.

"Ah, esteemed princess, clearly you are sheltered in the Ophar's Palace," he said. "Chariot dragons have their tails removed for all manner of reasons."

"Have I not asked for the reasons?"

"Forgive me, princess," he said. "Firstly, their tails are long and strong and may become tangled in the wheels or strike the driver unless docked or wrapped. Docking is easier. It usually is done upon hatching, for then it is swift and almost bloodless."

I shrank on her shoulders at the thought.

"Secondly, if for whatever reason, the dragon escapes, without his tail he cannot fly so it's easy to catch him. It is more responsible to avoid such a loss whenever possible."

"Why can't he fly without his tail?"

"He needs it for balance, propulsion and direction. Without it, a dragon merely lumbers about on the ground, and we all know, they are not very able on the ground."

It was true. We are not very able on the ground. We were made for the skies, and my chest ached at the thought of losing a tail in the service of the reeds.

Not all of the tailless dragons slept. A few watched us, their eyes dull and without life. I tried not to look at them as we passed.

"Don't worry, esteemed princess," Toht carried on. "It's much easier to remove the tails when they're young, so healing is complete. That way, they are dependent from an early age."

"But you have flutterbys here," said Shesst. "Why have these little ones not had tails docked upon hatching?"

"Ah, there are many uses for young dragons, princess," said Toht.

Beyat leaned in.

"Wait until you see what they do to the marakt dragons."

"Marakt?" said Kida. "I don't know that word."

"A chariot pulled by two dragons," said Adriam. "Invented for the games in Remus. We call them biagars. They fairly fly across an open field."

"They're unbeatable in a conventional battle unless met with the four-wheeled khasets from Ikasos," said Shesset. "Oh yes, I know what a marakt is. I pay attention to my studies."

She turned to Adriam.

"And no, they were not invented in Remus. I'm surprised you're allowed to teach my brother anything."

Adriam laughed but Beyat growled, but no one said anything when we passed through the marakt stalls. The stench was overpowering and the dragons barely recognizable as such. Not only were they missing their tails, but a wing as well. Some left, others right, but each dragon lived with two legs, one wing, and no tail. Their backs were striped with welts both old and fresh, and without exception, they did not lift their heads as we passed by.

I was grateful to leave that building and cross into the third. Here were the chariots. They were small boats made of gold, leather, and poles, resting on two great wheels of wood. They lined the walls in perfect rows, polished to gleaming in the windowlight. Chariots and harnesses, arrows and whips, armour and helmets and sandals and spears. I knew the Elements drove these dragons hard before the spokes.

Finally, we left the buildings and the wide courtyard to be led outside to a large expanse of barren plain. The Ophar, his wife and children took seats beneath a canopy, and the rest of the party sat on wooden stools in the sand. Boys with shaved heads waved fans to keep the heat from sticking, and girls with shaved heads tended us with water and beer, bread and figs. For my part, I was allowed to leave Shesset's shoulder and snuggle deep into Kida's lap, wishing to forget the sight of the chariot dragons and their lifeless eyes. I wondered about my little blue and gold friend, happily flitting around with no thought of what lay in his future. Perhaps they didn't all end up in the traces. Perhaps some of them kept their wings.

Amok and Khamet were also allowed to leave Beyat's shoulders, but they perched like statues beside him. There was no rest for my brothers, no arms to comfort, no gentle hand on the horns. It was not the last time I wished that they had died like the blue or the green on the banks of the Nahr.

The sun was hot and the conversation dull, and my painted lids were heavy as the afternoon wore on. I must have slept, and my dreams were filled with whips and wheels and a terrifying life without wings.

At some point, the Ophar shouted, and I lifted my head. The chariots had begun to roll and all reeds under the canopy sat forward to watch. I could see the tailless dragons bent forward in the traces, feet braced against the axle, necks strapped to twin shafts that carried along their flanks from chest to box. Wings beat just above the dry track and the wheels churned up dust in their wake. At some point, I realized it was a race, as six chariots thundered forward and fainted back. Whips snapped and wings struck wheels as the dragons flew madly onward. I don't know who won or who lost, but I knew then that these dragons had no better fate than the golden fields of Ever Spring for them when they died.

Another chariot was brought out, but this time, it was the marakt. A pair of drakes pulled the cart, and I could not look away as they swept into view. Two dragons, each less a tail and one wing, lashed together so that they moved as one. They looked like a single dragon with two heads. Up, down, up, down, their wings beat an unnatural rhythm and they surged forward pulling a single chariot with two reeds. One held the reins, the other held a bow with a quiver of arrows strapped to his back. Following them, six reeds dragged a creature that thrashed against the ropes. It was large and lean, with great long horns, neck spines and a skin of brown scales.

"A Knebes Sand buck," said Shesset. "They're a delicacy in my father's kitchen."

I watched, fascinated, as it reared and tossed its magnificent head. Suddenly, the ropes fell away, and it was loosed, bolting from the chariots at breakneck speed.

The Ophar cheered as the marakt tore off in pursuit. Soon, they were little more than puffs of dust on the horizon.

He sat back.

"When I was your age," he said to Beyat. "I hunted with my father. It is one of my most treasured memories of him."

"Too bad I have no such memory," said Beyat. "Perhaps I will make them with my son when I am Ophar."

For my part, I hid deep into Kida's arms once again, wishing for my own bed, my pool of shahket milk, and the familiar Court of the Great Gold. At some point, I heard the cheers and knew the marakt had returned, but I didn't open my eyes. I could imagine them dragging the carcass of the sand buck, could hear them presenting its head to the Ophar as a gift. They roasted it for us that evening and we all dined well, even me. I was not hungry, but I ate the buck that had been slain for us. I knew then that I, like my brothers, had begun the ancient alchemy of turning to stone.

That evening, we attended a service in the temple proper, with worship offered to the goddess Neburanna. Cauldrons of scented oil were lit, palm branches burned, cups of wine offered, prayers sung. Neither the Ophar nor his family participated. They merely watched from golden chairs in the centre of the room. Several priests carried in a brazier of sizzling coals, set it before us with a song of thanksgiving. Toht approached with a priestess, each carrying an iron poker and a roll of paprush. They held up the scrolls to show an imprint burnt onto the page.

Toht turned to the prince.

"Beyat-Rath of House Bey, Son of Thutmen'nahr II, Rath'nahr and Othorys. Spear of the World."

He held up the poker. The end was wider, etched, and clearly the stamp that had burned this mark in the paprush.

"This is your seal," he said.

The painted woman gripped his arm. He said nothing, merely watched with eyes as cold as my brothers.

The priestess moved forward, turned to the princess.

"Shesset-Isset of House Bey, Light of the Heavens and Daughter of Neburanna, sister-wife of Rath'nahr and lover of the Most High God."

She held up the poker.

"This is your seal," she said.

For her part, Shesset sat back and smiled.

Together, the priests plunged the pokers into the brazier. The coals sizzled and spat.

Josiat stepped between them, glanced first at Kida, then at Adriam. I chirruped as Kida gathered me in her arms once again. It was my favourite place in all the world. Nothing bad could ever happen when I was in Kida's arms.

"The God's Land is blessed with favour," said the vizier. "And Neburanna was pleased to send us this most blessed feat. A gold and two silvers at one time, in one family. This has never happened before in all Gifah's history and is truly a sign of miracles to come."

The pokers were drawn slowly out of the brazier. The ends were glowing red.

"Anekh Sun, Amok Moon, Khamet Moon," said the vizier. "We seal you to your house, forever to serve and be served as worship to the Great God Rath'nahr, by the power and will of his sister-wife, Neburanna."

Shesset sat forward.

"Keep her steady," she said to Kida.

"Don't worry," said Kida. "She's a good girl."

As the priestess moved towards me, Kida tucked my head under her arm, squeezed my body firmly into hers. I did not even struggle. Nothing bad could ever happen. Our heartbeats were as one.

"Let it be so," said the Ophar.

Nothing bad.

But the poker.

Heat, heat, heat, heat. There were no other words to describe it as the iron brand was pressed into my thigh. It was pain like none I had ever felt before. I struggled and thrashed but she held me still. The smell of scorching flesh stung my nostrils and my eyes rolled back into my skull. Acid rose from my belly, burning my tongue and scalding my throat. I wanted to die. I wanted to burn. I wanted the fire to race up my body and burst from my mouth as it should for all dragons, and it would be my power and I would be dangerous and beautiful, and no one would ever burn me again.

Relief washed from skull to talons now as Kida held me up, trembling and frail, to show off the brand. The Ophar cheered but I could hear the whimpers of my brothers and the first thing I thought was that they were not yet completely stone. Perhaps there was hope for us all.

Over the thunder of my blood, I came back to my senses, and I was aware of Tetterhu Toht chanting at an altar above a hammered gold basin. In one hand, he held up a narrow blade that gleamed in the oil light. In the other, a sweet, familiar blue and gold shape that trilled and twisted as he hung upside down from his feet.

"May Neburanna accept the sacrifice of her children," the priest droned. "And may the gods be honoured by the lives and deaths of their servants."

A flash of the blade and a spray of red and the trill ended like that.

Just like that.

We made it back to the palace late that night and rather than sleep on the divan with Kida, I chose to sleep in my linen-filled nest by the balcony. It was strange and cold, but I was strange and cold, and the next morning, not even the waters of the pool could clean me.

6

HAND OF THE PAINTED WOMAN

It was hot and there was no breeze, as Kida, Shesset, and I watched the reeds finish Netjeh's tomb. They were at the end, and it was almost impossible to see him now behind the walls of mud brick. I told myself I'd miss him, even though he did nothing. He was a reminder that some dragons could grow old and not die under a hail of arrows, be sacrificed to the gods, or maimed in the name of sport.

"Tomorrow, the last stone will be slid in place," said the princess. "There will be a ceremony to honour him."

"That means Anekh will be the Great Gold," said Kida.

"The Great Gold of the House of Bey. That's important."

Kida looked down at me, ran her fingers along the ridge of my eyes. It felt good to think that maybe I would be one of those dragons that lived.

"Will she be sealed in a tomb like that?"

"One day, yes," said Shesset. "When she is too large to live in the Hall of the Ophar."

I should have been content with our lessons and our luxury, but since the Temple of Neburanna, something had darkened within me. It was big and terrifying, but I told myself I was small and unable, so I did nothing about my privileged life. But sometimes, I would ache for those little dragons flitting about in the skies. Here in the Ophar's palace, there were more than I could count, but sometimes it seemed there were less.

"Although I can't imagine her sleepy like Netjeh," said the princess. "She has a heart of fire, like her mother the sun."

She was right. My dreams had turned to those of fire. Heart of fire, wing of flame. There was a burning in my chest almost constantly. My throat ached, my mouth watered, and even though I could spit acid on the workmen below my terrace, I had never produced even a spark.

Sythstone creates fire, and fire is the spear of the gods, Kida had said. Once a dragon has tasted fire, she is dangerous and can never be trusted.

What was sythstone and how could create it fire? But moreover, would I be dangerous and not to be trusted? After the searing brand while in Kida's arms, nothing was the same as it had been before. My dreams were dark, and so were my thoughts. I wanted to taste the fire that would make me dangerous. Maybe then, no one would sacrifice me to the service of the gods.

Maybe it was good that Netjeh was being sealed. They would value me all the more once he was gone. Then, I would be worshipped.

That night, under the winking gaze of the moons, I awoke.

The palace was sleeping, and I was on the floor beside the divan in the room of the princess. I was too big to sleep in Kida's arms now and far too big for the basket on the balcony. Shesset had arranged for a special pillow that was stuffed with dried irawat flowers and I enjoyed having it all to myself. It was large and it was soft – a fitting nest for my royal dragon bones. I slept like a stone most nights, but that night, there was something. I raised my head and blinked in the darkness.

The room was dark and that was strange. Normally, an oil lamp burned in the centre, but for some reason, it had not been tended and had gone out. I listened again, turning my head to amplify sound in all directions. I would always hear things during night at the palace. The patrols of the guards. The quiet workings of the staff. The distant murmur of the city through the hours of sleep. If I listened close enough, I could even hear Netjeh's breathing, the rumble of ages as he slumbered and dreamed, almost closed up now in his per ameht of stone.

Tonight, nothing, not even the sigh of the moons through the balcony. I breathed in deep, catching the odor of bronze on the breeze.

There, the squeak of a foot on the floor. The creak of a string drawn overtight.

The shape of a man against the moonslight.

I launched from the floor, a flurry of wing and talon and gold-painted scale. The arrow loosed as I struck the intruder, clacking wildly off the high ceiling. He dropped his bow and blindly swung a blade at my belly. Heat and pain spilled from the wound, but I tore at his chest with my talons, snapped at his face with my teeth. A second shape sprang over the balcony, and I barked for my reeds, my cry sharp as a twisted spear.

Kida sprang from the divan, snatching an iron lampstand and swinging it wildly as the second man rushed the royal bed. She fought like a dragon, my Kida, but she was young, and he was not, and his sword snapped like a hungry sobeth.

I needed to protect her! I sprang away from the first man, but he grabbed my leg and yanked me down towards his chest. He was too big for me. He could crush me with the weight of his body. He squeezed the thin bone of my leg, and stars popped behind my eyes. Through waves of pain, I sensed his sword arm raise, and I knew one thrust of the blade would bring a swift end to my path. His hands and weapons were the advantage, but I was a Great Gold of Gifah. I plunged my beak forward, sinking my teeth onto his nose and tearing his face down to his lips. He howled and released me, as a voice cut through the dark.

"Anekh! *Teer*!"

Fly!

An arrow whipped past my head and pinged off the stone of the balcony. I launched upwards, wrapping my tail around the man's throat to pull him taut, and he cried out as a second arrow thudded into his belly. I felt his weight increase and released him to slump to the floor. I flapped my wings madly, praying they would hold, and hovered over the dead man like a hummingbee over paprush.

"Drop your sword, wyrm of Syth," snarled Shesset. She was braced on the bed, golden bow drawn, arrow nocked and aimed at the second man. Kida held the lampstand like a pike, but she bled from many dark ribbons.

The man wheeled and fled, flinging himself over the balcony as a third arrow loosed from the bed. I heard the crunch as his bones hit the stone below. Kida rushed to gather me in her arms and guards poured into the room.

I'm sure none of us slept that night. The thin bone of my leg was broken, and Kida took me down to the stables of the royal vaskars. They bound my leg in paper-soaked linen, and smoothed yellow salve into the slice at my belly. In turn, I tried to clean Kida's wounds, but she refused, not understanding that dragon tongues are cleaner than cloths dipped in foul-smelling tar. I wished the vaskars' hushed conversations could have lulled me to sleep but the palace was alert, the tension like a taut cord. Even my quiet Kida was strained, and I knew that something had changed tonight for all of us.

I just wasn't sure what.

At some point, Kida carried me down to the Ophar's throne room. Many reeds were gathered, and she slipped quietly between the pillars, close enough to hear, but far enough to hide in the shadows. The Ophar's family, Adriam, the vizier, and a flank of golden guards were present. But, I noticed, the painted woman was not.

"The assassins are known to the general," said Josiat.

"They're from the Sedenes quarter," said the general.

"There're always assassins in the Sedenes quarter," said Beyat.

"But look." The general held up a small satchel. "We found these in one assassin's sash."

I peered forward from Kida's arms as he poured the contents into the Ophar's outstretched hand.

"Amber scorpioch beads," he said quietly.

There was footfall, and Nefheru was ushered in by four reeds with spears.

"Husband," she said, and she dropped to her knees. "Glory of the Land of Gifah. This is not as it seems."

"Tell me how it seems," he said.

"We've found more beads in her bed," said one of the reeds.

"Scorpioch eggs," said another. "In amber."

"How does this happen?" asked the Ophar. "When only weeks ago, my daughter was almost killed by scorpioch eggs *not* in amber?"

"She has tried to kill me thrice," Shesset hissed. "So, she can be mother to the next Ophar."

"How dare you?" snapped Beyat.

"I don't know how any of this happened," Nefheru wailed.

She looked from Ophar to vizier and back again.

"I swear on my life, husband. I swear by the Great God Rath'nahr."

The Ophar said nothing, merely sat in his chair, eyes fixed on his wife. Beyat moved to take her hand, lift her to her feet. The kohl ran down her cheeks like rivers.

"I swear…"

"Father," said Beyat. "Tell her you do not believe this thing."

"I believe this thing," said Shesset.

"Enough," said the Ophar, and they all remained silent for a long moment. My leg and belly were aching, and I wished to tuck my head into Kida's arms, but she was as taut as a strung bow. I leaned my chin on her wrist and waited. Finally, the Ophar sighed.

"Nefheru," he said. "After Shesset's mother died, you lifted me from darkness. You were the petal of my heart. I delighted in raising you from concubine to wife, setting the title of prince upon the head of our son. But you have made no attempt to conceal your disdain for the Daughter of Glory."

"No, that's not—"

The Ophar raised his hand.

"But it is true." He leaned forward. "This morning, we close the per ahmet on Netjeh, the Greatest Great Gold in Gifah's long history. When the last stone is slid to close him in to the Ever Dark, you, Petal of my Heart, will join him."

She collapsed once more to the floor.

"No!" snapped Beyat. "I refuse. I am Prince of Gifah and she's my mother. She won't be treated this way."

"She is a lowly concubine once more," said the Ophar, his voice as dull as unpolished stone. "One who has conspired to kill the heir of Gifah. She will accompany Netjeh to the UnderRiver. If she is innocent, her spirit will be weighed, and she will continue the journey to the Fields of Ever Spring. If she is not…"

Nefheru moaned from the floor.

"If she is not, she will be devoured alive by Sobeth and his hungry sons."

"I forbid it!" barked Beyat.

"You forbid it?"

The Ophar pushed to his feet and even the prince stepped back.

"You forbid it?" he seethed. "One word from me and you will join your mother in the per ahmet of a dragon! You and your silver drakes!"

"House of Glory," said Adriam. I had forgotten he was there. "You are both Sons of the Gods and your wisdom is without equal. But your divine passions may have clouded your vision to another, more equitable path."

The two men glared at him. I suppose it was a breach of something, a rule or a code. I didn't know. Like numbers and laughter, the rules of reeds were a mystery.

"Exile her, oh exalted Ophar. Exile her to Remus, my land, my home. There, she will be treated justly but fairly, as befits the mother of a prince, and the wife of a king."

He glanced between them both. Just the men, not the woman.

"She can live out her days in solitude and penance, but she will live."

"You can guarantee this?" asked the Ophar.

"I can," he said. "My father is magistrate of Bangarden. I can even accompany her if it pleases you both, and I will return with his seal of acceptance."

"Father, no," Shesset growled. "Don't do this."

For his part, Beyat said nothing, continued to glare with eyes like daggers. After a long moment, the Ophar returned to his seat.

"This is acceptable to me," he said. "Josiat, prepare a scroll for the magistrate of Bangarden, requesting asylum for the royal wife on account of treason against the River Crowns of Gifah. I will expect detailed reports of her expenses and consent to cover her costs for as long as she lives."

He narrowed his eyes.

"As befits the mother of a prince and the wife of a king."

Adriam nodded, flashed his sobethi smile.

"I'll make arrangements at once."

The Ophar looked to Beyat.

"Remember this, my son. My compassion runs deep but the scales of justice must be balanced. Otherwise, we risk the anger of the gods."

He looked to the general.

"Take the Queen to her suite. Allow her to pack whatever a single chariot can carry. She shall leave before the sun rises, before Rath'nahr sees what has become of his favour."

Silently, Kida slipped behind the pillar and returned to Shesset's room where she fed me fresh fish and sweet cakes. Despite my rewards, a veil of darkness soon fell over the palace. There was still blood on the smooth mosaic floors and splattered across pillar and wall. Shesset spent the night in the company of her father, and I'm certain the bodies of the attackers were taken apart, bone by bone. I knew then that the Wheel turned for reeds as well as dragons. It could crush as quickly as it could raise, and life changed with every turn.

That morning, they slid the last stone in place on the Tomb of the Great Gold, and I never saw Netjeh again. The painted woman, however, was already gone.

7

THE NAHR

"Adriam has returned," said Josiat.

Shesset paused. We were in the Court of Yellow Palms. She was holding a brush and had been painting elegant swirls around my eyes all morning. I could barely keep them open. I could barely lift my wings.

"That's soon," she said. "What? Two months?"

"Yes, princess."

"I hoped he'd stay in Remus."

Josiat grinned.

"The Queen has been set up on an island off the Remoan coast."

"Why should I care?"

She bent back to her work, strands from her long hair sticking to the paint. I never knew if it was real. All the other reeds shaved their heads, perhaps to look like dragons. Sometimes, they left tails and tufts. Sometimes they wore wigs of shiniest black. But I had never seen Shesset without hair. It was a mystery.

"I only say this to tell you that, with Adriam returned, I will not be needed in your brother's education. I can concentrate solely on you, my princess."

"Then, I want to learn about Remus," she said.

"Light of the Sun, you should learn about your own land. The God's Land."

"I know about the God's Land, Josiat. I want to know about our enemies."

"Remus is our ally."

I watched the knife smile cut across her face.

"Yes, of course. That's what I meant. Penet, Nabir, Lamos, and Remus. Our allies." Her eyes gleamed as she turned her attention back to her painting. "Remus is a long-time ally, isn't it?"

"But of course, princess. Why else would they have sent Adriam as counsel? Why else would they accept a traitor queen for exile?"

"Politicians have reasons for all things," she said.

"Of course, you're wise, my princess."

"I've heard strange things about Remus," said Kida. She was sitting next to me, helping me balance under the brush strokes. Her hands were soft and strong. "Is it true they ride dragons?"

"Apparently so," said Josiat. "But I've never seen it."

Ride dragons?

"Well, I believe it," said Kida. "Anekh would let me ride her."

"She's not big enough," Josiat snorted.

"She's young now, yes," said Kida. "But when she's older…"

"You will never ride a Great Gold of Gifah. Know your place."

She lowered her eyes.

"I'll ride her," said Shesset. "I'll be Ophar and I'll ride the daughter of Selis Anekh. My vaskar will train her and I'll ride her, and all the people will marvel at us both. Isn't that right, Anekh Sun?"

I cocked my head and blinked. Ride dragons? It was a wonder to consider.

Josiat shook his head, but he grinned.

"I look forward to seeing that, my princess. It will be a day unlike any other."

And with that, he left our company. Kida smiled and slipped me some candied wyrm. I chewed but it was without taste, for dragons are creatures of reckless imagination and the idea had captured me whole.

Reeds riding dragons. Netjeh was so large he'd never even have noticed a reed on his back. I tried to think of my mother. Memories of her had been fading so that she was little more than a splash of melancholic green, but yes, from what I remembered, she'd be a good size for a reed like Kida. And reeds seemed to know how to harness everything – from the wind to the river, from trees to each other. Chariot dragons were driven with whip and wheel and leather and rein. But one on one, skin to scale?

I closed my eyes under the royal brush, lost in the idea of arcing through the skies with a reed on my back.

With Kida on my back.

My dreaming was interrupted by the cries of young dragons from a rooftop above. I knew their voices immediately.

"Those poor drakes," said Kida.

"Adriam." Shesset scowled. "He's filling Beyat's head with dissatisfaction and rumor."

"Why did the Ophar accept him all those years ago, then?" asked Kida. "If he risked turning the prince against his own country?"

"Nefheru convinced him," said the princess. "She said it was important to have powerful allies."

She snorted.

"Nefheru wanted me dead to make way for Beyat."

"But your father stopped her."

"My father delayed her. He didn't stop her. She's still alive, isn't she?"

Kida stroked my spines, scratched my growing horns.

"I wasn't idle when I spoke of Remus," said Shesset. "They want our riches, our land, and our taxes."

Kida squinted up at the distant roofline, shading her eyes from the sun. The cries were plaintive, and I lashed my tail, called back to them.

"Beyat thinks my father's old and indulgent, and he is certain I will never rule."

Shesset laid the brush down and straightened, cast her eyes across the Court of Yellow Palms. She sighed.

"My father is a good man and a fine diplomat," she said. "But he's a man of peace. He trusts too easily. He believed that Nefheru loved him and that Beyat loves him still and that Rath'nahr would never turn his back on his people."

"Don't you?"

"I believe Rath'nahr wept for a reason when he created us."

I flapped my painted wings at the sound of my brothers' cries. They were loud and shrill, and I could hear terror and need in equal measure. Kida also looked to the high terrace.

"What is he doing to them?"

"Training them for war."

"Are you serious?"

"I am."

"But Gifah's not at war. We haven't been to war in years."

"So why is Beyat preparing for one?" Shesset's knife smile returned. "Let's go ask him."

And she bolted to her feet, leaving her paints and brushes to the cloud of women who trailed her like shadows. Kida held out her wrist. I hopped from my perch, golden chains swinging beneath me, and together, we followed the princess across the yard.

Into the coolness of the palace, she led us up a series of steps and by the time we reached the top, even Kida was out of breath. A guard threw a glance but did not stop us as we passed out onto a wide rooftop terrace. From this height, I could see the entire city of Wa'ast, rippling in the morning heat, and my heart leapt at the sight of the Nahr that wound like a ribbon in the distance. In the middle of the terrace, Beyat savagely spun a silver chain over his head, and at the end of that chain, Amok.

Around and around and around Amok went, his wings beating furiously, and I couldn't tell if he was flying or being spun like a toy.

Beyat saw us and turned, stilling the wild arc. He raised his fist and Amok landed, wings extended, beak wide. Slowly, the prince turned towards us, wrapping Amok's silver chains around his wrist. He whistled.

A silver arrow shot through the air past me. Khamet was free and he circled us again and again, bleating in a sharp, piercing voice. He had something in his talons, but it was a blur. Beyat whistled again and Khamet winged towards him. He came to rest on the prince's shoulder and dropped the blur into Beyat's hand.

It was a flutterby, one of the many young dragons that twittered through the courtyards. Its tiny head lolled, and I felt the acid rise in the back of my throat.

"Sister," Beyat said.

He didn't move, waited for Shesset and Kida to approach. I spread my wings and arched my neck, spines rising like a corona.

Beyat tossed the dead flutterby to Adriam, who was sitting casually on the western parapet. He caught it, studied it a long moment before tossing it over the side. He rose and ambled over to the prince, the sun gleaming off his fair hair. The wind brought an unfamiliar scent with him. It set my teeth on edge and made water spring from my gums.

"Remus sends greetings," Adriam said. "As does your stepmother."

"I'd heard you drowned in the Nameless Sea."

"The sea had no stomach for me."

"The sea and I are the same in that regard."

She turned to her brother.

"What are you doing to your poor dragons?"

"My poor dragons," Beyat began. "Are fit and ready, like dragons should be."

"You're too hard on them," said Shesset. "They're young. Their bones are soft."

"Amok and Khamet are made of iron," he said. "Unlike yours. She's a doll to be dressed up and carried."

"Anekh is the Great Gold. She must be protected."

The scent was captivating, at the same time both sharp and sweet. I breathed it in, filling my nostrils and throat with it, felt a strange stirring of acid in my belly.

"Protected?" Beyat gestured at me in Kida's arms, and I bristled. "Will you be carrying her when she's a yearling? Or will you have Josiat commission a little cart that your poor vaskar will pull?"

"What I do with my dragon is my choice, brother," said Shesset. "At least, she's not forced to play out war games like clay soldiers."

"I thought you were the strategist. That's what father says, isn't it? Tell me, does she sleep in your bed?"

"Of course not," growled Shesset. "She has her own nest by the balcony."

"I meant your vaskar." And he smiled. It was the first time I'd seen it. Shesset's smile was a knife. This was a spear. "She could sleep in my bed."

Adriam laughed.

"And you could sleep on the floor," Shesset said. "It's as hard as your skin."

Beyat's eyes glittered as he stared at Kida. I hissed again, wishing for his finger between my teeth. I was older now. Stronger. I would snap it clean off, given the chance.

"Perhaps one day, I will sleep with two advisors," he said.

"Like the Crowns of Sand and Storm," said Adriam. "One bronze and one gold."

The scent was stronger now, distracting, infuriating, and distinctly coming from Adriam.

"Look," said the Remoan, and he nudged the prince. "She knows."

"She's a dragon, Adriam," said Beyat. "Of course, she knows. All the stupid flutterbys in the courtyards know."

Adriam's hand went to a satchel wrapped at his waist.

"They do. Truly. They follow me like shadows since I've returned. It's only because they're afraid of the twins that I find peace."

"What is it?" snapped Shesset.

"Just a gift from Bangarden," said Adriam. "For your brother and his drakes."

"I'm happy I got them," Beyat said. "Gold is for old men and vain girls. Silver for daggers and spears. It's a warrior's metal."

"Silver is the future," said the Remoan. "Remus will help you with that."

"Perhaps Remus will join Gifah," said Beyat. "In the marriage bed."

"Hah," snapped Shesset. "Your dreams are for fools and little boys."

"My father is in talks with your father," Adriam said. "But I've told him I don't want you."

"I will never marry a Remoan," snapped Shesset. "Nabir and Penet present far more attractive options."

"Nabir is gone," said Adriam. "No one hears from them anymore."

"Nabir has withdrawn," said Shesset. "But they were riding dragons before Remus stole its first egg."

Riding dragons again. Sometimes I wasn't certain about this world of words. I'd never imagined a chariot before I saw one. Or scorpioch eggs in amber. But somehow, I could imagine a reed riding a dragon.

"Besides," Shesset went on. "An Ophar marries for political reasons, so perhaps I won't marry at all. Gifah has no need of such alliances."

"Perhaps you'll marry a woman." Adriam turned his eyes to Kida. "It's not forbidden in Remus. Is it in Gifah?"

"When I'm Ophar, I will do as I please," said Shesset.

"That's what you say but, in the end, you won't," said Beyat. "You're boring and afraid, just like Father."

And he stepped back, held out a hand to his side and snapped a finger. Khamet leapt to his wrist. He reached over to unhook the silver chain at Amok's leg. My brother sprang to his shoulder, trilling and clicking with wild energy. My brothers looked magnificent and menacing and my heart broke at the sight.

It was then that I noticed their collars, slim and silver and tight at their throats.

"Remoan bands?" asked Kida.

"Remus is generous with its resources," said Adriam. "The drakina's collar looks like it would feed an army."

"*Are* you feeding an army?" asked Shesset.

"Just training the Moons of Gifah," said Beyat. "What have you taught this Great Gold, vaskar?"

"More things than we care to tell you, brother," said Shesset.

"I was talking to the vaskar."

"It doesn't look like she's talking to you."

He laughed and it startled me. I've said before, I don't understand the laughter of reeds. It frightens me, just a little.

"Can she even fly?"

"Of course, she can," said Shesset. "Her wings are strong."

"Her wings are painted," he said. "They weigh more than the statues at Thenes."

He stepped back, spread wide his arms. My brothers spread wide their wings. They looked like mirrors.

"I've never seen her on the wing. We are high above Wa'ast and there is a good strong breeze. Let me see her fly."

Shesset turned to look at me, but Kida shook her head, eyes pleading.

"Give me my dragon," said Shesset.

"My princess..."

"She is strong and clever and knows the palace as I do. Give her to me."

"My princess, no—"

"No? You dare tell me no?"

Kida passed me over and I fumbled on Shesset's wrist. I didn't know what to expect. My heart was racing as Shesset carried me to the edge of the roof. From there, I could see the Court of the Great Gold and the per ameht of Netjeh. I saw the palace and surrounding city gleaming in the morning sun. Rooftops were flat clay and shaded with poles. Smoke rose from kilns and bakeries and kitchens and braziers. The roads were congested. They rippled like wyrms as wagons moved through them. Lastly, like a dragon himself, I could see the glistening ribbon that was the River Nahr.

No, I echoed Kida. I was too young. The world was far too big for me, the sky even more so. I had never flown before. I was a carried dragon, a Great Gold. It was my privilege. It was my right.

Shesset released the links at my feet and the chains fell to the roof like bells. She looked at me, her eyes bright and dancing.

"Show him how you fly, daughter of Selis Anekh," she said. "Show him why there will always be a Great Gold in the House of Bey."

And before I knew it, she flung me out over the roof's edge, and I fell.

I fell, tumbling, tip over talon; my stomach lurching as I plummeted like a stone towards the yard below. I fell, eyes stinging, head spinning, teeth cracking in my mouth. I flung my wings wide, reaching with every claw and scale and spine for the sky. To my utter surprise, I caught it.

I caught the sky. I caught the wind. I caught the smoke of the fires and the shade of the roofs. I caught the sun as she beat down and I caught the heat as it swept up, and suddenly, I understood. As she beat down, I beat down. As the heat swept up, I swept up. Up and down, down and up. The secret to flying was to understand the Wheel of the Elements and to harness it.

Like a chariot, I could harness it.

I beat down once, twice, three times, spiralling off towards the per ameht's golden peak. Beat, beat, beat, but my heart beat faster and I barely noticed the shouts of the workmen as I tumbled through the air around them. Too much with the right wing, too little with the left, raise the head, tuck with the feet. My tail was a rudder and I remembered how the chariot dragons lost them for sport. Soon, I was beyond the palace walls, following the narrow streets and arcing above the heads of reeds and beasts alike. There was a rhythm. Beat beat, breathe in. Beat beat, breathe out. Soon, my world shrank to these alone.

The city rushed below me, and I surrendered all thought, allowing my dragon body to discover this new element. I barely knew it as I angled a wing over the city's harbour, altering my course to match the river. I wove between the sails of the boats, feeling a thrill when the reeds pointed as I flew by. The sun was high, and the water was clear, and my heart leapt to see my reflection in the smooth, blue surface. The sky was my birthright, my heritage, my kingdom. While on land, I belonged to the Ophar, but here in the sky, I was queen. Anekh Sun, daughter of Selis Anekh. I pulled no skyboat. I served no god. My rule was wing and beat, wind and wave and Wheel.

At some point, there was no city and there were no boats, and the sands of Gifah stretched all around, save for the ribbon of green on either side of the river. My shoulders burned with the motion of flying, but I knew it was because of my life of sloth in the palace of the king. I dropped my chin, feeling the rest of my long body follow suit, and soon, I was skimming the surface of the Nahr. I reached out my back talons, felt the spray as water cooled my belly and washed the paint from my wings. I lowered my beak, snapping up mouthful after mouthful to slake my thirst. I was wise, however, and kept a keen eye out for sobethi. I had no desire to end up splash and bubbles like my green brother. Not today, of all days. The day I learned to fly.

More boats, some big this time, and soon, another city of reeds appeared along the banks. I wove between the boats, feeling quite proud until a net slapped the water beside me. I had no desire to be caught and sold as seket in a market, so I raised my beak and rode the heat up and away from the fishers. The air was so much cooler up here, and below, the river was a narrow, winding ribbon of blue and green. Still, I followed, marveling at the vast golden land of Rath'nahr and the remarkable per amehts that rose up along the dunes.

I thought of my mother once again. I knew that one day, I would go back and build a per ameht just for her.

Mechanical, methodical, elemental and pure, I flew low to the water when there were no boats, and high above it when there were. I didn't fear the reed people, but the princess had told me to fly, so I flew, thinking of nothing but beat and breath, wind and wing. The burn was gone now too, replaced by the cord and snap of my perfect design. I was glorious. Seb had said it. The Ophar had confirmed it. There was nothing in all the world to compare with a dragon. It was no wonder the reeds worshipped us. Neburanna, sister-wife of Rath'nahr, had chosen well.

More boats, more cities, little towns and villages. Truth be told, I believe I could have flown forever. The God's Land of Gifah stretched out as far as I could see, flat and pitted like hammered gold, but along the Nahr, she was green. Green and lush, with fields that hugged the river like a sleeve. Reeds worked in those fields, and I knew they were feeding the cities with fruit and bread, corn and meat. Beyond the sleeve, there was sand and scrub and roads and hills, more fields but less green. Wild pastures of belled flaxen bucks and slow-moving, great horned uru. I wonder if the princess Shesset had seen any of it. It would help her studies immensely, I reckoned, to see something in real life, as opposed to map and scroll.

Kida knew this, I told myself. Kida knew.

After a very long time, the Nahr split in two like the spokes of a wheel. The Wheel was testing me, so I let the wind choose, followed it along the northerly branch, but it split again, and again and again. I rose on the heat to get a better view. It was then that I saw the most amazing thing.

The river was no longer a river. It had opened to become a vast, wide, endless stretch of green. From east to west, north to south, I could see no bank nor shore ahead of me, and I knew the time of flying had come to an end. Besides, my stomach was rumbling. It had been so long since my last meal, so I dipped a wing to arc down to the water. I had become very skilled at swimming with my mornings in the pool and I landed on the surface with barely a splash. I kept the shore in sight as I settled, folding my wings across my back, feet paddling expertly in the current. Waves took me up and down, much like the air, and I breathed deeply, noting the heavy smell of salt. I scooped a mouthful of water but gagged when I tried to swallow. I shook my head, clenched my eyes tight, and squeezed the salt out through my nostrils. Surprisingly, the water was sweet after that, and I was able to slake my thirst, though not the growling of my belly.

I gazed down through the ripples of the water. There were shapes swimming around my feet. Fish! I had never caught a fish. But here they were, circling my talons as if tempting me, so I plunged my beak into the waters, snapped down. Slow, slow, slow, like diving through honey.

I pulled my face up, snorted the water, and blinked at the pain behind my eyes. I shook my head and looked down again. The fish swam, mocking me.

I studied my reflection as it rippled beneath me. The paint had streaked from my eyes down my throat to the collar of gold and jewels. A collar that could feed armies, but I couldn't even catch a fish to feed myself. I was helpless as a wild dragon. I knew nothing. Nothing at all.

The faint sound of voices echoed across the water, and I looked up. On the horizon, I saw a line of boats. The breeze carried the scent of bronze and oil, and I ducked low to the water, straining to see them better. They were bigger than fishing boats and smaller than barges, with sails that turned gold in the sunset. Large eyes were painted on the curved prows, making the ships seem as though they watched everything on the sea. They looked like ships of war, and I wondered if they were enemies or allies of Gifah? Shesset would know. Maybe Kida would too.

I waited until they became little more than glimmers on the surface of the sea. When they were gone, I raised my head and glanced around.

Water. Only water, and a distant shoreline that led home.

It was a very interesting moment for me, then. For the very first time, I was alone, bobbing what I would later learn was the Nameless Sea. There were no dragons. There were no reeds. I even doubted if there were sobethi. Perhaps this was the end of the world, where Rath'nahr spent his nights. Perhaps this was the realm of Aketh and Hapeth, dragon gods of water and floods, so I called out to them, my warbles echoing across the waves. Perhaps this was another spoke on the Wheel, and if I chose wrong, I would be destined to spend my life forever lost, far from the sands of Gifah and the reeds that tended her.

The princess had commanded me to fly, but she had never said return.

If I didn't, I would never see Kida again.

Kida. My reed. My world. She, who carried me like an infant, who fed me wyrm at risk of her life. She, whose heart drummed me to sleep at night, who served the princess yet loved me more. We were both caught in this tangled world of kingdoms, where a life could end with the flash of a blade. As I paddled and bobbed, I wondered at the strange relationship between Shesset and Beyat, Ophar's heirs both. But then again, it was the same as my brothers and I, and they were alive and thriving in the Ophar's Court.

I looked up. The sky was streaked with purple, and I knew soon, the skyboat carrying Rath'nahr would be gone from the heavens, pursued by his brother and the twin moons of Gifah. Just like me, the sun was pursued by her brothers, the moons, and so I sang a lament to them all, my voice echoing across the rippling waters, returning to me empty.

Empty on the Wheel of the Sea.

The Wheel was strange and mysterious and unpredictable and cruel, but I was not. I was a good girl. I was royal. I wanted to go home, and for me, home was Kida. Home was Shesset the sharp, Josiat the wise, and the proud, proud House of Bey. I stretched out my neck and pushed with my feet, bringing my wings down until I was sky borne once more. I returned the way I had come, finding and following the branches until they became familiar and one. I didn't have to concentrate this time. It was as if I'd flown all my life. I knew the princess would be proud.

I could carry her one day. I would.

The sky was black as the moons rose, chasing each other like young drakes. They were so like my brothers, so I leaned into my flight, strangely eager to see them again. I could fly with them. We could bumble and snap as we had done as hatchlings on the banks of the Nahr. While the river reflected silver in the moonslight, the lands on either side were as dark as the sky, making the horizon indistinguishable. The cities along the banks looked like dragon scales flickering with oil lamps inside the homes. The smell of fire set my teeth on edge, and I remembered the strange scent from Adriam this afternoon. He was from Remus, and Remoans rode dragons. Did their dragons have fire, and if so, why didn't we?

After many, many hours, Selis Anekh and her skyboat of sun painted the sky pink. I had flown all night over river and dune, and soon, the great, marvelous, congested city of Wa'ast lay before me, sparkling like gems along the river. I spied the Ophar's Palace and arced a wing over Nehjet's per ameht. I spun through the Court of the Great Gold and whipped between the pillars and palm trees and urns. Finally, up to the balcony, to the railing of polished stone, where reeds would stop and admire as I fanned my wings in the daylight.

Home.

The breeze wafted the sheer draperies and oil lamps flickered in the dawning light.

"Princess," came a voice.

It was one of the other attending girls, and I looked around the room. Swiftly, the princess rose from her bed.

"Anekh Sun," she whispered. "You're back."

I snapped my beak at her. I was hungry. I wanted my Kida.

Shesset turned to the girl.

"Quickly, fetch the vaskar."

"But my princess, she's—"

"Now!"

The girl fled the room and the princess moved towards me on the balcony.

"I'm sorry, Anekh Sun," she said, her eyes shining like the Nahr. "My father ordered it. I had no power to stop it."

She reached out a hand and I pushed into it, welcoming the warmth as she smoothed the spines along my head and neck. I cooed as she scratched the prongs of my young horns. She wouldn't hold me. She never did, so we stood for a long time, she content to smooth and scratch, I content to let her, until the slap of feet echoed on the mosaic floor.

I could smell her from so far away, my reed, my Kida, but this time, her scent was mixed with blood. I rose up on hind legs, spread wide my wings, as she entered the room. Her shift was tattered, her eyes fixed on the floor, hands clasped tightly against her thighs. I trilled with joy, for I knew Kida meant food, and I was a hungry, tired dragon.

"Leave," the princess said to the serving girls. "Leave us and don't return until noon. Tell Josiat I'll have no lessons today."

They obeyed, and there was silence for a long moment. I snapped my beak once, twice, three times. The smell of blood was very strong.

"Look. My dragon is restored," said the princess. Her voice was not its customary sharpness. "And so is my vaskar."

"Yes, princess," said Kida, but still, she did not look up.

I sprang from the railing and flew to them, proud to show off my new, strong, purposeful wings. But when I took my home on Kida's shoulder, she hissed with pain.

"Come closer," said Shesset. "Let me see."

Kida said nothing but obeyed as Shesset leaned around to pluck at the linen shift. It sucked away from the skin, and I smelled fresh blood once again.

"I told them," said the princess. "I told them it was me."

Kida clenched her teeth, gaze fixed on the floor, but she could not stop the Nahr from overflowing its banks. Twin rivers gleamed down her cheeks. Still, she said nothing.

"How many?"

"Only ten," Kida said.

"Ten too many," said the princess. "I'm so sorry."

"You did nothing," said my reed. "The vizier—"

"Exactly! I did nothing!" Shesset seethed. "Nothing! You warned me but I didn't listen, and now, you have taken the lash for my pride."

Now, the Nahr flooded her banks as well. She took Kida's hands in her own.

"Never again," she said. "I will be Ophar one day and I will be a good one. I will change the way we rule, but I start right now with how I live. Can you forgive me, oh dear Kida, royal vaskar and lover of dragons?"

Finally, Kida looked up, those great dark eyes wondrous and round. She nodded.

I was happy to see Kida smile, but I was very hungry. I slipped my head in between them, snapped my beak once, twice, three times.

This summoned the Nahr all over again. Sometimes I think I will never understand reeds. Words and arrows, laughter and tears and blood.

Kida rested, tended by the princess with salve and more tears, and exchanged her tattered shift for one of the princess's fine dresses. She also joined Shesset in the royal bed that night. It was a good progression. From the floor to a divan to a bed in a matter of months. As for me, I was delighted to have the divan all to myself.

But I've said that dragons are not good at counting, and many things can happen in the span of one day. Things uncounted, things unseen and unknown, for during that day, there was a time, however brief, when there was no Great Gold in the Ophar's Court. The Wheel has spokes of sand and water, blood and gold, but also, I realized soon enough, it also has a spoke of silver. And that spoke was rolling across the Nameless Sea from the land of Remus, towards the great, terrible, sparkling city of Wa'ast.

8

FALL OF THE HOUSE OF BEY

Once a year comes the Weeping, when the Nahr floods its banks and brings silt-rich waters from the mountains of the east. I believe the gods live, not in the heavens above or the rivers below, but in those mountains. Rath'nahr, Selis Anekh, Neburanna and the host of gods surely lived in the mountains. There must be much sadness among the gods for all the weeping water that was sent. However, I also believed that they could simply stop the Wheel at any time, freeing us all from its relentless weight had they the desire to do so.

The Palace was very heavy now.

Kida said that, with this Weeping, I was now a yearling, but that meant nothing to me. A year was ten and two of months, and a month was ten and ten and ten of days. As I've said before, counting things is not the strength of dragons. I only know that it was difficult for

Kida to carry me, and even perching on Shesset's shoulders was a game of balance. I was young and proud and glorious as the sun in the sky. Every day, I would sit on the balcony, waving my painted wings at the reeds below me. They would stop and marvel. Some would fall on their knees with praise, others would raise their hands and sing of my fame. Sometimes, they held up wyrm or fish or sweet cakes, and since I now wore no chains at my feet, I'd sweep down above them and snatch the treats with my talons. Soon, I only accepted cakes. The reeds would squeal with fear as I soared down, laugh with joy as I spun in the air above them before returning to the balcony and my feast. My teeth were often sticky and sweet, my belly most often full.

But now, all this was changing. With this new season of Weeping, the reeds rarely stopped and marveled or offered me cakes. No, they rushed about in groups, preoccupied and whispering, and I tasted bronze on the wind. From my balcony, I watched encampments setting up all along the northern and western flanks of the city, with marakt chariots and soldiers with smoke and swords. I heard the word 'armies' and 'battle,' 'Remus' and 'war' far more than ever before.

I knew there was change on the wind but still, the defiant sun of Gifah rose and set over them all.

During that time, I also watched Khamet and Amok, as they often swept through the skies of the palace. The flutterbys disappeared at the first flash of silver, but my brothers were fast, and they killed many each day. Once, they knocked a green out of the sky just above my balcony and I watched it plummet to the ground below. The silvers were on it in a heartbeat, Khamet pinning the green tail with one talon while Amok danced around, biting the youngling trapped under their claws. Amok snapped and Khamet pecked, but they did not kill. It was a game, I knew, like the flaxen shakhets and the bells in the sand. The green hatchling flapped and peeped, and its blood speckled the stone with a Weeping of its own. As I peered over the railing, I was horrified at the sight, but more so at the waters springing up in my mouth.

"Net," cried Shesset, and she leaned past me, flung a clay cup at them from above. It shattered and my brothers launched in a flurry of silver, taking the flutterby with them.

"I hate those drakes," she said under her breath.

"The royal vaskars hate them too," said Kida. She too moved over to me and smoothed my hackled spines. "They've had to increase the number of eggs and hatchlings they buy from the traders because the Moons kill so many."

I watched them arc over the courtyard to disappear at the Prince's Terrace, and I envied them a little. I had never killed a fish, let alone a flutterby, but my teeth were strong, and I was certain I could. I remembered my mother and the dead things that she brought.

Shesset ran her fingers along my neck, stopping to spin my collar around my neck. It was loose and thick and heavy with jewels.

"Remus is everywhere," said Shesset. "Even the Moons wear silver."

"Seb said Remoan collars prevent the calling of fire," said Kida.

"I knew it," said the princess. "Adriam's brought sythstone from Remus."

Kida ran her hand along my forehead, twisted her fingers around my back-swept, yearling horns.

"He did admit it," said Kida. "He was preparing his dragons for war."

"War is here," said Shesset and she leaned out over the balcony, looked out over Wa'ast to the dunes beyond.

"Nefheru's exile was convenient," she said after a long moment. "There are rumors that she is the one leading the army across the Salt Dunes."

"Joined by Remus?"

"Encouraged and supported by Remus, yes. Why try to conquer a rich land when you can invest in its instability and profit when it falls?"

Kida's hand slowed. I nudged her, irritated at its stopping.

"Beyat will take the throne," said Kida.

"He will try."

"And he'll kill you," said Kida.

"He'll try that, as well. He'll also need to replace Anekh with the Moons as symbol of the House of Bey."

"That's impossible."

"Not if he kills her. Erases our history in gold and rewrites a future of silver. He said it himself. Gold is for old men and vain girls."

"Is that why the army is on the Wa'asti Plain?"

"My father is preparing, but half-heartedly. He doesn't want to believe it. I'm only privy to some of it."

"You should be privy to all of it," said Kida. "You have a good mind."

"I also have Josiat and Anekh and you," she said, and she turned, took Kida's hand. "Between us, we may yet save the kingdom. But it won't be easy, or swift."

"The Wheel turns on its own," said Kida. "We can't push or pull it either way."

Shesset smiled and together, they left the balcony. I remained, my eyes straining the skies for a sight of my brothers. The Wheel was rolling again, crushing all in its path, but this time, the Wheel was silver.

***

I will never forget the night that the House of Bey fell.

The Remoan army made the Wa'asti Plain and the Ophar led the stand against them. For two days, they did not fight, for neither side wanted to be the aggressor. I wondered if the painted woman was indeed in their company, and if the Ophar had spoken with her. It was a moot thought, for after two days of inaction, posturing and impasse, the real war turned on the wings of dragons.

It was evening and the skies were Gifahn gold when I caught the scent on the river breeze. Not flutterbys, not chariot dragons. More like the heavy musk of Netjeh but many Netjehs thick in the clouds. Soon, the drone of wings shook both floor and pillar like a massive chariot. The golden skies grew dark then, and I pushed my dread deep, deep inside. Suddenly, Josiat burst into the room.

"Is the princess safe?" he cried. He was accompanied by two reeds with arms filled of tattered cloth. "Princess?"

"Safe," said Shesset, rising from her settee. "Josiat, where is my father?"

"With the army, princess. He has ordered your removal."

"I'll not leave him."

"The Dragon Flights are coming, princess," he said. "And our army will be turned to ash. We leave now."

"I won't leave my father," she hissed. "This wasn't the plan!"

"A barge is readied at the dock to take us to Karadoum, on the Island of Sand and Storm."

"No!" And she clapped her hands together. I knew this command. I lit from the balcony balustrade and glided over to Shesset, landing on her with one foot on each shoulder. I spread my wings wide and raised my head over hers, barked three times to the painted ceiling. The vizier and his guards shrank back.

"My princess," said Josiat, eyes lowered. "I took an oath to your father, but so did you. This time, you must listen and do as I say."

He swung a satchel from across his shoulders, pulled a cord to reveal a flash of metal. Bronze and gold. I'd seen it before.

"The River Crowns of Sand and Storm," said Shesset, her voice barely a whisper. "Those belong to the Ophar."

"They belong to you now."

"No…"

"You'll need them to restore your claim to the throne."

She glanced up, sharp eyes filling with the Nahr.

"The Remoan dragons have darkened the sky," Josiat said. "Once they break, he will die."

"I won't run," she said. "I'm no coward."

"You are the Glory of Gifah," he said. "And now, you are her only hope."

Kida stepped to Shesset's side, spear and bow in her hands.

"I will protect you with my life," she said. "As will Anekh Sun."

I barked again.

Shesset released a long breath, set her chin like a statue.

"We are daughters of the goddess," she said. "We retreat now, regroup and return to restore peace to Gifah. But I will kill my brother."

She hissed now.

"I will kill him and Adriam and Nefheru and the Moons Amok and Khamet. I will rule as a dragon rules, and Gifah will be feared all over the land."

She was almost a dragon herself. She had more fire than I.

"And you will," said Josiat. "But today..."

The vizier passed Kida a pair of tattered shifts.

"Today, you are terrified servants fleeing a falling house. As for the Great Gold..."

He held up a woven rug.

"She is a dusty, old spice carpet. Hide her well, or we all die."

Kida called me to her wrist, and I reluctantly obeyed. As she took the rug, there was a splitting screech and the skies opened up over the Wa'asti Plain. Like a volley of arrows, dragons fell from the clouds. Large dragons swept down over the army, their wings churning sand into glass and their breaths blasting reeds into ash. Smoke billowed over the dunes as the dragons soared in perfect formation, spraying fire across the Gifahn troops again and again and again.

Suddenly, the balcony rattled as a massive shape swept over us. I could see the red scales and lighter underbelly, the flap of wing leather and the whip of a striped tail. I could feel the heat as it swept by, setting the Painted Palms aflame and circling around in the purple sky for another pass.

"To the barge," said Josiat.

***

Today, you are terrified servants fleeing a falling house.

Light and shadow warred as we raced through the halls, and reeds ran in every direction, weeping and wailing as dragonfire rained down from the heavens. Carved pillars were splattered with blood, stone columns chipped by blades. The air was thick with smoke and oil burned in slicks across the floors. There was chaos everywhere as reed fought reed, and all fled the turning of the tide.

Shesset, Josiat and the guards were far ahead, with Kida and I following, so as not to arouse suspicion. I was loosely bound in the makeshift carpet, but I could see the night sky seething with wing, coil, and flame. Blazing oil vats dotted the yard, contrasting everything with flashing light and deep shadow. As we rushed through the Court of the Great Gold, a huge, blue drakina landed on the stone with a swirl of wind and a boom that echoed across the yard. Kida skidded to a halt, almost dropping me in her panic.

"Kida!" cried Shesset from across the courtyard.

The great blue head swung towards us, and the man astride her was clad in silver and gold.

"Go!" shouted Kida. "I'll meet you at the river!"

The princess whirled and disappeared with the vizier, as the drakina leaned towards us, nostrils wide, breath hot.

"Portia likes your rug," called the rider from his mount. I could see his teeth flash. Smiles were like laughter. I trusted neither.

Kida clutched me to her chest, bound as I was in tassels and thread.

"You're not afraid of her," he said. "You're brave. But then again, you carry both a carpet and a spear. You must be a mighty warrior."

She said nothing.

"And I would dearly love to see what damage a girl can do with a carpet of war."

I could feel her heart pounding through the thickness of the rug.

"We do not wish to kill you," he continued. "Remus doesn't make war on Gifah's citizens."

"Only on Gifah's king," Kida snapped. "And his loyal army."

"Kings come and go," said the man. "So do armies."

"Then go," she said. "Back to your land across the Nameless Sea."

"We should," he said. "But we follow our king's orders, and so we are here."

"Go."

"Your wish is my command. But here…"

He peeled a small satchel strapped to his thigh, tossed an object into Kida's hand. His teeth flashed again.

"Now you have three weapons, dear lady. A treat for the stolen dragon in your rug."

And he turned his head, tugged a rein. The drakina grumbled but unfurled her great wings and launched herself into the sky, the wind sending sand like hot stingers into our eyes.

Kida looked down.

"Sythstone."

There was a shout and she looked up. Row upon row of soldiers marched into the courtyard, carrying an unfamiliar standard on a bronze pike. The Remoan army was in the palace, and Kida moved swiftly towards the outskirts of the court, tucking the spear behind her back. Familiar silver wings flashed overhead, circling above the invaders, as a second group came out from the palace and the Terrace of the Prince.

"Remoan brothers," called Adriam. "Dear friends and liberators of the Gifahn people. I thank you for your service to the River Crowns of the Empire."

"Tell me my father is dead," came a voice.

Beyat, clad head to toe in silver, snapped his fingers, and the Moons lit on his shoulders like mirrors. Their beaks were open, eyes shining in the firelight.

"Burned to embers with the rest of his army," said the sun-headed man.

"People are stealing things, Adriam," Beyat growled. "Your dragons were not supposed to touch the palace."

"Apologies, my prince—"

"Ophar. My father is dead. I am Ophar."

"Most Esteemed Ophar," said Adriam, and he bowed. "In the heat of battle, armies are notorious."

"Where is my sister?"

"Hiding. She is as skinny as a wyrm."

"Find my sister and bring her to me. Find her dragon, slit its throat, and sell the scales for seket. And where is my mother?"

"Here, I'm certain she—"

Beyat swung around, spread wide his arms.

"Nefheru-Nassat, Wife of the Traitor Thutmen'nahr II. Mother of the Most High Beyat I of House Beyat! Show yourself to your son! Now!"

Back pressed against a pillar, Kida held her breath. So did I, even as I peered out from the end of the rug.

"You are responsible for this destruction, Adriam," he hissed. "I will have my staff count all that is missing, and the amount will be deducted from the tithe."

"I—"

"Mother! Show yourself! Mother!"

"Silver Spear of Gifah," came a voice over the crowd. "Esteemed Seed of Rath'nahr. I'm here, my son, my life."

The soldiers parted as a chair of silver, carried by four reeds, entered the courtyard.

It was the painted woman. The four reeds carried her through the crowds and the burning chaos to her son. They lowered the chair to the ground. She extended her hand for Beyat to take, and he helped her to her feet.

From across the court, I saw Amok's beak open, tongue extended tasting the air. With all the dragons in the city, and with me literally wrapped in spice, it was unlikely that he could pick my scent out of them all. Still, I shrank deeper into the carpet. Kida slipped around the pillar and quietly, made her way out of the court in the dark.

All around us, those once loyal to the Ophar abandoned their positions as the Remoan army marched through the halls. Servants wailed as they ran, some with baskets, others with urns; scribes rushed in all directions with scrolls of paprush clutched in their arms. Silver-clad soldiers pushed them all to the ground and stomped on paper, clay and reed alike. It was chaos and I was grateful when we passed under the great lintel of the palace and onto the narrow streets of Wa'ast.

Soldiers had reached here too, and Kida kept to the alleys to avoid them. Torches were sporadic and the moons played hide and seek through the night clouds.

She walked swiftly, her feet slapping on the hard dirt of the city road, but soon, the smell of the river was stronger than that of oil or smoke. City buildings grew sparse, replaced by huts, docks and jetties. I pushed my head out of the carpet as the flashing ribbon of the Nahr opened up before us.

"Where are they?"

She stepped up to the embankment and peered over the river's edge.

"Oh no," she moaned. "We're too late."

She laid the carpet on the stone and kicked it with her foot. I rolled out and sat a moment, disoriented and dizzy, but I spread wide my wings and breathed in the stories of war.

I launched upwards on outstretched wings. There were riverboats and skiffs staked all along the bank, some nestled among reeds, some roped to the basalt stone, and others anchored further out in the water. It was dark but I knew sobethi hunted at night. I perched on a post, folded my wings across my back to watch.

"The Sand and the Storm made the Mighty River Nahr," said Kida. "And the Mighty River Nahr made me."

She leaned out over the river, weight on the spear she still carried.

"They're going to the Island of Sand and Storm," she said. "Karadoum and the Island of Sand and Storm. And that's east."

She looked around at the river, the docks, the skiffs.

"I remember from Shesset's maps. Karadoum is east, where the River Sand and the River Storm meet to become the Nahr."

She looked up at me.

"Come, Anekh. We can catch them."

And she turned and trotted down the steep stone steps of the embankment, the spear clutched in her hand.

Suddenly, a flurry of silver wings dropped from the sky, knocking her off her feet and sending her tumbling down the steps. It was Amok and I launched from the post to meet him in the air, teeth bared. He dipped downward, raking my tail with his talons as he hurtled past. I tucked and spun but he was behind me again, and I was not prepared for the blast of flame that hit my flank, scorching my scales with incredible heat.

My heart thudded at the realization.

My brothers could breathe fire.

I peeled away and raced towards the water, Amok in furious pursuit. It was a terrible dance, whirling and spinning and tumbling through the air, and all the while, he sprayed flames across my path.

"Anekh!"

The dark shape of Kida called to me from the bottom of the steps. I circled back towards her, feeling his teeth snap at my tail. He was trying to kill me. My own brother, turned from a silly, wrestling chick into a weapon of war, and I could barely breathe as we soared over the embankment. Kida was there, and she thrust the spear swiftly up, its tip flashing in the moonslight. Amok squealed, his wing sliced open, and I wheeled in the air as he crashed to the stone. He rolled over and over towards the river, body flailing, tail whipping, wing flapping like a torn sail. Kida towered over him and drove the spear into his breast. He thrashed wildly as she dragged him to the river's edge at the point of the spear, leaving a gleaming slick of blood in his wake. With a cry, she plunged him into the dark waters. They bubbled and the spear shook, but she held firm, and soon, there was quiet.

"Neburanna, forgive me," she said quietly, and she yanked the spear out. I flew to land on her shoulder. In the moonslight, I could see blood on her forehead and cheek. She reached up, laid a trembling hand on my spines, and released a long, deep breath.

"Anekh. My Anekh. We have to go."

I sprang into the air, and she turned to make her way along the water's edge. Tethered to an embankment post was a small boat made of bound paprush. Once again, she glanced around before slipping the rope from its mooring.

"I claim this skiff for the House of Bey."

First one foot then the other, she stepped into the boat and dipped the spear's tip into the water, pushing down on the shaft. The skiff glided away from the embankment and onto the inky surface of the river.

I swept down to perch on the prow, spreading my wings until the balance adjusted for my weight. Kida used the spear as a pole, moving the boat like a barge, but we were set against the current, so it was slow going once the river grew deep.

"We'll never catch them like this," she said. "Anekh, *luf.*"

And she held out the spear.

I cocked my head at her.

She shook the end.

"Anekh Sun. *Luf.*"

Catch?

I sprang into the air and grasped the end of the spear with my back talons, my wing strokes carrying me up, but she held me straight. I didn't understand.

"Anekh, *teer!*"

Fly!

But I was flying.

"No, forward. Pull the boat!"

I twisted in mid-air, gripping the spearhead and beating down my wings. She hung on to the other end, braced herself against the bindings as I pulled and flapped. The boat jerked under my efforts, then jerked again, and suddenly, I understood. I was to pull this little boat against the current of the river. Soon, we were gliding across the surface of the Nahr.

From the river, I took one last glance at the city of Wa'ast. The night sky over the palace flickered with gold and grey - flames and smoke reaching up to the stars. A war of reeds, a storm of dragons. The death of the Ophar, and the fall of the House of Bey.

It was dawn before we caught up with the princess' barge and I was exhausted. Kida tumbled over the boat's edge and crawled to Shesset's side under the dark canopy. She called me and I wearily obeyed. I was almost as big as she, but I didn't care, grateful to be taken into her arms once again. Her heart was the drum of my life, and it wasn't long before I surrendered to sleep. As I did, I realized this newest change had occurred in the darkness. The Wheel had turned once again, this time crushing the mighty House of Bey in its path.

9

THE RIVERS OF SAND AND STORM

I suppose I should have been sad for the trials that
befell my reeds during their time on the barge. It had
taken only one day for me to fly from Wa'ast to the
Nameless Sea, but it took many, many more days to go
upriver to this Island of Sand and Storm. We were still
'servants fleeing a falling house,' and, to avoid the
Remoan Dragon Flights that searched for us along the
river, we soon traded the barge for a smaller fishing
boat. It had few luxuries, no banners or royal standards,
and the striped linen canopy covered only Shesset, Kida
and Josiat. We also left many of the princess' attendants
and ladies-in-waiting behind in those villages. The boat
was small and so, our party needed to be small as well.
Still, we had six strong rowers, and they worked non-
stop, for the current was against us and the river was
strong. But the little sail caught the breeze like a
dragon's wing, and we moved through the waters like a

Son of Sobeth. The princess was sullen the entire time, saying little even to my Kida, and she stared with dull eyes across the Nahr at the villages, markets and dunes that swept past.

Because of the Dragon Flights, Kida rubbed my skin in fish oil several times a day to disguise my scent, followed by a dusting of ashes to hide my golden scales. During the nights, I fell asleep watching the moons and singing to the stars in my beauteous dragon voice. And yes, I should have been sad for the reeds; for the princess and her court and for the fallen state of the House of Bey, but I couldn't. In fact, I believe I was the happiest I'd ever been, for now I was a river dragon.

They had left in such haste that they had taken no food. They had also taken nothing to trade with the many merchant boats and river towns along the way, and I knew they were desperately missing their cakes. I can tell you how much reeds love their cakes. Flat, white cakes, sweetened with honey and dates, or round, golden cakes dusted with spices and salt. Smooth cakes wrapped around figs, and crispy cakes washed down with beer. They had none of these, and I wonder if their bellies dictated their sadness. I loved sweets as much as any reed, but now I had no desire for cakes or figs or beer. Now, I had a river brimming with fish.

Because of my experience with shakhet milk pool and my limited time on the Nameless Sea, I thought I was an accomplished swimmer, but the first time I dove for a fish, I realized that I was, in fact, deluded. Water was thick and heavy, and caused more drag than a strong wind. It took several attempts before I did little more than bob back up to the surface. Kida watched me as I floundered, but I was hungry, and therefore committed. When I set my sights on a flat, grey tarfish flashing in the waves beneath me, I dove, and everything changed.

My inner lids covered my eyes of their own accord and the world of the underwater came alive to me. Fish, rushes, vines, sticks. Bubbles and rocks and bits of weed. It was as alive as the sky, more so, and I became a sobethi coursing through the waves. I kept my wings tight against my body and realized that my tail worked far better when I waved it side to side, rather than up and down like a dragon. So, I used my powerful tail as both propulsion and rudder, and I bore down on that tarfish who darted along the bottom. Faster and faster, I went, using my long neck to follow the fish as it dashed out of reach. Instinctively, I narrowed my eyes, opening my mouth as the spiked tail flicked before me. I felt the water spin across my teeth, felt the current sting my eyes. The tarfish dashed to one side and I rolled, sucking in great amounts of water and suddenly, it was there, fat and wriggling, between my teeth.

I crunched and the fish burst.

I cannot tell you how it felt as I crested above the waves, my prize proudly displayed for all to see. It flapped and flailed but I had it tight, its blood flooding my tongue with taste. Gripping it hard, I forced the water between my teeth and out my nostrils, as flesh squished and bones crunched with the force. And I threw my head up, tossing the fish to the back of my throat and swallowing it all in one gulp.

I floated for a minute, wings folded across my back, very proud of myself, and I heard Kida call my name. I looked towards her. She leaned over the edge of the boat, her smile as big as the sun.

"More, Anekh," she called to me. "Catch more. *Luf.*"

Catch.

Catch fish.

I leapt into the air, arced my long body and dove once more, entering the water like a golden spear. This time, the hunting was easier, and I caught a second tarfish within minutes, and then a third. Each time, I crested the water and swallowed, enjoying the crunch and slip of the fish in my jaws. Soon, however, my belly was full, and the next time I crested, I bobbed, holding one in my teeth, proud to have caught but not inclined to swallow. Contentedly, I looked to Kida.

"Here, Anekh," she said. "Bring it here. *Tat!*"

And she gestured with her hand.

The rowers paused as I paddled over, my powerful legs and talons churning through the water. The boat rocked as I sprang to perch on its side. She reached for the fish, and I spat it onto the floor.

Josiat grunted with satisfaction. He took it and passed it to one of the princess' women. I think her name was Tamal.

"Gut it," he said. "We can dry it on the canvas and eat tonight."

"There are thirteen of us," said Tamal. "One fish won't feed us all."

"She will catch more," said Kida, and she cupped my beak in her hands. "Anekh, *luf.*"

I warbled at her and sprang from the edge, flipping backwards to enter the water with a great splash.

I soon learned how to swallow fish while underwater but keep them in my crop, whole and uncrunched. This allowed me to catch many fish in one dive and vomit them all back up onto the floor of the boat. It reminded me of my mother, when she would open her mouth and feed us digested skarabs and wyrm. I was tending these reeds as if they were my hatchlings and I was sad for them that they weren't dragons. Still, they gutted the fish, and hung the flesh to dry on the boat's canopy and by evening, the entire crew shared a meal because of my hunting. Morale improved considerably because of my new skills, and despite the sour mood on the boat, I was inordinately happy.

Several times a day, the sky would darken and a Remoan dragon pair would streak along the surface of the river. I knew they were still searching for us, and Kida would grab me and tuck me under a woolen wrap.

She didn't need to rub my scales in fish, for I was a fisher dragon now. I stank of their oils and entrails and blood. Each night, I slept soundly in Kida's arms. I was as big as she, but still, I felt protected and safe. I know she was warmed by me, perhaps reassured that she had not lost me like everything else. I wished I could warm the princess the same way. She seemed lost as a withered palm in the breeze.

One morning, after a splendid catch of fat stonecarp, I dozed on the warm floor of the boat. Kida sat under the canopy next to the princess, folding something over and over in her fingers. The scent caught my fished-logged nostrils, and I lifted my sleepy head.

Josiat frowned.

"What is that?" he asked.

"Sythstone," said Kida. I sat up now. The stone crumbled in her fingers, and it set my mouth watering.

"You have sythstone?"

"From one of the Remoan dragon riders. I don't know why but he gave it to me."

Acid pooled between my teeth, dripped out onto the deck.

Josiat frowned. "Have you given any to the dragon?"

"No," said Kida. "I never learned much about sythstone, other than it creates fire, and that once a dragon tastes fire, she is dangerous and can never be trusted."

"This is why it's forbidden," said Josiat, and he sat back to stroke his beard. "Ophar Nekah'nessar III outlawed the mining of sythstone after the House of Keph burned down the Royal City two hundred years ago."

I snapped my beak. This sythstone had captivated me and the heat rose in my belly to meet it. The acid on the floor of the boat had begun to congeal, turning into wax as it cooled in the shade.

"Beyat's drakes had fire," said Shesset, her first words spoken in days. She hadn't moved from her position under the canopy and sat, arms wrapped around her knees. "He had an army, too."

The vizier lowered his eyes.

"So, how did Beyat do this?" snapped the princess. "How did he summon an army, arrange a coup, and kill my father all without the vizier knowing any of it?"

There was silence on the boat. Even the wind held her tongue.

"Adriam of Bangarden, princess," said Josiat.

"I told you Remus was our enemy," said Shesset. "They turned my brother against us, and in doing so, usurped my father's throne. I told you."

"And, I did tell your father," said Josiat. "But he wouldn't act on it. He believed he still had time before Remus grew so bold as to wield the prince."

"He was wrong," she spat. "You should have counselled him better."

"Yes, my princess, I should have. But I loved your father as a king and a friend, and I love his children even more. I prayed to the gods that Beyat would not be so weak, and in doing so, I failed you all."

Shesset stared at him for a long time, before turning her face away to watch the riverbanks once again.

"You will not love me this way, vizier. I demand your mind, not your heart."

For her part, Kida quietly slipped the sythstone into the satchel at her hip and I returned to the water, disappointed and finding solace there.

On the seventh day, we came upon another river town, and we could smell the smoke from a bustling market near the water's edge. Shesset called Kida, Josiat and I to her side. I perched on her knee and pushed my head under her hand, asking in my dragon way for a scratch.

She smiled sadly and obliged.

"We need to buy food and weapons," she said. "Swords and spears, at the least."

Josiat shook his head.

"We have nothing to trade," he said.

"We have Anekh Sun," she said.

"No!" said Kida but Josiat shrugged.

"Surely, she could spare a scale or two," he said. "Seket commands high price in the markets."

"Sell me instead!" begged Kida. "Please, princess! Don't touch Anekh!"

"Peace," said the princess, stroking my bony head and running her hand along the yearling spines on my neck. They were not so soft anymore and were growing into a mane of thorns. "I will never sell any part of Anekh Sun. She is the daughter of Selis Anekh and glory of the House of Bey. But this…"

Down my throat to the gold collar studded with lapis and garnet and pearl.

"This was a gift from my father. It will bring even more than a dragon."

Kida nodded swiftly and she smiled. I thought I saw the rivers brimming behind her lashes.

"Besides, I still need a Great Gold if I intend to restore the House of Bey," Shesset added. "Vaskar, remove her collar."

Kida unhooked the elaborate neckpiece I'd worn since my dedication, passed into Shesset's waiting hand. With a deep breath, the princess looked up and, for the first time in days, in her eyes, there were stars.

"Josiat, bring us to shore," she said. "Today, we begin my family's restoration."

The vizier smiled, but his smile could not compare to Kida's. Nothing ever could.

Under the power of oar and sail and royal command, the barge veered towards the north bank, and the markets.

***

On the evening of the ten-and-second day, we felt the first bump.

The Nahr was wide and marshy at this point, and the sail was not catching much wind, so the rowers were pressed to exhaustion. Both Kida and the princess sat outside the canopy, counting the stars, and watching the moons dip in and out of the clouds. They were like eyes, these moons, and tonight, one was wide while the other was barely a sliver, and I thought of my brothers. Amok was dead, killed by my reed as he sought to kill me. I thought of my mother and all her efforts to keep her clutch of five alive. Now, there was only Khamet and I, the others crushed under the spokes of sand, water, war and need. If dragons could weep, I would have that night.

I wasn't alert when the first bump came, gentle at first, tentative, like a thing testing. I raised my head from my wing claws, breathed in the whispers of the night. There was a second, this time a scraping along the bottom of the boat, and I heard muffled voices as Josiat rose to speak with the head rower. If we had been in the barge, I wouldn't have concerned myself with the dangers of sobethi, but this was a smaller vessel, shallow and easily tipped. So, I scanned the dark surface, watching for eyes, spines and the familiar side-to-side waves made by their powerful tails.

There, a third and the boat shook. I barked three times to alert my reeds before I leapt from the deck and plunged into the water.

The Nahr at night is a terrible thing.

Bubbles become nightmares. Weeds become spears. I was grateful for my inner lids that magnified the faint moonlight and illuminated a world painted in black and green, highlight and shadow. I could feel the current of the river running west, and the wake of the barge running east. Above and beneath and all around me were the tiny eyes and powerful black tails of sobethi, churning up the waters and hungry for prey.

I did not hesitate, for to hesitate would be death. I shot forward, ramming one with my yearling beak. I rolled and went after another, a creature almost my own size, catching its tail between my jaws. He was heavy and his long, scaled body lagged in the current, but I burst above the surface and unfurled my wings, dragging him away from the boat and onto the bank. I released him and wheeled, diving back in and hearing shouts of the reeds echo in the night.

Two sons flashed through the dark waters towards me, and I ducked low beneath them both. One flipped and followed, his tail a lethal whip. I swam to the boat, feeling the currents favour me this time and I burst from the waves next to the boat's shallow edge. The sobethi followed, his jaws and teeth rising out of the waters to snap furiously at my tail. My Kida was ready and with a flash of moons' silver, she plunged her spear into his mouth. He fell backwards with a great splash, and I tasted blood in the water.

Kida wasn't the only reed ready, and the rowers were as proficient with their spears as they were with the oars. The surface churned as I dove back in, as many sobethi thrashed side-to-side, impaled, and trailing blood in their wake. Through the waters I raced, grabbing the wooden shafts and swimming around and around each creature until the spear came loose. Swim up and burst out to drop the spear onto the deck before arcing around the sail and plunging back in. I was able to retrieve five spears this way, although two were broken, and soon, the Nahr grew still once more.

However, the boat was taking on water.

Shesset's few attendants scrambled to stem the leaks but there were cracks in between the deck boards. They stuffed spare linen into the seams, but they quickly became soaked, and I knew this had been the sobethi plan. Sink it, capsize it, the only thing that mattered to them was to get the reeds in the water for a soft and easy meal. Clearly, they'd had experience with boats before, but, while small skiffs and rush-bound canoes might be an easy target, a fishing boat was a different thing. Still, the water did not stop.

"Wax," said a woman. "Do we have candles or swarm wax?"

"Wait," said Kida. "Anekh, come here."

I hopped down from my perch on the boat's edge and lumbered over to her.

"Dragon acid turns to wax," she said, and she looked at me. "But I've never trained her to spit."

"You're a vaskar," said Josiat. "You can teach her anything."

"Hurry, please," said one of the rowers.

Kida thought for a long minute, and I waited, hoping she'd run her hands along my eye ridges or rub my young horns or scratch the tender scales between my jawbones. She did neither, but then, she slipped her hand into the satchel at her waist, pulled out the small chunk of sythstone hidden there.

I sat forward, saliva immediately springing up on my tongue.

"What are you doing?" asked Shesset from under the canopy. "Do you want her to burn the boat to cinders?"

Kida smiled, held the stone in front of my face.

"Can you smell this, Anekh? Sythstone?"

I could, in fact, smell it. It was tantalizing and sickly sweet, salty and sharp and heady and intoxicating. I snapped my beak, once, twice, three times. Nudged her hand with my nose.

"No fire, vaskar," said Josiat.

"No fire," she said.

She spat on the seams.

I snapped my beak, feeling the acid bubble up my throat and bite the roof of my mouth.

"She doesn't know what you're asking," said Shesset.

"No, but she used to spit on the workmen below the terrace," said Kida. "She thought it was a game."

It was true and I loved it. In retrospect, I'm not sure the workmen did.

She spat again, the waters of the Nahr black as they bubbled up through the cracks. She held up the stone, waved it in front of my beak. I shook my head, drool and acid flinging in all directions. The women behind me shrieked but I was fixated on the stone dancing before me.

"Spit! *Htah!*" She spat again, and this time, I understood. The acid spilled from my teeth, so I spat a great wad onto the linen over the seam. It sizzled and steamed.

"Yes! Again! *Htah!*"

I spat again, and again, as a spring of fiery acid flowed inside me that I knew would never dry. Soon, all the cracks were covered in sticky white resin, and they cooled quickly, forming a barrier against the river and the sobethi that hunted its waters.

"Well done, dragon," said Josiat. "And well done, vaskar. I will not doubt again."

Kida smiled and looked over at Shesset. The princess nodded.

I watched eagerly as my reed broke a shard off the sythstone and held it out for me. I nibbled tentatively with my tiny front teeth, savouring the sweet, sharp taste on my tongue. I snapped my jaws, blinking at the sensation. It wasn't enough, and I closed my jaws over her hand, gnawing at the shard with my great back teeth. I took it now, chomping and crunching with eager glee. It shattered into smaller and smaller pieces until it was like sand, coating my teeth and sizzling along my gums. There was a flash of light behind my eyes as the acid raced up my throat once again, threatening to split my golden head wide with the pain. Sythstone and acid at the same time, and the roof of my mouth scorched with heat.

I sprang backwards to the edge of the boat.

"Anekh, *kah!*"

I shook my head but could contain it no more, so I spread wide my wings and I exhaled, but this time, a plume of yellow fire sprayed out instead of acid. My eyes popped and my chest burned, and I breathed it out again, lighting the darkness like a beacon. One last time, and I took my time, savouring the crackle of the sythstone along my teeth, the tide of the flames as they rolled across my tongue, and the wave of coolness that swept up in its wake.

And then it was gone.

I sat back, gagged to rid my mouth of the sharp, cinder taste. My eyes were heavy, my limbs like dead weights, but I looked back at Kida. The entire boat was staring at me.

Yes, as I said, this time along the river was the happiest of my life.

I slept soundly in her arms that night, and in the morning, the first of the gods came into view.

10

KARADOUM

There is nothing in all the world like a statue of a dragon. We are magnificent and sleek, our smooth lines are ideal to be carved in stone, then shaped by the wind. Reeds, likewise, make fine statues as they are lean and rippling, and while they don't have wings or elegant tails, their bodies do have a certain grace. There are many, many other creatures in Gifah, all of which could be subjects for statues. But I have never seen any creatures like those statues built by the reeds of Karadoum.

They called them gods but in reality, they were basalt statues with reed bodies and not-reed heads. Dragon, sobethi or rassa heads, uru, iribis birds or scorpioch heads. Some heads wore golden hoods, others wore crowns and all statues held something, whether staff, spear or paprush scroll. Gleaming in the Gifahn sun, they rose out of the waters, their massive figures dwarfing even the pillars of the Ophar's Court. I saw first one, then a pair, then four, finally columns and columns, all leading us further upriver to the fork of Nahr where he split into the sibling rivers of Sand and Storm.

I'd known it was coming for days because, at some point, the waters of the Nahr had begun to change. Streams of gold threaded the currents, and I could tell from the taste that it was sand. The fish had changed too, smaller and less barbed. I knew we were nearing the place that Kida had called Karadoum, the Island of Sand and Storm. It was an important city as well as a strategic port, and it also housed the Library of A'Toth which was tended by the Scribes of Karadoum. It sounded like an ominous place and on the evening of our ten-and-seventh day, the island-city finally came into sight.

Torches and oil lamps beaconed us towards them, but it was twilight before our boat made landfall. The night air was cool and smelled of incense. A legion of armed guards holding spears, khopeth swords and torches awaited us.

"Majari," Kida whispered at the sight of them. "The Hand of Rath'nahr."

Josiat hoisted his satchel, swung it over his shoulders and the princess scowled at him.

"You don't need to bring that," she said. "It is safer on the boat."

"It is safest with *you*, princess," he said. "And where you are, I will be."

"Do not let them see," she hissed.

He smiled and stepped past her, up and onto the dock.

Kida turned to me.

"Anekh, *psat*!"

She clapped her hands and I lit to Shesset's shoulders, wings spread, and neck arched so that my spines rose like a crest. I was her crown, her mantle, her glory. I was also altogether too big for her, but she had trained her whole life and, while she was slim, she was strong. Still, I hissed at the guards as we stepped off the boat and was satisfied to note that more than a few of them stepped back.

"Esteemed majari," said Josiat. "The House of Bey honours you with the God's Light. Bring us to the Scribes of Karadoum."

The first guard thudded his staff on the stone dock and the legion split, allowing us passage between them. A black-robed priest led us down a long walkway flanked by statues, but soon, we entered a squared building with a narrow door. A brazier crackled in the centre of the room, and lamps hung from chains in the ceiling. I counted nine reeds standing in a semi-circle, and the room was flanked by those Kida had called majari.

One man stepped forward. He was dressed in a loose shift of white linen, with only a woven cord around his waist as a belt. He held a golden flail and nodded somberly at us all.

"Emissary of the House of Bey," said the man. "Welcome to Karadoum. I am Lo Karaket, servant of A'Toth and curator of the God's Library."

Josiat bent at the waist.

"I present to you Princess Shesset-Isset, Daughter of Thutmen'nahr II of the House of Bey and Ophar of the land of Gifah."

"You are mistaken, my lord," said Karaket. "Thutmen'nahr II no longer rules the House of Bey, and the House of Bey no longer rules the land of Gifah."

I could feel Shesset tense beneath me and I tightened my tail around her ribs.

"The gods do not suffer treason lightly," said the vizier.

"Treason is a subjective accusation, my lord."

I was prepared, then, when Shesset stepped forward.

"Treason is an abhorrent accusation," she said. "But it pales in comparison to blasphemy, lese-majesty and regicide."

The scribes were silent at this. She raised her chin.

"My father, Thutmen'nahr II, was a good man and a noble king, much loved by the people of Gifah. Now that he is dead, he sits at the side of Rath'nahr as a god of the heavens, along with Netjeh, the Greatest Great Gold in the history of the God's Land."

At the name of Netjeh, I barked once, twice, three times. The scribes stepped back as if afraid.

"I'll speak without pretence or decorum," Shesset continued. "I intend to restore the House of Bey with or without the assistance of Karadoum. How it falls for you afterwards depends on how you fall tonight."

Karaket gripped his flail.

"Karadoum is neutral," he said. "We support the current ruler, whomever the gods have chosen."

"So, I cannot trust in your support?"

"Once you sit upon the throne, you will have it."

"Until then?"

"To do otherwise is, well…" He smiled. "Treason."

I wasn't a reed. I didn't understand their politics or polemy. But I did understand tension and the room was tighter than the string on a new bow.

"Is it treason, gentle scribes," Shesset began, "To allow the daughter of a god to spend time in the Library of A'Toth?"

They exchanged glances.

"Time spent in the Library of A'Toth is a gift for all who look upon it, even more so for those who may decipher its pages."

She smiled thinly, like a knife. Her eyes were daggers.

"It is a good thing, then, that someone has taught the daughter of a god to read."

I thought I saw one man smile, but it disappeared as quickly as it had come.

"The gods have given us this library, and so, we honour them by opening it to you." The man spread his arms. "Allow Nephi to illuminate your path."

And he gestured to a young scribe with a shaved head and long face.

"My vizier, my vaskar, and I will visit the library immediately," said Shesset. "I intend to set out on the Sand for Penet in the morning."

"You intend to raise an army in Penet?"

"The House of Bey's intentions are reserved for those loyal to the House of Bey." Her knife-smile widened. "Unfortunately, that does not include neutral scribes serving a false king."

Karaket also smiled once again.

"You are a credit to your House, Shesset-Isset, and I look forward to the day of your rule."

He turned to the young man.

"Nephi, please show the Daughter of Glory to the Library. A'Toth will be honoured by her presence and his peace will be challenged by her tongue."

More men smiled this time, but I knew it to be true, every word.

"I will push my luck, gentle scribes, for some chalk and sheets of paprush for my vizier. We wish to make notes from A'Toth's great wisdom."

"It will be done as you request."

"And lastly, I trust also that a few cups of beer might be spared for my attendants, both here and on our humble boat? The Nahr is strong, and we have journeyed many days."

"Not only beer, princess," said the man. "The bakers of Karadoum make the best fig cakes in all Gifah."

"I look forward to them, then."

She turned her razor gaze on the boy with the long face.

"Nephi, now please. My dragon is heavy and my shoulders groan with her weight."

He ambled towards the door. I spread my wings and snapped at him, and he moved much faster after that.

***

It was very late when we entered the labyrinthine halls and darkly lit rooms of the Library of A'Toth. It was an impressive compound containing scrolls, parchments and records going back hundreds of years. Some were stored in tubes and slid into holes in the stone walls. Others were folded in large envelopes made of linen. Others were bound in leather and stored under small statues, protected by the gods, if not the elements.

The reeds spent hours poring over these papers by the light of many scented oil lamps. The words 'Penet', 'Nabir', 'treaty' and 'restoration' became dull but soothing wordsong for me, so I dozed on the top of a high pillar.

"Do you think King Marwethad will honour the Palm Treaty?" Shesset asked as she looked up from her scrolls. "It doesn't specifically mention a change of ruling house."

"This is the issue," said Josiat. "Both Palm Treaty and Sand Accord call for support in case of open warfare. This is different."

He sat back and sighed.

"Still," he said, "It was the House of Bey that signed those accords, not the House of Beyat."

"Agreed," said Shesset. "There may be old loyalties that we can leverage."

"It's the only thing we can hope for."

She thought for a long moment.

"What about Nabir? There is no explicit treaty, but my father always spoke of them as allies."

"Not allies," said Josiat. "But not enemies, either. We have had little to do with the Nabiri since the Dragon Trade ended over a hundred years ago."

I opened one eye at the mention of dragons.

"Again, that was an exchange between the House of Bey and the Nabiri," said Shesset. "They may have heard of the usurpation of Gifah and the murder of my father, but they would have received no party from Beyat. Surely not yet."

Josiat stroked his thin beard, thinking.

"He may have sent the Remoan dragons," he said.

"He wouldn't," Shesset growled softly. "Nabir would not welcome an invading army as emissary. It's political suicide."

"Beyat's a spoiled child, not a politician," said Josiat. "But you're correct, my princess. I think Adriam would council against the sending of dragons."

"And he has no infrastructure to support him," she continued, "No dragonets to send to Nabir, Penet, or even Lamos across the Nameless Sea. And we took to the river before he did. We should have the advantage of time if he goes by boat."

"The advantage of time only," said Josiat. "He has the throne. He has the army."

"I have the birthright," she said.

"A murdered king's blessing is nothing compared to a living king's blade," he said.

She said nothing.

Around another brazier, Kida sat with Nephi amid mounds of paprush and chalk. Kida was dragon-like in that she couldn't read, but Nephi was a helpful translator and tried to answer her questions. I gazed down at them, glowing in the warm light of the braziers.

"Dragons came from Nabir," she said to him. "They live wild in the mountains and tame in the cities."

"That's the story," said Nephi. "Although according to the Record of Amenophor, it's much more complicated than that."

She leaned forward, her large eyes gleaming in the lamplight.

"They ride them, just like the Remoans do. It was terrifying and exhilarating at the same time. The stories made me want to ride a dragon."

Nephi snorted.

"Well, you won't be riding dragons in Penet," he said. "They are forbidden to even enter the land."

"How do you stop a dragon from entering your land?" asked Kida.

"I don't know," said Nephi. "But you won't be bringing *her* to the palace of King Marwethad, that is certain."

He pointed at me atop the pillar. I flattened my spines at him. I did not like this Nephi. I would bite his thumb very hard.

"But she's a symbol of the throne of Gifah," said Kida.

"Not anymore," he said. "Best to sacrifice her now to the gods' favour and sell her for seket in the Market of Give and Take. You could buy an army with her golden scales."

"You're a vain boy," said Kida. "Anekh will never be a sacrifice."

"All dragons become sacrifices sooner or later," said Nephi. "As a vaskar, you know better than most."

Kida looked down, silenced.

I hated this word seket, and it bothered me to hear it now. Selling of dragon scale as a cure for disease, but that was all I knew about it. I wondered if that was why the flutterbys were sacrificed in the temples? But then, I'd never heard seket mentioned other than in conversation about me. Were the reeds healed by any dragon scales, or just by golden ones? I could believe it, but that didn't make it right. The conversations lulled and the wordsong stilled, but I did not close my eyes.

It was a very long, quiet hour.

Now, I have said before that dragons have excellent hearing, so it was the crunch of sandal on stone that first roused me. Most reeds go without footwear of any kind, so I was alerted and opened my eyes to see a glint of silver in the darkness. I barked and rose up, spreading my wings as five soldiers stepped into the light. They trained their arrows on me.

"Helots of my esteemed brother," said Shesset and she too rose to her feet. "Am I being ordered back to face a sham trial?"

They carried both spear and khopeth sword and their skin was painted with stripes of silver.

"Please come with us, princess," said a silver man. "We have a barge waiting."

"On who's orders, helot?"

"The orders of Beyat, First Ophar of the House Beyet, Son of Thutmen'nahr II, Rath'nahr and Othorys, Spear of the World."

"On what count?"

"Treason."

"There was no treason," she spat. "Ask the Ophar's vizier if you doubt."

"I have my orders, princess. You, the vizier and the vaskar are to come with us. If not, we are ordered to kill you all and return with your heads."

He raised his sword.

Josiat touched her arm.

"Princess, perhaps we should go. We can state our case in the Ophar's court."

She scowled.

"I will not be dragged back on the whim of a murderer." She raised her chin. "There are majari in every corridor. They will kill you before you can give the order."

"I see no majari, princess," said the silver man.

"What's more, the drakina breathes flame. I suggest you leave before she roasts you where you stand."

I lowered my head and snarled, let the flames roll and lick across my tongue. He remained still for a long moment, and I watched the battle play across his face.

"Forgive me, princess, but you leave me no choice. Archers, kill the dragon."

I sprang from my pillar as arrows sliced through the darkness to clatter against the stone where I had lain. I arced my wing and plunged, calling the acid in a burning wash up my throat. It was only my second time breathing fire, and I had little control of it, but the sythstone on my teeth sparked and I sprayed flames wildly onto the heads of two archers as I swept past. They howled as the fire melted their skin, and I swept up again, vindicated.

Suddenly, my shoulder burst with unexpected heat. I had been struck by an arrow and my head spun with dizziness and waves of pain. I tumbled to the floor, striking a soldier in my clumsy descent and together, we crashed in a flurry of golden scales and silver paint.

I could have stayed down forever. I could have curled upon myself in a tight ball, squeezed my eyes against the agony. But I heard Kida scream, so I struggled to free myself from the soldier beneath me. He grabbed my throat and tried to roll over to crush me under his weight. I snarled and sank my teeth into his chin. He shrieked, releasing me, and I spat him out to scramble away. Nearby, two archers writhed on the ground, their faces burnt from my fire. I swung my head – two silver soldiers remained between me and my reeds, their swords drawn. One lunged towards the princess, but Josiat threw himself in front of her and the curved blade sank home.

Finally, the majari flooded in through the corridors like the Nahr during the Weeping, and they struck down the two soldiers left standing. With efficient grace, they moved between the moaning three, plunging spears through flesh and fabric to clink on the stone floor. Soon, the library was quiet. Small fires had sprung up on the library's scrolls and Nephi scrambled between them, attempting to douse them before the entire room caught the flames. Karaket strode from the shadows, but my attention was taken as the vizier sank to the floor.

"No," commanded Shesset. "You're not allowed to meet the gods yet. You still have work to do. Get up."

He smiled, reached up to stroke her face.

"Glory of the House of Bey," he said. "You are far more clever than you know. Wear the Crowns of Sand and Storm with pride, Daughter of the Gods."

Tears of the Nahr ran down her cheeks.

"And you will be with me when I take that crown. Do you understand? Josiat, I command you. Josiat..."

Her voice became a whisper as his hand fell away. She caught it, clutched it tightly to her cheek.

Kida crossed the floor to me. I tried to move but my wing buckled beneath my weight. I arched my neck to see the shaft of the arrow sticking out of my body. I snapped at it, grabbing it with my teeth but light burst behind my eyes, and I snarled again. This was how my mother had died, pierced by the arrows of men, and the fury rose in my breast. I called the flames and sprayed the shaft. The thin wood sizzled and curled.

Kida grasped my beak.

"No, Anekh," she said. "I have to pull it out."

I growled at her. Truth be told, I would have bit her, had she not had my beak clasped in her hands.

She pressed one palm against my shoulder. Blood bubbled from the wound, and I hissed.

"Anekh, be still."

She wrapped her other hand around the shaft of the arrow, and with a deep breath, she yanked it free. Blood sprayed across the floor. Pain, pain, and more pain. I snarled and snapped at her, and it was then that I noticed the majari had surrounded me, their own khopeth swords ready to cut me to pieces.

"No," she gasped, and she pushed to her knees, laid her hand on my neck. "She's good now, aren't you, Anekh? She's good."

I growled again. My wound was stinging, and the blood flowed from my shoulder down my wingbone to my claws. I bent to clean it with tentative swipes of my tongue. The tang of blood was nothing compared to acid, ash, and flame, but it was new and sharp and a sign of how dragon blood was so easily spilled in Gifah.

Shesset rose to her feet.

"How did they get here?" she growled, and she looked up at Karaket, her eyes burning like dragonfire. "How did my brother's soldiers know we were here?"

"Esteemed princess—"

"Did you send them?"

"The Scribes of Karadoum are neutral—"

"Neutral unto death?" Her hands curled into fists at her sides. "You turn a blind eye to treason, but you cannot pretend to have no part in the murder of a king's vizier. The wisdom of A'Toth has left this place and the heavens weep at your fall from the heights."

"We have saved you," he said. "The majari did not have to intervene, but they did. You should be grateful."

"The majari serve the Crowns of Sand and Storm." She tugged the satchel from Josiat's body, pulled at the cord to reveal the gleam of green and gold. "They serve me."

There was silence in the library of A'Toth.

One majari nodded at her. He was a tall man with glyphs tattooed on his cheeks and chin.

"She speaks truth," he said. "We serve the Crowns."

"There are more soldiers coming," Karaket said. "Leave now before you lose more than a vizier."

The princess looked down at me.

"How's my dragon?"

"She's injured but I think she'll be fine," said Kida, and she stroked the spines of my neck. I growled and continued licking. The bleeding had almost stopped.

"You can't carry her," said Shesset. "Can she fly?"

"I don't know, princess."

"Assault on a Great Gold," she snarled. "Another in Karadoum's list of treasons. Get her up. We leave now."

"I will take them to their boat," said the tattooed majari.

"Make it swift, Abshir," said Karaket. "We're all in danger now."

With Kida's help, I took a tentative step. My wing claws curled under the strain, and I growled again. I tried to follow Kida towards the dark doorway, lumbering and limping in an awkward, land-borne gait.

"I'll carry her," said Abshir, the tattooed man, and he stepped forward, bent towards me. I flattened my spines and growled again.

"Anekh," said Kida.

"Peace, young dragon," he said, and laid a hand on my spines. "Like you, I serve the River Crowns of Gifah."

"Hurry," hissed Shesset.

I turned my head away. I was big but he was strong, and my tail lashed against his legs as he gathered me into his arms.

The princess turned to survey the library. Karaket stood in the centre, surrounded by majari, while despite Nephi's efforts, the chambers were still littered with small fires and smouldering scrolls.

Paper everywhere.

"What do you treasure most, oh esteemed Karaket of Karadoum?" asked the princess.

"Clearly not politics or personalities or royal houses, princess," he said.

"What do you treasure?" Each word bitten and precise.

"Knowledge, princess," he said. "Knowledge and the preservation of knowledge."

She nodded.

"Think of this as a gift from the House of Bey. Perhaps, one day, you will gain more than knowledge. Perhaps, one day, you will gain wisdom."

And she looked at me.

"Anekh Sun," she said. "*Kah.*"

The fire rose up my throat, rolled off my tongue and burst between my teeth like a song. The scribes screamed but Abshir held me tight. I sprayed the walls, and the parchment roles inside them caught, flames tunnelling deep into the stone. I sprayed the floors and the scattered paprush caught, rushing like an oil spill. I sprayed the tables and both treaties and fig cakes and wood caught, leaping like hands reaching to the heavens. I sprayed tight and far, and the records in Nephi's arms burst like fireworks and all the men shrieked as flames danced all around them.

"Run," said Shesset.

And they bolted down the corridor, feet slapping on the stone floors. Reeds rushed in all directions, not knowing how to meet the chaos, and shouting as they scattered. Soon, we were out into the cool air of dawn.

We raced to the docks to find a boat moored next to ours and a silver soldier stepped onto the embankment at our approach. His sword was drawn, his face furious. I didn't wait for the command and blasted the sails with my flames. He howled and fell backwards into the river. Our own crew scrambled to the oars as Shesset and Kida climbed aboard.

For his part, the majari slid to a stop at the end of the dock. I was almost as big as he was and I flailed in his grip, but he was strong and held me firm.

"Princess," he said. "I am bound to Karadoum, unless you give the word."

She spun round, her eyes flashing like blades in the firelight.

"You serve the Crowns," she snapped. "Join us and serve."

He stepped over the rail and onto the deck.

Both Shesset and Kida collapsed, and I sprang to the prow of the barge, wings wide, beak open. As the boat pushed out onto the River Sand, the towering statues watched us go. Karadoum glowed like an angry sun as flames from the library reached into the night sky. Soon, Selis Anekh peeked above the horizon, pulling the skyboat of Rath'nahr into the dawn. But we were away, gone, escaped down the river and it was two years before I set claw in Karadoum again.

11

THE RIVER SAND

The northern fork of the Nahr took us onto the River Sand. It was called this because of the silt carried in the current, giving the water a yellow cast. I could see it. I could taste it. The fish were different, flatter and oilier and they slid down my throat like wyrm. The river itself grew wider as well, and the riverbanks were lush with trees. There were palms and cedars, acacia, gumyum and peppers. Along the banks, villages came and went, but there were no large cities, which I thought was surprising. I was also surprised to see small per ahmets dotting the shorelines. I wondered if they housed kings or dragons, and if so, whom.

There were many creatures along the riverbanks that I had never seen before, and I listened as Kida told me their names. There were huge, round serat'horns, ridge-backed river wraiths and a type of stone buck with tiny horns, iridescent scales, and a neck so long that it could reach the leaves on the highest branches. We awoke every morning with the chittering of riversnakes and the skittering of water wyrms. We went to sleep every night to the drone of salt beetles and the song of the stars.

I did see sobethi so I was wary. I perched every evening on the side of the boat, watching for the familiar ripple, and listening for the dreaded splash that accompanied their hunts. We had survived one attack. I wasn't convinced our little boat would survive another.

I saw no dragons, however. No Remoan Flights searching for us along the river and no wild ones like my mother nesting along the banks. There weren't even the little flutterbys that used to fill the palace skies. It broke my heart to think that they were bred for sacrifice. Happy young dragons enjoying life and adoring their reed masters until the Wheel rolled over them and crushed them for the simple act of being. And while my wing was healing, I could not forget the fact that I had taken yet another wound in the cause of the princess. I would forever wear her seal, burned into my thigh as a scar.

Each night, as I watched the moons rise over the God's land, I ached for my brothers. Amok was already gone, sold down the UnderRiver for a chair of gold. I wondered if Khamet would fare better, and if I would ever see him again. I wasn't sure how I would feel if I did. My brother was my enemy, a thing that should never be.

In the days on the River Sand, I became skilled at breathing fire. The shards of sythstone seemed permanently attached to my back teeth and since I could call the fire at any time, it only took a spark to produce a mouthful of flame. I would sit on the edge of the barge and wait for debris to float by. Sticks, reeds, lilies, unsuspecting water wyrms. As we rowed one way and they floated another, I'd track them with my eyes and adjust my breath for angle and reach. Soon, I was able to hit almost anything. Fire was the sigh of the sun, the breath that burned. My right and my heritage, claimed and true. However, I do admit to some regret at the bleats of the unsuspecting wyrms as I turned them to ash.

I also learned to cook the fish that I caught. While I preferred them cold and raw, the reeds didn't, and one blast of flame was faster than leaving them to dry all day on the canopy. With the loss of Josiat, I knew I needed to do more to help protect these poor, lost reeds and filling their bellies was an easy thing.

The majari had joined us. His name was Abshir. He was older than Kida but younger than Josiat, and he was nearly as quick as me when watching for sobethi. He also worked the oar like the other reeds, and I think they were all grateful for his presence. Nothing was said, true, but dragons are skilled at interpreting silence.

In that vein, I realized that Shesset was turning to stone.

One evening, as we passed the lights of a riverside village, she, Kida and the last of her attendants sat beneath the canopy, watching Selis Anekh disappear beneath the horizon and her brother moons take flight across the sky. Amok the smaller was a sliver that night while Khamet was wide. Kida stroked my growing horns and scratched my thickening spines. Half the oarsmen rested while the other half rowed, keeping the northeasterly direction strong against the current. It was a moment of sadness and calm, much like the first days on the boat.

Kida looked up.

"Why did you choose me?" she asked, the first words spoken in the whole of the day.

Slowly, Shesset turned, eyes blinking slowly.

"What do you mean?"

"During the dedication, why did you ask for me? You had royal vaskars and other women in waiting. Why did you choose me?"

"I want what I want." Shesset shrugged. "Why do you ask?"

Kida sat forward.

"You once told me that when you became Ophar, you would be a good one. That you would change the way you rule, starting with how you lived."

Abshir glanced from vaskar to princess and back again, but the princess simply stared at her.

"You have a good memory."

"Did you mean any of it?"

"Every word."

Kida thought for a moment.

"You also told Josiat that he was not to love you the way he loved your father," she continued. "That he was to love you with his mind, not his heart."

Shesset narrowed her eyes.

"What of it?"

"Do you wish the same of me?"

"I wish both from you."

"Why did you burn the library?"

Kida had stopped scratching my horns. I nudged her to continue. The princess shifted, looked out over the waters.

"I…We needed…"

Kida waited. Abshir glanced between them both. The oarsmen rowed. The sail flapped. The riverbanks slipped by. I've said it before. Dragons feel tension. We feel it acutely, like a wing or a claw.

Finally, the princess turned to face her vaskar.

"No. I was angry. They had mocked my father's death. They belittled my position and the legitimate call to war. And they killed Josiat! Dear, good, gentle Josiat!"

Her tears flowed now.

"I rebuked him for loving too much! I called him weak, and he died in my arms, protecting me!"

Her eyes were glistening and fierce.

"I was so angry, and I wanted them to feel the pain that I felt. The pain I still feel! I wanted them to lose what was important the same way I had lost those things. I wanted Karadoum to burn the way Wa'ast burned."

Kida nodded.

"And they did burn, princess. Only now Gifah has lost a treasure and we have lost a valuable resource."

"I am looking forward, dear vaskar, not back."

"So, you are fighting for yourself, then, not Gifah."

"I *am* Gifah," she snarled.

"Josiat was Gifah," said Kida. "The Library of A'Toth was Gifah. Gifah is more than you, my princess."

There was silence for a long moment and Kida took a deep breath.

"I'm saying that, if you want to be a good ruler, then you must think beyond yourself. People can be resources, and we are just as valuable as a library or a bag of crowns. Yet, I got the lash because you tossed Anekh over a wall to prove something to your brother. Josiat is dead because you wanted to prove something to the scribes. What other resources will you waste because you have something to prove?"

The princess stared at her, face frozen like a river statue, but to her credit, she said nothing.

"You're the daughter of a goddess and have learned strategy your whole life," Kida went on. "Please use it for Gifah, otherwise we're no better than dead. You are so clever. You've a mind like no one else I've ever met."

"You talk to dragons," muttered the princess. "So that's not saying much."

There was a pause, a long bitter silence, then a sound like a snort. It was Kida's laughter, and it startled even the oarsmen. Reeds. I will never understand this part of them.

Shesset sighed.

"Continue to speak freely, vaskar," said the princess. "I will try to listen."

"I think that's a good start."

Shesset sat for a moment longer, before rising to her feet. She crossed the deck to the side of one of the oarsmen. She laid a hand on his arm.

"Rest now," she said. "It's time I took a turn at the oar."

They all stared at her, but finally, the oarsman left his position, resting in the shadows beneath the striped canopy.

Shesset gripped the oar, began to row and breathing returned to the royal boat.

It was in the early red hours of dawn that I realized we were being followed.

***

I've said it before. Dragons have excellent hearing.
Dip, splash, swing.
I raised my head.

Dip, splash swing; echoing above the sighing of the river.

I growled, flicked my tail, and beside me, Kida stirred.

"Anekh?"

I pushed myself up and spread wide my wings, opening my beak to breathe in the sights, sounds and smells of the river. It was dark, the water darker, but the distant glint of moonslight on metal was clear, as was the flash of stars across the waves.

Kida turned to nudge the sleeping princess.

"No," Shesset moaned. "Rowing is the hardest thing I have ever done. I would chop off my arms if I could only hold a blade..."

"Princess, we are being followed."

Immediately, Shesset sat up and Abshir rose to his feet. Together, they peered back across the River Sand.

"Perhaps another barge heading to Penet?" said Shesset. "The bridge is sure to be close."

"Bridge?" asked Abshir.

"A construct that spans the river. The Waterwall Bridge is the border between Gifah and Penet."

"There've been many boats on the river, princess," said Kida. "But Anekh's never reacted like this."

I could hear them. Splash and dip, splash splash dip.

Three boats filled with soldiers. I could smell the bronze of their swords. I could hear the silver on their tongues.

I growled again.

"Curse Beyat," the princess hissed.

"All hands to the oar!" snapped Abshir.

The resting reeds sprang to their posts and the barge surged forward under the power of frightened men.

I barked across the waters, even as my chest thudded like a summer storm.

"Tell her to burn them," snarled Shesset. "They will be little more than ashes floating on the river."

"Anekh," cried Kida, and I spread wide my wings. Just then, an arrow whipped past my head, disappearing into the dark water beside the barge. Another followed suit, and then another. Kida grabbed my tail and pulled me back into the boat.

"She's already wounded, princess," she said. "She can't risk taking another arrow."

"And we can't risk falling to Beyat," said Shesset. "We'll all die then, not just my dragon."

"Your dragon is strong and fast," said Kida. "She can pull the barge and add her strength to the oars and the wind."

"Do it," said Shesset. "But if they come too close, I will unleash her. There will be nothing left for the sobethi."

Kida scrambled past the oarsmen to the bow of the boat.

"Anekh," she gasped. "Anekh, come here and pull." She held up a hemp rope.

"*Luf!*"

Just like we did before, the night Wa'ast burned.

I sprang into the air and snatched the rope with my back talons, wheeling around the sail to the prow. I felt the boat jerk as I stretched out my neck and laid into the wind.

"Pull!"

The river spray cooled my belly and the boat moved swiftly now, aided by oars, sail, and dragon. The River Sand was choppy, making our way difficult, but behind us, three boats edged closer with each stroke. I fought the rise of acid in my throat. I could drop this rope, sweep around, and burn them all, but the princess had said no, and we all obeyed the princess.

I am convinced now that dragons know more than princesses.

The sun rose as Selis Anekh pulled the great god Rath'nahr into the sky, and the heavens painted strokes of pink, orange, and gold to welcome him. The song of the River Sand increased to a roar and ahead of us, I saw a shadow rising from the river to the skies across the land. It was a mountain range, a tall wide flat escarpment like the step of a god, and dividing it, a ribbon of gleaming white. Spray rose up where it hit, breathing clouds of white in the early morning pink.

We were nearing the foot of a waterfall, and my heart sank. Clearly, the River Sand continued his way up and over and into the land of Penet. There would be no way to carry this boat up a mountain like that, not on the strength of six reeds and a dragon.

"The Waterwall!" cried Shesset. "The bridge should be very soon!"

I narrowed my eyes through the waterwall mist, trying to focus despite my aching wings and racing heart. There! Just moments away, I could see a band of shadow stretching across the river, almost silhouetted in the waterfall's white spray.

"Once we pass beneath its stone, we are safe to claim asylum!"

"Will Penet's soldiers recognize the claim?" cried Abshir over the roar. "Will Beyat's honour our sanctuary?"

"They must," said Shesset. "Or we're dead. They'll kill every one of us."

"Anekh will burn them before it comes to that," said Kida.

Another sound could be heard over the roar of the waterwall. The drum of wings, the heartbeat of my people. I threw a glance behind me. Three great shadows bore down on us from the west.

"Dragons!" cried Abshir.

They were far away but gaining swiftly. An arrow splashed into the river beside me, and I dropped my head, throwing more power to my shoulders and forcing my wings to beat stronger, faster, harder. I didn't even feel the wound reopen and the blood begin to ooze.

As we closed in on this thing called a bridge, I realized that it was huge and made entirely of quarried stone. It spanned the wide River of Sand from side to side, with massive, curved archways like posts that straddled the water. I had never seen anything like it. In my memory, there were no such 'bridges' along or crossing the Nahr. This looked as if it had stood forever, and the waters flowed around its legs like morning fog. On the stone ramparts, I could see reeds silhouetted in the morning sun. They gathered along the edge as we neared, holding spears and bows of their own.

A dragon bellowed, the sound echoing along the river. They were closing in, and I knew one blast from their mouths would end our race in ash. Pushing past her people, Shesset scrambled to the prow, bracing as the boat rocked and bumped across the choppy waters.

"No, princess," said Kida. "The arrows—"

Shesset rose to stand at the very front of the boat and held Josiat's satchel high above her head. The linens fell away to reveal the marvelous bronze and gold headpiece, the River Crowns of Gifah. Slowly, dramatically, she set it on her head, and spread her arms wide.

In the mist and dawn light, she was glorious.

A Peneti arrow splashed to the right of the prow, another to the left. It was clear they didn't intend to kill, simply to deter. One by one, chain mesh curtains rolled down between the arches of the bridge, intending to block passage beneath and prevent entrance to the land of Penet.

"Men of Penet," she cried out to the figures on the wall. "I am Shesset-Isset, daughter of Thutmen'nahr II of the House of Bey, and Ophar of the land of Gifah!"

I flew harder. The reeds rowed faster. Only the centre arch remained open.

"I greet you in the name of Rath'nahr, father to both our peoples and wise ruler of all the gods!"

The hull of the boat thudded now as arrows rained from above and we beat faster still. Faster as the drum of wings grew loud and close. Faster now, as the last mesh curtain roll down on the last arch. I swept beneath it, and the curtain rattled as I struck the links with my spines.

"I claim asylum under the Palm Treaty and seek an audience with King Marwethad under the Accord of the Sand!"

That final curtain paused, and the rowers ducked as they swept beneath. Shesset did not, and the oarsmen caught the mesh curtain, sweeping it over their young monarch's head. Then, we were under the stone and darkness fell upon us even as the rowers carried us forward. My wingtips struck the waters with each stroke and I'm sure I held my breath as the metal curtain splashed into the river behind us. The silver soldiers were now barred but the dragons above were not.

Silently, we swept out from under the bridge, holding our breaths in the early morning light. There was no blast of fire nor snap of teeth. There was no hail of arrows or volley of spears.

"Anekh Sun," called Shesset. "Release. We are at the mercy of Penet."

I released the rope and swept up to the bridge to hover over the stone parapet. It was lined with Peneti soldiers, their arrows and spears trained on the three great dragons hovering just beyond, their great wings blowing spray across the stone. I could see the Remoan riders, deep in their leather saddles, cursing as they were prevented from entering Penet by the unspoken rule of kings.

A great blue drakina bellowed again, and I recognized her from the night Gifah fell. Portia. Her name was Portia. They had let us go that horrible night. They had let us live.

Her rider leaned forward.

"We have no quarrel with Penet," he called over the drum of Portia's wings. "We are charged with returning the rebel of Gifah, and her stolen dragon."

On the bridge, a reed in red held high a staff. It had a golden stalk of wheat at its tip, and I wondered if it was the symbol of Penet.

"Likewise, Penet has no quarrel with Gifah," he said loudly. "Nor does it wish to make war with Remus, long an ally. However, the Waterwall Bridge has been crossed and asylum has been claimed. King Marwethad is now sovereign over the lives of these fugitives and this dragon. Depart to your lands, with a promise from our King that all pleas will be heard, and justice will be served in his good time."

"Not acceptable," cried a silver soldier from one of the boats. "The princess has stolen the River Crowns of Gifah. She is under penalty of death from Ophar Beyat of House Beyat."

"That is now in the court of kings," said the man with the staff. "You know a dispatch has already been sent. Leave now. This will be my last request."

Suddenly, an arrow whipped through the air from one of the Gifahn boats. I wheeled as it whipped past me, striking a man who stood behind. He cried out and fell backwards and the line of Peneti archers released their volley, pelting the three Gifahn boats with tens and tens and tens of arrows. Reeds screamed, waters churned, but it was over in moments. The River Sand was fed. I lit back on the stone of the bridge and peered down at the three boats. They drifted away on the bloody current, taking the slain soldiers with it downstream.

The three Remoan dragons had not moved, and they hovered over the carnage, unswayed by the sudden turn of the tide. The man with the staff looked up.

"You are far beyond the borders of Remus, skyborn," he said. "And I'm certain you don't want to cause yet another war for your emperor. Leave now with your honour, and that of the Remoan empire, intact."

For a long moment, the only sound was the beating of great wings. Portia's eye blinked slowly in the dawn light as she hovered over the waters. I marveled at her grace and strength. One blast would render this line of reeds to char. Three dragons could melt the stone beneath their feet. And yet, this was not her fight, and she waited under the saddle of her rider, a Remoan mercenary.

Swiftly, the rider yanked her rein and the three dragons peeled away, splashing waters with their great wings. Then, they were gone, receding like shadows as they flew back along the river towards Karadoum. I barked before whirling in the air and dropping back to my boat, landing on the prow on the safe side of the bridge. A thin river of blood ran down the scales of my chest and belly, and I gripped the rail with my back talons. I didn't tuck my wings, however, and kept them wide as a fleet of small boats left from the southern bank. I wasn't sure if I had any fight left, but I was a Great Gold. I was noble, royal, proud, and good, so I arched my neck, causing the spines to stand up like the rays of the sun.

The first boat had rowers, archers and a reed holding a spear. We bobbed for several moments on the surface of the Sand as they closed in around us. Abshir and Kida stood behind the princess, flanking her on either side, but for her part, Shesset remained as if stone, arms crossed against her chest. Wearing the Crown of Sand

and Storm, she looked as regal as any of the statues of Karadoum.

"Princess Shesset-Isset," said a tall reed in linen and gold, his voice loud to be heard over the roar of the waterfall. "Welcome to the garrison of Waterwall. I am General Burhaan, commander of the Waterwall Border Patrol. Under the Accord of the Sand, I welcome you in the name of King Marwethad."

She nodded, ever so slightly.

"It is a four-day journey upriver to the royal palace in Moradin," he continued. "And the route is rich with waterfalls and mountain crossings and marvellous cities of silver and gold. I will accompany you and your party when we depart first thing tomorrow morning. But if it pleases you, today you should rest. Tonight, I offer an evening of refreshment here at the Waterwall."

Shesset nodded again, but I could see the tension in her shoulders. I could taste it in their words.

"I thank you for your kindness," she said stiffly.

"It is our great privilege. But there is one thing that will prevent you from making the journey with us…"

He turned his eyes on me.

"Dragons are forbidden in Penet."

"Why?" asked Kida.

"Penet is a land rich in resources. We are known throughout the world for our fruit trees and our crops, our flaxen shearers and our long-horned uru. You see, our greatest assets are agricultural, and as such, dragons are a threat to our way of life."

"My dragon is no threat, oh wise General," said Shesset. "She is the daughter of Selis Anekh, goddess of the Sun, and, as a Great Gold, she is the very symbol of the House of Bey."

He smiled.

"I understand, princess, but there are no exceptions. Not even when your father made excursion here seventeen years ago. He understood the need to keep his Great Gold in Wa'ast. We can arrange to accommodate your drakina while you go on to enjoy the hospitality of our kingdom."

"Please, princess," begged Kida. "We need her."

Shesset said nothing.

We bobbed up and down on the surface of the waters, he in his boat, we in ours.

"We have been on the river for almost a month," Shesset said finally. "Can we make shore to rest and discuss this like children of the gods?"

His smile widened.

"Our homes await, esteemed daughter of Gifah. You and your crew are welcomed to enjoy the hospitality of this modest border town."

"And we will discuss how you will properly accommodate my dragon."

"That will be our foremost conversation."

And just like that, the politics were over, and the relief flooded through the boat like the Weeping. Kida moved swiftly to my side.

"Anekh," she said, brows drawn as she examined my open wound. "Oh, my Anekh."

It didn't hurt, so I let her tend me as the rowers followed the fleet of boats to shore.

The entire complement disembarked and made their way towards a building of white-washed bricks, and I stayed, perched on the prow, until I could see them no more. I swung my head to survey the docks, not surprised to see the darting eyes of every Peneti in the vicinity. No dragons in Penet. This was a sad country, then, and I raised my head and bugled a long cry before leaping into the air and splashing into the river. I caught three fat shore wyrms and made sure to eat them, loudly and lustily, in full view of the reeds. Then with my belly filled, I curled up on the canopy. The smells from the village were intriguing, but I was tired after so long on the water. I missed my divan. I missed my shakhet baths. I missed the Ophar's court and Netjeh's slumbers and the little flutterbys swooping between the rooftops. I fell asleep to the roar of the Waterwall, and the river's song filled my dreams.

At noon, I roused again to fish and preen. The air was warm, the river spray cool, and I sunned myself, wings spread wide and beak open. My wound was almost closed, and I welcomed the looks from reeds passing by on the river or moored in their skiffs or walking on the shore. No dragons in Penet, indeed. They were clearly amazed, and perhaps a little afeared, and I wondered how they could stop a dragon if she flew into their lands. Politics is a past time of gods and reeds, not dragons. We are no respecters of borders.

Kida didn't return by late afternoon, or early evening, or even midnight, and for a while, I stayed curled up on the canopy in the aft of the boat. The moons called me out, however, and I watched them chase each other overhead. Amok and Khamet, twins of silver and shade, and my heart ached. While they shared the sky, they would never be together, and they would never catch their sister the sun. And so, I sang for them that night, for my brothers and my mother and Netjeh and for all the dragons who lived and died in this great, terrible land. My song slid up and down the dragon scales, heartfelt and lonely and infinitely sad, and once, just once, I could have sworn I heard an echo.

How could one stop a dragon?

I slept fitfully that night, alone on my boat, and it was early morning when I heard the familiar steps of my reeds on the docks.

"Anekh."

I rose and stretched, slapping my tail, and shaking my neck spines. They were growing in beautifully. I knew because I would often gaze at my reflection when the river was calm. Spines and spiral horns and shimmering scales. I was a Great Gold. I was a treasure, surely deserving the worship of the reeds.

"Anekh."

Kida stepped down onto the deck, and I looked to see the princess, the majari, the general and a few other reeds on the embankment. There was a strange, wheeled cart behind them, with bronze bars and a flat roof. An older reed in a long linen shift left the group and followed Kida onto the boat. He had a full beard and fuller belly and he stood behind her, holding a few strips of leather and chain in his hand.

Kida knelt down beside me, ran her hand along my neck. I nuzzled her, enjoying the feel of her fingers on my skin. She took a deep breath.

"Anekh, you are a good dragon. A very good dragon."

I knew it to be true, despite all the hardships that had befallen me.

She rested her forehead on mine.

"We have to go east to the king's city of Moradin, but dragons—"

Her breath caught in her throat.

"Dragons are forbidden."

Silly reed, I thought. I was bonded to her and the House of Bey. Where she went, I went also. I took one of her hands in my teeth, content with the holding, while she stroked me with the other.

"But they are good and gracious hosts. They have made a historic exception."

With my tongue, I could taste the salt of her skin, the spices of the meals she had eaten, the oil she used to clean her hands.

"You will come with us," she went on, stroking my chin and jaw and eye ridges. "But you will not fly."

I looked up at her. There was something in her voice. I could smell salt and tension. Sometimes reeds were a puzzle.

"You will not fly. You will not swim. You will not walk. And no, I will not carry you." She smiled with her mouth, but the Nahr spilled from her lashes. "But you will ride in comfort like a princess, pulled by an uru in that lovely cart."

The cart did not look lovely.

The man with the beard and the belly stepped forward. He pulled a silver band from his satchel.

"This is Anis Ixaak, King Marwethad's Wardyr of Beasts," Kida went on. "He has found you this new collar."

"It's from Remus, where the Dragon Flights come from," Ixaak said. "They have perfected the care and husbandry of dragons."

He passed the band to my Kida. She turned it over and over in her hand.

"It's not as pretty as your old one, but still, I think it'll serve us well."

I peered down to study it, took a nip with my tiny front teeth. Kida laughed.

Such a strange thing, laughter.

With both hands, she opened the band and placed it around my throat. It fastened with a click.

It was tight, and I shook my head. My first collar was not like this. My first collar was gold and jewels, soft and loose. I reached up to scratch at it with my hind talon, but Kida took my foot in her hand.

"No," she said. "You must leave it and wear it always. And these…"

The reed called Ixaak passed her the chains. I recognized them from my time with the House of Seb and my early training in the Court of the Great Gold. She fastened first one, then the other, around the slim bones of my leg, just above my taloned feet. I lifted first one, then the other, shook first one, then the other, hearing the chain rope rustle and clink.

I didn't need these anymore. I was a yearling, a Great Gold, a good girl, a royal dragon. I bent down to gnaw them off, but Kida caught my beak in her hands.

"No, Anekh. You must not struggle. This is the only way you can come with us."

And Ixaak passed her the strips of leather. She slipped them over my beak and around my head, tugging it tightly as it sat just beneath my young horns. I shook my head and snapped at her.

Except I couldn't.

I pulled my head back, tossed it again, tried in vain to open my mouth. I couldn't. The leather straps had my long muzzle bound shut and I turned a wild eye to Kida, to Ixaak, to the princess and the majari and all the reeds standing along the dock. I sprang back to perch on the barge's rail, but the foot hobbles had me fast. Kida reached for me, but I battered her with my wings and tossed my head. I could fly. I could still fly, and I launched up into the morning sky, but the Wardyr had a holdfast, and his grip was sure. I thumped back onto the deck in a rattle of chains as two other reeds rushed forward.

I would burn these leathers off and the hobbles too, so I called for the fire, but the fire would not come, and acid pressed out between my teeth. My eyes stung with the force of it.

"Please be still, Anekh," cried Kida. "I promise once we're in Moradin, you'll be free again."

"Cover her eyes," shouted Ixaak. "She will calm once we cover her eyes."

And the reeds on the dock leapt into the boat, with their many hands and many covers and many commands. I saw Kida weeping and Shesset on the dock, hugging her ribs, eyes shining like liquid daggers, her mouth a tight, grim line. They wrapped one eye, then the other, and then I saw nothing. And they folded my wings and lifted me from the boat like when I was taken from the banks of the River Nahr. They carried me in darkness once again, bobbing yet bound, to the cart of bars and the weeping of reeds and the laughter of the Wheel around me.

12

PENET

At some point, they removed my blinders, but
nothing else, and so, I travelled in that little cart,
watching with dull eyes as we headed into the foothills
of Penet. We were a part of a king's caravan with reeds
in carts, and reeds on foot, and their voices rose and fell
like the river. Occasionally, Shesset would laugh, but I
never heard Kida and I wondered if she laughed too. I
wondered if she wept. I must admit I didn't much care.
The feel of her hand setting the chains was burned into
my skin like the brand of the princess on my thigh.

As we travelled along a red, mud-brick road, the
River Sand rushed nearby, now churning white as both
river and road climbed into the mountains. It smelled
good to be near the water, and my heart ached with the
desire to swim and dive, to fish and to fly. But in this
cage, I couldn't stand, could barely fit my folded wings,

and the tip of my tail flicked out between the bars. Chains bit into my scales, leaving patterns in their wake.

The carts were pulled by long-horned urus, and I'm certain the beast following me was terrified as I watched him from the back of my cart. His eyes were round and ringed with white and constantly fixed on mine. I wondered if he thought I was going to eat him. I wondered that myself. I had only ever hunted fish. I knew the reeds ate urus, but I wasn't sure I could ever eat something so steadfast and hard-working, despite the growling of my dragon belly.

Besides, I still wore this dreaded collar and head muzzle. I couldn't even open my beak.

Penet was land of red. The road was red. The stones were red. We passed groves of ruby cloud fruit and fields of russet grass, the kind that was harvested to make sweet cakes. We passed villages of scarlet brick and clay, and always, the reed people stopped to watch as we rolled by. We passed *per ahmet*s grouped in threes. They were smaller and sharper than those in Gifah and made of red stone. I wondered what beasts were enshrined within them, since it seemed dragons were not. It was a rich, red, bountiful land but I cared for none of it.

Like Shesset, I was turning to stone.

Night came, and with it, the moons. Two blinking eyes, slivers of their usual orbs, lids closed as if to stay hidden, or to hide from sight the world of men. Only then would Kida would come to me, bringing water in a leather flask, but she was not allowed to open the cage door or remove my muzzle. She slipped her hand in and poured the water over my beak, hoping some of it made it to my tongue. I turned my head away, however, wing claws crossed beneath my chin. Hope was a thing for reeds and free dragons, not Great Golds in uru cages.

"It won't be long," came a voice and Ixaak appeared from the shadows. "Besides, it's hot on the road to Moradin. She'll drink soon enough."

Kida scratched my elbow with the tips of her fingers.

"Where will she go, once we reach the King's palace?"

The big man smiled.

"Why, to his bestiary, of course," he said. "King Marwethad has a wonderful menagerie."

"But no dragons?"

"They are forbidden."

"She's a good dragon," said Kida. "She wouldn't cause any damage to your kingdom."

"Dragons are how the House of Bey took Gifah from the House of Thenet," said Shesset as she too approached my cage, followed by Abshir the majari. He was her shadow, now, speaking little but watching all. "Dragons are power."

"And power corrupts," said Ixaak.

She raised a brow.

"But not you, princess," he added quickly.

"Are you sure?"

I flicked my tail, not looking at any of them.

"She's angry because of the muzzle," said Kida. "And this stupid collar."

"You can't take them off," said Ixaak.

"You are speaking to Shesset-Isset, daughter of Thutmen'nahr II of the House of Bey and true Ophar of the land of Gifah," said Abshir. "She is a threat to her brother, the usurper Beyat, and you know the resources he has sent to kill her. I can assure you he has sent assassins, and while I am majari, I am only one. This dragon is far greater protection than I could ever be."

Ixaak thought for a long moment.

"You may remove the muzzle," he said. "But the collar stays."

Immediately, Kida's hands were through the bars and behind my horns.

"But she stays in the cage," he added.

"Until Moradin," said Shesset.

"Until Moradin," said Ixaak.

My reed pulled the leathers from my face, and I shook my head, snapped my beak several times. My tongue was dry and stuck to the roof of my mouth.

"Feed her," said Shesset. "She is a growing drakina."

I rapped my tail on the cart. It was the smartest thing a reed had said for days.

And so, it went like this for many days, travelling by cart during the day, talk around my cage by night. Soon the road grew busy with carts and reeds and urus and buyers and sellers, and all stopped to stare as we rolled past. In fact, at one point, we halted, and a heavy cover was draped over the roof. That was the last I saw of the red road to Moradin. I suppose that was the last they saw of me, so maybe that was the intent.

At one point, I could have sworn I smelled dragons.

I'd only known a few grown dragons in my life. My brothers, my mother, the great Netjeh, and the Dragon Flights of Remus. Dragons have a scent unlike any other creature. Even under the sun-dappled cover, I lifted my head and breathed.

Yes. Dragon. I was sure of it.

But then it was gone, replaced by the smoke and smells of the city.

We rolled into the King's palace in the early evening. I could tell because of the rising noise and reverent music, then quiet as we rolled into the shade of a cool building. I had lived long enough in the Ophar's palace to recognize the sounds of a king's hall. I could hear voices announcing the arrival of the princess, and voices announcing the entrance of the king. Once, a corner of the woven cover was lifted and a young face peered through, but I heard Ixaak yell, and the face disappeared. I waited for a long while after that, my tail tapping in frustration outside the bars.

I'm sure I dozed a bit when the cart suddenly jerked forward, rolling again through shaded halls until sunlight warmed the cover and I knew that, once again, we were outside. Before I knew what was happening, the cover was yanked off and the door of the cage thrown open. Blinded by the sun, I lunged forward, snapping my wings open and leaping from the cage. Up, up, up I went, intending on getting as far away from my prison as possible but I was yanked to a halt midair by the chains at my feet. I bleated my displeasure and wheeled in the air, wings beating to keep me in place. I looked down to survey the scene below.

Sandstone and whitewash and tile and brick. Pillars painted with greens and blues, tall palms waving in the breeze. It was an open courtyard much like the Court of the Great Gold and many reeds stood in a half-circle, Kida, Abshir and the Wardyr Ixaak among them. Shesset stood next to a man in sweeping robes and they both gazed up at me, hands shielding their eyes from the sun. The man in sweeping robes threw back his head and laughed, and I wished I had fire to burn the tongue from his mouth.

"Anekh Sun," cried Shesset. "Daughter of Selis Anekh, goddess of the Sun and servant to the great Rath'nahr, symbol of the House of Bey and the great land of Gifah. Come and greet Marwethad, King of Penet and Son of the River Sand."

And she held out her arm.

I flapped my wings, glancing from Kida to Shesset beneath me. I had been caged. Me, a Great Gold of Gifah, caged like a sacrifice.

"Anekh Sun," said Shesset and she held her arm higher. "Come."

I knew what she wanted. She wanted me to land, to be petted, to be admired. She, who had caged me, a good dragon.

I was a good dragon.

I bleated to the sun but descended, reaching with my talons until I caught her arm. I was entirely too heavy for her and kept my wings moving and wide for balance. Shesset threw a glance at Kida. My reed rushed to help, and I hissed and squawked as they held me between them.

"This is Anekh Sun, my Great Gold," said Shesset and she turned her eyes to the robed man named Marwethad. "You may touch her."

"She will not bite me?"

"She will not."

He reached tentative fingers and I nipped at them.

"*Naht,*" said Kida and she flicked my chin.

I shook my head, watched Marwethad reach forward again. I hissed but did not nip as his dry fingers touched my ribs.

"Oh," he breathed, and ran first fingers, then hand, along my side, under my wing, up my neck to the spines at my throat. "Oh, she is warm."

"And strong," said Shesset. "Without this foreign collar, she could destroy an army."

Marwethad nodded but said nothing, engrossed in the study of me. He touched my chin, my young horns, the ridges over my eyes. I bared my teeth at him, and he gasped.

"How old did you say?"

Shesset looked at Kida.

"One and a half years," said my reed.

"Old enough to breed?"

Kida was silent. I growled deep in my throat, not knowing this word.

"Vaskar?" prompted the princess.

"Old enough, yes," said Kida. "But the drake must be young too or—"

A cry echoed from beyond the court and shadows swept across the sun. All reeds looked to the skies and my heart leapt to my throat.

Three winged shapes, circling, silhouetted in the sun. Dragons. I knew it! No one could stop a dragon, no policy or agreement, no bridge nor invented division.

"Remus?" barked Shesset and Abshir rushed to her side.

"Not Remus," cried the king, and he held his hands out. "Not Remus!"

These dragons had a distinctly different scent and I beat my wings furiously until my reeds released me. I rose on the stifling hot wind to meet them, but I couldn't, bound to the earth as I was by the chains in Kida's hand, and so I flapped and flailed at the end of the tether, wishing I could meet them in the clouds above.

They circled lower and lower, one blue, one grey, one red, and their wings lifted the sand into swirls beneath them. I called to them, singing the only song I knew. The blue sang back and, as he descended, I noticed a red banding stripe running the length of his body from snout to tail. He was twice my size, as was the red, but the grey was larger still, with a pale underbelly and spots on his wings.

To my utter shock, there were reeds upon their backs, but no silver. These were not Remoan riders. These were not Remoan dragons.

I folded my wings and allowed myself to sink back to Kida's arms. She gripped me tightly, but, I think, not because I was heavy.

Everyone stepped back as the trio touched down on the tiled ground and the sound of their breath filled the courtyard. First the grey, then the other two, spread wide their wings and lowered their heads and I noticed the shape of a hand painted in gold across each eye. The riders slid from their backs, their sandals raising dust as they struck the stone. Together, they strode over to the princess and the king, while the red rider followed several paces behind, both hands on the swords at his hips.

The king spread wide his arms.

"Dejenai! Nakosa! Penet welcomes you!"

"It's been too long," said the older man and the two embraced like brothers. He was shorter and grey with a thick chest and a bad eye. The blue rider was younger and taller, and he did not embrace. Rather, a swift nod and the flash of a smile, but his eyes had fallen on me.

King Marwethad turned.

"This is a miraculous day, when all of the nobles of the God's lands assemble together in peace. I am blessed to introduce King Dejenai and Prince Nakosa of the Nabiri Skyborn to Princess Shesset-Isset, daughter of Thutmen'nahr II of the House of Bey of Gifah."

"Your father is with Rath'nahr in the Great Halls of the Sky," said King Dejenai, the man with the bad eye. "He will be missed by those of us who have not made that journey."

Shesset nodded.

"I did not know you knew my father."

"By correspondence only. I had no occasion to visit Gifah, and he had no occasion to visit Nabir. Such is the life of a king."

"Why do you chain your dragon?" asked the prince and all turned to him.

Shesset straightened.

"In Gifah, we do not chain our dragons," she said. "But we are not in Gifah."

"Forgive my son," said Dejenai. "His tongue gets the better of him at times."

"As does mine," said Shesset.

"In fact," said Marwethad. "I was just discussing with the princess how to set up a limited breeding program in Penet. We've been closed to change for so long."

"As a child, I had heard you rode dragons," said Shesset. "I'd thought it a myth."

"And we prefer to keep it that way," said Nakosa. "It offers a surprising advantage on the battlefield."

"I need such an advantage if I'm to reclaim my country."

"That's an ambitious thing," said Nakosa.

"I am an ambitious woman." Shesset's eyes gleamed. "Ask anyone who knows me."

Dejenai laughed.

"Your father must have loved you very much."

"I loved him more than my life."

"And your brother?"

"A murderer, usurper and traitor."

"He's bought an army from Remus. How will you defeat such strength?"

Her smile was that of a knife.

"With armies of Penet, the navies of Lamos, and the dragons of Nabir."

"Such an ambitious woman!" Nakosa laughed now.

"We can discuss this, and many more things, over dinner," said Marwethad. "The dragons can stay in my bestiary in Diddad Wat. There are many cages and pens available."

"Our dragons do not live in pens," said Nakosa.

Kida lowered her eyes. Kingdoms and policy, laughing and knives. It was confounding then. I confess it still is.

"Well, Ixaak will think of something," said Marwethad. "Dragons, and people of the dragons, go with him. Kings, princes, princesses – all the God's children," and he grinned, "Will come with me."

I watched the God's children disappear beneath the painted pillars, while Ixaak shrugged, turned, and walked the other way. Kida kissed the top of my head and followed.

***

There were many courtyards in the palace of Marwethad, King of Penet, and Ixaak brought us to one of them. He'd spread the chaff from the sweet grass of the fields, and I thought it perfectly suitable bedding under a wide, open sky. The Nabiri dragons met us there and I marveled at their size and freedom. Grey, red, and blue, striped and spotted, they were almost the same as the Remoan dragons, and I studied them like I had never studied anything in my life.

Ixaak had also brought several slaughtered beasts that I assumed were uru, and the Nabiri dragons made short work of them. For me, I hadn't eaten anything save slivered wyrm in days, and I fell upon the flesh with relish. My razor teeth sliced large chunks and I tossed my head back, eager for them to slide down my throat. They didn't, and I retched, bringing them back up and onto my tongue.

"The collar," said Ixaak when Kida asked. "It prevents them from swallowing large pieces of food whole."

"But why?" asked Kida.

"To keep them dependent, I suppose," he said. "Dragons are dangerous predators."

As I spat out the flesh and proceeded to nibble it with my tiny front teeth, Kida's fingers toyed with the band.

"Anekh is not dangerous," she said softly.

"She could be when she's older," he said, and he gestured at the Nabiri dragons. "The bands would also prevent their fire if I had the authority to collar them. You cannot tell me that, even now, their fire is not dangerous."

Kida said nothing. It didn't matter. I was so hungry that I grabbed a piece, tossed it onto my back teeth and chewed. Dragons don't chew. We don't have the teeth for it. We tear and swallow, grind and slice. And so, it took a long time to chew and chew and chew that piece of uru, and the acid bubbled up in my mouth, turning it all into mush that slid down my throat like a paste.

I gagged and shook my head, eyes watering at the sensation.

It was twilight when I'd finally eaten my fill. Kida had settled down in the sweet chaff, her back against a pillar. I curled next to her, wings folded across my back, head in her lap. The stars were out, and the moons were high, one slowly opening now while the other still winked. The sky was clouding over, claws of red and pink and purple, and I wondered what it would be like to fly through them, if the clouds would brush my scales like wool or slip over my wings like linen. I had never been so high. Truth be told, I had never been so free either. Not like the dragons of Nabir, even with riders on their back.

There was a sound, and I snapped my head, growling.

"Forgive me," said prince Nakosa of Nabir.

"For what?" asked Kida.

"For startling you," he said.

She held her tongue, I knew. Restraint was her signature, discipline her strength.

"You're Lamoan," he said after a moment.

"My mother was from Thima," she said. "A city on the shores of the Nameless Sea. My father was a Gifahn trader who worked the markets along the coast."

"How did you come into the service of the princess?"

"I worked as a vaskar in Wa'ast and studied my way in," she countered. "Not all are born in a palace."

"Forgive me twice then," he said, and he turned his head. "I need to check on Anshassar, Kharsis, and Bask."

"The dragons?" asked Kida. Her eyes gleamed at the words. "They are remarkable."

"Bask is mine," he said. "Bask, son of Bash. He's young, so I can only pray he'll behave."

And he smiled. Kida ran her hand along my spines.

"I've never worked with dragons so large. They are culled before their third year in Gifah."

He shook his head. "For all your accomplishments, Gifah is still a land of many chains."

"How does it feel to ride them?" she asked.

He folded his arms and looked over at the blue drake, nibbling on the grey's wings like a brother.

"Free," he said, after a while. "That is why we are called Skyborn. It is like nothing you've ever known, until you know it. You are reborn once you have flown."

Kida said nothing, continued to stroke my head.

"Will you stay with her?" the prince asked.

"Her?" asked Kida. "My dragon?"

"Your dragon?"

"The royal dragon, the princess's dragon. Not mine. She—she's not my dragon." She glanced up. "Is that what you mean?"

"Yes. No. Both," he said, and he shrugged. "Marwethad and your princess are in talks to see the Kingdom of Penet support her claim for the throne of Gifah. They've sent a message to Illyrio of Lamos, requesting ships. It will take months, if not years, for the plans to be approved and the armies to be readied. Tardek is the war city of Penet. That is where your princess will go if she is to fight for the right to rule."

"I don't understand," said Kida. "I go where she goes."

"But your drakina doesn't. Your drakina goes to Diddad Wat, where the King's bestiary is. In exchange for the armies, Marwethad gets to breed your dragon when she's ready. She'll go south while your princess goes east."

Kida hugged me tighter, and I held her thumb. I wanted to slink over to the drakes, sit in their shadow while the sun still sang.

"She's a fine drakina, but she's still young," he said. "I hope she's not used up to restore some golden chair. It's not worth it."

He gazed over at the drakes, sighed.

"Well, it's been an honour to meet you, Kida of Lamos." He gave a small bow. "And you too, Anekh Sun of Gifah. I pray you success and long life."

Kida looked up.

"Are you leaving?"

"At dawn," he said.

"But—"

"This is vanity," he said. "There will be no Nabiri dragons joining your campaign, and because of that, you will fail."

He bowed again.

"Sky bless, sister."

He left the pillar and strode over to the dragons, speaking to them in soft, musical tones. They purred at his approach, trilled as he ran his hands along their scales. How I wanted to go with them, mount the clouds, sweep the mountains. But I was here in a stall with sweet chaff and sadness. Still, I had Kida, and I knew she'd never let me go south while she went east. She would never do such a thing. Never.

I should have remembered the Wheel and how it turned, how it crushed all things under its spokes. I wouldn't have slept if I had remembered. I wouldn't have dreamed had I known.

We were parted the next morning at dawn.

13

THE BESTIARY

The bestiary was south of Moradin and not surprisingly, I made the journey in chains, collar, and muzzle. And yes, in an uru cart.

It was an uneventful trek along a single, palm-lined road, flanked on both sides by arid hills and desert plains. Red sand and red rocks, markets and pointed per ahmets. All leading to Diddad Wat, the summer home of the King.

It was as large as the Ophar's palace, surrounded by a river carved by reeds.

Once there, I was dragged into a cage that allowed me to turn around, and no more. It was as high as my wings were high, and as long as I was long, from point of beak to tip of tail, with a stone base and iron bars for walls and roof. There was also a floor-to-ceiling metal mesh screen that could be pulled across the floor when

they cleaned it, and it took three reeds to do this task –
two to lever the mesh and one to scrub the stone floor.
Truth be told, they cleaned it every day, so I was in no
danger of sickness or ill health. Also, I was still a good
dragon. As best I could, I lifted my tail and shat outside
the bars.

The cages lined the periphery of a large courtyard,
and to be fair, each cage was nestled beneath a leafy,
damal tree that gave us shade during the hottest times of
the day. There was a wide expanse of gardens in the
centre of the court, and while the flowers, shrubs and
exotic grasses were a respite for eyes, it was the central
fountains that were the true blessing. There, fresh water
leapt and bubbled all day, and often, the spray was
carried on the breeze to keep us cool. Ixaak was a
conscientious wardyr, and I do believe he had our best
interests at heart.

Besides, I knew Kida was coming back for me. She
was my reed, and I was her dragon. It was only a matter
of time.

Most days, I lay in the coolest part of the cage,
hoping for the overspray from the fountains. I had long
since stopped studying the others collected in this
courtyard menagerie. There were two different
serat'horns, a flat-backed river wraith, a very old sobethi
(who was the first and only sobethi I'd ever pitied),
several armoured plainsbucks and a tawny rassa. I was
the only dragon, and people paid to come and see.

This wasn't how Ixaak made his living, however. He was a dedicated servant of the king, and he delighted in showing off the king's collection to his many friends, colleagues, and political associates. Ixaak himself was very generous with both time and possessions, but there were many reeds needed in the upkeep of such a place. It was they who made a small fortune on the side, slipping customers under the gates and over the walls when Ixaak and his family had gone to bed.

It was an entirely sedentary, tedious life for a dragon. For any creature for that matter, and the rassa would pace from end to end of his cage, from the first breath of Selis Anekh to the rise of the brother moons. He was big – almost as large as me, with great powerful forelegs, a ridged spine and curved fangs that hung like daggers over his bottom jaw. Of all the creatures in Marwethad's collection, he was the only one I feared. I was glad we had an empty cage between us.

I was never forced to wear the muzzle. Many hands had removed it after placing me in the cage, sliding the mesh wall to keep me in place and freeing my beak. The hobbles above my talons were still there, though, as was the collar, or silver band. It was heavy and tight, and pressed upon the middle of my throat, preventing me from swallowing anything larger than diced wyrm or fish. I remember the first time a bucket of wyrm slop was slid into the cage. I looked at it, then at the reed who had brought it. But I made the best of it and ate it, right down to the last sticky scrap of pink. I then played with the bowl for a while. It was, to be honest, the most interesting thing I'd done that day. But the novelty of wyrm slop in wooden buckets wore thin very quickly, and soon, I'd simply eat and be done.

After many days, Ixaak came by to inspect my compound. He had with him a very small reed who walked with a crutch and a twisting gait.

"Well, Gaviid," he said to the boy. "Here she is. A Great Gold from Gifah."

The boy gripped the bars with both hands.

"She's so beautiful, abbahay," he breathed. "What's her name?"

"I don't know, Gaviid. What would you call her?"

He thought a long moment.

"Emay," he said. "It means golden, I think."

"You're a very smart boy."

Gaviid smiled.

"Do they really ride her?"

Ixaak laughed.

"No one rides dragons, Gaviid," he lied. "But this one has pulled her share of river boats, or so I'm told."

"The Nabiri ride dragons."

"Also, a myth. It's too dangerous."

"I would ride her…"

"You would ride her?"

The boy nodded.

"You mean, you would fly?"

And with a swift motion, Ixaak grabbed the boy by the arms and swept him up into the air.

Laughter again, and I wondered if the man would throw the child into the rassa cage. Instead, he swung him up and onto his shoulders, snatching the crutch from the ground as they turned to leave.

"Can I feed Emay, abbahay?"

"I'll get Cawil to give you some lessons. But you have to be very careful."

"I will, abbahay. I promise."

And then they were gone, leaving me with the fountains and the bucket and the bad-tempered rassa pacing next door.

Day turned to night, night turned to day. I watched as the dance of the sun and the moons became routine, a mundane tedious repetitive cycle changed only by the waxing and waning of the brothers. I smelled the fruit grow and ripen and I saw the grass turn to seed and blow away in the wind. I heard natural thunder for the very first time, and for the very first time, I felt water fall from the sky in the form of rain. There was no rain in Gifah. All water came from the Weeping, and so, the first time the clouds opened and the waters came down, I was afraid. Soon, I learned to delight in it, and I would close my eyes and open my beak and let the water splash into my mouth and run down my throat.

And I lived outside in those rains, enjoying them far more than the scorching heat of summer or the arid

winds of winter. I lived through the howl of the karads –
windstorms that filled the skies with sand and buried
entire villages in dust. I slept in those times, when they
would seal our cages in cotton tarps to protect us from
the sand. I slept and I dreamed, and I thought of Netjeh,
too large to move, to weary to try. I often thought of
Kida, her great dark eyes, her gentle hands, her spirit of
protection and her quiet strength. She was coming back
for me, I knew. But then my throat would grow tight,
and I'd curse the band that she'd placed there, and dark
thoughts began to intrude, bringing with them the first
shadows of doubt and needles of fear.

But I chased those thoughts out of my mind. They
brought nothing but ache and loss and memories of
young dragons and death. So, I slept, and ate and grew,
all in that little cage in the compound of the king's
wardyr. The only highlight in my day was Gaviid.

He was allowed to feed me every other day, and he
would wait patiently for Cawil and the others to slide the
mesh into the centre of the cage, forcing me back against
the far wall. I went willingly, for now, my bucket of fish
and wyrm slop was one of my only diversions. Cawil
would unbolt the cage door and Gaviid would scramble
in and wait again for the bucket to be passed into his
arms. He'd slide it in through the little square hatch and
watch with wide eyes as I dove in with relish. I wish I
could say that I took my time. I really should have, all
things considered, but my entire life was centered

around two buckets of bloody, slimy flesh. It was hard to remember that I had once been a Great Gold.

Even in the rains, Gaviid would come. Sometimes, he'd reach in to touch my scales and I'd rest my nose close to the bars, warming him with the breath from my nostrils. I loved those moments, remembering Kida and how she'd stroke my eye ridge or my horn buds or my chin. Gaviid learned to trill, and we'd play trill and repeat for as long as his father would let us. Once, he brought me a whole fish and I foolishly tried to swallow it but was forced to retch it out and grind it into mush with my many great teeth. It took me the better part of an evening to finish that fish, something that once had been gone in a gulp. Still, it was different in a time when nothing was, and I was grateful.

Gaviid was often sick, so his father soon forbade him from spending much time in the menagerie, and certainly not in the rains. Days would go by, and I wouldn't see him, but when I did, I was as happy as a caged dragon could be.

One night, while I dreamt of Kida and the River Nahr, I caught a scent that didn't belong in the bestiary.

Dragon.

I lifted my head. It was dark with only one moon smiling down on me, and I heard the rush of wings in the wind.

I rose to stand, pushed my face against the bars, and breathed in his scent. There, his shape silhouetted against a starless sky and in near silence, he landed in the courtyard, wings wide, tail lashing. He lumbered to the fountain, and in the moonslight, I could see he was the deep green of jungle leaves. He breathed in the scent of the water, lowered his head, and spat a wad of acid at the base of the fountain. Marking his territory, I knew, because it cooled to soft, pungent wax in the night air. Then, he drank deeply, great gulps of cool, fresh water. The bucket I got daily was stale, and my throat ached at the thought.

After he drank his fill, he tossed his head up and down, splashing the water over the sides. He was playing, and my heart ached at the sight. I wondered if he'd ever swam, if he dove for fish or taunted sobethi or played in the reeds along the banks of a river. He was a wild dragon in a land that forbade them, and to me, he was a beautiful thing.

The plainsbuck bleated from a cage across the court and he lifted his head, snorting as he sifted the scents of the various creatures in the bestiary. His nostrils flared and he swung his head in my direction. I flattened against the floor of the cage.

The green drake took one step, then another, his knuckled wing claws thudding on the earth as he moved towards me. He cocked his head, first one way, then the other, before stretching his neck out to the bars. And then, he trilled. It was soft, quiet, a rumble like distant thunder rolling from his tongue and I rejoiced at the music of his voice.

I trilled back.

He lashed his tail and tossed his head and my chest threatened to burst. He pranced in a wide circle, neck arched and crested with spines. He was magnificent and he knew it and I wanted to push myself from these bars and leap into the night to fly with him and never return.

He circled back now, pressing his beak to the edge of the bars. I did the same. He breathed out a long, deep breath and I inhaled him. Smoke, musk, sythstone, acid. Wild. Freedom. Sky.

I was a dragon in a cage.

There were whispers and the flash of a torch, and I knew Cawil was bringing a secret, paying guest to view the king's collection. The drake stepped back and snorted before rearing up on his strong back legs and leaping into the air. His wingbeats sent wafts of dragon musk down as he disappeared into the night.

I, too, had been a free dragon once.

I did not sleep or dream after that.

He did not come the next night, or the next, but he did come again a few weeks later, landing quietly in the courtyard for a long drink at the fountain. I trilled at him, and he swung his head, streams of water spraying from his beak. He arched his neck, his crest and winged forelegs stiff as he strutted to my cage. Once again, he pushed his muzzle between the bars and droplets of water gleamed in the moonslight. I darted my tongue across his chin to catch one, savouring the taste, fresh and sweet as spring rain. He opened his mouth so that water spilled between his fangs, and I lapped it up eagerly. His scales were like pebbles, and I nibbled them with my tiny front teeth. I heard him purr as he pressed his jaw, then throat, against the bars.

The grooming of dragons. So different than Kida's brushes and paint.

He returned every few nights after that, and I wondered if he had a route that he maintained. With Penet's persecution of dragons, he would have needed to hunt at night and stay hidden during daylight, so I had taken to thinking of him as Mehen, the great dragon protector of Rath'nahr as he travelled the underworld during the long, cold nights. It was one of the things I remembered from my time in the drakmet, when Seb told stories by the brazier.

Between the visits of Mehen and young Gaviid, I had something to look forward to other than green water and buckets of wyrm.

There was a month when the rains were late, and drought stretched its killing fingers across the land. To my despair, the central fountain dried up and the damal leaves withered, leaving us baking in the heat without relief. In fact, it was so hot that many of Ixaak's servants did not show up to care for us, leaving Cawil and young Gaviid to do all the work. Beasts grew hungry, and I could only imagine Mehen in the wild with no reeds to tend him.

That night he came, as green as a jungle vine, and he immediately made for the fountain. I heard him grumble in the base of his throat, watched him gnaw at the basalt with his powerful teeth. He turned his head and looked at me and through the moonslight, I could see his sunken cheeks and hollows around his eyes. It was then that the plainsbuck bleated. It was then that everything changed.

Slowly, Mehen approached the buck's cage, head low, tail lashing. The leggy creature bleated again and again, darting from one end of its small pen to the other. In the next enclosure, one of the serat'horns wailed as the dragon advanced. He pulled back his head and opened his great mouth and the dark courtyard flashed with the breath of dragonfire. In a burst of flame, the plainsbuck went down, head and wild legs thrashing, and the moment a hoof came through the bars, Mehen struck, catching it in his jaws with powerful force.

Oil lamps came on all throughout the great house, accompanied by the shouting of the reeds, and still Mehen did not release. The buck's dying cries ceased, and the air was filled with the scent of charred flesh, but he tugged and tugged until finally, the sizzling leg came off in one go.

"Go! Go!" cried Ixaak as he and Cawil rushed into the yard. "Cursed beast, begone!"

Mehen tossed the leg to the back of his mouth, hoof out one side, bloody thigh out the other, and he charged Ixaak, snapping his wings and leaping skyward before they met. He was silhouetted by the moons in an instant, but my heart had shattered in a thousand tiny pieces. I knew what was coming. I knew how this would end.

"What is it, abbahay?"

Ixaak looked down at Gaviid, with his crutch and his great, round eyes.

"A dragon," he said. "But it is over now. Go back to bed."

"A wild dragon, abbahay?"

"Yes. We will need to inform the king."

"Will he send archers?"

"I suspect so." He laid a hand on the boy's shoulder. "Now, go. I have to help Cawil with the buck."

"Well, at least the rassa will eat tomorrow," said the boy as he headed back to the house.

Within three days, there were soldiers in the bestiary. Archers with their bows and quivers, swordsmen with their blades and spears. They placed vats of water in every corner, left baskets of fish by every door. To lure the wild dragon or disguise their scent, I didn't know, but I knew it would be bad. There would be no bars or cages for my jungle-green dragon, only death at the point of many blades.

Each night thereafter, they waited for him in the shadows. Each night, I hoped he would not come.

But of course, he did.

Wide-eyed moons that night, as if the night goddess, Naret, watched with interest the affairs of reeds and dragons. As if the twins, Amok and Khamet, watched as well, eager to witness the death of one of their own. It was then that I hated the moons and the night and the goddess. All bad things happened under their insatiable gaze. My mother's death, the fall of the House of Bey, the Burning of Karadoum, and now this. I was Anekh Sun, daughter of Selis Anekh, Goddess of the Sun, and I was powerless because of the reeds and their cages, their collars and the night.

Mehen died that night as swiftly as he came. I barked to warn him when I heard the rustle of his wings, but it didn't deter him and the moment his talons touched down, the arrows loosed, thudding into his green body like the beating of a drum. He bellowed and coiled to spring, but a second volley shredded the leather of his wings. The soldiers rushed him next, swords drawn, and he sprayed them with a blast of dragonfire. Some fell to the ground, screaming as they burned. A third volley of arrows and he swung his great head, flame spewing from his tongue, tail lashing as his body hit the stone. The spearguard came next, hurling the weapons from the darkness, then moving closer as his struggles slowed. They stabbed him repeatedly until the last twitch of a talon, the last flutter of a wing. The smell of blood overpowered even that of the fish.

There was silence then, save for the moaning of a lone serat'horn, and the weeping of a young boy under the arch of a door.

It was then that I knew Kida was never coming back.

14

THE KARAD

If the death of Mehen was the beginning of the end of my months in the bestiary, then the 'end' of the end was the night of the karad. The day had started off unnaturally quiet, with not even a breeze to cool the skin. The drought had meant that the reeds could barely keep us watered and the old sobethi died that week because of the lack. They did not move him from his cage and his body quickly became a haven for piks, skarabs and sand wyrms. I hadn't seen Gaviid for many days and I hoped he hadn't succumbed to this heat as well. I would be sad if that were the case, but I had already lost one friend in this horrible place. A second wouldn't have surprised me.

The wind started just before noon, turning the sky the colour of stone. Inside the cages, creatures either paced furiously or made themselves as small as possible. I was one of the latter, folding my wings across my back and curling my neck and tail into a tight coil. By mid-afternoon, the sky was green, bringing with it pellets of sand that stung like skorpiochs. Soon, a bank of red cloud rolled towards us like a tide.

Ixaak and Cawil came early to feed us and to lower the awnings meant to protect us from the sand. The wind howled now and the grit that came with it was strong, shredding the cloth within minutes. Useless, I thought, and I tucked my head beneath my wings to shield my eyes.

Cawil paused, one hand on my gate, the other cradling a bucket in his arms. He tossed my bucket in, spilling its contents across the stone floor, and struggled with the latch on the door of my cage.

"This is pointless, wardyr!" he cried. "None of them will eat in this!"

I didn't move, caring more to stay tucked into myself and out of the sting of the sand.

"The last karad howled for six days," shouted Ixaak from the wraith's pen. "The king lost all of his collection in one week! I can't let that happen again!"

"But wardyr—"

"Do your job, Cawil! Marwethad pays you well!"

Cawil snarled and moved on to the rassa. He tossed the bucket and slammed the gate with such force that I felt the bars rattle from here. For his part, the rassa did not budge, preferring to stay curled up just like me. For the first time, I admired his way of thinking.

The sky fell upon us then like a collapsing wall of sand. Baskets rolled across the compound, the damal trees bent and snapped, and the fountain – our beloved fountain, respite during the hottest of days – tipped and shattered across the tiled ground. Sand piled up next to me and I thought of my mother, green and young and buried under the banks of the River Nahr. I wondered if that would be my fate as well. The last Great Gold of the House of Bey, trapped and buried in a cage like a wyrm.

The karad howled and the sky raged, and I could hear the two reeds shouting to each other over the wind. But over it all, or perhaps under it, I heard a strange sound that was not wind or sky or reeds, and I opened one eye. The rassa gate had blown open and, through the buffeting fists of sand, I could see the great beast move towards it.

The men struggled against the wind and threw their bodies against the door to force it closed. Through the bars, I saw lethal claws flash, shredding wool and linen and flesh. Ixaak howled but the wind howled louder, and I quickly lost sight of them in the chaos of swirling sand. I thought I saw two figures lurch across the court, but they disappeared from view as the dust rose like a wave. I tucked my head back under my wing for the rest of the night.

The karad lasted for many days and it was impossible to tell noon from night. There was sand and darker sand and the wind's howls deafened me, so that I'm not certain when it stopped. I remember trying to raise my head, but a crushing weight pressed down on me. In fact, it took me back to my days in the shell and the journey up through the sand of my birth.

It seemed the Wheel was as cruel and relentless as ever.

And so, at one point, I stirred, and the sand spilled. I moved, and the sand spilled. I stretched and pushed myself to my claws and the sand spilled. I shook and the sand flew like it had all week. Now, I was the karad in one weary, golden dragon body.

It was the dead of night. The moons hovered low and heavy, and the stars danced as if they'd never been gone from the sky. As I looked around the courtyard, it was unrecognizable, merely dunes along the walls and drifts across the stone. I barked into the silence, calling for the river wraith or the serat'horns or the rassa to answer, but none did.

Pillars shone in the moonlight, rising from the sandy courtyard where they had not been before. Some tall, some not, some erect, others leaning, I counted nine pillars of solidified sand in the bestiary's yard. I pressed my face to the bars to see them better. Glass. They were pillars of golden, gleaming glass, spun by the karad and worn smooth by the wind.

Between three of them, where the fountain used to be, I saw a mound rise out of the dunes. It was the rassa. He was not in his pen, and he shook for several long moments to rid the sand from his pelt. Slowly, he padded off towards the courtyard's outer wall, pausing once to look back at me. Then he was gone, swallowed up, a tawny shadow lost in the night.

They found Ixaak early that morning, buried at the entrance to the rassa pen, dead from the rassa or from the karad, I'll never know. I never saw Cawil again, either, or the rassa, or the river wraith. The serat'horn survived, however, and he was shipped off to the Border Markets to pay for some of the bestiary's debts. Since the buying and selling of dragons was forbidden in Penet, this was not an option for me, and I waited many days without food or water before someone came to look at me.

"It's a shame," said a reed, one of two. He was small and stocky with a hoop in one ear. "Ixaak was a fine man. Very generous and compassionate. He lived for these creatures."

"He died for them, too, apparently," said another. He was tall and broad with tattoos on his cheeks and lips. "What happened to his son? The little crippled boy?"

"Too many debts," said the hooped man. "I saw him the other day in the Beggar's Quarter."

"He won't last a week."

"I know. His body is frail, but at least his heart is light."

The tattooed man nodded.

"I pray Othorys is swift and merciful," he said. "I heard there was a rassa?"

"Gone."

He grunted.

"I have a buyer for a rassa, but not a dragon. Unless…"

The hooped man waited patiently.

"Unless I take her to the Market of Give and Take."

"There is no Market of Give and Take," said the first. "It's forbidden."

"As forbidden as the sale of a dragon," said the tattooed man. "Besides, where do you think I'd be selling the rassa?"

"You are going to get yourself killed, my friend," the hooped man grunted. "The Market throws dangerous dice."

"Games which I live to play." The tattooed man stroked his chin. "I could ask Kunyane. He runs a travelling circus."

"The maab?"

"They tour the Glass Road across the Wyldelands, all the way to the River Storm."

"They could handle a dragon?"

"You said she's tame, yes?"

"A Great Gold of Gifah. She probably lived better than you or I."

The tattooed man studied me, and his eyes shone like pebbles.

"She is very beautiful," he said. "Perhaps Sakariye wants her himself."

The hooped man grinned.

"Sakariye is a glass trader and a thief. What would he want with a tamed dragon?"

"A very skilled glass trader and a very rich thief," said the tattooed man. "A tame dragon could guard his hoard."

"He could skin her and sell her scales for seket. There's great profit in the selling of cures."

"Seket be praised, she'd be worth a fortune. But it would be a shame to kill her." The tattooed man glanced at the other. "Are the Gifahn soldiers still looking for her? I heard something about Remoan dragons…"

"It's been almost a year. I was surprised Ixaak hadn't showed her to them, out of his foolish, generous heart. He trusted everyone, that man."

"He did, indeed. Has she bitten anyone?"

"I doubt it. Ixaak said Gaviid would spend hours here with her. That boy loved her, and she never once hurt him."

The tattooed man stepped forward, placed a hand around a bar. I brought my beak close, breathed in the scent of his fingers. Honey, tobacco, oil, cypress.

"A tame dragon," he said softly. "A Great Gold."

One finger moved, timidly touched the curve of my lip.

"What does she eat? And that's a Remoan collar, yes? Is there a key?"

The hooped man shrugged.

"So many questions," he said. "Sadly, I have no answers."

"Hm. Would Gaviid know?"

"More than me."

"Find out about the key. The Beggar's Quarter, you say?"

"Last I heard."

"We could just let her go..."

The hooped man stared at him. His mouth opened, then closed. He ran a hand over his forehead.

"That...that would be very easy."

"She died in the karad."

"She died in the karad. Hmm."

They turned to walk away.

"Well, let me know if the very rich thief Sakariye wants her," said the hooped man. "I need to figure it out before the king's soldiers come back."

"Well," said the tattooed man. "Why don't you buy Sakariye a drink and convince him."

And Sakariye put an arm around the hooped man's shoulder.

"He's thirsty."

I watched them trudge away over the mountains of sand. I lay my head back down, content with my fate to meet Othorys and have my heart weighed against the scale of truth. I was a good dragon. Kida had said it herself. I was a good dragon.

I was good.

But Kida wasn't coming back.

Two days later, a cart rolled up to my cage. It was pulled by a long-horned uru, and I could smell water and dried salt wyrm. I lifted my weary head. The very skilled glass trader and very rich thief called Sakariye slid the bolt open and held both doors open for me. It didn't take much coaxing, and I dragged my aching body from cage to cart. It was small and creaked under my weight, but it contained a barrel of fresh water, and I plunged my face in and drank it dry, barely hearing the latch as the door closed on my life in the bestiary. He chained one back foot to the inside of the cart, and flapped canvas over the sides. As the cart rattled off, I curled around so I could peer out the back and watch the streets of Diddad Wat go by.

Back out towards the palm-lined road, but we veered south this time, cutting through the narrow lanes of the summer town. It was much the same as Wa'ast and I thought of the time I'd escaped with Kida the night the Ophar died. Huts and awnings, market stalls and alleys. Smoked fish rolled in sheets of paprush, and headless wyrms swinging upside down. Incense and oil, tobacco and sweet cakes. The smells told the stories of the busy lives of reeds, and I closed my eyes, content to read it with my nose. We were almost at the end of the town when a new story reached my nostrils, and I opened my eyes. The flies were thick, and the sun was baking but this road was pressed with reeds. They were young and old, and they stood, sat, crawled, bound in tattered linens, and begging at the sides of the road. As we passed, some followed us. One grabbed the bars of my cart, and I shrank back.

"A golden dragon!" he cried, and I was surprised to see he had no teeth. "She has seket in her scales! One touch and I am healed!"

"Seket!" croaked another.

"Seket!"

"Seket!"

The cry was taken up and soon, a horde of reeds followed us, their many hands reaching in through the bars, trying to touch me. A whip cracked above their heads, and they shrank back, bloody and wailing.

Except one.

"Emay!" came a thin voice and my heart leapt in my chest.

A young boy, dirty and bruised, hobbled after us through the pressing mob, his crutch flailing like a sobethi tail.

"You can't take her! She's mine!"

I pushed up against the bars and called to him.

"My dragon," Gaviid cried again. "No! Bring her back! She's going to fly me away! We're going to fly! Emay!"

My heart ached at the sight of him, moving as fast as he could through the crush of bodies on the road. Suddenly, the crutch slipped and he fell, swallowed up by the crowd in our wake. I called again and again and again, but there was nothing. I laid my head on the floor of the cart and closed my eyes, trying in vain to rid myself of the sight of him, the little boy who wanted to fly, and the Wheel that had crushed him as it turned.

15

THE GLASS ROAD

The rains started the day we left Diddad Wat.

In all my life, I had never experienced rains such as those in Penet. The goddess of the Gifahn skies, Naret, never wept over her children the way she wept now over this land of Penet, and I wondered if it was because of their lack of dragons.

I wondered many things in those days on the Glass Road, for once again, I was trapped in a cart pulled by an uru. I wondered if this was the same cart as before, when I was unceremoniously brought from the Waterwall to Moradin, and finally, to the bestiary at Diddad Wat. If so, it had grown smaller. I was pressed in on all sides by the bars and the roof and the floor, and changing positions was problematic. I began to understand Netjeh, so big for his per ahmet that dreams were his only escape.

Perhaps the cart had not grown smaller. Perhaps I had grown bigger.

I wondered how long I'd been at the bestiary of Marwethad. Months, yes, but the ringed man had said a year. Long enough to outgrow an uru cart. Long enough for a princess to raise an army. Long enough for Kida to forget.

We were headed south, I think. Or perhaps west. I couldn't tell anymore, and truth be told, I didn't care. The view outside the bars changed gradually, the flat golden red of Diddad Wat turning into the thirsty foothills of the Glass Road. I overheard Sakariye saying that it was an overland road linking Penet to the Sun Steps of Nabir on the banks of the River Storm. A 'short-cut' across the Wyldelands, he'd called it, but I didn't know what a 'short cut' was, as opposed to a 'long cut', when in fact, he wasn't cutting anything. I only knew that we were nowhere near the River Sand, or the mighty Nahr, and yellow grass went on forever like the dunes of Gifah. Still, in the distance, I could see a range of low mountains just beginning to green with the coming of the rains. I wondered if they were as thirsty as I.

Pillars of glass dotted the landscape. They were like those left by the karad in the wardyr's courtyard, and I understood why it was called the Glass Road. Some tall, some short, some jagged, some clear, the pillars clustered in uneven groupings across the plains. I wondered about the strength of winds needed to produce them. Even in the rains, the pillars were surrounded by tents, and I knew there were reeds working to sheer thin slices and chip large slabs. Carts pulled by uru and serat'horns journeyed in all directions, delivering the glass to cities and ports alike.

We joined a caravan early on, the maab owned by a reed called Kunyane and his wife, Kiin. It was a travelling exhibition, a showcase of jugglers and magicians, contortionists, and exotic beasts. It was a very colourful band, with blue-dyed tents and jewelled lanterns and golden wheels pulled by creatures painted with circles and stripes. Kiin was equally colourful, with tattooes on her brow and chin, hoops around her neck, and hair piled high with wrapped ribbons. I never liked Kiin. She always carried a spear and smelled of saffron, lantern oil and blood. Every morning, she would strike the bars of my cage with her spear and laugh. I think she enjoyed hearing me snarl. She took delight in watching me hiss.

They talked frequently about the Market of Give and Take. Sakariye kept pressing the idea of taking me to the Sun Steps, that the Nabiri would pay a ransom for the Great Gold of Gifah, but Kunyane and Kiin disagreed vehemently, citing the profit to be made in the selling of cures and seket scales. Frequently, their talks became arguments and the tension in this maab became uncomfortable for all reeds involved. As for me, everything was uncomfortable now and the last thing I wondered was whether dragon souls were weighed the same way reed souls were when we died. When we died, I was certain we'd sink down to the UnderRiver, but what happened to us afterwards? If light enough, were we allowed passage, like the reeds, across the great Salt Sea to the Fields of Ever Spring? If that were the case, I hoped I would see Netjeh again. I hoped I'd see my mother.

And so, we stayed on the Glass Road for many days. When we would come upon a settlement or village, the maab would stop, unhitch the uru and circle the carts. Sakariye would pitch a large tent overtop the cart, and while I couldn't see out, conversely, no one could see in. Soon, a crowd would gather and even in the rains, reeds paid to enter the tents to watch the magicians, dancers, contortionists and beasts. They were especially eager for their first glimpse of dragon. I'm sure he got rich, richer than he had been before as a 'very skilled glass trader and a very rich thief,' but as for me, I became a little less 'dragon' each day. Fading, empty, listless, thin. I used to think I was turning to stone but now I knew I was turning to sand.

At night, once he'd emptied the villagers' pockets, Sakariye would sleep atop my cart, for the ground was rocky and wet and swimming with beetles. Before he'd take to his strange bed, however, he'd light an oil lamp, sit in front of the cage, feed me strips of salt wyrm and talk. He regaled me with stories of the adventures of a man who had a little boy. The boy loved to collect glass rocks, ride urus, and make whistles out of the reeds along the River Sand. There were many adventures, but they always ended the same way, with the little boy losing his footing and getting stuck in the heavy silt of the river until a sobethi freed him with its great, horrible teeth. There would always be tears then, and my heart broke for Sakariye and that little boy. I wondered if his riches eased his sadness or doubled them.

The nighttime stories reminded me of my early years with Kida and Seb in the drakmet of Wa'ast. It was a pleasant connection, perhaps the only pleasant thing in those weeks on the Glass Road. The collar had become very tight, and breathing was difficult. I didn't care to eat anymore – it was too difficult to swallow even the salt wyrm that'd I chew into paste. I'd lost the taste for it in my mouth. Even the rains couldn't wash it down, but I could feast on the stories forever.

"Come, my girl," he'd say to me. "Please eat."

And he'd hold a sliver of wyrm to my beak, waggle it as if waggling made it any better. Sometimes I would take it, very carefully with my tiny front teeth, and he would touch me then, run his fingers across my scales while I tried to choke down the wyrm.

Sometimes, I'd let him stroke my neck, smoothing the stiffening spines and running his thumb across the silver band that cut into my throat.

227

"Right here," I'd hear him say. "There's no key, just a click. It would be so easy…"

He'd withdraw his hand then.

"A little closer," he'd say. "Wait until we're a little closer. Then, you'll soar over the Sun Steps and be with your people. And maybe I'll join you and fly over the water's edge. Maybe, I'll get to see my boy again. But my heart is not light, for I am a thief and there is no place for me in the Fields of Ever Spring."

I enjoyed those nights because the alternative was misery. Some nights, he would spend the evening with Kunyane, drinking wine and playing bone dice. It was then that Kiin would slip in, smelling of saffron, and dim the oil lamp that cast the tent in a warm glow. Then, she'd lift the tent flap for reeds of her own, collecting gold as they stepped in. They'd laugh when she'd poke me through the bars with the blunt end of her spear, squeal when I'd rage against it, and my chest burned with heat from trapped flame and fury. I longed to burn them, as I'd burned the papers of Karadoum. I longed to bite and tear and rend, but I was more caged than in Diddad Wat, a Great Gold of Gifah reduced to a spectacle for barter and trade.

One night after her customers had left, Kiin stayed and turned to the cart that had been my prison these last weeks. I growled at her, bringing my head down as low as the cage allowed.

"That's too small for you, isn't it, dear Nagira," she said, poking my face with her spear. "But don't worry. You won't be there for much longer. The Market of Give and Take is only two days away."

She leaned in. I bared my teeth, almost tasting her flesh in my jaws.

"Then, we will be rich, and your troubles will be over." She smiled, the tattoos stretching across her chin. "Win, win."

And with that, she left the tent, but I could still smell the saffron.

Fury is a kind of fire. Both start in the belly and rise, burning the chest and tightening the throat before finding release through the mouth. For me, now, in this tiny cage with my leg chained to the cart and the collar squeezing the life from me, both fury and fire came up as acid, rolling across my tongue and dripping between my teeth. The bars sizzled with each drop, and I cocked my head. The acid that was still a weapon, and I was still a dragon. Maybe not a 'good' dragon anymore. The good dragon was a construct, built over my bones like a per ahmet. It was then that I realized that once upon a time, oh so long ago and for only a few short weeks in the nest on the banks of the Nahr, I had been wild.

The good dragon could be forgotten, along with her vaskar.

I set to work on the bars of the cage.

Sakariye returned later that night, staggering into the tent, and barely making it up to the top of the cart. I was angry with him as well, and that night my dreams were filled of saffron and blood.

And so, I dreaded the next morning, when the tents were packed away and the urus hitched to the caravan of carts, because it was one day closer to this Market of Give and Take. I didn't know what it was, but it sounded ominous and final and not at all something I wanted to see. Like the royal boat on the river Nahr, the acid burned for only a short time before cooling into wax, and I was making little progress on my attempt to escape this cage. Still, as we rattled along the Glass Road under a canopy of blue stripes, I kept at it, working one section of bars with acid and tooth.

That evening brought more rain, more reeds, more gold, more spectacle, and it was even longer and louder than before. When the crowds finally died away and Sakariye turned down the oil lamp for the night, both Kunyane and Kiim entered the tent. The reeds held long, narrow jars and the contents smelled the same as Sakariye after an evening spent in their company.

"Look at these," barked Kunyane. "Glass flasks! I feel like an Ophar!"

"Filled with the best beer from Karadoum," sang Kiin. "We traded one of the old uru for it."

Sakariye clapped his hands.

"Good trade," he said. "But first, food for me and the dragon."

"Tonight is our last night together," said Kunyane. "Beer is our meal of choice!"

Sakariye grinned.

"I'll drink to that."

"And besides," said Kiin, passing him a flask. "You're two days from the Sun Steps, and the Storm. She'll be free to eat her fill once you ransom her."

"What's another night without salt wyrm?" asked Kunyane.

"She doesn't eat it anyway."

"True, true, true," said Sakariye. He lifted the flask to his lips, took a long deep drink, and smiled. "Good trade."

"The uru was old," said Kiin. "No legs for pulling anymore and not enough meat for a soup."

Together, the three of them climbed to the top of the cart and conversation flowed down like the rains.

I pushed on the bars with my beak.

Nothing.

I pushed on them with the top of my head.

Nothing.

I opened my mouth and slid my teeth up and down, feeling the iron grate and the bars flake. They tasted sharp on my tongue. Still, I would not be daunted, and I added the acid to the working of my teeth. As the night wore on, the laughter above me grew louder, more unsettling, and at one point, a glass flask tumbled past the bars to shatter on the rain-soaked earth.

Moments later, a body followed, and I raised my head as Kunyane and Kiin climbed down from the roof.

"He's out," said the man, nudging Sakariye with his sandal, but beside him, Kiin pointed.

"Look," she hissed. "Those bars are almost chewed through!"

I recoiled into myself, dripping acid through my teeth. I would kill them both. I would eat the smiles from their faces. I would tear the laughter from their throats.

I lunged forward and the cage shuddered at the impact, but Kiin met me, thrusting her spear between the bars into my chest.

Heat. Heat. Fire and heat.

I arched my neck and caught the shaft between my teeth, crunching down with all the force in my aching, starved body. It shattered in half, and I bellowed my fireless fury as the reeds staggered back.

Heat. Heat. Fire and heat. Red changing everything before my eyes.

Just like the arrow in the library of A'Toth.

I recoiled and thrashed against the cage bars.

Heat. Heat. Fire and heat. Red changing everything before my eyes. Cold descending like the rains, not even a dry salt wyrm to live on.

I tasted blood on my tongue but the Wheel rolled on.

16

THE MARKET OF GIVE AND TAKE

In the Book of the Creation of the World, the dragon, Aphorys the Dark, always existed.

He swam through the black waters, alone and master of all the realms. He was exceedingly pleased with his worlds until one day, he saw something he had never seen before, and that was light. Bewitched, Aphorys swam towards the light only to find himself, reflected in a mirror. Where he was shadow, however, his reflection was light, and he thought she was as beautiful as the fire that burned inside his belly. And so, he named her Selis Anekh, goddess of the Sun. But the moment the words left his mouth, the mirror shattered into a thousand shards and Selis Anekh was released into the worlds, bringing light and life with her as she went.

Even today, she ushers her most beloved creation, Rath'nahr, across the sky in a boat blazing as the sun.

Every night, they are pursued by Syth and his dragon twins, the moons Amok and Khamet into the darkness still ruled by Aphorys. If they catch him, they will surely kill him and his goddess dragon. Aphorys will swallow them whole and then, he will swallow himself, becoming Orophys, Dragon of the End. When that happens, all light, and life, will surely end with him.

In all truth, some days I am Anekh. That day, I was Aphorys.

Every bump of the road, every rattle of the Wheel, sent stars bursting behind my eyes. The spear was embedded in the hollow between my wing and my neck, in the very same place that the silver arrow had been, and I couldn't move without blood bubbling up on my tongue. I remembered my mother then, and me as a young hatchling, biting at the arrows in her body in my innocence. This was how she died – terrified and in agony.

My heart broke anew for the plight of dragons. We were around since before the creation of the world, and yet, slave to the children of Rath'nahr.

My wing was not the only thing burning that day.

I had not seen Sakariye since his fall from the roof of the cart, and now we rolled along a packed dirt road, worn smooth by the wheels of hundreds of vehicles. I was still covered in canvas, so could see nothing, but even in my weakened condition, I could tell we had entered a city much like Wa'ast or Moradin or Diddad

Wat. Reeds were noisy creatures. Their shouts rose over even the bleating of uru and kitchen wyrms, their laughter above the drums of incessant rain.

They were going to kill me for my scales.

The rain bounced off tents and awnings and heads and feet. The roads splashed like the whispering Nahr.

They were going to kill me, a Great Gold of Gifah, daughter of the Sun. They would skin me and sell me off, scale by scale, as a balm for sickness and a cure for disease. They would flay my flesh and grind my bones and lie to make a profit from the suffering and naiveté of their own people. Dragons were many things – noble, grand, godly, proud, but mystical we were not. I was a creature of shakhet milk, not seket. It was absurd. It was futile.

Smells of a market – smoke, spices, offal, salt.

They were going to kill me for a lie.

Fruit, meat, fish, blood.

Not if I killed them first.

And so, I rested on the cart ride into this new city where the Market of Give and Take made its home. I rested and I chewed. I fought against the stabbing pain in my body as I chewed the bars with acid and dagger teeth. I scraped the slate floor of the cart near the bars with my wing claws, blinking back the fire with every movement. My mother, brother Amok, dear Mehen and my little blue striped friend had all died at the ends of blades. I wouldn't succumb to the same fate.

Then again, I was only cargo, a Great Gold of Gifah, a product to be bartered and sold. Even Kida knew that.

It was afternoon when the rains stopped suddenly. So did the cart, and I knew we were under a roof of some sort. I was grateful. The long road to this market was exhausting, and I was determined to meet my fate.

The uru bleated as the cart was wheeled into a circle and I could smell incense, oil and fire. Shadows of reeds moved along the canvas, and footsteps crossed a stone floor.

"Welcome, friends, to the Market of Give and Take."

It was a deep voice with an unfamiliar accent.

"The business that is done in this particular Market is forbidden, and therefore, has never, nor will ever, happen. Is that agreed upon by all?"

Answers of yes all around and I counted eight distinct voices, including that of Kunyane and Kiin. I would know them in a heartbeat. Their voices were, and are, burned into my memory like Shesset's seal on my skin.

"I am your moderator, Symon of Malao," he said, and he staked a torch deep in the ground. "I neither Give nor Take."

Another voice.

"Haran Sweet of Mundus," he said. "Take."

And another.

"Salaris Pyr of Tabathae. Give and Take."

"Seth Kunyane of the Glass maab, along with Kiin, my partner. Give."

And so, it went. Soon, each voice had sounded off and they all began to barter with each other in hushed tones. Flasks were opened with a hiss, gold was exchanged with a clink, and laughter rose with incense and oil into a heady mix.

"Your turn, Seth Kunyane!" the one called Haran laughed. "What is a maab performer doing at the Market of Give and Take?"

"Have you brought a dancing jaffebuck to sell?" cried Salaris Pyr.

"Or a juggling river wraith?"

"Ooh, perhaps he has brought us a contortionist?"

They murmured and clinked flasks as Kunyane laughed. He stepped over to the cart.

With dramatic flair, he flung the canvas from the roof and swung a torch towards me. Light kissed my eyes and I flung myself at the bars of the cart, roaring as I never roared before.

Their screams were satisfying.

They scrambled back, swinging both spear and sword but Kunyane waved them back.

"Respect," he barked. "She's a Great Gold of Gifah."

Their spears did not waver, but soon, one man peered closer.

"I have never seen a dragon," he breathed. "But here, a Great Gold."

I lashed my tail, bared my teeth at them all. I would eat their faces but spit out their hearts.

"She's bleeding," said Pyr.

"She tried to kill me," growled Kiin. "She has the temper of a shrike."

"Is this the one the Gifahn soldiers are searching for?" asked Symon the moderator.

"The very one, born and raised in the palace of Thutmen'nahr II, forced to flee with the princess after the coup."

"I heard she brought the wrath of Remus down upon Gifah," said Salaris Pyr of Tabathae.

"Why haven't you turned her in?" asked another. "Surely, there is a price for her head."

"She's too valuable for a bounty," Kunyane said. "And I am a man of bountiful good sense."

"What are you going to do with a dragon?" asked a man in pink silk. "Can she dance for you?"

"What is any of us going to do with a dragon?" said another. "We'll have Marwethad's army on us like flies if they find out."

"Why are you selling her?" asked Symon. "You should add her to your maab. People would pay to see a dragon."

"Too much work," said Haran Sweet. "Feeding her would cost a fortune, and you never know what the Glass Road brings."

"Seket," hissed Kunyane. "She's worth a fortune in cures."

Several men nodded, stepped forward with their torches to see me better. I swung my head between them, snarling.

"Every day she grows, so do her scales," said Pyr. "You're sitting on a lifetime of profit."

Kunyane snorted.

"Every day she grows, so do her teeth. What do you know about dragons?"

"Do I look Nabiri?"

"Too much work," agreed another man. "She's a dangerous creature. Wise men don't gamble with danger."

"Too risky," added another. "Especially with both Marwethad and Beyat the Usurper after her. Turn in the head only and sell the scales."

Symon nodded. "Every single scale will make you a fortune. You'll never need to work again."

They all murmured at this.

"We all buy her," said Sweet. "The Market pays your price, and we do this very thing. We will live in houses bigger than Marwethad's palace!"

"We have the means," said Pyr. "We can kill her in the morning. She's half dead already. It will take days to divide the scales among us."

"What do you say, moderator of the Market?"

They all looked to Symon.

"Name your price, Seth Kunyane of the maab," he said. "The Market gives, and the Market takes."

Kiin grinned at me in the torchlight. I growled at her, curled my claws on the hard floor of the cage.

"No!"

They turned now as a ninth reed entered the Market. He was tall and square with tattoos on his cheeks and lips.

"She is not for sale. She is not for trade. She does not belong to Seth Kunyane of the Glass maab, nor his viper of a wife. She belongs to me, gifted by Ixaak of Diddad Wat, the king's wardyr."

Two dozen guards peeled from the shadows thrown by the pillars, swords and spears raised, as the man stepped into the room.

"Sakariye Tull," said Symon and he waved at the guards. "He is known to me. Let him pass."

"I repeat," said Sakariye. "The dragon is mine, stolen from me along with my cart and my uru, by these thieves and liars."

He swept a hand at Kunyane and Kiin.

"He is lying, kind moderator," said Kiin. "She was traded to us last night for a cask of summer beer."

Sakariye continued over to the cart.

"I know what's in your beer, witch."

He looked at me for a long moment, his dark eyes locking with mine. I was angry. I was fury. I was fire. But I was dying.

"I can prove that she's mine," he said quietly as he rolled up his linen sleeve. "How many of you have ever touched a dragon?"

Murmurs from all.

"Kunyane? Kiin? No?"

"You never touch a dragon, fool," snapped Kiin. "They are not kitchen wyrms."

"No," said the glass trader and thief. "They most certainly are not."

And he raised his hand to the bars. I growled, low and rattling in my chest.

"What have they done to you?"

He gripped a bar with trembling fingers. I stared at them, bared my bloody teeth.

"The Sun Steps are calling, my girl. My goddess…"

He slipped his hand through.

I could bite it clean off, even with the spear.

"And that collar is far too tight."

The scent of his fingers. Honey, tobacco, oil, cypress.

He had never hurt me. He had told me stories.

I nudged his fingers with my beak. He was cold where I was hot.

There was silence for a long moment as Sakariye stroked my muzzle. I didn't know what to do. I didn't know what to think. My wing claws curled under, and I dropped to the floor of the cart with a rattle in my chest. My head was so heavy, and his hand was a balm.

"Get these imposters out of here," barked Symon. "Fifty lashes each for lying to the Market of Give and Take."

The guards fell upon them, catching them both by the arms.

"Wait," cried Kiin. "You can still be rich!"

"The Market is still open!" said Kunyane.

"Kill the glass trader and then, the dragon."

"We only ask a small fee, being the ones who brought her here."

"We do not kill each other," growled Symon. "Here, we do business."

"Death is good business," spat Kiin.

"Seket is life," said Kunyane. "People need their cures."

"Well?" asked Symon. "The offer stands, Sakariye Tull. The Market will make you a rich man."

"I'm already a rich man," said Sakariye. "And I withdraw this false offer. The Market is closed."

"The Market is closed when the Market closes," said Sweet. "And you are not the Market."

Sakariye reached up to tug at the canvas flap.

"There are always rules, Haran," he said. "You cannot Take what I do not Give."

"There are rules, thief," said Sweet.

"Name your price and we will Give," said Pyr. "Otherwise, the Market may be closed to you forever."

"Then it's closed forever," said Sakariye. "I'm tired of it anyway. Time to settle down and enjoy my profits. Maybe I'll buy Ixaak's place, start a collection of my own."

Sweet stepped forward. Three guards followed, their spears gleaming in the torchlight, and I pushed myself to my claws, snarling.

"Give us the dragon."

Sakariye glanced up.

"The matter is ended, Haran."

"Give us the dragon," said Pyr, and he too stepped forward.

The others pressed in. Symon moved to the front of the cart, unhitching the uru with the rattle of cords. I could hear its pitiful moan as it wandered off into the darkness of the temple.

"Your uru is gone," said Symon. "And if you're wise, you will follow it. But the cart, and its contents, stay."

"You're fools," snapped Sakariye. "You think this is a Remoan collar but you're very wrong. You forget she's a Great Gold, heir to the flame of Rath'nahr and trained by the vizier of Thutmen'nahr II to protect the royal daughter."

He snatched a torch from Haran's hand, swept it from side to side.

"I was supposed to bring a rassa but he is dead, burnt alive by the breath of this magnificent beast. Ixaak taught me her commands and with one word from me, she will turn you all to ash. Is this how you wish the Market to close? In a glorious blaze of dragonfire and a pathetic puff of ash?"

I snarled again and the men fell back. I wished I did have my fire. Reeds in the Market burned as easily as water wyrms on the River Sand. I had learned that these last years. My teeth ached with sythstone as acid bubbled up between them, dripped onto the cart's slate floor to sizzle and smoke.

"He lies!" barked Kiin. "She has no fire because of the collar. He told us so himself."

"The Market demands a Take," said Sweet. "Symon, you have no choice."

"I have no choice," said Symon, and the guards moved towards my cart. I bellowed at them, threw myself against the bars. They rattled under the impact. I looked down.

Splinters. Finally.

Sakariye raised his hand to the cage door bolt.

"You can try to take her," he said. "But can you do it before I release her? She's young and her scales are strong. You throw one spear and may kill me, but you'll have one live, angry, free dragon—"

She was fast, I had to admit. Kiin snatched a spear from the hand of a guard and pitched it across the room. Struck with lethal force, Sakariye staggered backwards before collapsing onto the stone floor with a thud.

The scent of his fingers. Honey, tobacco, oil, cypress.

I bellowed, acid spraying from my teeth and I flung myself into the bars again.

Smoke, musk, rathstone, acid.

Mehen.

Fire as a second spear pierced my wing. I rammed the bars again.

Gaviid. Josiat. Netjeh.

And again. One bar sprang from its mooring.

The little blue and gold from the Temple complex, and the dragons under harness in the chariot races. Dragons sacrificed for blood and worship and pleasure and sport.

And again. Two now, then three.

My mother killed by arrows. My brothers turned by a prince.

The Ophar. Shesset. Kida. Betrayers all.

With a final lunge, the gate shattered, and I spilled out onto the stone floor, a deadly golden coil of teeth and claw and scale and rage. Rising slowly, I unfolded my great golden wings, arched my deadly spines, lashed my long-silent tail. I dropped my head low to the ground and bellowed at them all as both guards and sellers scattered like sand in a windstorm.

All except Kunyane. He was not as fast as his wife and I lunged at him, catching his leg in my teeth. I whipped him side-to-side like a wyrm until the bones rent from the hip and blood sprayed across the floor.

I barreled forward, leaping onto the fleeing back of Symon the moderator and knocking him face first to the ground. He screamed as my teeth sank into his neck and my back talons shredded the flesh of his buttocks and thighs.

Kiin next and I lunged for her but was yanked back to the floor as she fled the temple. Snarling, I turned to look – the chain on my foot was still attached to the cart. I bit at it, but it was sound and strong and would need many days of acid to work myself free.

The Market was closed now, the traders gone, with only the pitiful moaning of an uru somewhere in the dark.

I swung my head around, taking in the low, pillared room where I had been Given and Taken back. It looked like a temple, with painted ceilings and no windows and coloured tile on the floor. It was empty now, for even the guards had fled, and I lumbered over to where Sakariye lay in a river of blood.

He reached a bloody hand for me, and I lowered my beak to breathe in his scent.

Honey, tobacco, oil, cypress.

His fingers trembled as they slid across my neck.

Stories and tears and glass and loss. A little boy and the teeth of a sobeth.

Thumb on the edge of the silver band at my throat.

Stories. His stories.

"Go," he said. "Anywhere, my girl, but go."

Seb's stories, and Kida's.

The silver band clicked.

Never mine.

The collar fell away, along with his hand. Air flooded into my throat, burning with coolness, the muscles weak from constriction. I filled my chest again and again, feeling the crackle of sparks along my teeth.

I looked down. The glass trader and thief was gone. I hoped he would find his way to the boy in the Fields of Ever Spring, but I needed my own story.

I took a step, blinking back the pain shooting from my wing and shoulder.

The cart yanked behind me. I growled.

I leaned in and took another step. And another.

The cart had wheels. I made it move.

In the Market of Give and Take, I lowered my head, stretched out my trembling wings and leapt into the air.

And for the first time in my life, the Wheel turned for me.

17

BREAKING THE WHEEL

I could not tell you how difficult it was, for the first time in a year, to fly. Not only fly but fly beneath a low ceiling between pillars of painted stone with a spear in my neck and a wheeled cart behind me.

I dipped, I turned, I spun, and I dodged, my wings stiff and unresponsive. Twice, I hit the pillars as I swept past and both times, suns exploded behind my eyes. But I pushed through with each downbeat, strained with each up. The cart rattled behind me, loosing pieces of wood, slate, iron and spoke against each pillar it struck. Still, I was flying, and I was free, and the Wheel was mine to serve or shatter as I wished.

I saw guards, ran them down with a taloned swipe at their heads. I saw Sweet and Pyr race towards the golden light of the streets and I flattened my spines, streaking towards them like an arrow. I swept overhead and caught them, crushing their heads with my talons, and leaving their bodies like bloody shat in my wake.

The trailing cart bumped over them like dirt.

Finally, the streets, and I landed between the entry columns, the cart scraping to a halt behind me. I could not fold my wings across my back, so I held them out at my flanks, trembling and stiff. People saw me and screamed. Unlike laughter, I am never confused by their screams. It is a sound with obvious meaning, and the street instantly erupted in chaos. It was like the rough waters of the Nahr as reeds fled the marketplace, scrambling over each other to get out of my way. I bellowed at them, and my rage echoed through the streets. And not only did I bellow, but I released the flames that had been trapped inside me for over a year, since Kida had fastened that cursed band around my throat. I roared and sprayed, swinging my head, first one way, then the other, and all manner of stalls caught fire under my breath. Carts, barrels, awnings, fruit, meat, and awnings burst and blazed, causing light and shadows to dance across the streets. It was early evening, the rains incessant, and the flames sizzled in the downpour. Smoke billowed all around and I lifted my beak, sifting the hundreds of scents for one alone.

I found it.

I snapped my wings and lumbered out into the street.

One step, two, and I launched skyward, bringing my injured wings down in a powerful stroke, knocking the braziers and fruitstands in their path. Higher and higher I went, each wingstroke causing the spear to bounce and stab. My eyes popped with the strain, but the tang of blood was fire on my tongue, and I met the rain with relish. Beneath me, the shattered cart swung like a bell, smashing stalls and walls, but I stayed low, sweeping through the narrow streets, tracking the one scent that was burned like flame into my mind.

Saffron.

The streets were a maze, and the moons were rising, but she was a beacon by her scent alone. I ignored the pain when a wing struck a statue, paid no heed when the cart bounced off a stone wall. Below me, reeds shrieked and pointed and ran but the rain felt good against my dry scales, and I longed for the river where I could dive and be free.

But first, saffron called for blood.

There, her ribbons flashing in the dark streets, she ran like a plainsbuck, glancing over her shoulder as the cart smashed behind her. I dropped like a stone, catching her arms, and sinking my talons into the flesh at her shoulders. She howled and I beat my wings, carrying both her and the weight of the cart up, up, up above the rooftops. She twisted in my grasp and snagged the shattered spear, sending pain racing through my bones. Beat, beat, went my wings, and I reached down with my beak, snapped my teeth at her thrashing legs. She clutched the spear with both hands, screaming and twisting like a wraithe.

With the cart and the chain and the reed and the spear, I was losing altitude. My head spun from pain and hunger and weakness. I did the only thing I could do.

I released her.

She flailed for a moment, clutching the spear, and swinging helplessly above the city. Her weight shifted my balance and I banked to avoid striking the peak of a clay spire. Suddenly, the spear jerked free from my shoulder, taking both flesh and blood as it went, and then, her weight was gone. I did not see her hit the ground.

I was nearing the outskirts of the city now, so I forced myself to climb. The cart was cumbersome, and I was weak, and I couldn't gain the height needed to soar into the clouds. And had it been other circumstances, I'm sure I would have found the city beautiful in its own way. No, from here, I could see the mountains, lush and green in the abundance of rain, and more than this, I could smell the river.

The river.

Oh, how I couldn't wait to skim along the surface, drag my talons in the waves, dive for fish and taunt sobethi along the banks. Perhaps I would find another dragon like Mehen, a fine jungle drake full of life and pride and himself. Perhaps a blue like the Nabiri Bask, ridden by the serious prince of the Skyborn. Or perhaps none, and I lived out my days alone in peace and dignity. There could be worse fates for a Great Gold of Gifah. I was certain I had just escaped all of them.

Alone.

With the city gone, the land stretched out before me, mountains rising in the distance, glimpses of pink and purple gleaming under the gaze of the moons. The river was there, I knew, the elusive Storm, carving the mountains like a blade. I had never been to mountains. I had never seen the Storm, and I was alone, draining blood with every wingbeat and dragging an unwieldy, crippling cart.

I was flying by instinct now, wing and breath, beat beat beat. Following the scent of the river, wing and breath, beat beat beat. I was a wild dragon now, alone and free and flying in the twilight. My head was light, and thoughts trailed behind me like a chain. Like a broken cart.

I almost didn't see them then, the small, pointed per ahmets of the Glass Road and the Wyldelands. The cart struck one as I flew overhead, shattering the rest of the wood and smashing the stone peak to the ground. I circled back on it, exhausted but awake, and landed on the shorn top, wings wide and aching.

I swung my head, hissing to the rain, barking out a challenge, but there was no reply. I called again and again, with the same result. I was alone so I settled myself, carefully coiling my tail and gingerly folding my wings across my back. I could sleep here for the night. It was high and it was safe, a perfect perch for a dying dragon, but my heart would not settle, and my eyes would not close.

It was my first night outside the company of reeds.

I nudged the oozing wound under my wing, sprayed it with a film of acid. With the rain still beating down, the acid cooled almost immediately into the thick, gummy wax that had patched up the hole in the river barge. I had saved the reeds then. I had been brave and resourceful and good. I was brave and resourceful still. But good?

Good was a term given me by the reeds, but here, there were no reeds. They had been washed away with the rains, along with the good.

I thought of Sakariye who told me stories by lamplight, his fingers clutching at the bloody spear. I thought of little Gaviid, so brave with his dreams of flying, falling beneath the mob in the crowded street. And Kida, my Kida, my reed, my world, giving me up to follow a princess for a kingdom that had turned its back on us both.

There was no reed to control me, no reed to direct me, no reed to protect me. I was alone, and it was a strange, unsettling thing. I was in the Wyldelands, alone and free, with the remains of a cart to remind me what I'd lost.

At least, I thought as I tucked my head beneath my wing, there was no saffron.

***

That night, I dreamed of Kida. We were in the palace of the Ophar, sleeping on the divan at the foot of the royal bed. She was weeping as she held me in her arms, and I was struggling, but I didn't know why. She was my reed, my life, my world, and she flicked my beak with her finger. Then, she rapped my head. Then she slapped me.

I opened my eyes.

Stones.

I was being pelted with stones.

Sometime during the night, the rains had stopped and now, the goddess Selis Anekh was rising with the dawn, turning the clouds pink and orange as she flew. I lifted my head and looked down. There were glass pillars dotting the fields, and at the foot of the per ahmet, a trio of reeds, throwing rocks at me and shouting in a strange tongue.

I growled and pushed up to my feet, the chains rattling around the broken carapace. They bolted but regrouped quickly, scrambling for rocks and chunks of stone. I could have burned them, I realized, but it seemed a cruel and needless thing, so I snapped open the leather of my wings. Blinking back the ache, I launched into the air above them. The remains of the cart and rattling wheels swung dangerously close to their heads as I soared over them, and their shrieks were music to my ears.

I think it was the first time I understood the concept of laughter.

I flew on from there across the greening plains, leaving the per ahmets and glass columns behind. The land was rising, and I could smell water strong on the breeze. I vowed to fly until I reached the river or succumbed to my injuries along the way. And so, I flew by instinct, starving and bloody, dragging a chain of wood and wheels behind me, leaving thought and memory behind with each downward beat of my wings. Beneath me, the land was gold and green and rocky and lush. I had never seen so much green. Gifah was gold and Penet red, so this was a new thing for me. I could not help but think of Mehen, and my heart ached for his proud, wild beauty. I also vowed that, one day I would be as wild as him or I would die trying.

Still, a part of me felt empty, as though I were missing something. As if I were wrong, somehow, less.

All morning I flew over this new land, rising higher on cooling winds. Beneath me were mountains with trees like a blanket, and valleys torn into the earth as with dragon claws. I saw small villages and single huts, but I kept flying. I didn't miss the company of reeds. What I did miss was their food and my belly had long ceased growling. I'd lived on wyrm for years, learned to exist like Netjeh on as little as a grain of sand. My head was growing lighter, however, and I knew that I could easily die of hunger or thirst before my wounds killed me. So, you can imagine my joy when I saw a herd of uru wandering the rocky hills.

I was not a wild dragon. I didn't know how to hunt but I knew how to fish. Surely, it couldn't be that different.

One uru grazed alone, a fair distance from the others. It was brown and grey, with four great scaled horns and a spinal ridge that was worthy of a dragon. Also, around its neck, it wore a bell, and I knew this creature belonged to the reeds. I remembered my mother, bringing home flaxen creatures with tender flesh. I remember my brothers and I playing with the bells for days.

I remembered her unseeing eyes, body riddled with arrows and spears.

The reeds had killed my mother because of a creature with a bell.

The reeds had killed Mehen because of a creature in a cage.

I had killed a reed who'd smelled of saffron, yet I was still aloft.

And so, I lowered my head and dove, feeling the weight fall into my talons. I stretched them wide, eager to catch its ridged spine in my grasp, eager to drop my full weight on its long, curved neck. I was a wild dragon,

teeth and talon, scale and claw. I would kill it in a
heartbeat, without mercy, without a thought.

It looked up at me.

Its eyes large and round and brown as new earth,
trusting, serving, seeing, fearing. The life of an uru,
slave to the reeds.

I couldn't.

I lost my nerve and swept up, forgetting the shattered
cart trailing behind. A jerk of chain and crack of bell
reminded me, for in an instant, they struck the uru, chain
catching around its low neck and snapping upwards as I
ascended. I was yanked back to earth, dropping onto the
scrub with my talons wide, wings outstretched.

The creature moaned pitifully as it lay, twisted in
chain and wood and wheels, and its forelegs thrashed
feebly against the scrub. Nothing else moved, not its tail,
not its hind legs, not its heavy-horned head. I launched
into the air, flapping once, twice, three times but that
was it, for I was tethered to the cart and the cart was
tethered to the uru.

I landed again and barked to the wind. The other uru
had gathered, watching our fate from a respectable
distance and I barked at them too. Pathetic creatures,
bound and belled to serve the reeds. Not I. I was wild. I
was free and yet, here I was, as bound and belled as they.

I lumbered over to the uru, saw the white of its sad
brown eye. It was bigger than a fish, but I was bigger
still. I brought my jaws down on its throat, feeling the

soft scales of it pelt burst beneath my teeth. Flesh next, tougher than fish, darker, redder, bloodier, and the scent almost blinded me. This was not a fish. I had never killed like this. I had never.

I placed one foot on the creature's flank and pulled my jaws away, bringing red and pink along with them. I tossed my head back, swallowing the mass in one go. I gagged up the flesh and tried again and again. I bit and tore and swallowed and gagged. I had been a year in a Remoan collar. My throat was constricted and tight.

The urus watched me with sad expectant eyes.

I snarled and snatched a chunk of flesh, tossing it to the back of my throat. I crunched and crushed and chewed, just as I had in the bestiary, just as I had in the cart. I called the acid and felt it sizzle, turning the flesh into liquid and I raised my beak, letting the ooze slide down my throat like oily water.

I did it again and again and again until I'd eaten my fill and my belly was warm with the sun and the uru. I launched into the air once again, brought my wings down with all my strength, but I was still stuck. I twisted, raged, snarled, tugged, there was no moving the dead weight at the end of the chain, and I dropped to the ground once again.

I brought my head down to bite at the heel brace. Nothing. My teeth merely slid off, scraping the metal, and catching my skin. Acid! I called it and it came, scalding its way up my throat and stinging my eyes as I sprayed it across the chain. The metal sizzled and hissed but turned to wax and I remembered it had taken days to weaken the iron bars of the cage. I bit at it again and again and again, wincing as my teeth shredded my own flesh and I shook my head, snorting the taste from my tongue.

I looked up. There were skarabs and sand wyrms scuttling around the carcass, hoping to scavenge an easy meal. The other uru had gone back to grazing and I wondered at that. I was still a deadly predator, a dragon bigger than them. Did they know I was trapped by this infuriating device, or was it the fact that one had died so the others were safe?

The purchase of life by payment of death. One loss for much life.

I looked down at the brace above my talons, tight and oozing with my own blood.

Loss for life. It seemed the way of things in this world of reeds.

I blinked back the agony as my teeth sank into the flesh above my heel talon, tore through tendon and sinew alike to saw across the hard whiteness of the bone. My head spun as my jaws worked and my blood mixed with that of the uru, staining the scrub grass a familiar Penet red. Skarabs were already at work on the uru, crawling across its flank and skittering between its ribs. Even now, some of them nipped at my tail with their tiny pincers, and I knew that, if I didn't move, I would be bones by midday. I lashed my tail, sending them sailing against the grass and the rocks. Their bodies were snatched up by the sand wyrms, their tiny wings and bobbing heads comical as they gobbled up the beetles that had tried to gobble me.

The Wheel rolled over all of us, it seemed, making no distinction between wyrm and uru and dragon and reed.

My jaws struck bone and I almost succumbed to the emptiness of sleep. But the chittering wyrms and skittering skarabs kept me awake, and I attacked my leg with renewed fervor. I had lost all feeling in it now. There was just waves of heat and nausea and the taste of blood until I felt the sickening slide of the brace and then nothing. Nothing at all, but lightness and air. I lurched away from the carcass on two wing claws and one foot, and I pulled my severed leg tight against my belly. I looked back. The abandoned talons were already curling in the bloody grass. The skarabs were already on it.

I leapt into the air, relieved to find no burn from the chain, nor tug from the cart. The wheels were gone, and I flew high, higher than before. The skies spun but I flew, yielding to the wind and the sun and the beat of my wings. I crested hills, and dove through valleys, alternately green and yellow and the grey of scoured stone. I flew for hours, thinking nothing, feeling less, waiting for blood loss to send me crashing to the ground. Soon, a valley stretched below me from horizon to horizon, and in the valley, a ribbon of light. My heart leapt within me at the sight of the river, rushing and furious and white.

The Storm.

I knew the way that led to Gifah. I could tell by the strange tug inside my breast. Gifah was northwest. Northwest to the Nahr and to Wa'ast, to pillared temples and sun-drenched courts. To order and familiarity and great houses and gold. But it also led to Karadoum and Khamet and the prince who ushered the Fall of the House of Bey. So, as I soared over the valley and felt the cool spray rising from the waters, I raised my wing and angled south. South to freedom and the unknown and to the angry, defiant, untamed spirit rising inside me.

I could not tell you, however, if it was good.

And so, I flew south for a day and a night, the moons of the world smiling down on the River Storm and the dragon that flew as though dead.

It was dawn when I came to the Steps of the Sun.

18

A THOUSAND STEPS

The stories were true, all of them. The Steps of the Sun were dragons.

Nine dragons were carved into the mountain, one atop the other, larger than the great statues of Karadoum or those at the temple complex of Neburanna. They were intricately carved, elaborately painted, and unique from each other in form and pose. Gold, silver, lapis, verdigris, cobalt, red, ebony, ivory and copper. Each was glazed in a different colour but the glaze was worn from wind and time. Each was easily the size of Netjeh, if not larger, and their glorious bodies formed a massive stairway from the river to the top. The Storm roared on either side of this stairway, a double waterfall larger than any I had ever seen. Along the crest, a temple spanned the entire breadth of the escarpment.

They had carved a path for Rath'nahr. He was carried to the heavens on the backs of dragons. I knew it now, and the truth of it was breathtaking.

I could see reeds moving along the stairway, tiny dots clad in white, journeying up the stone ramps that fronted the statues, and I wondered if it took them an entire day to reach the top. Boats and barges were hauled up from the river to the escarpment's edge, and I saw uru pulling great wheels of chain and rope. I remembered similar modifications made when we'd navigated the cascades of the Nahr and the cataracts of the Sand, but no cascade or cataract could rival the sheer size and splendor of this waterwall. It was a fitting nod to the ingenuity of the reeds, the power of the river, and the majesty of dragons.

I continued towards the waterfall, for neither the canyon nor the river went anywhere else but up. The roar grew louder, the spray cooler, and the early morning sun beamed down to almost blind my eyes. I could die now, I thought as I soared closer. I could close my eyes and let the Wheel crush my weary bones, let the fall break my neck, and let the river fill my lungs with water. It would be a fitting end for any dragon, even one as young as I, and I closed my eyes, prepared for the shock that would send me to the Fields of Ever Spring.

Suddenly, I heard a dragon call, and I angled my wing, sweeping up moments before I would have struck the rock. Reeds turned as I swept past, and I unfurled my damaged wings to catch the updraft. When I crested the waterfall, a red drakina rose to greet me. She had a rider on her back.

My chest ached as I hovered before the temple, for beyond it, was a vast, green land. Mountains had replaced the low hills of yesterday, purple peaks tipped with moons' silver. The River Storm was wide and shining, and morning mist rose from the waters like dragon's breath. And there were dragons, many, many dragons, some with riders, others without, roaming the skies.

Nabir.

A blue drake rose to hover next to the red, and then a striped green, all with riders perched on their backs. I should bow, I thought. I should land on the temple wall, spread wide my wings, and lower my head in deference and respect. I should follow them and see what sort of life they would find for me in this strange, new, humbling land. It would be a mercy, and after all I'd been through, mercy was a rare and precious thing.

No.

These dragons had reeds on their backs and for a few short, miserable days, I had tasted life out from under the harness of reeds. I would never be caged again.

And so, I beat down my wings, arcing into the skies above the trio and soaring over the temple and the waters of the River Storm. The three arced wings in pursuit.

They were faster than me, and stronger, well fed with intact wings and both feet. I had been caged for almost a year, chained, banded, and fed mash like a hatchling. And yet, they did not catch me, seeming content to flank me at a distance. Like an arrow, we swept along the River Storm, and over the winds, I could hear the reeds shouting to each other. I thought I heard the word 'Gifah', but I didn't care. I kept my head low, eyes fixed, wingtips splashing the surface of the river. To my left, the red drew closer, and I saw the rider with a coil of hemp rope in his hands. I glanced to my right. The same. I felt them closing in like the pincers of a skorpioch.

With a deep breath, I dove into the water, tucking my wings and lashing my powerful tail side to side. It felt so good to be in the water once more, and my inner lids slid across to protect my eyes from the waves. Silt, weeds, rushes, rock. Bubbles streamed from my nostrils and the rippling current soothed my skin. For a moment, I reveled in the simple pleasure of the river.

It was a very brief moment.

For I bent my neck and whipped my tail, circling back the way I had come. I lifted my head and burst from the waves, trailing the water behind me like rain, and I stayed low over the river, casting my eyes around to spy the dragons. I did not, for a minute, think I had lost them. I also knew that I couldn't stay over the water, so I arced a wing away from the bank in the direction of the mountains.

I passed over small boats, and when I reached the far shore, over huts as well. The land was lush and rocky, the air humid and thick, and I rose with the mountains, slipping in and out of clouds that hovered between the peaks. Entire cliffsides were covered in shrubs, and vines strung across canyons like linens in the Ophar's palace. But one thing took my breath away, nearly overwhelming my weary mind, and it was the trees.

I had never seen so many trees. In Gifah, trees were palms or figs, and they were used sporadically for shade and decor. Here, there were trees everywhere, on the mountains and in the valleys, along the river and rising out of the rock. As far as I could see, there were trees, and I swept down over them, sweeping them with my wingtips, marveling at how they moved. It reminded me of Mehen, and I wondered if this had been his home before he'd come to Diddad Wat and me.

The peaks were high and narrow, ridged like the back of a great dragon covered in all the green. I swept between them, needing to find a place to stop. I knew the trio of dragons was still above me, soaring silhouettes like spots on the sun. I didn't care. I'd been flying for a day and a night. I had taken a spear to the chest and a spear to the wing. I had chewed my foot off for the skarabs and the wyrms. I needed to stop. I needed to rest. I needed help and I needed solitude.

It wasn't until I saw steps, however, that I arced a wing, and I've since wondered at that. Steps carved into a cliff side, and the steps led up to a black opening like an open mouth. I soared up past the steps, circled around the peak to study the darkness. Flanked with carved pillars and a stone lintel, the opening was wide and rectangular, and I realized it was a temple built into the mountain. Within the darkness, a single light flickered with the promise of warmth and welcome.

I was still drawn to reeds. Still, I chose them to soothe that emptiness inside.

I flew to the opening and leaned back, wings wide, talons reaching for the ledge. I touched down, feet hitting the warm stone – Foot! Only one, and my bloody heel struck now, sending lights flashing behind my eyes and pain shooting throughout my body like arrows. I pitched forward, scraping chin and breast and belly as I slid before coming to a stop in a tangle of wing and tail and limb. I lay for a long moment, waiting for the waves to subside. They did, leaving pebbles of ache and the throb of my pulse in my throat. A dark silhouette moved towards me.

"Mother?"

The night fell like a hammer.

* * *

I dreamed of shakhet milk, rubbed into my skin.
I dreamed of kohl, painted across my eyes.
I dreamed of brands, searing into my thigh,
imprinting names of ownership, belonging and service.

And I dreamed of Amok, beautiful, dangerous, angry and dead.

Death. The smell of death and blood and smoke and sharp mustard.

I opened my eyes to the sound of humming.

"Mother."

I raised my head, swung it to see a reed kneeling beside me. He was thin and bony, with a grizzled grey head shaved to the scalp. He was binding my leg in linen, and I growled at him.

"Rest, dear Selisanaa, mother of the sun," he said, and he smiled a toothless smile. "You must heal. You are safe in Gesse for as long as you need."

I noticed his eyes. White and cloudy, like mist over the Nahr at dawn.

He turned back to my severed limb, ran his boney fingers along the bandages.

"I've cleaned your injuries here, here, and here..." He moved his hand along my flank to the shoulder, patted the spear wound on my wing. It was no longer coated in wax. "And dressed them with a *buji* poultice. I've sent the *niwanii* for some palm oil and lemon. They should be back soon."

He moved back towards my thigh, hovered frail fingers over Shesset's brand. I growled and rolled over onto my other flank, lashing my tail as I did so because it hurt, and I was angry.

"Forgive me, Mother. I am too familiar."

He pushed to his feet and, as I watched him shuffle across the rocks, I swept my gaze around this new, old place. It looked to be a cave turned into a temple, with a rough stone floor and rocky ceiling that sloped low over my rook. The curved walls were carved with images, but unlike the temples of Gifah, there was no paint or colour to be seen. Several iron braziers glowed with coals, lighting the cavern deep into the mountain.

He shuffled back to me, lowered a deep carved bowl to the floor by my beak.

"Drink, dear Mother," he said, his cloudy eyes watching but not seeing. "Life begins and ends with the Storm."

Water. I dropped my face into the bowl and drank, sucking the water up in sweet streams between my teeth. It flowed over my tongue and down my throat, and I waited for the familiar pinch of the collar as it restricted even fluids passing its dreaded ring.

No pinch. The collar was gone. I kept forgetting.

"I wish to see you," he said. "But I cannot with my eyes, only with my hands. So, if you growl again, I will stop."

And his hand touched me once again, moved across my scales, warm, light and dry like flower newts. He wasn't Kida. He wasn't a vaskar. I should have been angry, but there was peace in his touch. Clearly, I was not as wild as I had hoped.

Besides, the water was very good.

"I think you have had a strange life, Mother," he said quietly. "You are not a wild dragon, and neither are you Nabiri Skyborn. I've known my share of both, but the world is filled with new and wondrous things. I am merely a speck in the eye of the gods."

I finished the water and tipped the bowl with my beak, enjoying the feel of the liquid making its way down the length of my long throat. I remembered Mehen, splashing his beak in the fountain, simply playing as wild dragons do. No, I was not wild, but neither was I caged. It was a strange place to be.

There was a shadow at the cave's squared mouth, and I growled again.

"Come up, Kekket," said the old reed. "She's not wild."

It was another reed, a woman this time, middle-aged and rounded, and she stepped up into the temple with caution. She wore bright colours and a hat that held a large basket on the top of her head.

"Well, she hasn't eaten you yet, M'tawe," said the woman. "Not that there's much on you to eat."

"I've been told I could make a good soup."

With tentative steps, the woman crossed the stone floor, removing the basket and laying it by one of the braziers.

"I brought the lemon as well," she said. "But the *niwanii* are afraid to take the stair now if a dragon waits for them at the top."

"Then I'll go hungry for a while. The gods know what is need and what is want."

"What's wrong with her neck?"

"I think it was an ill-fitting collar," he said. "It must have been on for months. Years, maybe. It has left its mark."

I lifted my head and sniffed the air. Lemon, yes, but meat. Uru, by the scent, and wyrm. My belly rumbled. It had been so long.

"Bring it here, Kekket," said the old reed and he waved the woman over. "I suspect she's hungry."

"This is your *sadaka*," said Kekket. "The villagers gather it for the Monk of a Thousand Steps, not a runaway dragon."

"The villagers gather it to keep the Monk of a Thousand Steps alive and in Gesse," he said.

"To keep his wisdom alive and in Gesse," she corrected.

"The Monk has made many mistakes in his life, but this…" He laid a hand on my neck. "This is not one of them."

The woman sighed and came closer, finally laying the basket at his feet.

"I will not weep when she eats you," she said.

"You will laugh.".

He plucked a red haunch out from the weave, stretching out his arm and bringing it up to my beak.

"Eat, Mother," he said. "The people of Gesse keep their oracles well."

Meat. Uru meat. I snatched it up, my eyes rolling back in my head as my teeth tore through the muscle and my jaws crunched into the bone. I shook my head, spines snapping against my neck. Eagerly, I crunched and cracked and chewed, throwing back my head and tossing the mangled haunch down like I had in my early days. I waited for the catch and gag of the collar.

But the haunch went down.

It hurt all the way, but it went down.

I snapped my beak, once, twice, three times and swung my head to study the monk.

"I know," he said and patted my neck. "Whatever was there was too tight. I had to battle an evil spirit to relax the muscles. You should feast much better now."

I rolled back on my tail, brought my remaining foot up and scratched with my talons. The scales were tender, the spines misshapen, and ridges rose up like mountains over a valley that ringed my throat. But, thanks to Sakariye, there was no collar. It was all coming back.

"It will take time to heal."

Sakariye had removed it in the Market of Give and Take. I had killed and eaten an uru on the plains of the Wyldelands. I could feel the sythstone on my teeth.

I rocked forward and called it – the sigh of the sun, the breath that burned – and it came, leaping up my throat and bursting into my mouth. I held it for a long

moment, feeling the flames lick the roof of my mouth,
delighting as they bit my tongue and baked my teeth. I
released it then, spraying the rocks and the basket and
the simple furnishings and the altar. The monk laughed,
the woman shrieked, and I pushed myself to stand,
balancing on one foot and wing claws, severed limb
tucked up into my flank. I lumbered across the rocky
floor, swinging my great wings to use their claws as feet.
Walking. I never walked. But here, now, maimed as I
was, I walked. It was an awkward lurching gait – talon,
claw, claw, talon, claw, claw. I made it to the wide,
square opening and leaned out, clutching the ledge
tightly, and I breathed flame once again, spraying the
sky and the mist and the mountain and the stair. I filled
my chest and breathed again, my tongue scorching, my
eyes watering but my heart bursting with joy at the
effort.

And I bellowed out over the deep valley, rage and
heartbreak and sorrow and triumph. I believe it echoed
forever.

In the temple of Gesse and with the Monk of a
Thousand Steps, I was free.

I turned and lumbered back to my corner under the
low ceiling and the rock. I turned in a circle, cradling my
leg close to my body, and dropped to the stone floor,
satisfied.

Well, not entirely.

I dropped my head into the charred basket, throwing the last of the meat to the back of my throat and swallowing without chewing. It went down like thorny sobethi, but it went down all the same.

Char. Smoke. Ash. Ember. It was music on my tongue.

I sighed, a deep, rumble that rattled my chest, and sounded like distant thunder. I wrapped my tail around myself and tucked my head under my wing.

"She will kill us all," muttered Kekket, beating the scorched wood with rocks until only wisps of smoke remained.

"Ah, what a profound exit," said the monk.

"This is not wisdom. It is chaos." She straightened and wiped her hands on her multi-coloured skirt. "Shall we bring more tomorrow? Targa has sacrificed an oryks for you and Gabaya has the first of his new moon plums."

"Please," he said. "And have the *niwanii* bring sticks and rushes and branches with them when they come."

"Why?"

"For her bed," he said. "Let them know that the Monk of a Thousand Steps has a guest."

And he smiled.

As for me, I closed my eyes, savouring the taste of cinders in my mouth and dreaming of the sun.

19

MOTHER

The Gesse Valley was rich and rocky, verdant and fierce, and I explored a little more each day, not willing to go too far and inadvertently trespass on some wild dragon's terrain. I established a small territory for myself, marking cliffs and canopies with acid that sizzled first before turning to wax. I had seen Mehen do it at the fountain in Diddad Wat. I still remembered his scent.

The skies went on forever, and I marveled at the cold the higher I went. On the tallest mountain, there was white, and it was a most wondrous thing. White and cold, slippery and smooth. It was as if the clouds had come to earth and, while I was a Great Gold with the desert wind in my blood, I loved to settle my scales into the white, feeling the clouds become water. I knew then that rain wasn't created by the goddess Naret weeping for the reeds. In reality, it was sky dragons. The twin moon dragons and Selis Anekh herself, soared through the clouds, churning them into water and raining them down onto the land below. Truly, dragons were the guardians of all life, and I took to calling this mountain, the White Horn. I could see all the world from its heights.

Strangely, I still felt my foot. Even after it had been gone for months, I would sometimes forget and try to land with both, only to stumble awkwardly to the ground. Or I would feel sensations—spasms, cramps, or aches from a limb that no longer existed. It was strange, but my life was strange, so I adapted. I was good that way.

I returned to the monk's cavern each night, where he would share his *sadaka*, or basket of fruit, meat, and sweet breads. I did not touch the fruit or leafy things. Dragons are not impressed by banais, qale, or moon squash. Gingeh cakes, however, are a different matter entirely. Dragons are much impressed by gingeh cakes.

At night, he would sit cross-legged beside my nest of sticks and regale me with stories of the lands of Gesse and Nabir. He spoke often about the first dragons that made the world. His stories were different than what I had been told by Seb and Kida, Ixaak and Sakariye, and yet, the words strangely similar. Selisanaa instead of Selis Anekh, mated to Stellores instead of Styl Horys – sun dragon to lord of the night sky. He spoke of

Ankhares, not Ankh Horys, as titan of the seas. When he moved, he left trenches in the oceans so deep that no light could reach, and no fish could live. The monk spoke of Nerisanaa, not Nerys Anekh, as goddess of the earth, and insisted that the Gesse Valley nestled between the ridges of her spine. He called them the Spines of Nerisanaa, her peaks the Seven Sisters, and while dragons are not good at counting, I thought there were far more than seven. He talked about Apophores, the dragon before all things, and Orophores, the dragon after all things. He never spoke of Rath'nahr or Syth, Othorys or Neburanna or any of the Gods of Gifah. In fact, other than the dragons, most of what he believed was different from what Kida had believed, and, also, from what Sakariye believed. I wondered then how much was true, how much was tradition, and how much was story. Reeds loved their stories. I must admit that I loved them too. Perhaps, I was part reed. Perhaps, my time with them had made me so.

The monk was called M'tawe, and he taught these stories to people that climbed the stair each day. They brought him their *sadaka*, or offerings, in exchange for his stories. They also sought his wisdom and decisions on matters that ranged from taking a wife, to buying a field, to solving a conflict. It was monotonous and I rarely paid attention. They were all frightened of me until, one day, I unknowingly answered their prayers. One day, I killed a mountain wraith.

Wraiths are dangerous beasts with dagger fangs and long, strong, dragon-like bodies. Their legs are tiny, plentiful, and barbed, and they undulate like waves when they move across water, sand, or branches. They are usually found along the banks of rivers but can live in the dunes as well. Here, I would sometimes see them gliding through the treetops of Gesse, snatching up small animals and feasting on the nests of other creatures. I had little experience with wraiths, save the one I'd shared the bestiary with in Diddad Wat. They weren't sobethi, so I had no inclinations about them either way.

One morning, after I had refused half of the monk's *sadaka* (it was all tubers, roots, and inedible greens), I lumbered over to the ledge and sprang off, tucking my wings and diving straight down over the reeds who were making the climb. I loved this moment – the lurch of my belly into my throat, the rush of breath in my chest, cold wind across my eyes. The reeds shrieked and ducked into the rock, and I cruelly admit I loved that as well.

I plunged along the steep mountainside until I lifted my chin ever so slightly. Then, my wings snapped open, catching the wind, and relishing the lurch of my belly at the change. I swept upward then, swimming through the air as though underwater, my tail rising and falling in time with my heart.

Clearly, a dragon was meant for both sea and sky.

I soared through the valley, sweeping my gaze along the ravine's moss-covered rock and low-hanging cloud.

Even up the steep slopes, a canopy of trees created a blanket of green and I thought of Mehen once again. I'm not sure why. I had known him such a short time, and that spent on opposite sides of a cage, but I was a mature drakina now. More than once, I had thought of taking a mate.

Not yet, I told myself as I swept over thatched-roofed huts and wyrm coops, dipped a wing at the belled uru grazing in thorny pastures. I'd never eat one of these uru. They belonged to reeds of Gesse, and I would respect that. Still, the wild uru that roamed the steppes were fair game for me, and I had hunted more than once on these wild, rugged peaks. Despite their speed and their horns, uru were easy prey for a dragon. They never thought to look up, so dropping down from the skies and snapping their necks offered them a swift, merciful end, and me a thick, tasty meal.

I had also become skilled at 'flushing', in which I'd sweep over the jungle and smack the treetops with my tail as I went by. The canopy would burst with flower newts and crested wyrms, and I would feast as I circled overhead, snapping my jaws into a veritable sea of frightened, flying things.

I swallowed them all in one gulp, intact, whole.

If a dragon could laugh, this would have been the time.

And every day, I flew to the highest ridge of the Seven Sisters, the White Horn, and marveled at the panorama around me. To the west, the wide ribbon of the River Storm that, according to M'tawe, travelled to the lands of the Nabiri Skyborn. To the east and north, a dusting of cloudy white along the tops of the surrounding mountains. Still, the sky above these low clouds was amazing and I was content to sit atop the White Horn and fan my wings in the goddess' sunlight, surveying the Gesse Valley beneath and imagining it the spine of the ancient Nerisanaa, mother to all the earth.

Sometimes, I saw dragons.

Dragons in the distance, streaking, dancing, hunting, and I watched them with a stabbing heart. Part of me wanted to join them, but it was a move into the unknown. Were dragons creatures of the herd like reeds? Were they solitary like rassa, or familial like sobethi? Or were they content to be near each other, yet distinctly apart, like uru? I had no idea and so I watched, drawn yet wary, mature yet inexperienced in the ways of my own people.

I often wondered if we were a people.

Certainly not like the reeds, whose communal lives took on a life of its own. Towns, cities, temples, and armies, these were things unknown to other creatures, and I often wondered why. Was it their curious hands that allowed them to build, or their ability to communicate that allowed them to exchange ideas in order to build? Dragons had ideas. Dragons had imagination and dreams and hopes and fears, but we did not build. My mother's attempt at a nest of sticks was doomed to fail, while a reed could build a per ahmet of stone to house even the largest of us.

It was a mystery. Now, I had the freedom to ponder it.

That morning – the same morning I had refused the *sadaka* – I flew along the valley and heard a cry. I arced a wing and soared between the Seven Sisters, listening for the cry yet again, adjusting my flight to track them. It came from an uru field deep in the Hamabi Gorge. There were only a few families in the Gorge, reeds who struggled to tend their roaming herds. I remembered a man speaking to M'tawe about a pair of mountain wraiths making raids in the night. He had petitioned the monk's prayers and guidance but that was weeks ago, and I hadn't been paying attention because of the gingeh cakes.

I swept down into the gorge, and as I arced over the hilly field, I was surprised at the strange, spiked plants growing out of the rocks. Spikes and spines and barbs and needles – truly, this was the back of a dragon. Uru had scattered between them, anxious and bleating, and I smelled the copper tang of blood. I circled back once more, spying a carcass, its young neck and limbs twisted awkwardly against its flanks. I landed, wing claws taking my weight as I settled onto the scrub.

I wondered why the carcass was still there. Wraiths hunted to eat, like dragons. So, here was a young uru buck, dead, and no wraith for the eating. I swept my eyes between the spikey trees.

There was a wraith waiting on the rocks.

He sat, coiled like a basket, his small eyes shining like glass, mouth grinning with razor-edged teeth. I had no idea why he was waiting. Surely, the young buck had made an easy meal, but he sat, coiled and still, watching me with unblinking eyes.

There was motion in the high grass, and I saw the writhing coils of another mountain wraith as it wrapped itself around some prey. It was the largest wraith I'd ever seen, more than able to bring down a grown uru. But this time, he had a reed in his grip, a boy no more than ten summers. The powerful jaws were closed around the boy's foot, and the long body was already wrapping around th legs, beginning the relentless process of crushing the life from him as it moved. The boy's mouth was wide, his arms rigid, and in his hand, a stick.

It was then that I remembered Gaviid, the valiant little reed who walked with a crutch, lost in a crushing mob of sickness and need. I hadn't been able to help Gaviid. I'd never been able to make him fly.

I lumbered forward and lunged, sinking my teeth into the wraith's spine. It tightened its coils, lashed its tail across my eyes, but I held fast, crunching muscle and bone and many tiny scrabbling legs in my teeth. I called the acid into my mouth, flooding the flesh from inside and out. Its scales sizzled and the muscle split but still the creature constricted, and I knew the boy was going to die unless I killed it.

In the same way that I'd blasted river beetles on the Sand, I called the fire. Tightly, sharply, I burned the flesh between my teeth. Smoke curled up around my beak and I bit down as hard as I could. Suddenly, my jaws snapped together. I shook my head and the coils fell away in two parts. The boy dropped to the scrub, and I sank back, folding one wing across my spine and waited for him to move. He didn't move.

I looked back over to the rock at the base of the spikey tree. The first wraith was gone.

There was a stab of pain as it sank its grinning mouth into the bones of my bad leg and with a slap of constricting black, the wraith wrapped itself around me like a chain.

I reared back on my tail, scraping the grinning head with my free talons but it did not relent, and its many tiny, barbed legs dug into my scales like hooks. Coiling, wrapping, twisting, crushing, every movement caused its body to contract. I snapped my wings open and rose into the air, but the writhing creature clung fast, and I dropped earthward once more.

Heat, heat, pressure and heat, the wraith wrapped around my bones, its long body coiled across my ribs next. I threw myself to the ground, thrashing with wing and claw as slowly, this creature turned my bones to sand.

I arched my neck and curled into a ball, clamping my jaws over its skull, and calling the flame once again. It rolled up my throat to bathe the head in flame. I smelled burnt flesh as its scales sizzled, but the coils tightened even more. I bathed it's head in fire once again and my jaws crunched down until I tasted blood, salt, and jelly on my tongue. Finally, the many legs quivered, and the coils fell away to roll over and over on itself in the throes of death.

Two wraiths. Two.

I rolled up onto my talons and swung my head to look for the boy. His eyes still bulged, his limbs were still stiff, and the wraith's jaws still held fast onto the bloody stump that had been his foot. I leaned over, lowered my beak down to breathe him in. There was no scent of death like there had been with Ixaak or Sakariye, so very carefully, I nudged him.

He drew in a great shuddering breath, and then another. He looked up at me and blinked once, twice, three times.

He screamed.

I rolled back and snapped my wings wide, leaping into the air with a push from my taloned foot. Beat, beat, beat, my wings carried me up above the field again. I heard voices but I did not look back. I didn't want to see the crushed uru, the bloody wraiths, or the frightened boy whom I had saved.

I flew directly home that day, back to the nest of
sticks in the Temple of a Thousand Steps. Several reeds
were there, some petitioners and two *niwanii* who served
and cleaned and cooked for the monk. I ignored them all
and lumbered across the stone to my nest, climbing up
and curling my long body into a tight ball. M'tawe
called to me but I tucked my head under my wing. Later
that night, he came to me with his basket of food, but I
had no appetite. I'm not sure why. Dragons are hungry
creatures, and an offering of food is never in vain. Still, I
couldn't eat, and I wished to be gone, lost in a world of
fish and water and trees and wild.

Reeds compromised us.

He must have sensed something, that monk on the
stair, for he sat with me in the nest all night.

The *niwanii* came the next morning with another
basket and fresh water. I wanted neither and I could hear
M'tawe speaking quietly with Kekket. I didn't care. I
was good. I had helped. I had killed the pair of wraiths
and saved the boy with the stick. For some reason, I
wanted them to know that. I wanted their praise or
wonder instead of their fear, when in truth, I should have
left the nest and the monk and the company of reeds
altogether. I'm not sure why I didn't, although, in truth, I
think I knew.

I tucked my beak back under my wing and wished for
sleep.

Later that afternoon, I heard voices, and when I peered out from under my wing, the temple was filled with reeds. They carried spears decorated with the tufts of uru tails. My heart thudded in my chest. They were still filing up the steep stair and there was no way for me to leave without taking some of them with me. I was trapped once again, caged by the people I had sought to protect.

I pushed to stand, balancing on wing claws and one foot.

Two men stepped forward, and M'tawe shuffled in between. There was a ripple in the crowd and another figure hobbled through, stick tapping on the stone floor like a claw.

It was the boy.

I lowered my head and growled, lashing my tail behind me.

I was big enough. I had fire. I could kill them all. Surely, they knew this. Surely, they knew.

The boy looked me up and down, nodding once. I realized that, like me, his foot was gone at the heel.

"Yes, *abwana*," he said finally. "This is the dragon."

"Mother," said the monk. "Selisanaa of the Sun."

The two men stepped aside, and three women approached carrying baskets. They knelt and laid the baskets in front of my nest, and I could smell meat and bone and fish and wyrm.

"Gold Mother," said one of the reeds. "You have slain the wraiths that have plagued our town, and saved the life of Teti, our young shepherd. We prayed to your master, but it was you who answered our prayers."

"Mother Selisanaa," said the other man. "Stay and bless us with your protection for the length of your days."

"Yes, Mother," said the boy, Teti. "Stay."

With his stick under his arm, he hobbled up to me and reached out trembling fingers. I breathed him in, warm and sticky-sweet and smelling of uru. I pushed my beak into his hand, and he sobbed.

"Mother," they all said, and one by one, they came forward, laying baskets at my claws.

"Selisanaa of a Thousand Steps."

I looked to M'tawe. He was smiling like a slivered moon.

I was no longer a Great Gold of Gifah. I was Mother Selisanaa.

And I happily accepted their *sadaka*. In fact, I think I ate all of it that morning.

For two days after that, I ate better than the monk. I woke early and left to fly over the valley, soaring over the Valley of Gesse and through the Harambi Gorge. I wove between the Seven Sisters, all the while watching for wraiths and rassas, sobethi and wyrms. And for two nights after that, I came home in the golden light of sunset, as Selisanaa of the Sun blessed me and my land and my people with light.

On the eve of the third day, there was a dragon waiting for me.

20

BASK, SON OF BASH

I recognized the scent immediately. I had met this dragon before but now, I was wary of both wild and Skyborn alike. I angled a wing and swept up behind the temple's jagged peak. I had come this way so many times before, knew where to perch to peer down at the Thousand Steps that led to the temple and the monk. It was very high, the valley sheered steeply below, and the greens were overshadowing the greys. Still, it was the mountains. Rock was the root of all things.

I landed carefully, my severed limb still causing me strife, but I clutched the edge of the rock face with my wing claws and peered down. I could see the dark shadow of the temple entrance, and at the edge, blue wing claws, regal and folded.

Regal like his rider.

I dove straight down, the wind biting my eyes like teeth. Before the top step, I twisted and clutched the edge with my taloned foot. I spun through the opening, head lowered, and wings spread wide, hissing as I came to rest. The blue shrank back, tail whipping behind him, and I smelled the boil of fire in his throat.

"Bask, no," said a voice and a reed stepped between us, hands up as if to placate. It was Nakosa, son of Dejenai, Prince of Nabir and First of the Skyborn. I remembered him from Penet and the palace of the King.

I bellowed now at the dragon in my lair. Bask the blue, with black spines and hand prints painted in gold across his eyes. He was bold to think he was welcome in my lair. I was the Mother Selisanaa. Me. He had killed no wraiths for the Narambi herders. He had saved no child. This was my temple, my den, my nest. He had no right to be here when I had already staked my claim.

He flung wide his wings and bellowed back, the membranes of his jaws rippling and red.

Nakosa stepped between us, laying a hand on Bask's neck. M'tawe did the same, both hands out, seeing everything with the flats of his palms. It was all I could do not to bite them clean off.

"This is our Mother Selisanaa, my prince," said the monk. "I've been told she's as gold as the sun."

"Her name is Anekh Sun, daughter of Selis Anekh of the House of Bey."

The prince grinned.

"I've met her before," he said. "In the palace of King Marwethad. She's a Great Gold of Gifah."

"I wondered," said the monk. "She has a naming brand on her thigh."

"The name of Shesset-Isset, daughter of Thutmen'nahr II of the House of Bey and appellant to the Throne of Gifah." Nakosa tugged at the blue drake's harness, removing it, and setting it on the stone. "I've met her as well."

"The people of Gesse care nothing for Gifah nor their royalty," said the monk. "But this magnificent creature protects them and, so, they adore her."

"She was bred to be worshipped," said Nakosa.

It was true.

I was tired and wanted to get to my nest but this blue drake was in my way. He had been so much bigger then, so majestic and regal. But I had been young and easily impressed. Now, I was a Mother Goddess, and he wore a rein.

I snapped at him. He snapped at me, flames licking between his teeth. I had my fire. I could breathe the same.

"The princess will want her back."

"She is a free spirit," said the monk. "She's not mine to give."

Nakosa slipped the rein from his dragon's jaw.

"The princess has an army."

"A dragon has the wind."

And M'tawe turned to me, hands spread wide.

"Fly, Mother," he said. "You belong to the Scales of Nerisanaa and the Mountains of the Moons."

I bellowed and leapt backwards, plummeting straight down, my spines whipped flat against my neck. He was right behind me, this Bask. Bask, the Nabiri Skyborn mount of a prince. I could feel him, his heat, his breath. I could hear the sound his body made as it thundered in the wind at my tail.

I swung my neck and arced a wing, my body curving into the ravine just above the canopy of trees. I leaned forward, eyes narrowed, as I threw everything into my wings. Beat, beat, beat, beat. Faster, stronger, swifter, fiercer. I would lose this tamed blue in the Seven Sisters and wait him out in the Narambi Gorge.

Up and down and in and out I flew, weaving between the great peaks like rushes in the river. The river! I doubled down, flying harder than I had ever flown before. He was still behind me, his breath like fire on my tail. This audacious blue drake thought it was a game and I a prize to be won. My heart leapt when the glimmering ribbon of the River Storm came into view.

I soared over the huts along the riverbank, over the boats and barges and skiffs, ignoring the reeds who raised their hands as I swept overhead. Finally, the water, a great wide stretch of brown and white, churning and wild and fast. He descended to my flank, his wingbeats easily keeping up with mine, and I realized that, while I had grown in both size and wisdom, he was still older and larger and far more experienced. This *was* a game for him. I *was* a prize. He was bold but I was smart, a goddess worthy of worship, and before I knew it, I arced downward and plunged into the river.

Thick and dark the currents moved, my wings tucking instinctively to my sides, my tail sweeping in powerful strokes as I swam through the waters. Oh, how I'd missed this, the water and the waves, the many sensations that rippled across my scales to cool my seething blood. I could swim like this forever, fishing for starred eels and hunting sobethi. River wraiths, too, now, were my enemies. I would kill them without a thought if I saw them on rock, tree, or riverbank.

For a brief moment, I forgot about that cocky blue drake. I was simply a creature of the waves and the sea.

Joyfully, I burst up from beneath the surface, spinning water in all directions. The sky was streaked with purples and pinks, and I was the sun, golden and warm and glorious. He was hovering half a bank away, and when he saw me, he trilled a curious call. He beat his wing downward, unhurried and pensive, flying with head low as if studying the water. He reached down with his talons and dragged them across the surface, spraying water across his belly and tail. I headed back upriver, slowly now, allowing him to catch up and I watched him dip his wingtips into the waves, then his chin. Clearly, it was a new thing for him, this river of delight, and I marveled at something so simple. Then again, I had been a Great Gold. He was ridden. Magnificent, yes, but bound to a reed in ways I had never been.

Still, I had been sun to Kida's moon. I could never forget that. Even painful memories lived.

The moons were rising now, smiling twins in a vast indigo sea. Together, we flew side by side to the boats and the bank and the huts. Back to the ravines and gorges of Gesse, and the jagged peaks of the Seven Sisters. This was my land, and it was filled with wonders. I showed him the cliffsides with the strange spikey trees. I showed him the rocks that crawled with green, and the clouds that hung low like the breath of a dragon. Up, up, up I took him, skimming the Scales of Nerisanaa and onto the steep plains of cooling white. Finally, up to the highest peak, the White Horn, where the air was thin, the land was vast, and the heavens went on forever.

He was the sky. I was the sun. We were wing to wing when he bit me.

Just a nip at my shoulder but it was enough.

How dare he? I was Selisanaa and Selis Anekh, mother and goddess rolled into one. I snapped back at him. He bit my neck this time, and I spun in mid-air, snarling and raking his flank with my talons. He threw back his head and bellowed, his voice echoing through the Sisters, but it wasn't fury or pain. It was something else, something I had only become aware of when I met Mehen, when I had tasted the fountain water on his chin.

I bellowed too now, twisting into the drake as we soared through the night skies. My wings battered his, his tail whipped mine and our jaws batted and bit as we spiraled up to the stars. He spun around and sank his teeth into the back of my neck, not piercing but firm, and I marveled at the sensation of his talons on my flanks. I arced backwards, taking us back down to the White Horn and into the deep blanket that crowned her.

We hit the soft whiteness hard, sinking as if in water, necks and tails entwined like a pair of wraiths. We thrashed together, rolling through the white and crashing across the rock. There was no rider; there was no monk. There was only breath and bellow, couple and claw. Only the stars and the white and the fire in my throat and I released it, spraying flames into the night sky. It turned the white to water and a flood poured down over the rocks. Bask pinned me to the rock with his great weight, and I yielded, his belly moving across my spine like a mountain, his breath scorching my scales like a karad. His teeth daggers against my neck, I bent my head back, mouth wide, flame rolling across my tongue.

I arched my back and welcomed him.

I'm not sure how long we remained on that mountain, but the moons were across the sky when we returned to the Temple of a Thousand Steps. I landed first, crossing the floor to take my nest before he could. The monk yawned and the prince looked up wearily from his place on the rock.

"Oh dear," said the monk. "Kekket will not be happy."

"Why?" asked the prince as he rose to his feet.

"We'll need sand tomorrow," he said. "Lots of it. Unfortunately, there are many stairs."

The prince shook his head and gathered the harness.

"I won't take her," he said. "I must tell my father, however, and I can't say what he'll command. But for me, for now, she stays."

"You will make a fine king, Nakosa Skyborn."

"So, you say." He grinned, tugging and strapping the leathers into place. "Until you pay tax."

I watched from my nest as the prince swung up onto his mount. It seemed a perfect fit, I thought. The spines dwindled along our necks, and the dip in our shoulder made a perfect resting place for a reed's leg. I wondered at the weight. Bask was large, and the prince was grown. I wondered if I could carry the monk. He was thin as a river rush. I was certain I could.

Bask turned and lumbered awkwardly to the temple's edge. His great wings came down and together, they launched over the side, disappearing into the beams of morning sun. The last I saw was the flick of his tail, brash and taunting and showy and gone.

"Here, Mother," said the monk and he set a barrel of water by my wing. "You'll have a thirst."

He was a very wise reed, and I plunged my face in the barrel, drank deeply the cool, sweet water. I had called much fire tonight. We had both turned the White Horn into a flood, had likely sent some rocks crashing down the mountainside in our wake. I hope I'd crushed some wraiths while doing it.

I finished the water and the monk offered me a gingeh cake, which I also accepted greedily. He patted my neck once, twice, three times before he turned and shuffled back to the bag of dry rushes that served as his bed.

Yes, I knew I could carry him.

I could carry Shesset. She was thin and spindly, like the monk.

I tucked my head under my wing.

I could probably carry Kida if she cared enough to try.

Sleep came quickly, and that night, I dreamed of blue.

***

I realized, as I leapt from the edge of the Thousand Steps, that I had rarely ever touched another dragon.

It had been so profound to me. The grate of his rough scales, the sting of his talons, the lash of his tail. Even still, other than my brothers, I had never felt the skin of another dragon. All my contact had been with reeds or in a very few instances, prey. I had no experience with my own kind as equal until that night with Bask.

Kekket and the *niwanii* had filled my nest with sand. I didn't know why but it was nice. Cool, first, then warm, and I found myself digging little holes into it with my claws, nudging it into piles with my beak. For some reason, it took me back to that first day when I left the shell and crawled through an eternity of sand to meet the sun and the great, smiling teeth of my mother.

Several weeks later, I flew over the valleys and gorges of Gesse, leaving the weaving of the Seven Sisters for another day. With the river in my wake, I angled my wing and headed south.

I had seen glimpses of dragons before, so I rode the air currents for several hours until I caught their scent. For us, the sense of smell was keen, as keen as a reed's vision, and I coursed through the skies – south, southwest, southeast, now east – until I caught the trace of dragon spoor.

I leaned into the wind, my wings carrying me further with every beat. Soon, I was farther than I had ever been, past the last wax marker I'd left for myself as Mother of Gesse. I was free and unfettered, with no collar or muzzle or hobble to bind me. It reminded me of the time when I was young, and I flew along the Nahr to the Nameless Sea. That had been an adventure. This? This was terrifying and exhilarating at once.

The scent of dragons grew stronger, and mixed with that, brimstone. This mountain was different than the Seven Sisters, wider even than the Spines of Nerisanaa. Smoke and cloud billowed from its peak and my heart leapt into my throat. I bent low to the wind, feeling wave after wave of heat as I arced up over green cliffs and black rock, and rounded the smoldering peak. What I saw beneath me shook me to my core.

Truly, it was the Mouth of Aphorys, the door to the underworld where Rath'nahr journeyed each night.

It was a lake within a lake – a fiery, boiling, red crater contained within a ring of fresh water. Beautiful, terrible, opposing yet entwined, and steam hissed where they met, creating clouds in the process. Rocks floated in this lake within a lake. Wisps of steam carried up from the surface and currents spun in twisting vortices down, down, down to the black depths.

No, I thought, not the Mouth of Aphorys. If the Seven Sisters were the spines of the ancient Nerisanaa, then this was her Eye.

The stench of brimstone was overpowering, and I almost turned away until I noticed the dragons.

There were nests in the cliffs surrounding the twin lakes, tucked into crevasses and fissures and cracks. There were nests on wide ledges and nests in protruding rocks. There was even a young drake sitting atop one of the floating stones, fanning his wings in the heat.

I perched on the rim, cocked my head to take it all in.

Tucked under a cleft in the rock, a red drakina noticed me first and she raised her head and sang. It was a warbling, eerie and beautiful sound, taken up by a grey, and then, a nearby blue. Soon, the entire crater echoed with dragonsong and I spread my wings wide, hoping to catch all of its music with my skin.

A great green drakina landed beside me, wings wide, head low. On the other side, a bronze drake, but he did not land, preferring to beat his wings at me from the air. I knew nothing of dragon ways, nothing of the etiquette of my own people, so I bowed to the drakina, wings also wide, head low but eyes averted, respectful and still. She stretched out her neck and breathed me in, her nostrils warm with the lake's strange heat. The drake dropped to the stone and nudged me from behind. I growled, and he barked shrilly over the crater. Soon, I was surrounded. Blues, greys, greens and reds, nudging and nipping, sniffing and snuffling. Earlier, I had complained about a lack of dragon touch. Now, it was entirely too much.

The bronze drake shook his spines and nudged me again. This time, I snapped and the green drakina leaned past me and caught his face in her teeth. But it wasn't an attack, and I watched with wonder as she arched her neck and trilled, her green spines alternating between sharp and flat, sharp and flat. Immediately, the drake yielded, relaxing his body and folding his wings. He trilled in response, and she held him down for a long moment before releasing him. He took off, complaining as he disappeared into the crater and a nest tucked deep within the mountain. The drakina barked once, twice, three times and all the dragons that had surrounded me took to the air, returning to their nests and rocks as if nothing had ever happened.

The drakina remained, however, and she nudged my flank, pushing my branded thigh with her beak. She breathed down to my severed limb, and I watched with curiosity as she paused, mouth open to enhance the scent. It seemed to be an inspection, and I remembered the mornings spent in the drakmet of Seb, poked, prodded, inspected, and cleaned. She nudged my tail next so I lifted it, wondering if she could tell that, only weeks ago, I had been mated. Finally, she snorted and stepped back, folding her great wings across her back.

She cocked her head at me, and, for a very brief moment, I saw my mother.

Then, she turned and flew off, back down to the crack in the cliff where she lived.

Where she lived with her eggs and her hatchlings, and I felt odd.

I needed a nest.

I looked around at this strange, wonderful, terrible place.

I had indeed been mated to Bask, son of Bash. I needed a nest for my eggs.

I would have eggs. Soon, I would have hatchlings and Bask would be their sire.

I knew it in my bones.

But I had no idea what to do. Just like my mother, I had no idea. But there was one thing I did know – the monk would help me.

I unfurled my wings and leapt from the rim. I was the Mother Goddess and I was going home.

21

OMENS

Several weeks passed before the first egg came, then another day before the second.

That last week was uncomfortable as the growing eggs pressed into the bones of my hips. I spent days pacing the temple – laying, sitting, stretching, circling. Kekket and the *niwanii* had brought dozens of large pitchers filled with sand to the top of the Thousand Steps, moving the sticks to create a centre both deep and soft. It was like the Eye of Nerisanaa, warm sand surrounded by cool sticks, and I found myself digging one pit, then another, as I moved and rolled and moved again.

All the while, the monk waited on his stool by the brazier, telling stories and talking to the breeze. He was frail, I thought. Frailer than normal. I didn't know how long reeds lived, but his movements were slow, and his breath smelled of bones. Still, he adored me, and I knew I would serve him for the rest of his remaining days.

Finally, there was one morning where I didn't touch the *sadaka*. I couldn't sit. I could only lie, but even my tail was uncomfortably placed.

"It's time, Mother," said the monk, and he patted my neck.

With a deep puff of breath, I arched my back, lifted my tail, and shuddered as a wave of pressure rolled down my spine. Then it was gone. I looked behind me to see a large, speckled, leather oval, nestled in the sand.

An egg. A dragon egg. My dragon egg. Mine.

I needed to bury it deep in the sand, and I turned to dig with my wing claws. It would have been easier had I been able to balance with both back feet, but still, I made do, scraping down to the temple rock with my claws. I nudged the egg until it tumbled into the hollow and I covered it with sand and sticks until it was a mound. I thought a moment, remembering my earliest crawl from the depths, so I levelled the top with my beak for an easier hatch.

No. It would be cold. I dug a new hole and rolled the egg in, nudged more sand over the shell.

I glanced up. The monk was smiling. Sometimes, I wondered if he could see.

I snorted and stretched out, covering the nest with my long body, and tucking my head under my wing.

I did sleep that night, but a second wave of pressure woke me early. Another egg arrived within minutes, smaller and speckled, and I buried it next to the first. I was hungry after that and ate the contents of two *sadaka* baskets. Then, I believe I slept for a full day, and when I woke, I thought I'd dreamed it all. I was glad the monk was asleep, for he would have smiled more as I dug and nudged to find the two eggs, safe and whole in the sand.

I coiled myself around the mounds, and I'm sure it was days before I left. Kekket brought me the baskets and was good enough to hold them while I gobbled them down. Once, in my haste, my teeth accidentally crunched through the staves and she barked at me, holding up two rings and some splintered stalks. I grunted and laid my head back down on the sand, rebuked but unapologetic.

The people of Gesse continued to come, making the long trek up the One Thousand Steps, now thrilled at the thought that their Mother Goddess was truly a mother. They said that dragon eggs were good omens, and I had given them two.

Within weeks, the baskets could not fill me, so I began to hunt again. It felt good to be soaring over the valley after laying for so long curled up with the eggs. I also resumed my duty of protecting the people and remember vividly the day I swept over the fields of a man named Terek. He grew moon plums and guavas, and sometimes, his wife would bake plum cakes for me. I liked plum cakes, even though the seed gum stuck to my teeth like paste. They were sweet and chewy and not at all green. Nothing green is fit for dragons.

Terek was working in his orchard, and there was a strange, familiar scent on the breeze. From the sky, I could see a shadow stalking towards him through the trees and the tall grass. I dove down like a spear, landing on it, breaking its spine with the force of my weight. This time, it wasn't a wraith but a rassa, with its long fangs and golden hide. I remembered the rassa in Diddad Wat then, felt a strange pang of guilt. It was fleeting, however, and I sprang back up again, its heavy, furred body in my talons. I swept over Terek's head and dropped it to the ground in front of him. He waved at me, and I knew I would have a nice basket of plum cakes within days.

It was sunset when I returned, to find the monk, weeping. There was a welt on his head and rivers in his eyes. Water was proof that reeds came from the Nahr, but closer to the Nameless Sea where all was salt and fish and sky. I leaned my great face onto his, breathed in the sharpness of the tears and the copper of his blood. I wondered if he had fallen again. He was frail, like a leaf in the dry season.

"Mother," he moaned.

I pushed past him and climbed up onto my nest, dug with my claws into the soft, warm sand. I needed to turn the eggs. I needed to turn them.

I needed to find them.

"Oh mother…"

I tore the nest apart. Sticks, stones, sand, bark.

"Gone," he moaned. "She was a new *niwanii*. I didn't know her. I didn't know."

I spun a tight circle on the mat of wood and rock. My eggs were gone. They weren't in the temple, and I swung around in front of him, and bellowed. I bellowed until my breath pushed him to knees. I bellowed until he clapped his hands over his ears. I bellowed until blood trickled from his nose.

I sprang from the nest, my tail smacking him against the stone wall as I went. But I didn't look back, and I barreled to the mouth of the cave and bellowed again so that my cry echoed long and far over the valley. I breathed deep the twilight for the scent of my eggs, caught it on the breeze east towards the river. I launched into the dark to follow.

***

It was a community without a name, which was strange because reeds have a need to name things. There is power in a name. Which is why I was Mother Selisanaa the Goddess. I was power and now, I was fury.

It was night, with only one moon for light and I wondered if it was an omen, too. One moon, one brother. If I could save one egg, even just one, I could rest. Out of my mother's five chicks, only two survived their first year.

So, I swept over the tall fence that surrounded the village, over the thatched roofs and earthen paths inside. The fence was made of bound tree trunks chiseled to a point and standing on end. It might keep a rassa out, but nothing could stop a dragon. No. Reeds built things to keep us in, but I was done being kept.

I landed with a growl, and stalked through the small town, tail lashing, my footfalls thundering in the quiet night. The scent was almost masked by woodsmoke and ananais oil, but I found the hut near the fence line. It was made of mudbrick and grass, and there was a small, untended garden with withered seedpods by the wood-stick door. I could hear voices from inside, and I crouched low as the door swung open and a woman stepped out.

She froze.

She was the one, I recognized her scent from the temple. The scent of egg and monk and fear. She spun on her heel and disappeared back into the hut, screaming furiously from within. A man emerged, spear in hand, and he shook it at me, shouting as if I should be afraid. I was Mother Selisanaa the Goddess, a Great Gold of

Gifah. I rose over him, and he jabbed the spear at me, but I caught it and snapped it in my teeth.

I bellowed now, a sound that awoke the entire community and others peered outside their doors before ducking back in again. I bellowed at them as the man disappeared into the hut.

"It's your fault!" screamed the woman from inside. "I told you she would know! I told you we would die!"

I could hear the sound of a table being dragged to block the door. As if a table could stop a dragon. As if a door could.

I snapped at the roof with my great jaws, ripped it off like the tines of Kekket's basket. Their screams rose into the night, echoed now by the shouting of the villagers. They had found their courage, but I had found my eggs, and I stepped my wingclaw onto the mud brick wall, buckling it like wet sand. The couple staggered out onto the path, each carrying a satchel, and they turned to run. I swung my head to follow.

Suddenly, my hip stung with the bite of skorpiochs. I swung around to see a villager holding a spear in his hand.

"Go home, Mother!" he shouted. "Leave and we will save your eggs and bring them back to the monk. But leave!"

My blood ran down the shaft, and I roared at him. He fled down the dirt path, and I roared again, shaking my head, and blinking away the needles. More villagers hurled spears at me, so I pulled my wings down in a great, earth-scattering stroke and leapt up into the sky. Up, up, up I went, even as spears were flung towards me from below. I winced as one, then another pierced my flank and thigh. Most bounced off my leathery hide and rained back down on them like Gifahn arrows.

I found the scent in a heartbeat and flew after the pair as they raced towards the gate and the jungle that lay beyond. Several villagers ran after them, some with spears, others with torches. I didn't care. I wanted my eggs. I swept down on the man and caught him in my talons. He screamed as I carried him up, just like Kiin and the Market of Give and Take, and he dropped the satchel. Far below, the woman caught it and bolted down the hard dirt path towards the fence, the gate, and the jungle beyond.

I flew over her and dropped him on the path in front of her. Just like Kiin, I did not care to hear the crunch.

The woman skidded to a halt.

"Mak?"

I swept down to block her path, landing with a thud that shook the trees. A crowd was forming around the man on the ground. I could smell his blood as the woman dropped to her knees beside him.

"Mak, no."

"What have you done, Ejjae?" cried a villager. "How do you anger the Mother?"

"The eggs are worth more than her scales!" said another. "Mak said he could sell them up river, and we would all be rich!"

I growled now, lashed my tail furiously. The flames rolled on my tongue, licked the roof of my mouth, danced between my teeth.

"Give her the eggs, Ejjae," said another. "Don't be a fool."

"He's dead," moaned the woman called Ejjae. "The dragon has killed my husband."

"Just give her the eggs," said a man.

"Get her out of our village," said another.

"Do you know how hard it is, carrying the *sadaka* for a dragon up those steps?" She looked up. Her eyes were filled like the Weeping. "Can you imagine three? My mother breaks a little every day with such heavy baskets."

One by one, the villagers moved aside as I lumbered towards the woman. I towered over her now, my breath rumbling as she clutched the satchels to her chest.

"People are wrong. The monk is wrong. A dragon is not a good omen."

She met my eyes, her own fierce and proud, raised the satchels over her head.

"Ejjae, no!"

"A dragon brings only death," said the one called Ejjae. "Go back to Gifah where you belong."

311

And with a roar of her own, she smashed the satchels into the dirt.

I heard nothing. I felt nothing. I was a dragon turned to stone.

With a deep breath, I set her ablaze.

She twisted on the hard-packed road, flames catching her hair and her clothes and her skin. The villagers screamed and raced for water, but it was too late for Ejjae. She was a twitching husk in a matter of heartbeats, alongside her husband broken on the road. I bent down to gather the satchels in my teeth, tossed them back onto my tongue and leapt into the night sky. I noticed the cold wind now, and the black sky. The lone moon and the hollow valleys. I tried not to taste the bitter salt ooze through the weave of the sacks, tried not to imagine the sliding shells over dewy wet bodies. I could save them. I was their mother.

The temple was dark when I returned, no candle or oil lamp, no brazier or stories to warm me.

"Mother…" His voice was thin, but I was busy.

I lumbered over to my nest, dug and scraped, scraped and dug as I tried to reassemble what I had torn apart earlier. When I had finished, I rolled the satchels from my tongue onto the sand. They were both wet and dark, with a sharp, oily scent, but I had no hands, no miraculous reed fingers by which to open them. I trilled and turned to nudge the monk.

"Mother," he said again.

He clasped my face in both of his hands, leaned his forehead against mine but I pulled my head to the nest. He came with it, released me to pat the sticks, stones, and sand with his boney hands. They found the satchels and slowly, he worked the leather strings until the mouth of the bags opened. He worked them gently, until the shells slid out.

Two chicks, blue with gold stripes. I held my breath as one little head curled weakly in the sand. They were not ready. I knew this somehow. They were not fully formed, and the splitting of the shell and loss of the slime inside brought them to a slow, sticky end. I climbed up onto the nest, coiled my long body around the two little shapes. Reached down to breathe warmth over them both, trilling and cooing and pleading like a distant wind. The curling one opened its mouth, and I saw its tiny teeth and pink tongue. Its eyes were open, even as it stilled.

I swung my head to the monk.

"I'm so sorry, Mother," he said, and his hands trembled as he crawled over my limbs into the nest. "I should have read the leaves. I have failed us all."

I whined as he slid his frail body between my wings and my flank, but he was light as a dry reed. I barely felt him nestle in. I whined again, but it was plaintive and sad as everything that was in me broke that night.

I lowered my head over my chicks.

Bad omens. I was a bad omen.

313

My birth had brought about the death of my mother and brothers, the emtombment of Netjeh and the downfall of the Ophar. My life had been traded for Josiat's and Ixaak's and Gaviid's and Sakariye's. In my lifetime, Mehen and the little blues and all the dragons of the Temple of Neburanna. Great Golds were not good omens. Great Golds were bad.

I did not sleep, fearing the step of Kekket or the *niwanii*. They would come and they would know. I had burned a woman tonight. I had dropped a man from the sky. And I had blamed the monk, had roared at him until he burst, my fury all but snuffing his breath like a candle. I was not a good dragon.

Kekket did come that morning, but early. She was frantic and worried and let out a long wail when she found us. I didn't raise my head. I didn't move. My chicks were cold under my chin, the monk was cold against my flank. She lowered her basket and dropped to her knees. I waited for her shouts, for her curses, for her strong fists to beat my face and neck and beak. But instead, she lifted her head and sang.

"Mother in the Temple of a Thousand Steps,
Monk of the Temple breathe his last.
Spirits soar on the wings of gold,
Mother in the Temple of a Thousand Steps."

I raised my head and joined her.

My song slid up and down the dragon scale, sometimes sharp, other times round. The temple echoed with our song, and I admit, I sang louder than I normally would in the company of reeds. I sang long and loud, and continued, even after Kekket left that evening. I sang it all night, leaving the nest to stare out over the valley, sending my lament through the Seven Sisters and the Spines of Nerisanaa and beyond.

I returned to the nest at dawn, curling myself around the three dead souls, and giving myself over to a bone-weary sleep.

By noon, many reeds had made the trek up the mountain. Some were from the town, some from the river. There was no *sadaka* that day, but I'm not sure I would have eaten. I was weary. Weary of this life with reeds and hope, weary of this life with cages and spears. Go back to Gifah where you belong, Ejjae had said. But she was wrong. But did I belong in Gifah? I had lost my mother, my home, my reed, my position, my friends, my clutch, my future. I did not want to hear the whispers of those who wanted me dead, nor those of the ones who wanted me gone. Without the monk, I was untethered, unpredictable, dangerous. Without the monk, I should be gone.

An argument broke out later that day, as the spearman from the village recounted the tale of me breaking down the house and burning the pair. They didn't care that my eggs had been stolen, just that I had burned a woman while she yet lived. I would have burned them all at that moment if I had cared to. If I cared.

But Kekket was strong, and she chased them all out. She told the *niwanii* that she needed to plan M'tawe's journey to the afterlife. It needed to be done right, and I allowed her to move his stiff, dry body out of the nest. She spent the rest of that day wrapping him in strips of leechy leaves, then linen, then wool. They broke his bones easily and curled him into a basked the size of my foot. They poured oil on him and set candles all around, sang songs well into the night. Then, they left, and I was alone with the dead, until the dragons came.

22

SKYSONG AND SKYBORN

It was very late when the dragons came.

I believe I had slept, but at one point, heard the sound of talons on rock. I opened my eyes, to see a great, green face, flickering in the light thrown by the candles. I lifted my head. It was the drakina from the Eye. Behind her, a dozen dragons here in the Temple of a Thousand Steps.

She lowered her head, breathed in the scent of my dead chicks, and trilled at me. It was sad, it was heartbreaking, but I had no will to trill back. I had no will at all, and I watched with disinterest as the others spread out into the temple, pushing, sniffing, nipping, exploring. A young red nudged the basket of the monk, but it creaked, and he backed up swiftly and launched himself out of the cave. A blue nibbled the water bowl, tipping it and spilling water across the floor. Another joined him in the splashing. A small brown sprang onto

317

a wooden chair, which teetered for a moment before shattering under his weight, while another nudged one of the monk's candles, fascinated by the flame. It tipped over and rolled dangerously close to the basket, and the wick flickered against the oil-damp weave.

The green drakina turned and barked, and one by one, they left the temple until only she, I, and an old grey drake were left inside. She ran her beak along my cheek, nibbling and nipping with her tiny front teeth. There was no intimidation, and once again, I was reminded of my mother. I was as inexperienced as she had been. The drakina snorted and turned, padding over to the grey. He was perched on the edge of the temple, wings folded majestically across his back. She did the same, settling in the entrance, front wingclaws gripping the ledge.

And then, she sang. Starting low and rising in pitch, it slid up, then down in tenor, sometimes sharp, other times deep. It took me back to the Ophar's palace and the nights of harp, sistrum and cymbal. The drakina's lament was picked up by the drake, then another outside, then another, and soon, the entire valley of Gesse was echoing with dragonsong. They were making music for me.

I rose from my nest to perch beside them. I didn't sing but I marveled as the night sky was filled with dragons dancing.

Sweeping, soaring, swirling, spinning, they sang, and they danced over the Thousand Steps until the moons joined in, peering out from behind the night clouds to shine their light on the spectacle. The drakes, proud and preening, tossed their heads and beat their wings as they spun about the sky. The drakinas, regal and strong, chased each other's tails and soared up and down the steep mountainside, catching tiny rocks and sending them bouncing down the stair. Even some of the hatchlings were flying now, and I watched them try out their young wings, finding their balance and learning their rhythms. I remembered. It had been so different for me on that day when Shesset threw me from the roof.

Down below, I could see lanterns flicker on in houses and farms, towns and villages all throughout the valley, and I wondered what those poor reeds thought. I wondered if Kekket was standing down below, hands on hips, cursing the monk who had allowed me to stay.

They sang for most of the night, and it was only when Selis Anekh chased the moons from the sky that they left. Just a flick of a wing and one by one, they were gone. The grey drake next, and finally, the drakina. She rose and scraped her talons across the rock before launching herself into the valley. I never saw her again, but I know that, somehow, she had saved me.

I returned to my nest, nudged the chicks one last time. They would never sing like these fine dragons. They would never soar. My mother would have eaten them. She ate the green that died early on. So, I did too, snatching up their tiny bodies and their leathery shells in my jaws, and swallowing them whole, returning them inside where they had begun.

I padded over to the basket and the monk. The monk I did not eat, although I think he would have wanted it. The oil had soaked his wool and linen and leaves, and there was a thin wisp of smoke rising from the bottom, where the candle had smoldered for hours. I would miss him. His kindness and his humour, his stories and his boney hands. I was glad to have been with him at his death, but I wished he could've lived forever. But he wasn't a dragon. He was only a reed, frail and easily bent by the wind. I wished him good life in the Fields of Ever Spring.

I turned and leapt off the edge, soaring down the One Thousand Steps for the very last time. I didn't see the wool catch, nor did I know that the temple burned that day. His one last story met a lonely, fiery, and dramatic end. Many times later in my life, I wondered if, perhaps, he was more dragon than I.

***

I didn't know where I was going, I didn't know why I flew. I knew there would be a place for me at the smoking mountain and the Eye of Nerisanaa, if, and when I needed, but something drew me back to the water. The River Storm was healing. The River Storm was life. Fish and rushing currents, deep blue and soothing mud. Even though it was crowded with reeds and boats and cities, I hoped for something else along its rushing whitewater banks.

So, I soared through the valley of Gesse, as Rath'nahr lifted his hand to the dawn sky, streaking the world with pink and yellow. The land below was thirsty, and I knew the rains would be coming soon. I settled into a contented rhythm. Beat, beat, beat of my wings, the low, smooth undulation of my neck and tail as my serpentine body soared through the skies. It was efficient and tireless, and I knew I could fly like this for days. Dragons are made to fly. It never grows wearisome or burdensome. In the skies, we never need strive.

So, it was with a strange sense of contentment that I saw the River Storm, and his shining ribbon of brown. I lowered my head and narrowed my eyes, wings beating in time with my heart. Over the dry riverbanks and fences, the fishing huts and the border of yellow rushes that lined the shores. Once the rains came, the rushes would be submerged, and the river would swell to the fishing huts and the fences. The Storm was life, the same way the Nahr was life, and I wondered at the dragon god of the water. Ankh Horus in Gifah, Ankhares in Gesse. I was the daughter of Selis Anekh, but I wondered if my father had been him.

I dove into the water, like that night with Bask, and tucked my wings against my flanks as I sped through the currents. Side to side went my tail, and my inner lid rose to cover my eyes. I loved the world beneath the waves. The bubbles and the brown, the silt from a land I did not yet know. I remembered both Kida and Shesset spoke of Nabir and the Kingdom of the Skyborn. Bask had come from Nabir. Bask, the proud, boastful blue, with a gold hand painted over each eye.

I rose to the surface, blew out my breath and deeply inhaled another, but this time, did not leave the water. I began to swim like the sobethi, low and flat, with only eyes and nostrils out of the waves. At least, that's what I told myself. I'm sure my backswept horns and neck full of spines announced the fact that I was no sobethi to all the reeds who watched from the boats.

It didn't matter. I used to be a creature of stories, of reckless imagination, of dreams. I could be again, if I tried.

And so, I swam upriver for days, navigating the rocks and overcoming the strong currents with my powerful tail. I fished at will, slating my hunger on the sweetest of flesh. I slept in the rushes, warm and buoyed, and groomed by the pics and white flower newts that lived by the banks. The reed people left me alone, and I was grateful for that. And for a time, I was content.

One day, as I swam upriver, I tasted a new silt in the water. It was rich and mixed with clouds and I knew there would be a waterwall soon. The banks of the River Storm were rising again, with escarpments of red stone and embankments on either side. The sky overhead

constricted as the river cut through new mountains until
the sky was the ribbon and the river was all. By noon, I
heard it, growing from a hiss to a hum to a roar, and by
evening I saw it. Not as tall as the Steps of the Sun, but
tall nonetheless, it rained five plumes of white down to
the river below.

Just like at the Steps of the Sun, there were many
boats and skiffs, barges and sunsails being pulled up by
uru and wheels. Just like at the Steps of the Sun, there
was a temple built across the crest, beautifully carved
limestone atop massive stone supports. The waterwalls
flowed around and between these supports, and I
couldn't imagine the force of water that would rush over
the edge come rainy season. And sitting atop the carved
lintel, dragons.

I pushed out of the water then, beat my wings to rid
them of the spray, and they saw me. I rose, spinning and
soaring and daring these poor saddled Skyborn to stop
me. They trumpeted the alarm, but I rose up, up, up to
the top of the waterwall, and I soared over the temple to
the land beyond. And I marveled at that land. It was
miraculous.

Atop the waterwall sat a lake as large as a sea. It was
surrounded on all sides by mountains, and along the
banks, a city unlike any I'd ever seen. The buildings
were tall and spired, with circular walls and clay roofs.
The streets were crowded and colourful and the scents of
the markets wafted over the smell of fish. In the centre

of the lake was an island, and on the island was a palace much like the one I'd grown up with in Gifah. Bridges ran to and from the island, and along the roads, carts were pulled by both uru and plainsbuck.

But the skies were filled with dragons.

Red dragons, green dragons, blue dragons, grey. Some flew alone, others in pairs, and without exception, they were saddled, ridden by reeds like Nakosa and his father, and my heart skipped at the knowledge that I had found the fabled kingdom of Nabir.

A pair flew in above me; another pair fell in at my tail. I was unbridled, unsaddled, unridden and free, and I wondered if this was allowed in Nabir, or if I was breaking yet another unspoken rule of reeds. I dipped my head, aiming for the lake, when a trio appeared beneath me, and another appeared at my flanks. I was effectively surrounded by dragons, but I did not fear, nor did I rage. I was a Great Gold of Gifah. Captivity was not an option and I dared them to take me with net or spear.

Our strange company turned and shepherded me towards the palace on the lake. I let them, angling my wing, and dropping my head. One of the riders blew a curled horn as we circled the palace, and I could see reeds scrambling down below. The palace was large with many levels, domed spires in some areas and others open to the evening sky. From one of those open courtyards, a blue flew out to greet us. He had gold hands painted across his eyes.

It was Bask, son of Bash, and this time, he wore no rein.

***

Prince Nakosa made a special arrangement for me to stay in a place he called the Pike and share a stall with Bask. I was not Skyborn. I had never worn a rein, so I knew this was an accommodation because of my past. He had met me as a Great Gold. He had met me again as a Mother Goddess. I'm quite certain that my noble ties swayed any perceptions he may have had to my benefit, so I was appeased.

And I am happy to say that King Dejenai adored me.

I spent many days in the throne room, along with his great grey, Anshassar. It reminded me of the temples of Gifah, with high pillared ceilings, columns and tiles and statues of dragons, rassa, sobethi and men. Only here, there was little gold. All was ebony and oiled wood, palms and carved cacaciar. Dejenai would feed me delicacies made for his court. He wasn't supposed to, but sometimes he would pretend to slip. An eel roe cake would fly in my direction, and I would snap it out of the air before it touched the floor. I would grin at Anshassar, then, with eel roe paste stuck to my teeth. He would grumble at me, not because he was jealous, but because he was old. Not as old as Netjeh, but still, grumpy and slowing, and he growled every time I came near.

I could be the King's dragon, I thought to myself. I wouldn't growl or grump.

The days we spent touring the city, flying over rooftop and mountains, lakeshore and bridges. When Nakosa rode, we would fly over the temple and the waterwall, and I loved to gaze down to the bottom where reflected colours arced like ribbons in the spray. When Nakosa didn't ride, we would fly up, up, up to the clouds, chasing the sun and trying to spy Selis Anekh and the sky-boat. It was cold up there, and I wondered how Rath'nahr could live, when the reeds so loved their candles and fire.

Bask had a stone-hewn stall in the Pike, one of the mountains overlooking the city. All the Skyborn did, and again, in the same way as the Temple of a Thousand Steps, a connecting web of wooden stairs wound its way across the cliff face. Dragons are not good at counting, and I lost count of the stalls after ten and ten and ten and ten. But there were more, and I knew that in the ranges beyond, there were even more. We shared that stall, Bask and I, but I refused to mate with him. The fear of losing eggs was too fresh, the ache too deep. Fortunately, he didn't try, and I found myself enjoying his preening and posturing. The others were another story, entirely.

In fact, the Skyborn drakes were relentless.

Since I was a new drakina without a clutch, I was the focus of their attentions, and from sunset to sunrise, I had a procession of suitors. They would flap all around my ledge, trying to catch my attention, trying to draw my eye. I wasn't interested. I had been imprinted in my youth by Netjeh the Noble, and Mehen the Magnificent. I had been mated by Bask, son of Bash, the Skyborn mount of a Nabiri prince. Clearly, the call of a clutch wasn't as strong in me as my pride. I was Great Gold and would be until I died.

I was with them for months, when, one day, a barge was raised over the waterwall and onto the lake. There was something about it that I remembered, and I caught a scent that was at once familiar and strange. It was evening, then, when the curled horn blew, summoning Bask to the palace of the King. As was our new custom, I flew with him. My heart thudded in my chest when I spied the barge, anchored off the island's rocky shore, for carried in the boats and the docks and the ground of the palace, was the Golden Standard of Gifah.

Gifah. A barge from Gifah. My world was about to change.

There was an open terrace on the roof, where important, visiting dragons of important, visiting men, stayed. I often found myself here. The terrace was warm and sunny, or warm and rainy, and music would float up on the breeze from the courts below. It also offered a perfect view of the king's Court of Laws, where he entertained diplomats from all kingdoms of the world. Bask and I landed together, and he leaned over to watch the world of reeds play out below him. I stayed back, afraid of what I would see.

He swung his blue head, the golden handprint flashing in the sun. He trilled at me. I pressed myself low to the floor, flattened my spines, and slunk forward. Clutching the terrace ledge with my wing claws, I peered over the side.

They were from Gifah. I recognized the clothing. White sheaths, golden collars, flat sandals, transparent gauze. Soldiers were clad with breastplate and helm, but I noted no spear or shield, no sword or flail. No one would be allowed to bear arms in the Court of Laws or the presence of the king. Still, Anshassar coiled behind the king's large chair, and I wondered if the Ophar would have died had Netjeh been so near. I would always be in the room if I were ever a king's dragon.

Dejenai sat on the wide, carved seat, looking regal and impressive as the procession filed in. Nakosa stood at his side, hands clasped behind his back. Both king and prince wore patterns of black and gold, and Dejenai wore a headpiece of dragonscale and horn. My chest swelled at the sight. The Skyborn of Nabir. I was honoured to be with them.

Two men stepped forward carrying tall earthen vats. They laid them at the foot of the throne and stepped back into the procession. A woman stepped forward next, dropping to her knees, and lowering her eyes.

"Fermented shakhet milk," she said, indicating the first vat with the tip of a hand. "From King Marwethad's divine flock."

She waved at the other, but I'm certain I didn't see.

"And Desert Plum Wine from the lost vineyards of Suradan on the Glass Road."

I'm not sure I remembered to breathe.

"I bring greetings from Queen Shesset-Isset, daughter of Thutmen'nahr II and Glory of the House of Bey."

"Rise, daughter of Rath'nahr, and emissary of the Land of Gifah," said the king.

Kida smiled and rose to her feet.

23

KIDA

Kida.

She was taller, leaner, and dressed in red and gold. Her hair was also longer and braided into many tight knots atop her scalp. She stood before Dejenai like a queen and my heart swelled at the sight of her.

"You and your people will be welcome in Nabir," said the king, his voice echoing across the mosaic floors. "As long as you stay, you will be welcome."

"You are an honoured king of an honoured people," said Kida.

Her voice was strong, clear. She was not the quiet thing of my youth. She had grown. But so had I.

"My son says you are Lamos-born," said the king. "I have never met a Lamoan. They are as much legend to the Nabiri as Nabir is to Gifah."

She smiled a quick smile, and I thought my chest would burst.

"We all have legends," she said. "They are as life-giving as bread."

"It's how the world is built."

Dejenai leaned forward in his chair.

"But you are not here because of Lamos, are you, girl?"

The blood quickened in my throat. Kida wouldn't leave the princess unless there was a great need.

"The king speaks the truth," she said.

"So, tell me then. Why are you here?"

Me! I knew it in my bones. She had heard of the Mother of a Thousand Steps and had come to get her.

"I have been away from my home for so long," she said. "But my home is not Lamos, honoured king. My home is Gifah."

I was a Great Gold of Gifah. She had come to take me home.

"And we are taking it back from the usurper, Beyat, and his silver legion from across the sea."

Beyat.

"We?" asked the king.

"The princess Shesset-Isset, daughter of Thutmen'nahr II and Glory of the House of Bey."

The princess. She was here for the princess.

"Shesset-Isset rises like Rath'nahr to restore the God's Land to his people," she said. "And with the help of King Marwethad, she has raised an army in Penet to be her sword."

Not me.

"I ask again, daughter of Lamos, why are you here?"

"As we speak, the princess is heading to Karadoum, where a small Flight of Remoan Dragons guard the city. She leads a fleet of Peneti warships, and a legion of five thousand Peneti warriors follow in their wake along the banks."

"And?"

"There is a second cabal of Peneti soldiers – a secret legion – coming over the mountains, prepared to lay siege to Wa'ast from the northeast. King Marwethad has also assured us the aid of Lamos, my birth nation. They are already sending a fleet into the mouth of the Nahr."

"Forgive me, girl, but Lamos is a faithless nation. She looks to the needs of Lamos, no further."

"Not when their ancestral enemy, Remus, is involved."

Dejenai snorted and behind him, Anshassar tightened his tail.

"Beyat has sold his birthright to Remus," Kida continued. "Remoan Flights guard the holy city of Wa'ast and patrol the skies with their dragons."

"So, she sent you, a daughter of Lamos, to ask for ours?"

She'd forgotten that she'd once had a dragon. I would have guarded them all with my life.

"Yes, oh honoured king. She does."

The king of Nabir glanced at his son but said nothing for a long time.

"You have told me the how, not the why. I give you one last chance to answer my simple question."

"I have journeyed along the Glass Road with a small retinue to bring you this." Kida held out a scroll. "She proposes an alliance—"

Dejenai waved a hand, but Kida stepped forward.

"—a marriage."

Both men looked up.

"A marriage?" asked the king. "To me?"

"To Nakosa, most honoured prince of the Nabiri," said Kida, "A joining of two great kingdoms under one sun and two moons."

Slowly, the king sat back in his chair, drumming his fingers on the chair's hand rest. For his part, Nakosa could have been a carving for all that he had moved.

"And where would they rule this joined kingdom?" the king asked after a moment.

"From the halls of Karadoum," she said. "And the Island of Sand and Storm."

"So," said the king. "The daughter of Gifah gets a king, and the son of Nabir gets a queen. I'm certain the duties extend further than the marriage bed."

"Gifah is a pearl among kingdoms," said Kida. "You know this to be true. Any royal house that makes such an alliance will be established forever and will lack for nothing."

"Gifah is not hers to give."

"It will be, once we take it back."

"With Nabiri dragons."

"Commanded by a Nabiri prince."

My throat had grown tight, tighter than when banded with silver. All was politics in this world of palaces and princes. Dragons were merely pawns in the game, little more than winged dice.

Bask cooed at me, bobbed his blue head as I clutched the ledge, sending tiny pebbles down to the mosaic below.

Nakosa looked up.

"Perhaps, father, we should ask the dragons."

And he held out his hand.

Bask sprang from the ledge, his weight sucking the air in a cool sweep behind him. Anshassar bugled as Bask circled the throne room, a regal flash of blue and red, before settling onto the mosaic and arching his neck like the sky. Nakosa laid a hand on that great chest, and I felt a rush of pride. We are magnificent creatures.

Bask swung his great head up and the room echoed with his call. All eyes turned my way, including the largest in the world.

She saw me.

I ducked low and slunk back. I wasn't ready for her. I wasn't ready. I lumbered to the outer edge of the terrace, breathing deep the cool mountain air, feeling the lake spray prick my eyes. The sky was golden like the sun, and I welcomed the warmth of her breath as she ferried Rath'nahr into the dark, chased by the moons. Just like I had been chased from my home by my brothers. I felt a stirring within me.

Home. Gifah was my home. It still called to me, even after all this time. The sand and the dunes, the palms and the river. That mighty River Nahr, with its tides and its depths. It was why I kept coming back to the company of reeds, why I could never take my place among the dragons of Nerisanaa. I had been raised in the palace of the Ophar with its pillars, columns, and courts. My life had been Netjeh, Josiat, Shesset and Kida.

My Kida.

But was she?

I was no longer hers, so was it possible she was no longer mine?

Were dragons possessive? Did we so easily covet what we did not have?

I leapt from the terrace and soared over the city, sweeping up to the Pike and the stall that belonged to Bask. It was strange that I presumed I had access without him. We had mated, so I suppose there was familiarity. But even as I settled onto the pile of rocks that served as his bed, I realized it was not my nest. I had no nest, no den, no lair of my own. I never had. I was not like the drakinas of the Eye. Even the Temple of a Thousand Steps belonged to the monk. He had shared with me because of his great heart.

I missed him.

I closed my eyes and must have slept until there was a scent and I knew Bask had returned to the aerie. I raised my head to see Nakosa slide from his back and reach up a hand for Kida.

"Anekh," she breathed.

Not Anekh.

She stepped closer.

"Anekh."

I pushed to my claws, keeping my stump tucked close to my body.

She reached out a hand. I growled.

"Be careful," said Nakosa. "She's been free a very long time."

"I thought she was dead." Her eyes were still larger than anything, larger even than the Eye of Nerisanaa, and the waters of the Nahr gathered behind them. "They told me she was killed in a karad."

I had been. I died in that place.

"Oh, look at her horns. Look at her spines. She's so beautiful…"

Trembling fingers approached my beak and I growled again.

"Her foot?"

A foot she had chained, so long ago.

"And her throat? The scales are damaged, the muscles withered…"

Because of a collar she had clasped.

"I'd forgotten you were a vaskar," said Nakosa.

"Once," she said. "Yes, once I was a vaskar. I was happy then."

I watched her hand now through narrowed eyes, growled one last time.

"*Net,* Anekh," she said and stepped closer, arm outstretched, fingers reaching, reaching…

I snapped my jaws down on her hand. She cried out and a sword appeared at the prince's side.

"Wait!" Kida gasped.

She had grown but so had I. My mouth had closed over her entire arm.

She held her breath.

Her hand pressing between my teeth, soft and brittle and frail like a reed. They were reeds, persistent and fragile and easily uprooted. Just a little more force and a little less thought, and she would be like me. Maimed, crippled, less. Like Gaviid the brave. Like the Monk of a Thousand Steps, who saw more without his eyes than the sighted ever could.

No.

Not less. Never less when the spirit grows in the body's wake.

I growled again but let it roll around in my chest as I moved my tongue along her wrist and across her palm. Her skin tasted of sand and salt and ink and paprush. She was older now, forging a life with Shesset, she of the steely eyes and the knife smile. Daughter of

Thutmen'nahr II and Glory of the House of Bey. Rightful Ophar of Gifah.

Gifah. The land that breathed like a setting sun, that bit like a sharp wind.

I released her and turned my head. She sank to her knees.

"Oh, my Anekh," she whispered and buried her face in her hands.

Bask cocked his head and trilled. Nakosa laid a hand on his neck.

"My father will gift you a royal barge for the trip back, but he will not give you dragons."

Kida nodded, let her hands fall to her thighs.

"Then we will lose. The Emperor of Remus has sent Dragon Flights to guard the great city."

"Then the Emperor of Remus is the Emperor of Gifah."

"Beyat was a fool," she said, and she pushed to her feet. "He thought he could peddle the legions of Remus, but instead, they used his vanity to gain a foothold in the God's Land."

"Puppet kings happen all the time."

"Shesset will be no one's puppet." She turned to him. "Will you accept her offer?"

"I will," he said. "It's a good match. And from what I remember, she has a fierce spirit."

Kida nodded swiftly, mouth tight, eyes strangely bright.

"She does. She is a powerful woman. You will be very happy."

"More than that, I will be doing what is right for both kingdoms and I will be proud."

She nodded again.

"But Gifah is not your home," he said. "Why pour yourself out for a land not your own?"

I could see her struggling with the river behind her lashes. Oh, the Weeping of the Nahr.

"You love her," he said, and the rivers released.

"I love her," she said through her tears. "Yes, I love her. I can't imagine my life without her. She is proud and fierce and stubborn and sharp. But she is good and clever and wise and strong. Until Gifah is secured, I have no will of my own. Only loyalty to my queen, and duty to my adopted land. I will fight for her until my last breath."

"Then I have made the right decision," he said. "If she inspires such faith in her people."

She wiped her eyes with the palms of her hands.

"In me, at least. Maybe I'm a fool."

"You love dragons in all their forms."

She smiled.

"Maybe one day, we will make a royal trip to Lamos." He shrugged. "I understand it's poor now. Mostly ruins. Crumbling temples and floating markets and people selling pieces of history. Only a shadow of what once was."

"A Land of Once but No Longer."

"Once but No Longer." He looked at me. "Try to touch her again."

She swallowed and raised a hand. I intently watched as her fingers reached for me, reached, reached...

Touched.

She closed her eyes, and once again, the rivers spilled their banks.

It was like the kiss of the sun, warm and tingling across my scales. Touch. It needed no words, no language, no common tongue. It was a song of its own.

My Kida.

"Perhaps you will have a dragon after all," said the prince.

"I couldn't," she said. "She's lost so much already. She should be free."

"She is," he said, and now he stepped over, ran a hand along my neck, smoothing my spines, scratching my horns. Touch. Not only a song for dragons. "But she was never wild. She always comes back to people. The Monk of a Thousand Steps thought she was a *ha'arat.*"

"A *ha'arat?*" Kida glanced up. "A spirit that journeys between life and death?"

"Like that," he said. "But she journeys between worlds, between our world and the dragon world."

She looked back at me and smiled.

"Anekh Sun, *Ha'arat* of Worlds."

A title I graciously accepted. I bent my head to nibble my wing claw. I'm sure there was a bit of dirt.

"Would you try to ride her?" Nakosa asked.

"I'm not sure I could."

"You've already flown from the throne to the Pike on Bask. Are you afraid?"

"No, it's just…"

Her voice trailed off and he cocked his head. Much like Bask, I reckoned.

"It's not my place," she said finally. "She's a Great Gold, the dragon of a queen. I couldn't. It wouldn't be right."

"You are asking a Nabiri king for dragons to help wage a Remoan proxy war on behalf of a Gifahn princess," he said. "What is your place, exactly?"

She laughed.

It was music.

He turned and strode off to the wall of straps, peeled a set of black leathers from the hooks. As he made his way back, I growled and flattened my spines against my neck.

"She doesn't like the harness," said Kida.

"She doesn't have to like it," he said. "But she'll have to wear it. You're an inexperienced rider. You'll fall off at her first dip."

He passed her the rein and hoisted the harness that wrapped around a dragon's belly. I shrunk back and snarled this time. Bask trilled, confused.

"Besides," he said, "With a missing limb, her balance is wrong. You won't be an easy fit."

I would not wear these things. I'd worn a hobble and, in the end, lost my foot. I'd worn a collar against my will, and it had almost killed me many times over. A part of me was still Anekh, but another part was not, and I would be subject no more to the whims of reeds.

"Anekh?"

I left Bask's nest of stones and lumbered past the reeds in my three-beat gait to the mouth of the cave. Bask swung his head towards me, nipped at my shoulder but I snapped back at him, and peered over the steep side of the Pike. Below me, the Nabiri city stretched out in a circle around the lake, glistening like jewels around a royal throat. The lake itself gleamed in the setting sun, purple and gold and flickering white, and in its centre, the palace of Dejenai the King.

It was a Wheel of a very different sort.

I tipped forward, letting the earth pull me down, and down I went. The wind stung my eyes, rattled my teeth and I gloried in the sensation of down. Down, down, down, faster than my blood, faster even than thought, certainly faster than I would have with a reed on my back. I was no tame dragon, no chariot-beast or marakt-maimed. I was free, if not wild. There was no rein to turn me, no harness or leather to bind me to a reed. And the Wheel, that accursed crushing Wheel of the

Elements, had been shattered for me along the Glass Road when I chewed off my talons rather than yield.

I swept up then, avoiding the rocks at the base of the Pike and angled my wing towards the lake. Drakes warbled at me from their aeries, but I soared past. I needed no drake. I needed no reed. I needed the sky and the water and the power of my wings. I breathed deeply the lake air, the coolness of the approaching dark, the scent of eel roe cakes baked in the palace kilns. And lastly, the barge of Gifah, with its golden standard catching the last of the light.

Gifah. The bones of a thousand dragons crushed into sand by the Wheel and time.

I circled the boat, watched as the crew waved and wept as I flew by.

Gifah. The land of the gods and their children, the reeds.

I saw Abshir, and my heart leapt at the look of wonder on his face.

Gifah, the pearl of kingdoms.

I ducked low, touching the water with the tip of my wing, spraying the barge with sweet fresh water. The crew cheered and my heart shattered.

Gifah, the land of my birth, mother of the Nahr.

The Sand and the Storm made the mighty River Nahr, and the mighty River Nahr made me.

I heard Bask bugle from the palace roof and arced to meet him. He was there with Nakosa and Kida, and I landed carefully. Kida watched me with her great dark eyes, expectant and full of awe.

I lowered my head, extended one wing.

"Please," moaned Nakosa. "At least one rein…"

"Let me try without," said Kida.

"It's been nice to know you, Kida, vaskar of Gifah."

She stepped over to me, ran her hand along my neck to my shoulder, delighted to let it rest there a moment before reaching up and grabbing a horn. I leaned into her as she stepped on my wing and swung her leg up. It felt heavy and off balance, but she was neither, so I knew it was me. Slowly, she lowered herself down onto the hollow between my neck and shoulder.

I have to admit, it felt strange.

"Release the horns, now," said the prince. "They're too far forward to hold. You'll need to try to hang on by the spines but be careful. I've heard of many riders impaled by a sudden turn or abrupt stop."

I shook my head, and the spines snapped back and forth against my neck. I felt her hands grip the two nearest my shoulders and I relented. I stepped back and raised my wings, curious at how her weight went with me. I dropped down to the stone, lashing my tail now and feeling her weight settle across my back.

"May your gods be merciful to you, sister."

I turned to peer over my shoulder.

She was bent low across me, draped across my neck in her perch. Her knees tucked in the crook of my wings; her legs followed the bend of my shoulder.

"Please don't throw me off, Anekh," she said.

I lumbered to the edge of the roof. I felt strange, unbalanced, heavy.

"I can't believe you're doing this," said Nakosa. "Please, just let me tie your legs."

I stretched out my wings, a challenge to my brothers, the moons.

"I have carried her all my life," she called as the wind plucked at her words. "Now, it's her turn to carry me!"

I opened my wings and sprang from the roof.

Not a deep plunge like my descent from the Pike, and I arched my back above the lake, feeling the leathers catch the sky. I stayed low over the water, very aware of this reed on my back. My wingbeats were awkward as I tried to find a rhythm. Up, down, up, down, and my body followed in a serpentine flow. Still, her body didn't interfere, and, other than weight, it was as if she wasn't there. Beat, beat, beat, over the lake and the boats and the bridge to the shore.

I soared up and over the city, it's fires and lanterns glowing like stars beneath us, while the stars glimmered like lanterns above. I wondered if she'd caught her breath yet, if she'd remembered to exhale. She'd always been a quiet one. I felt her shift her weight, leaning forward to grip my spines better. She was almost flat on me, and I had to admit she would have been more secure with a harness. I felt a pang of guilt, but it didn't last long. It did make me wonder about riding dragons at all, and the partnership that surely had to have been in place for years. Was Nabir the first land to ride dragons? Was Remus? Were there no stories of the first dragons and their riders?

Below us, the palace gleamed in the moonslight, so I brought us back to the water, low enough so that the tip of my wings splashed the lake's surface with each beat. Soon, we settled into a rhythm that could have carried us all the way back to the Nahr had we the time.

Above us, the moons shone, reflected in the water below. In that moment, we were between worlds, Kida and I. A *ha'arat* dragon and her reed. It was mythical.

Glowing with torches and lantern light, the royal barge sat low in the water.

"There, Anekh, *khem!*"

I circled the barge, and spied Abshir watching us from the uppermost deck. He waved and smiled as wide as the moons. I was glad he still lived.

I leaned back, drumming my wings to bring me slowly to the top deck. Most reeds scattered and I realized they were not Gifahn or Nabiri, but Peneti, unused to the comings and goings of dragons. I touched down with foot and stump, then rocked forward to take our weight with my wing claws. Slowly, the barge dipped in the water under my weight.

I growled and swung my head towards the Peneti, keeper of cages and binder of dragons.

"The rumours were true!" cried Abshir and he strode forward. "Is this truly Anekh Sun, she who razed the Library of A'Toth and brought Karadoum to its knees?"

He had no fear, for he reached up to take my beak in his wide hands.

I let him.

"It is," said Kida. "And she is so much more, but first please, Abshir, can you help me off this dragon?"

He bolted to her side, and I lowered so that my belly touched the coolness of the deck. She was rigid, her hands stiff and bloodied from gripping my spines, her legs raw and chaffed from the iron of my scales.

But even as he helped her, he could not help but marvel.

"It is her," he breathed, running a hand along my thigh. "The searing is Shesset's."

He passed her over to a host of women, who gathered her to themselves.

"Do we have dragons?"

She glanced up, tried to smile.

"Well, we have one."

"Two," came a voice and the barge rocked once more, as Bask, son of Bash, landed on the deck.

24

THE RIVER STORM

We were three days now on the River Storm, and it was vastly different than her sister, the Sand. Whereas the Sand was wide and deep, the Storm was wild and frothy, with cataract after cataract, cascade after cascade, interrupting the smooth flow downstream. I was impressed how the reeds managed to move the barge from top to bottom of waterwalls with no damage. They used a series of ropes and pulleys and sheer strength, lowering the barge in stages with tension lines on both banks of the river.

Dragons didn't do things like that. We never try to recreate or manage our environments like that. We adapt. Reeds overcome. It was curious and gave me more questions than it answered.

We were too big for the barge, so I taught Bask the ways of the river. For a dragon that had lived in a city on the banks of a lake, he had never swum, and it took him a day to find his way in the water. The current was strong, the water sweet, but he took to it like a sobethi once he understood. We needed to use our tails differently than in the air – side to side, as opposed to up and down. It was counterintuitive since the sky is our natural element, but once the rhythm was found, it came easily to him. It was life to me, and I rejoiced to be back on the water.

Each day, we swam alongside the barge like river guardians, catching fish for our reeds and ourselves as we wished. We were larger than any sobethi now, so there was no fear, and to be honest, I dared any to try to hunt Bask or I. I did kill two that swam beneath me, and I happily crunched their stony scales with my powerful jaws. They didn't make a good meal but their blood in the water was sweet.

Finally, the rains started, casting the sky in shades of grey, and the clouds were heavy and cold. Still, it was a glorious time of my life, and I purposefully did not think about the war that was awaiting us beyond the Island of Sand and Storm.

Bask and I mated again. We had been hunting in the rushes (I secretly hoping for another chance at sobethi), and the blue drake had managed to snare a large anglefin in his jaws. He burst from the water, proudly tossing his head, and displaying his catch. I could hear Nakosa and Kida cheering from the barge. Cheering for such a silly thing as a fish, so I darted through the water and lunged at him, trying to snatch it from his beak. He tossed his head again, ducked and flapped like a hatchling. I barked at him, and he launched into the air, the fish flashing in his teeth.

I leapt after him.

Kida's people have their stories, Nakosa's have their legends, but dragons alone know the truth – our coupling makes the thunder and calls lightning. And it did that day. I chased him, that boastful blue, biting his tail and his feet and his flank, until he swung his head back and bellowed. The fish was gone, and I was furious, and I bellowed back, raking his belly with my talons. He beat down his wings, arching his neck and twisted his body towards me. I met him swiftly, gladly, fiercely, as thunder rolled, and lightning cracked the sky. We spun through the rain, necks wrapped, tails entwined, wings extended and racing. Our coupling took us to the moons and back. I never did get the fish.

We plunged back into the river, once spent, and the wave splashed over the barge. Bask rolled in the waters, preening his wings, and slating his thirst, while I sank low like a sobethi, savouring the sensations that echoed through my body. I was grateful that the rains had made the tide high and the current strong, so I could doze and be carried along, with only my tail waving slowly in the water. Before I did, I slid one eye up to the barge beside me, where Kida and Nakosa stood watching us from the rail. For the very first time, I wondered how reeds mated. I'd been completely unaware of such things when I lived in the Ophar's court. I wondered how they chose mates, how they paired up and when they laid their eggs.

The rains continued the next day when Kida flew again. She was ready this time, her legs wrapped in strips of linen, her palms in strips of leather. She also wore a woolen headcovering to keep her face and throat warm. She stepped out onto my back from the deck of the barge and slid across my shoulders as if home. I pushed out of the river then, my tail propelling me forward, my wings forcing the water down, and I emerged from the Storm like a skyboat, golden and glorious as the sun. We rose above the river with every beat of my wings, Bask and Nakosa a blue shadow beneath us. We soared and we dipped, we circled, and we dove, and not once did Kida fall off. Truth be told, I was gentle with her again. I had lost her once in the palace of Marwethad. I didn't want to lose her again.

We flew along the River Storm until we came to the last cataract before Karadoum. It was not a waterwall, so the barge could navigate it without pulleys. Still, Nakosa leaned to the side and Bask banked and went down, landing on a large rock cut on the riverbank. I followed, impatient for her to be off my back, for I had seen a school of moonfish and I was hungry. The reeds sat and talked, while Bask and I hunted, and when I was sated, I climbed back on shore to rest until the barge caught up.

Bask stretched out beside me, his tail across mine. The rain was warm. I was tired and full of fish, and I enjoyed the wordsong of our reeds.

"Do you think she'll catch?" asked Kida, rubbing the sensation back into her legs.

"I don't know," said Nakosa. "I heard that she had laid two in Gesse, but that they died."

"Hm," said Kida. "Sometimes, the inexperienced ones do lose the first few clutches. That's why we raised them in the drakmet ourselves."

"How could you raise an experienced drakina if you do it yourself?" asked Nakosa, picking at the greening grass with a dagger. "How could they ever get the experience?"

"They couldn't. They needed us to do everything for them. I suppose it was our way of keeping them dependent."

"Prisoners."

"Partners." She shrugged. "I was a child, doing an important job in a prestigious drakmet in the royal city. I don't make life, but I lived."

He smiled, picked at the grass.

"Do you talk to her?"

"Talk? To Anekh?"

"Yes," he said. "The Skyborn can talk to their dragons. It's how you make a bond, because once they're big, it's impossible to control them even with a rein."

"You talk, with words?"

"Without. With thoughts and wishes, with impressions. I want to go down, I look down, I think down, Bask goes down. I want to go east, I look east, I think east, Bask goes east. Like that."

She shook her head.

"I don't have that gift."

"I think you do. She wouldn't have bonded with you, otherwise."

She looked over at me. I raised my head and looked at her.

Nakosa grinned.

"See? Welcome to the Skyborn, Kida of Gifah."

I snorted.

Reeds.

I lowered my head and slept until the barge.

***

Two days later, the statues appeared.

I remembered them, towering out of the river like gods, with their reed bodies and creature faces. Dragons, rassa, sobethi, wraith. They were glorious and fearsome, and they signaled that at some point, we had crossed the border into Gifah.

More statues now, in twos, then fours. It would still be hours before we made Karadoum. The first dragon, a lone green sentry, watched the river from the top of a

statue, his rider clad in Remoan silver. It was early
morning, the skyboat of Rath'nahr hidden behind clouds,
and all was grey and heavy. Bask was in the water,
invisible because of his colour, and I was in the sky.
Kida and Nakosa had made a good plan, but I had never
fought a dragon before. Remoan dragons were trained
for war. I was trained to reign. There was a vast
difference.

Kida shivered with the cold and the wet, but we
needed to be high so the drake couldn't breathe our
scent. We approached from the southeast, as high up as
we could, and I felt my heart grow as cold as my rider. I
wasn't sure I could kill a dragon, for he was only doing
the will of his reed. I tried to remind myself that this
dragon brought death at the whim of the Emperor of
Remus and his vassal, Beyat. None of them had
anticipated a Great Gold, bringing it all back like
lightning.

I hovered a moment, high overhead, arched my neck
and dove like an arrow.

Down, down, down, I plunged. I thought not of Kida,
just of my prey. He was a wyrm, a wraith, a sobethi. He
grew larger as I flew closer, and the wind bit my eyes
and rattled my teeth. At the last minute, he swung his
head up and flung his wing. I swerved and felt Kida slip,
losing her balance on my rain-soaked back. I twisted
awkwardly, raking his rider with my talons, and yanking
him off his mount. I carried him for a wingbeat before

dropping him, twisting and screaming, into the river. Just like Kiin and Mak, the egg thief of Gesse. The drake sprang from the statue but reeled as Bask struck him from the waters below. They spiraled through the air, smashing into statues, and crashing against the stone. Bask had a grip on the sentry's green throat and the drake spewed flame wildly as he thrashed. Nakosa stood in the stirrups and plunged a spear deep into the green's neck, just above the shoulder, and blood sprayed across basalt. Bask released his grip, the prince yanked the spear back and the Remoan dragon plummeted into the river below.

Weighed down by his armour, the rider struggled in the dark waters, managing to yank his helmet off and toss it to the side. It was a foolish decision, as Nakosa pitched his spear once again. Both man and dragon disappeared into the deep.

I struggled to find balance as Kida swung from my spines, so I winged up to perch on a statue, allowing her the time to climb back on. Bask landed on the statue next to us, and the prince wiped the rain from his eyes. He turned.

"Her foot threw off her balance," he said. "Are you hurt?"

Kida shook her head but wrapped her arms around her ribs.

"No," she gasped. "But I need leathers. I need a harness. I will be a millstone if I slip or fall."

He nodded.

"I have a harness," he said. "I brought it from the Pike. But you did well. Both of you."

"This was one," said Kida. "There are two more at Karadoum."

"There are two of us," he said. "We will win."

"If Rath'nahr pleases."

"If the moons align."

The rain was heavy as we returned to the barge. There, they approached me with the harness from the Pike. I fought the dread as Nakosa tried to bind it across my back. I fought the terror and memory, fear and fury, and I broke out in a fierce trembling. I was a Great Gold. I would fight for Gifah. But the memories of cages, collars, and carts rattled my bones, and I could barely catch my breath. Even Kida's hand could not soothe.

"No," she said finally. "The gods know what I need. I'll ride her without harness."

"You'll die."

"My heart's light," she said. "And Othorys is just."

It was mercy, then, that we left immediately for the Island of Sand and Storm.

We were headed for war this time, and the plan was simple but riddled with dangers. We were going to meet Shesset's army, along with the boats from Penet, at Karadoum where there were two more dragons stationed. We were going to try the same strategy – approach from sky and river and aim to take the riders.

The dragons themselves had no will to fight any army. They were bonded with their riders, so if we took the riders, the dragons would yield. He counselled Kida to be prepared because I had swerved to balance my phantom foot and would likely do so again. More importantly, to also be aware that Shesset's army would not know we were coming, and they might assume that we were also the enemy. They would shoot us with spears and arrows before we got close enough for them to see.

We flew in the dark, without the brother moons to guide us, only the wide, dark, gleaming ribbon of Storm below. I didn't need light. I recognized it by scent alone, for we had been here before, also in the night. Soon, we didn't even need the moons because the glowing horizon drew us onward. I knew that, once again, Karadoum was burning. Perhaps it was destiny that I was here now as it burned again, and I took some comfort in that.

Together, we soared, higher than the smoke and higher than the pointed peaks of the temple library. Through the statues and pillars, I saw hundreds of war sails on the river with hundreds of footmen on the mainland side. Two large dragons swept above them, spraying fire on both, and the air streaked with arrows.

There were soldiers fighting on the river. There were soldiers fighting on the banks. There were even soldiers fighting in Karadoum itself and I wondered who the majari served now. The two Remoan drakes wheeled beneath us, a red and a grey, catching their breath before raining fire once more.

We hovered for a moment, Bask and I, trying to mark out the flight path of the drakes below. I was younger than Bask, and far less experienced in the art of war, so I peeled right, claiming the smaller of the two. Bask would be better suited to the large red spiralling down over the warships. Shesset needed as many of those ships as possible if she was to take on Beyat and his silver soldiers. As for me, I had faint hope of taking on any large drake who had been trained for battle all his life.

Bask dropped from the sky like a stone and caught the red drake's rider in his talons. He arced a wing and soared towards the stone temple, the drake following in pursuit. Bask looked as if he would hit the high walls, when he wheeled in mid-air, releasing the rider to smack into the stone. The drake bellowed as arrows pelted mercilessly from below, and he plummeted from the sky, crashing between the pillars of Karadoum.

I turned my attention to the smaller grey.

I plummeted down, hoping Kida would be secure across my back. The young drake beneath me was unawares, couldn't catch my scent because of the fires, and he veered towards another warship, blasting the red and white sails of Penet with his flame. Hot wind burned my eyes, and I folded my wings back, dropping all my weight into my talons. Closer, closer. He angled shoreward, banking deep and his wing hit mine just as I was about to strike. I spun and swiped at the rider as I swept past. I raked his shoulder and neck, and felt his helm yank under my claw. But the drake had seen me now, and he rolled in the air towards me. I wheeled, spraying both him and his rider with fire before tucking my wings and plunging into the river below.

I forgot that Kida was on my back.

The water was black and boiling, and from the depths, I could see the flames dancing along ship and beam. There! His silhouette crossed the light, and I burst out, soaring over him in a heartbeat, and snatched the rider from his back. His scream was cut short as I crushed the helmet within my claws and dropped him into the river. Because of his armour, he sank like a stone, and the drake spun in wild circles over the ripples and bubbles and blood.

Suddenly, Bask hurtled from the sky and onto the young grey. They crashed onto the shore in a tangle of wings, lashing tails, and fire. Nakosa leapt from his saddle as the embattled drakes thrashed over and over into the lines of chariots, and foot soldiers scattered to avoid being crushed in their wake. The urus and their carts weren't so fortunate.

"Go!" cried Kida, and I wheeled in the air, glad that she had managed to somehow stay on my back through the water. She sprang from my back as I landed roughly, and I lunged at the young grey. He swung towards me, but I was ready and caught his beak in my jaws. Just like the great green drakina of the Gesse crater, I arched my neck and, with his face in my teeth, I trilled, my spines alternating between sharp and flat, sharp, and flat. Immediately, he yielded, and I softened my hold so that it was firm not fierce. The young drake buckled to the ground, eyes closed, submissive. Finally, I released him, and he curled himself into a ball, hiding his beak beneath his torn wings.

Fascinating. The way of dragons.

Spears in hand, the foot soldiers rushed towards us, and Kida leapt from my back and met them, palms forward.

"Nay, nay!" she cried. *"Ikthalees Shesset-Isset, Kida mebendet de Gifah!"*

The Peneti warriors lowered their weapons, and she pointed towards the island, where the battle still raged.

"Go!"

They sprang onto the boats, and soon, the roar arose anew from Karadoum as hundreds of Peneti warriors swept across the island and through the temple grounds.

I heard the grey drake whining as it trembled between Bask and I. Nakosa approached him, laid his hands on the bloody neck.

"Peace, young warrior," he said. "Peace."

Behind him, Bask trilled.

Kida rubbed her hands along my shoulders.

"Thank you, Anekh," she said. "Once again, you have saved us."

I brought my beak up to her face, breathed in the sweat and the smoke and the fear. I released my own breath in a puff, and she smiled. She was my world. She always had been.

"And I thank you, Prince Nakosa," she said. "Even one Nabiri Skyborn is worth a thousand Remoan Flights."

"Our odds were good," he said, running his hands over the young grey. "First, two on one, then two on two. The odds won't get better."

The grey whined, and my heart ached at the sound. He was as young as I, likely bred for war and now, his rider was gone, leaving him without a rudder. Nakosa lifted the great chin in his hands, breathed into the dragon's nostrils, and the drake lowered its head, pressing his forehead into the prince's body. He patted the bloody neck.

"But we now have three dragons," he said.

As the first beams of Selis Anekh reached across the sky, a smoking barge pulled away from the island of Sand and Storm, pushing across the river by many men with long poles. A figure in gold stood on the prow, thin and bloody, wearing armour plates and a gauze scarf across her face. On her head, the River Crowns of Gifah, but I would have recognized her in an instant even without it.

The barge bumped onto the riverbank, and she leapt from the prow, moving like a rassa through the pelting rain. She stopped in front of us, and both Kida and Nakosa bowed.

"Prince Nakosa," said Shesset-Isset, daughter of Thutmen'nahr II. "You turned the tide and rescued my fleet. I owe you my life, and the lives of my people."

"I am honoured to serve the Glory of the House of Bey," he said. "And, if she deems me worthy, to one day marry her."

She grinned the knife grin that I remembered from so long ago. She swung around, her eyes falling upon me, and I could see them gleam from the heat of battle.

"Kida," she snapped. "Is that my dragon?"

25

THE RIVER CROWNS

The morning sky was red as blood. The rains had stopped, the fires were out and Shesset summoned the scribes of Karadoum to gather before her in the outdoor hall of the Temple Library. All the people of the city were gathered as well, and the army of Penet flanked the courtyard, standing between the pillars like statues, row upon row upon row. She stood under the wide stone lintel, with Abshir on one side and Nakosa on the other. She was dressed in gold and bleached linen and wore the River Crowns of Sand and Storm.

Because of those crowns, the majari had turned, offering her fealty and loyalty, service and swords. And even more impressive then, was the fact that Kida and I stood behind her as well, with Bask on my right, and the

young grey on my left. I could only imagine what we
looked like to those reeds who had never seen a dragon
before, let alone three towering before them, glorious in
our scales and wings and smoke.

A man was brought forward. I remembered him as
Karaket, lead Scribe and curator of the Library of
A'Toth. He had refused aid to the princess and had
allowed soldiers into the temple library. I had been
pierced by an arrow because of this man. Josiat had died
because of him. He stood like a statue while Abshir read
a list of crimes from a paprush scroll.

Once he was done, Shesset turned to the people.

"I am not a god," she said, her voice echoing across
the stone courtyard. "Nor am I a goddess. It is not my
divine right to weigh hearts or condemn men to the
UnderRiver because of the evil of their deeds."

She looked out across the sea of faces.

"I am Shesset-Isset, daughter of Thutmen'nahr II,
child of Neburanna, and Glory of the House of Bey. It is
my divine right to condemn men to death for treason and
murder. And so, I condemn this man, Karaket of
Karadoum, to death for treason and murder."

The man stared at her. I could see his knees were
shaking as he tried to summon his spine.

"Gifah has rarely sanctioned executions for high
crimes because Gifah has long been a land at peace," she
continued. "Gifah is no longer a land at peace, and it will

not be until I wear the false beard of Ophar and sit on the throne in Wa'ast."

Shesset laid a hand on my scales. I grumbled deep in my chest. She never touched me. I didn't understand.

She looked at Karaket.

"But you, Karaket of Karadoum, are sentenced to die by dragonfire."

The scribe moaned and buckled to his knees as a murmur rose from the crowd. Kida glanced at Nakosa, who nodded swiftly. I glanced at Kida, but she would not look at me.

Death by dragonfire? Bask's? Mine?

"There will always be a Great Gold in Gifah," she said to the crowd. "Anekh Sun, daughter of Selis Anekh, was raised in the Courts of Wa'ast and bears the seal of the House of Bey. I trust you remember her, Karaket of Karadoum. Because of you, she nearly died at the hands of the Usurper's silver."

Karaket was a weak man, it was true. He had been responsible for the death of Josiat. He had chased us out when we needed sanctuary. He had turned his back on the daughter of his king. Yes, he was a very weak man. But was he bad?

"Anekh Sun is the spear of Gifah," said Shesset.

Could I kill him?

I had burned the God's Library of Karadoum, and I had killed Kunyane with my teeth. I had sunk my talons into Kiin and Mak, had dropped them from the heights and broken their bones. I was not clean. I was not good.

Karaket reached for Shesset's hem.

"Please…"

But I had burned Ejjae to death when she had smashed my eggs. Even still, I see her kneeling form ablaze, the heady rush as her flesh melted into gum.

I called the flame, relishing the burn as it rolled along my tongue, scorching the roof of my mouth and dancing within the prison of my teeth.

"Anekh Sun is the spear of Gifah," she repeated. "And I hold the spear. Beyat, the Usurper, killed his own father and you supported him. You are so very guilty."

I lowered my head, close enough to bite. I could see the pores of his skin and the tiny hairs on his cheeks. I saw his mouth twist in prayer, saw the Nahr spill from his eyes.

"But I am not Beyat."

She stepped away from me, took her place on the step above the crowds, raised her hands wide.

"I am Shesset-Isset, daughter of Thutmen'nahr II, child of Neburanna, and Glory of the House of Bey. And while I have condemned Karaket to death, I commute his sentence and consider it paid, for while I am an Ophar of justice, I am also an Ophar of mercy. Remember that, oh people of Karadoum, for I will set my crowns here on the Island of Sand and Storm. This will be Gifah's royal city and the Gods' Land will flow once again with milk and honey."

A cheer went up from the people and a cool wave of relief washed through my body. I was glad I didn't have to burn the reed. I wasn't sure if I could do it.

No. I was sure, in fact, that I could.

Shesset turned to Abshir.

"Dismiss the people," she said. "And remind them to be generous with food for the army. Karadoum will benefit from the Peneti soldiers, so we need to treat them well."

He nodded, moved past her, while she looked at Karaket.

"Rise," she said.

He did but grabbed her hand and drew it to his forehead.

"Thank you, most glorious Ophar," he said.

"Remember mercy," she said, her eyes like shiny daggers. "Now, I will have you draft a scroll. We will deliver it to Beyat, calling for his surrender. If he agrees, he will be met with the same mercy. If he does not, he will be met with war."

"Yes, most glorious Ophar," said Karaket. "I await your blessed words."

She nodded, turned to Nakosa.

"You'll deliver it to my brother?"

"As agreed, betrothed," he said. "Bask and I will leave once the scroll is dry and sealed."

Bask? Leaving?

"By boat, it takes two weeks," she said. "But flying should take only a few days."

"We'll be ready," he said. "But it's a futile gesture. We don't have enough men."

"If we had Nabiri dragons—"

"But we don't."

"I will not be swayed."

"I won't try to sway you."

She grinned now.

"I believe I've chosen well, betrothed."

He grinned. Together, they turned and walked into the Temple, leaving Kida standing quietly under the lintel. This time, she glanced at me. Her eyes, so large, so wise, tipped down at the edges now, like the corners of her mouth. I swung my head for her touch, but she too turned and walked into the cool shadows while I was left with the dragons at the gate.

Alone, I took to the river. It was remarkable to be once again in the convergent waters of the Nahr, not his offspring Sand or Storm. The Nahr was vast. The Nahr was rich, and from his cool, sweet currents, I watched all things. I watched the sun cross the sky and watched the boats from Penet gather on the Nahr. I watched my Skyborn Bask and his rider disappear over the golden sands of Gifah. This was a restless, troubling thing. There were eggs inside me, chicks that would be bound to Gifah and the House of Bey until they were culled at two. Unless, like the Weeping, the land was met with change. Unless the daughter of Thutmen'nahr II changed them.

At some point, the young grey joined me. I thought his name should be Chance. He had been given another chance by Nakosa and Kida, and he was taking it without a reed to guide him. I taught him to fish, and he took to it quickly, as all dragons do when given the opportunity. We stayed in the water that night, fishing and resting between the Peneti ships. We watched the moons chase the sun and the sky fill with stars. I had forgotten that the sky was so big in Gifah. Now, its beauty ached within me.

That morning, I felt the urge to go to the Library, and I knew it was Kida. Nakosa had been right. The reed 'thought' up. The dragon went up. The reed 'thought' east. The dragon went east. I was a controlled thing, the 'Spear of Gifah', little more than a weapon in an army of thousands. I wondered at Chance, with no reed now to call him or bend him to their will. I thought of Bask, noble and proud and ridden, and I thought of the dragons of Nerisanaa, wild and free and not.

With Chance at my tail, I rose from the water and met Kida at the Library. We were leaving for the Temple of Neburanna, inching towards Wa'ast and Beyat and my brother. My heart was heavy and filled with dread.

We took to the sky then, Chance and I, sweeping above the boats and over the armies that marched along the banks of the river. Their progress was slow but steady, and every village they swept through offered food as supplication to the army and the gods. I knew they'd taken supplies from Karadoum, as the city had not only housed the former library, but it was a bustling marketplace of trade and commerce. The Temple of Neburanna would be the same. Still, all I remembered was the sight of dragons, caged and maimed for the sport of reeds.

The skies cleared as we made our way into the land of Gifah. There was no rain in Gifah, only the yearly Weeping that flooded the banks of the Nahr, refreshing the land and quenching its thirst. Three days the armies marched, and the boats sailed downriver, with Chance and I sweeping over them like protector gods. Kida didn't take to my back during that time, because of the princess, most likely. I could have left then, could have arced a wing and returned to the Eye of Nerisanaa and the colony there. It would have been easy, and I would have been justified. It would have been interesting to take young Chance with me. He hadn't left my flank since we'd downed him, and I wondered if he had ever lived free of his rider. I wondered if he ever knew his mother. It was clear he needed an anchor, as bound to the reeds as any flutterby or uru. I thought of M'tawe, how he'd said I kept coming back to them too. Anekh Sun, *Ha'arat* of Worlds.

Perhaps, I hadn't shattered the Wheel as I'd thought, and perhaps, it turned for me still.

And so, we arrived at the walls of the Temple of Neburanna at dusk on the third day since leaving Karadoum. The sky was streaked with clouds. The sun was low in the heavens, but so were the moons. I'd only been here once, and that was the day of our dedication, the day of games and 'celebration,' the day my brothers and I were branded with hot irons and sealed to the House of Bey. I'd hated that day all of my life. I was not happy to be back.

Seeing it from the air this time was a heady thing, as opposed to when I was carried from stable to stall in Kida's arms, and Chance and I circled the complex, casting long shadows across the large courtyard below. Reeds rushed into and out of the many buildings, and flutterbys called to us as they spun through the air in between. The fleet had already begun pulling up to the shore and the army was raising dust as it crossed the fields towards the southern wall. In a golden chariot surrounded by warriors was Shesset herself, wearing the River Crowns. I circled until they drew up to the massive gate before I lit onto the parapet above it. Chance landed on the far side of the gate. The stone cracked and pebbles rained down to the sand below.

"No!" cried a priest. I remembered him. Toht was his name. I remembered his pride and his cruelty, his zeal and his seal. He was trapped on the parapet between

Chance and I, and he waved his hands at the princess. "No, you are forbidden!"

"Open this gate," she cried. "Open it in the name of the House of Bey!"

"Leave this land, false queen! Beyat is Ophar!"

Beyat. I hated that name. I would kill him as easily as I had killed Ejjae. I leaned forward and bellowed, long and loud so that more pebbles rained down. I swung my head towards the priest and bellowed again, bringing the heat with it this time so that he trembled in his sandals at the threat.

"You will open the gate and welcome the rightful Ophar," she cried. "And the city of Neburanna will tend the armies and navies of their queen, or our dragons will turn you to dust."

This time, I rose on my back legs, unequal as they were, spread wide my wings and threw my head into the sky. I bellowed a third time, summoning all the dragons and dragonets in the temple with my song. Chance joined me and within a heartbeat, a flock of colourful flutterbys rushed us, swirling in the wind. I could hear the cries of those in the stables, locked behind chain and mudbrick and service. It was beautiful, wild anarchy, and I was the queen of it all.

I lowered to the parapet, swung my head back to the priest and snarled.

"Open the gate," Toht cried to the acolytes in the yard. "Open the gate."

They did.

Shesset and part of the army flowed through, like the Weeping of the Nahr, sweeping in and filling the entire courtyard with their bodies. I watched them for a while until Chance barked at me. He was hungry. So was I, but I had something else gnawing at my belly. I unfurled my wings and sprang into the air, circling once before coming to land in the centre of the courtyard, reeds scattering in panic as I did. There, I saw the young priestess who had branded me. She did not flee but stood, as painted and proud as I had been in my youth.

Shesset's chariot pulled up in front of me, and Kida stepped down. She moved towards me, hand upraised, but I was not here for her. I lowered my head, opened my jaws, and bellowed loud and long and, once again, the temple erupted in the cries of many dragons. Flutterbys streaked round me, adding their shrill voices to the song. Chance landed beside me, raised his head, and roared, and I am certain we cracked the foundations of that horrible place with our chorus.

I arched my neck, the spines standing out like the rays of the sun, and I turned my eyes to the princess.

"What does she want?" she asked as she stepped from the chariot, lowering the crook and flail to her sides.

"The dragons," said Kida. "I think she wants us to release the dragons."

The princess fell silent, gazing to the ground as she thought. Then, she looked up, and a grin slid across her face.

"The gods have chosen well," she said.

She moved past Kida, and this time when she touched me, I did not growl.

"Release the dragons."

"But princess—" said the priestess.

"Ophar," corrected Kida.

"These dragons—"

"Are no longer slaves," said Shesset. "Remove their collars and release them to the training grounds. Slaughter one hundred sand bucks to feed them and give them as much sythstone as you have in the stores. Then slaughter one hundred more sandbucks to feed all of us. Do this without question or I will cast you out of this temple without shoes on your feet."

The priestess nodded swiftly and disappeared. For her part, Shesset merely stood, stroking my golden beak with one hand, and looking at me with new eyes.

"Two queens were forged that day," she said softly. "I had forgotten that. But I won't forget any more. You are the true daughter of Selis Anekh, and I am grateful that you have returned to Gifah to rule with me."

Suddenly, a shadow crossed above us. I didn't need to look to know that Bask had returned. My heart lifted as he circled the courtyard, but then I noticed that his wings beat an awkward rhythm, and he stumbled as he landed in the middle of us. He smelled of sky and smoke, Wa'ast and blood.

"Quickly," Nakosa gasped. "Get the princess to safety."

He leaned forward, yanked the bolt of an arrow from his mount's shoulder.

"They're coming," he gasped.

And suddenly, the sky was filled with dragons.

26

ENEMY WINGS

It reminded me of Gesse, and the Eye of Nerisanaa. The darkening skies rolled with wing and tail and rippling scale. Dragons everywhere, sweeping from the clouds like a volley of silver-tipped arrows.

"War dragons!" cried Abshir.

"The Remoan Dragon Flights!" said Nakosa.

Reds, blues, greens, and greys, with harnesses of leather and plates of silver hammered over their scales. They swept down in perfect formation, raining fire in swaths across the army assembled on the plains below.

"We're not ready!" snapped Shesset. "This is not the way!"

"Your brother has no honour," said Nakosa. "But honour isn't an advantage in war."

He straightened in the saddle.

"Tell my father that I am proud to be his son."

"You tell him," said Shesset. "When he attends our wedding."

"It would have been a good wedding."

Nakosa yanked on the rein. Bask bellowed and launched himself into the dragon-filled sky, Chance at his tail in a heartbeat.

Kida turned to me.

"Go, Anekh. Fight for us, but don't die for us."

And she pushed me with both hands. She couldn't move me. I was too big.

I swung my head to the plains, to where loyal Peneti screamed beneath the flames. I tried to count the soaring, sweeping tails, but night was falling and so were the clouds. Ten, and ten and almost ten. We had three.

"Go!"

I raised my wings, bringing them down in a great stroke, and I sprang from the parapet, joining the fury of wings above me.

I remembered the night of the Fall of the House of Bey, when dragons filled the skies and rained fire on the army from above. I was merely a watcher then, wrapped in a carpet that smelled of spice. But to actually join a sky battle is like nothing I can describe, and it is far worse at night. Wings, flame, blackness, talon. The winds churn at every beat, the heat scorches the surface of your eyes. There was only a single winking moon to give us light, so bursts of flame flashed through the night with terrible illumination.

The sky was thick with sand raised on the beating of so many wings. It bit my eyes and stung my throat, making it hard to catch my breath, but catch it I did, and I called the fire that lived in my breast. I blasted rider and dragon alike as I spiraled through their midst. I raked flanks with my talons, tore wings with a flash of my teeth. It was easy at first, like a river full of unsuspecting fish, and I realized that these Remoan Dragons had never reckoned with enemy wings. No nation other than Remus and Nabir possessed war dragons, so I'm sure they were not expecting Bask, Chance and I to break their lines just by flying through them. Over the howl of the winds and the screams of the army, I could hear riders shouting commands, and I knew that the current would turn swiftly against us once *we* became the focus, not the army below.

So, I made it count, flying above their lines and waiting for the flashes of dragonfire that showed me a target in the darkness. I swept down then, snatching rider after rider from the backs of their mounts, releasing them to meet their gods in the dunes. Those I couldn't remove, I pierced with my good foot and talons, and their blood left trails like smoke in the sky. I was very aware of my lameness, however, and the fact that I still favoured a missing limb. For every rider I disabled, I failed a strike with my phantom foot. Still, I'm sure I removed more than one head from Remoan shoulders that night.

Chance flew deftly and with precision. He was a Remoan drake, after all, and these were his kin. I could see him weave between the dragons, using his speed and lack of rider to throw them off balance. A mounted dragon had to obey certain sky rules, not be as quick or agile as those without. As a result, Chance shredded many wing leathers and crippled many fighting beasts. But, like me, his prey were the riders, for riderless war dragons were simply dragons. They had nothing vested in victory or loss. Without a rider, they were like Chance – rudderless, feral, and free.

Bask, was another story. He attacked with fury as he barreled his way through the Flights, first down, then up, spiralling like a karad in summer, trailing blood like the Nahr. I saw him take a Remoan red down outside the temple gates, and launch back to the sky, leaving him to the mercy of the marakt dragons and their fury. He was relentless and savage and, in that moment, my heart soared. It was a very brief moment.

A grey drake struck my flank and I spun wildly as pain burst from my ribs. He lashed again, raking my tail with his talons and opening ribbons of red. I rolled swiftly, knowing that, with a rider, he could not, and I came up beneath him, dragging my teeth along the soft tissue at his belly. A back foot slashed my cheek, and I pushed my neck into it, using my horns and spines to puncture his ribs before a second set of jaws closed upon my wing.

Two, now. Two Remoan dragons, and I knew the current was turning. I released the grey and arrowed straight down, taking the second dragon with me. I spiraled as I went, knowing this was difficult for the rider to control, even with their harnesses and straps. Suddenly, I snapped open my wings and the dragon pitched beneath me, flinging his rider out of the harness to plummet into the sands. The drake bellowed and followed.

It was then that I realized he loved his rider.

They all loved their riders.

Flash and flame, fire and breath.

Dragons and reeds, fates entwined since the creation of the world.

There was a roar of wind and I looked to the river. Five shapes in the night sky peppered the Peneti warships with dragonfire. Sails blazed and reeds howled as fire danced along the beams. But over the smell of dragon and smoke, I could smell the water. It was deep and fresh and more home than the walls of the Ophar's Palace. I curled my aching body, bore down on the fight and the shimmering, flashing ribbon that was the Nahr.

I swept down towards the first ship, swerving just before I struck the sails. I angled my wing so that my talons hit the river's surface, spraying water up and onto the boat. Steam hissed into the sky, dampening the flames, but not putting it out. I soared back up and hovered, wings beating the hot wind as I spied for an opening. A flash of rolling breath rushed at me, so I tucked and dove again. The new dragon followed but I didn't care. The ships moved swiftly, and I aimed for the small black gap between them. Reflections of fires rippled across the waters, and I pulled my head up just as I plunged into the river, belly first. A massive wave rose to flood the decks and the waters immediately doused the flames. I tucked, dove under the boats, and came up on the other side, shaking my head and blinking in the darkness. A great weight struck from above and I went under once again.

A dragon, its talons at the base of my horns, stabbed into my skull, threatening to crack me open like a seed. But I was home in the River Nahr and he was not, and I let the weight take me down. I rolled in the water like a sobethi, tucked my wings tight and whipped my tail back and forth, carrying me deeper still with each lash. Soon, the attacker's flanks were underwater, then his wings, and I knew that his rider would be panicking now, strapped as he was on the back of a submerging mount. The moment the talons released was the moment I made my move, sweeping up from the waters with a furious slap of my tail, to spin in the darkness above him. I landed on his back, crushing his rider under my weight, and clamped my teeth on the drake's crest, forcing his head under the water. I knew what it was like to fill my chest with the river, the panic and bursting ache that followed every time. He thrashed wildly now, but I stayed on him and soon, I felt him yield under my talons.

With a deep breath, I beat my wings down, rising into the night over the river, pulling his great head up with me until he shuddered and spat out the water. He would not fight now, but it was not a victory.

There were still so many dragons.

Flash and flame, fire and breath.

It was dark and I couldn't see Chance or Bask. I couldn't even see the Temple of Neburanna. We were losing this battle. Shesset and her army from Penet could never win against Remus and their Dragon Flights. Nothing could win against dragons. Once again, I thought of Gesse and the Eye of Nerisanaa, where the skies danced with wing and tail and rippling scale.

A drakina struck me from above, her talons piercing my shoulder, her hot breath on my spines. It was a solid grip and I spiraled downwards, plummeting towards the bone-crunching dunes below. Suns popped behind my eyes as her claws dug deeper and acid bubbled up in my throat. I sprayed fire as I spun, hoping some of it might catch her rider, but suddenly, there was a jerk and a dark shape plunged past my line of sight. The drakina released me and I swung my head up, snapped my wings open to break my fall. Still, I landed awkwardly in the sand and looked up as thunder rolled overhead.

Not thunder.

Flash and flame, fire and breath.

Skyborn.

I breathed them in as they swept past, sifting the winds that they brought with them. Ten and ten and ten and ten. New dragons, fresh from the south, no trace of silver or Gifah or gold. No, my heart leapt as the Nabiri Skyborn swept through the darkness above me, chasing down Remoan dragons, forcing them to the ground or ridding them of their riders. I flattened myself into the sand as they thundered overhead in wave after wave. The skies were alive and roiling, and even in the darkness, it was a fearsome, exhilarating thing.

As Remoan dragons hit the dunes, Peneti warriors swarmed them with swords and spears. The surviving Flights turned wing and beat back towards Wa'ast, the Skyborn following in pursuit. All along the walls of the temple, oil lamps sprang up in the darkness, but I stayed in the sand a while longer. I was bleeding, spent, and the sand was cool and soft and dark.

"Is she one of theirs?"

The voice was like something from a dream.

"I think this is the Great Gold."

"Seket?"

"Gods, the worth."

"They'll never know. Just one scale…"

I opened one eye as the spear flashed, and heat burst behind my eyes. A spear, just like Kiin. I had killed her without mercy. I bellowed in pain until the acid spilled between my teeth. I had killed Ejjae too. The acid caught and I swung my head, spraying fire over a Peneti footman, who screamed and staggered back. Three others tried to run, but the sand was deep. I pushed myself to stand and sprayed them all now, snarling as they curled into dark hearts within balls of flame. The air smelled of burning flesh, and I watched, unmoved, as they turned to kindling, until they turned to ash.

They all wanted my scales to cure their woes. Even now, even still.

After all I had done, after all I had become.

I understood all too well why Rath'nahr wept. They were a heartbreaking people.

Over the descending quiet, a dragon song rose in the air. It was plaintive and sad, and I knew at once it was Bask. I launched into the air, ignoring the pain from my neck. The spear bumped against my shoulder as I flew across the dunes towards the temple, and I circled the courtyard, wary and stiff, before dropping unceremoniously to the ground.

"The Great Gold!" cried a reed.

"Tell the princess!" barked another. "The Great Gold is alive!"

There were several dragons in the courtyard, and I saw Chance, sitting back on his haunches, one wing held awkwardly out to the side. He bleated at me, and it broke my heart. I lumbered over to him, reached out my neck and blew softly into his nostrils. He closed his eyes, breathing me in.

"Anekh!"

I swung my head as Kida rushed from the temple, followed by Abshir. She raced across the courtyard and flung herself against my shoulder, wetting my scales with her tears. I looked down at her. She was so small to me now. I'm not sure why I hadn't seen it before.

"Abshir, grab this spear!"

The man did, and I snarled as he pulled it out in a few painful tugs. Kida ran her hands along my bloody flanks. I swung my head and caught one in my mouth, held it as I used to, content merely to have her arm rest upon my tongue. It used to be her finger. Oh, how life had changed.

She smiled sadly.

"Anekh Sun," she said, and scratched my chin with her free hand. "My Anekh Sun."

It was true that the Remoan dragons loved their riders. I loved mine too.

I heard Bask again, and lifted my head, sang out in response. Chance joined in, and our song echoed across the valley.

Half of a slaughtered uru was brought to me but I had no belly for food. Bask was weeping over the dunes and I felt it in my bones. I returned to the parapet as the skyboat of Rath'nahr sent its first spears of light across the heavens. It revealed a valley of glass - sand and flesh and chariot and leather, scorched by dragonfire and littered with the dead. I watched as Gifahn, Peneti and Nabiri worked together to gather the slain—reed and dragon both—and pile them together on the plains.

Near the scorched banks of the Nahr, I saw the great Anshassar next to a bloody blue shape. I left the parapet and winged over the smoking dunes to land beside them, sand puffing up under my weight. I lowered my head against Bask's beak, blew gently into his nostrils. I don't think he knew I was there. In the dawn light, I could see his missing eyes, his shattered horns, his shredded wings, and I knew that, today, there were two slain princes of Nabir.

I watched with a heavy heart as King Dejenai carried the body of his son to lay him gently on one of the piles. Anshassar breathed his flame across it and Bask raised his head one last time, poured out his sadness as a gift to Selis Anekh. He did not stop singing, and I joined him, watched as the black smoke carried the souls of the slain to the skies.

Anshassar joined his voice to our song. It was the sliding dragon scales of heart and beauty, wind and death. Another drake landed, then a drakina, and soon, there was a flight of Skyborn weaving their stories into the dawn. Bask had stopped singing, and slowly, painfully, he dragged his broken body into the Nahr. The waters turned red around him, and for a moment, he looked like a sobeth, only his long beak, neck and spines visible above the surface. As if called, the Sons of Sobeth slid from the banks in his wake, and I watched his body jerk and twitch as they dragged him down into the depths. For the first time, I did not hate them. The Wheel rolled for them too, beginning and ending, death and life. The river splashed and he was gone, leaving only a trail of bubbles in his wake.

My mother, my brothers, Mehen, now Bask.

I had mourned so often, that now, I couldn't. We become sand before we turn to stone.

We left for Wa'ast at noon.

27

SUN AND MOON

Dejenai rode out first. He was to lead the Peneti force and meet those that were joining the attack from the northeast. Also, if the day went to plan, there would also be a Lamoan fleet attacking from the river. The Nabiri king took ten and ten and ten Skyborn with him, and according to Shesset, the city of Wa'ast should have fallen by midday. My heart was heavy as I watched him mount his great Anshassar and leave the temple courtyard. He had just lost his son, the light of his eyes, the flower of his heart, and yet, he rode. He was a king among reeds. He had slipped me eel roe cakes. I would follow him anywhere.

We flew out at noon with a Flight of ten. Shesset was to come in to Wa'ast, riding her Great Gold, something no other Ophar had ever done in the history of Gifah and its Great Golds. She spent most of the morning unusually silent, moving amongst the marakt dragons, touching them with childlike hands. It seemed she was holding the Nahr back behind her eyes, and I wondered at that. Then again, she'd lost much along this journey. One day she would be a statue when she too turned to stone.

She sat on my back, tucked in behind Kida. It was strange to carry two reeds, and I was mindful of my speed. Skyborn flew above and below and around us, like Selis Anekh ferrying the god across the sky. The sun was high, but so were the moons that afternoon, and one seemed to be closing in on the skyboat of Rath'nahr. I wondered what would happen if a moon caught him during the day. Surely, the chase didn't end at night. Maybe the chase never ended at all.

The last of the chariots had left earlier, along with the remains of the Peneti fleet. They were pulled by marakt dragons, and I was proud to see them working in the service of something other than sport. It took several hours to make Wa'ast by river, even longer by road, and a contingent of surviving foot soldiers stayed behind to secure the Temple under Abshir. Reeds betrayed each other without thought, so it seemed like a good decision.

Chance stayed behind as well. He'd broken a wing and deserved to heal. The last I saw him, he was stretched out in the shade of the temple wall, eyes closed and covered in flutterbys. They were grooming the blood from his scales with their tiny front teeth. I never saw him again after that, and I hoped he was happy, wherever the Wheel took him.

And so, we flew.

It's strange to think that, with hundreds of troops marching wide along the north bank of the Nahr, and hundreds of sails flapping in the breeze alongside, there was silence. All day, silence, weighing like a blanket of gold-woven fleece. Even the marakt dragons moved like a soundless wave, followed by a tide of archers. Everyone was thinking. Everyone was wrestling with their fears. For me, it was personal.

Khamet the Shining, the Last Moon of Gifah.

Somewhere on the flat, sandy plains between the holy city of Wa'ast and the Temple of Neburanna, I was going to meet my brother.

My heart was filled with both anticipation and dread. I wanted to see him, to know that he was alive and thriving in the Palace of the Usurper, but I also knew that it would be a spear to my chest to see the deadness in his eye after so long under such a man. Could he be my brother in any way? Could he still be the wild tangle of life that had wrestled and bumped and lived on the banks of the Nahr? Would he remember me or Amok or our mother from the time before time, or had he been so broken and remade that his world was nothing but Beyat and blood?

And so, when we saw the cloud of black smoke over the desert's edge, I knew we were riding into a very different battle. Through the smoke, I could see dragons circling, casting shadows across the sand, and my heart thundered in my chest. Were they Remoan, or were they Nabiri? If Dejenai had triumphed, the city would be ours. If not, I would be joining Bask and Mehen in the Fields of Ever Spring.

I beat on, my wings moving as if they had a will of their own, dreading my approach as the city itself took shape. Wa'ast had always been a city of contrasts, with her basalt pillars and her mud brick, either painted in vibrant colour or left to wash white in the sun. Per ahmets set outside the city walls, along with the peaks of those few cradled within. I thought of Net'jeh, walled up before his dreaming eyes could see the fall of his beloved Ophar. It was then I saw the sails.

"Look!" cried Kida over the wind, and she pointed to the river.

All along the Nahr, the Peneti boats sailed alongside others bearing a design I remembered from my time on the Nameless Sea. They sat low in the water, with long curving prows and striped sails. But it was the large painted eyes that I remembered, as I had ducked low in the waves to stay hidden from their sight.

"They came!" Shesset barked. "Lamos came!"

"King Dejenai said they wouldn't!"

"Thank the gods he was wrong. Lamos hates Remus. I knew they would need little excuse."

"And there!" Kida pointed east of the city, where reeds surged against each other like waves. Reeds in silver, reeds in red, reeds in armour, reeds in leather scale. A second battle had taken place along Wa'ast's eastern wall, a land battle of sword and spear, chariot and bow. It looked to be over, and I saw the golden wheat standards of Penet raised over the sand.

"The second legion!" Shesset cried.

"He was true to his word," said Kida. "Thank the gods."

"Thank King Marwethad," said Shesset. "I may have to marry *him*, now."

We angled over the city walls, and I could feel her weight shift as she placed the River Crowns on her head.

"Time to become a god," she said, and held her arms wide. For her part, Kida bent low over my neck. She was wrapped in gold cloth and was almost invisible on my back. It was all for Shesset, I knew. The people would see and marvel at the sight of a conquering Ophar riding a Great Gold. It was prophecy fulfilled, they would say. The will of the gods.

Shesset had always been gifted in strategies. She was a knife among reeds.

As we soared over the city of Wa'ast, I looked down, remembering the narrow streets and terraced roofs, the palms and the farmers' markets. There was considerable destruction, with crumbled walls, blackened timbers, and small fires everywhere. We flew through the smoke, and

I spied the bodies of dragons splayed across roofs and roads alike, scales bloodied, wings bent.

But as we flew, reeds stopped and stared. Some pointed. Some fell to their knees. We swept through the city, slowly, methodically, allowing all to marvel and worship and weep.

My flight rose as we soared above the walls of the palace. There were no flutterbys to greet us and I remembered how Amok and Khamet would hunt them without mercy. There were many living dragons, some wounded Remoans but mostly Nabiri Skyborn. There was no gleaming silver, and I forced my dread deep, deep down. We flew around the Court of the Painted Palm and the Royal Drakmet, finally circling the courtyard that had been my early life. Our escort peeled away, and I landed roughly, with foot and stump and wing claw as brace. I was not used to carrying two reeds and I was relieved when Kida and Shesset slid off my back onto the ground. I folded one wing behind my back, arching my neck so that my spines stood proud against the afternoon sun.

Anshassar bowed in the way of dragons, head low, wings high, and I was glad to see him.

There were many soldiers in the court outside the palace, and King Dejenai turned towards us. Shesset passed the twin crowns to Kida and strode over to him.

"They are bringing him out now," he said.

"Alive?"

"That depends on him."

We waited for some time, and I sifted the air for the scent of Beyat, Khamet and the painted woman. I could hear the weeping of the reeds outside the palace walls, the shouting of generals and servants, the wail of dying dragons. The city had indeed fallen. Now, we were waiting to make it new.

I heard the crunch of sandals on stone. A legion of Peneti foot soldiers emerged from the rich shadows of the columned hall. They had only one man between them, and I flattened my spines at his approach.

"Adriam?" hissed Shesset.

He flashed his sobethi smile as he turned and bowed before King Dejenai.

"Greetings, esteemed generals and valiant leaders. You are on sacred ground. May I ask your names, please?"

"I am Yashir Yar," said one. "General of the Fourth Heavy Division of the Peneti Army, representing King Marwethad the Benevolent of Moradin."

"I am Illio Katekolis," said another. "First Captain of the Areesian Fleet of the Council of Lamos."

"And I am King Danaea Dejenai of the Nabiri Skyborn."

"I knew this," said Adriam. "There is a strong resemblance to your son, whom I had the recent honour of meeting."

"My son is dead," said Dejenai. "Killed by Remoans like yourself."

"Ah, the tragedy of war."

He bowed again.

"I am Adriam of Bangarden, son of Magistrate Aaronus Aronadai, Emissary of Emperor Tinova of Remus, and Vizier of Ophar Beyat I of House Beyat. Welcome to Gifah."

"This is madness," growled Shesset. "I am Shesset-Isset of House Bey, Light of the Heavens and Daughter of Neburanna, sister-wife of Rath'nahr and lover of the Most High God. I ride a Great Gold and bear the River Crowns of Gifah."

"So dramatic," said Adriam. "It's in your blood."

Dejenai narrowed his good eye.

"You are the Remoan counsel and tutor to Beyat?"

"Vizier, now, excellence. To the Ophar of House Beyat."

"Where is my coward brother?" growled Shesset.

"How you've grown, Shesset," he said and "You were but a child when I last saw you."

"Skinny wyrm. Isn't that what you called me?"

"We were both young and foolish."

He grinned and turned to the men.

"Forgive the informality but the Ophar wishes to negotiate terms."

"There are no terms," said Shesset. "There is surrender or death."

The Peneti general stepped forward.

"The Usurper has a dragon in there," he said. "It will not let us near."

"Khamet," said Kida.

"Tell my brother—"

"Your Ophar."

"My murdering brother," she continued, "That we will discuss terms once he has released his claim on the throne of Gifah and accepted the rightful rule of the House of Bey under the invading forces of Penet, Lamos and Nabir."

"He wishes to share the throne," said Adriam. "There is a precedent in the Book of the Rule, if I'm not mistaken."

"You are mistaken, and I will never share the throne."

"You were the one responsible for the Remoan Dragon Flights?" asked Dejenai.

Adriam smiled again.

"Of course, excellence. Remus is highly regarded among nations—"

Dejenai moved quickly for an elder. He stepped forward, his sword flashed, and Adriam staggered backwards, clutching at the fountain of red bubbling at his throat.

"My son is dead," said the king. "Now, so are you."

Adriam buckled to his knees, eyes wide, mouth gaping, before he pitched facedown onto the stone of the court. His sun-coloured hair stained red in its own blood.

"That may not have been the most sound diplomatic strategy," said Dejenai, sheathing his sword.

Shesset stood for a long moment.

"We will drag Beyat and his painted mother out of the throne room by force."

"He has a dragon," said Yashir Yar.

"So do I."

She turned to me.

"Kida, send her in."

***

There is a spoke for silver on the Wheel of the Elements. There is also a spoke for gold. That is wise, for the Wheel is wise. The Wheel is unforgiving, impartial, and fair. It just goes around and around and around, like the Moons of Syth pursuing the Sun of Rath'nahr.

The moon, Khamet, pursuing the Sun, Selis Anekh. We were so well named.

I snaked under the columned roof, waiting for my eyes to adjust from the brilliant afternoon light. I could smell him even here. I could hear the rumble of his breath. Sun beamed in through the skylights, brightening the colours painted on the walls, pillars, and ceiling, and deepening the shadows. It was this room where I had first been presented, a gift for a god, gifted to a goddess. How I ached to be here again.

I heard him snarl and I lowered my head. There was no disguise, no attempt to hide. Beyat sat on the Ophar's golden seat, his mother at his side, and wrapped around it like a giant wraith was Khamet.

"Gods, she's a cripple," said Beyat. "I remember when she said I was hard on my dragons."

Khamet pushed to his feet and my chest tightened. I was weary, while he was fresh. I had been injured just yesterday in the battle of the Temple, while he was strong and unscarred. He had two strong legs, a full rippling throat and a will of iron. I could see the fire roll across his tongue as he breathed it in and out, in and out.

He lowered his head and took a step towards me.

I moved between the pillars as if they were the trees in the forests of Gesse. I was not disadvantaged. I had hunted uru and wraiths, sobethi and sandbuck. A fast flutterby would have been his only challenge.

Light, shadow, colour, wash. His silver scales reflected them all.

We circled each other, tails lashing, heads low, the columns our fences, the ceiling our sky.

I was a Great Gold. I had been caged and I had fought myself free. I had been robbed, and I had avenged. I had given life, and I had taken. I had been free in jungles and in rivers, and I had served these reeds with every scale on my body.

Around and around and around we paced, circling each other in the Throne Room of the Ophar. Both Beyat and his mother watched us with wide eyes. I couldn't tell if it were anticipation or dread. This chamber seemed to summon those things. I remembered them when I had been gifted. I remembered them when Nefheru had been caught.

I had been young then, a fledgling, then a calf. Today, live or die, I was a goddess.

Khamet slowed, lowered his sleek head. I watched the tip of his tail, tapping up and down on the smooth stone. Like a wraith, he moved, but I had killed wraiths. I had torn their bodies in two. They were nothing to me.

He opened wide his mouth and sprayed his fire, but I met it with my own and the heat melted the paint on the pillars. I heard a shout from Beyat but Khamet launched himself across the stone, fire spilling from his tongue. My wings beat down in a powerful stroke and I sprang high, his jaws closing on the tip of my tail. I twisted above his head, dropping with all my weight, clamping my teeth at the base of his horns, and pushing his head to the ground. I tore at his shoulders with my wing claws, raked his spine with my talons. He rolled beneath me, and I released, hovering just beneath the ceiling as he recoiled. I had drawn first blood. I knew the next moves would be crucial.

He coiled and sprang again, but I was gone, streaking between the columns just like in the Market of Give and Take. He was at my tail, and we wove in between the pillars and palms, sending fronds and chips of basalt to the ground as we went. And suddenly, we were outside, reeds scattering as we burst from the hall, and the sunlight threatened to blind me as I whipped over the courtyard walls. I soared around Netjeh's per ahmet, spinning higher and higher until I saw the gold-clad peak. Khamet struck me then from the side, sent me careening into the limestone, and little pebbles tumbled down the sides. It knocked the breath from my body, and he was on me in a heartbeat, beating me with his wings, raking my belly with his talons. I blinked back the pain and caught the soft tissue of his throat in my teeth. I collected my haunches and pushed off the crumbling wall, rocking him backwards under my weight and taking him down along the steep inclines of the per ahmet's wall.

A dragon on its back is a vulnerable one, and I beat him down, down, down to crash on the blackened stone below. Reeds scattered like water wyrms as we thrashed wildly, locked in a death grip with each other. I called the acid into my throat when he raked my eye with a wing talon. I released him, gagging, and shaking my head in order to see.

He was gone now, and I leapt into the air to follow.

I couldn't see through one eye, but still, I followed, snapping at his tail as he soared back through the Court of the Great Gold. He turned his head, sprayed an arc of flame and I veered as heat scalded my neck. Khamet skimmed the ground, his wing claws striking the mosaic stone as he rushed onward, me matching his speed, beat for beat.

I saw the reeds ahead. They had pulled Beyat and Nefheru from the throne room and I saw them all duck and scatter as Khamet arrowed towards them. He angled his wing and arced upwards. Beyat grabbed his sister and shoved her towards the approaching dragon. Swifter still, Kida flung herself into the path.

Khamet caught her in his talons and began to rise.

Kida.

She screamed and twisted in his grip.

Kida.

Higher and higher went my brother.

Higher and higher went my Kida.

I flattened my spines. There was nothing now. There was no throne. There were no crowns. There was no Gifah nor Goddess; there was no before, no after. There was nothing but Kida and my brother and the sky. Higher he went, my silver brother, straight up like an arrow. Her blood sprayed my beak like the rain in Gesse, warm and fat and relentless in its fall.

We were so high now, high as the clouds. So high that the sky was cold, and the land was hazy, and it was then that he arced his long body to let her go.

He let her go.

He spun in the air as I swept to catch her, struck me on a downward spiral with his great horned head.

I spun too, spraying fire as I went, smelling the burning of his spines and scales. I twisted away, head angled downward, and plummeted like a stone from the White Horn.

She is a dot, a blur, a speck.

I flatten my spines, force my heart into my wings.

I have forgotten Khamet. I have forgotten Shesset and Beyat and the God's Land of Gifah.

There is only Kida, the wind, the ground, and me.

She reaches for me, and I stretch out my talons.

Her eyes, the largest things in the world.

The wind, whipping her linens like sails, like wings.

Her hands, soft and strong, best to scratch a growing horn or itch a flake of drying paint. Like claws of her own. Reaching. Reaching.

The wind, once my friend, my source, my life. The wind biting my eyes, flaying my skin.

Her mouth, small and fine, a tongue most often held, now wide in terror, in free fall, in faith.

I will save her.

The ground is racing, growing, laughing.

There is only her eyes and my will.

I will save her.

My talons stretch, stretch until they crack, until my eyes pop out of my skull.

My world.

Her eyes.

The ground is here, and I swipe one last time and sweep upwards, feeling her safely caught in the grip of my claws.

But the Wheel turns one last time.

28

DRAGON OF SAND AND STORM

As dragons turn to stone, so also turn our hearts. The Wheel, while unforgiving, is also fair. Impartial, equal, just. It ends where it begins, as all things do; finds flowering in its root. It is a circle, after all. The Circle of Life, the Wheel of the Elements. So, there was a certain symmetry in the act of my phantom foot. It was Kida who fixed the chain to my leg; I who was forced to chew it free.

I didn't catch her. I will never forget the sound.

I landed beside her, my legs trembling from the exertion, limbs twitching from the flight. There was a pit where she landed, with a ring of sand from the impact. I leaned my beak down into the pit and breathed in the scent. I had smelled it before. Josiat. Sakariye. The

Monk of a Thousand Steps. I listened for the drum of her heart, but there was silence. I blew softly into her face. Her eyes did not close, just like my mother's.

Her eyes round and very dark, no longer sparkling with life.

They had been, once. They had been my world.

Foot soldiers moved towards us, but I bellowed at them, sprayed fire in a great circle all around. It charred the scrub and burned the sand, turning it to glass.

I swung my head, looked to the city. There was a flash of silver in the sunlight as Khamet winged down into the palace.

I was stone.

I was the Wheel.

The wind tasted different as I leapt into the air. Dry and hollow. Sharp and sweet. My wings felt different as they beat upwards. Once upon a time, it had been beat beat, breathe in. Beat beat, breathe out. But now, it was beat, breath, beat, breath. Mechanical, like the workings of a chariot. Like the spokes of a wheel. I flew straight up to Selis Anekh, Goddess of the Sun, but she too was different. Cold, wide, bitter, burn. Everything was different now as I rose on the wind.

Or perhaps, it was me.

I spun slowly around under the prickling rays, breathing in and out, letting the sharp, dry, sweet air fill my chest and blow away the embers of my heart. Below me was the great city of Wa'ast, centre of all things, yet

root of none. I could keep flying. I could go higher,
straight up to my mother the Goddess, let the cold and
the light take me to the Fields of Ever Spring. It would
be easy but no. My place was the river.

My place had always been the river.

I arced in the air, bent my neck towards the Palace of
the Ophar. Slowly, at first, I beat my wings. Slowly, then
strongly, then fiercely I flew. I was an arrow. I was a
Spear, Daughter of the Sun. I was lighter than the Scale.
I was Seket. I was Goddess.

They never saw me coming, not even Khamet, as I
swept straight down, hidden in the brilliance of the sun. I
caught Beyat's head in my talons, hearing the snap of his
neck as I pulled him off his feet. The painted woman
screamed, and my brother bellowed, and I winged
towards the river. I let him go then and his lifeless body
spun as it fell, striking the side of a Lamoan ship before
hitting the water. Like my blue brother, a splash, some
bubbles, and he was gone. I paid homage to Sobeth with
this gift.

I heard Khamet behind me, so I dove in, felt the
currents wash my scales like a waterwall. I swam
through the dark waters, wings tucked, tail lashing from
side to side, mechanical, removed. Bubbles steamed
from my nostrils and still, I wished I could breathe it in.
I gloried in the river. Even still, I sing in her depths.

There was a splash, and I knew he'd followed me in.
Foolish Khamet. I was Goddess of the River, born on her

banks and forged in her currents. He was nothing. A palace pet. A flutterby without joy. A tool.

I burst up through the surface, spraying water like arrows into the sky. With a flip of my tail, I circled above him just like I had with the Remoan drake at the temple and landed on the back of his neck. He struggled to surface but I added my weight, keeping his head under the waves. Still, I carried him forward, letting the rushing currents fill his mouth, allowing the darkness to flood his chest. I wanted him to drink his fill of this wonderful, terrible, relentless thing that I loved. The mighty Nahr. Giver of life and broker of dreams. We had shared this life once, so long ago, when our mother carried us to our nest on its banks.

Still winging forward, I push him deeper.

Our brother, the green, had died in that nest. Our brother the blue, here in these waters. The silvers, eager and reckless and full of life, sharpened on the Wheel as a whetstone sharpens metal. Sharpened by Beyat and Adriam and the great, terrible House of Bey.

Faster I flew, and farther, dragging him between the boats and beneath the waves. I was the Wheel now, mechanical and removed. I was stone, hard, unforgiving, cruel. I had killed wraiths, I had killed reeds and I had killed dragons equally. In the same way, I would kill Khamet.

A flurry of colour rose from the banks, and from the corner of my eyes, I saw flutterbys.

*The Sand and the Storm made the mighty River Nahr,
and the mighty River Nahr made me.*

There were many ships moored along the banks, and
all reeds watched as I drowned Khamet the Shining, Son
of Beyat. But it was the flutterbys that I saw, swirling
and dancing on the rushes that lined the river. Dragonets
and fledglings full of life and promise.

I slowed my wings, looked down at the drake under
my talons. There was no struggle, there was no fight. I
released him and hovered over the river, ready to
plummet back down at the first sign. His silver shape
carried on below the surface for a few moments, then it
slowed against the current, bobbing, shapeless and dull.
It sank in the dark, silt-heavy waters, and I waited for the
splash that said sobethi. But the sobethi never came.

*The Sand and the Storm made the mighty River Nahr,
and the mighty River Nahr made me.*

I dipped down then, catching a horn with my talons,
and I dragged his floating body towards the shore. There
were Gifahn ships, and Remoan ships, Lamoan ships and
Peneti. There were fishing boats and market boats,
barques and barges, mooring posts and stone
embankments, but with teeth and claw and force of will,
I dragged him up through the boats and docks and rushes
to the shore. I released him then, and sat on my
haunches, one wing tucked behind my back.

All the world met on the waters of the Nahr, formed
from the abundance of Sand and Storm. I, too, had been

formed from the abundance of Sand and Storm, but
Khamet had been formed from stone.

I don't know where the song came from, then, when I
lifted my beak to the sky. I had sung it when I mourned
my eggs so long ago. Bask had sung it with the death of
his noble Nakosa. But it was more than a song of loss
but of life, and I sang for the drakina of Nerisanaa and
her wonderous, wildling band. I sang for the blues and
the greens and the greys, the reds and the browns. For
Chance the Eager and Mehen the Free. I sang for the
Nabiri Skyborn and even for the Remoan Flights. I sang
for the wingless ones, defaced and faithful, and the
innocent hatchling flutterbys, whose blood bought the
blessing of the gods.

My song echoed, unaccompanied, across the waters
until I heard the tiny voices of flutterbys. They swirled
around Khamet and me, warbling their fledgling songs
in high, tremulous keys. Our song caught in the sails of
many ships before I let it go to disappear in the warm
breeze. The flutterbys settled on me like pic-bugs, on my
head, on my spines, on my tail and on my wings. There
was no sound then, save the flapping of distant sails and
the sighing of the river. It was the silence of the world
breathing. I looked down.

Khamet's eyes were glassy, his tongue pressed
against the roof of his mouth. But I was certain the soft
tissue of his throat throbbed once, when I heard a sound.

I reached my beak to breathe in his scent, sending my own breath hot into his nostrils and eyes. I trilled at him. Slowly, he blinked, his lid scraping the glass of his eye like a stonesmith's lathe. His tongue flicked and water ran like a creek between his teeth. I trilled again.

I watched the spines along his neck flex and relax, watched him vainly try to lift his head. I trilled a third time, and the flutterbys scattered as he heaved himself higher onto the bank. He rested for a long moment, before shaking his great head and retching a barrel full of water onto the scrub. He looked from side to side, snapping his beak, then settled his gaze on me.

There was no sound, other than the breeze and the lapping waters and my brother, breathing.

He trilled. It was thin like a bubble.

Slowly, with great effort, he gathered his wings and launched into the sky. He circled once above the bank, before turning west to follow the river. He rose higher and higher, becoming a silver star in the clouds.

I never saw him again.

I did not return to the palace. Rather, I returned to the place where Kida died. Her body was still there. Understandably. There had been a great battle and she was only one of the fallen. But, for me, she was the only one.

Shesset was there with a company of men. She was on her knees in the sand, and for the first time, she did not look like a knife.

"No," she moaned. "No, this is wrong. This is not the plan…"

The Nahr spilled and sand stuck to her cheeks.

"Forgive me, dear Anekh Sun, Daughter of the Goddess. It wasn't worth it."

She shook her head.

"I loved her."

Love.

I had known that, once.

All around us, reeds moved to tend the injured, mourn the dead, pile the bodies, begin again. I couldn't see the Ophar's Palace, nor the Court of the Great Gold, but I was told later that Nefheru was buried alive in the sand outside the city gates. I didn't care. My life was neither richer, nor poorer because of it.

Reeds stood around, waiting on the princess. No, on the Ophar of Gifah. Even Dejenai, kind, wise, strong Dejenai, waited on her. In the distance, Anshassar lay, claws crossed, wings folded elegantly across his back.

I snorted and rose to my feet. Shesset looked up but I ignored her and balanced on my wing claws and stump to finally, truly, take Kida in my talons. I sprang into the sky, then, sending sand like needles in the rush of my wings. Each beat took me higher, and I returned to the river to follow my brother west.

The sun was high in the sky, and I flew for hours. The clouds had begun to streak pink when I found the spot on the banks where I had been born. The very spot where my mother had died. The palms were thicker, the rushes thinner, but I knew it in my bones. There was the mound that had buried her, and the depression that had been our nest. Five chicks hatched, two remaining. I was not good at counting, but that, I knew.

I hollowed out the depression and buried Kida deep. Sand was, after all, first of many spokes on the Wheel. It was fitting that it was also her last.

I turned to my mother and the shifting per ameht of sand that had formed over her. I gathered my breath and blew across the sand, longer and hotter than I'd ever blown. I rose into the air and flew in slow circles around it, painting the melting, gleaming mound with flame. I dropped back down, watched the mound harden into a shimmering surface that reflected the sun's fading light.

Glass.

A new spoke on the Wheel.

I lumbered to the edge of the river and stretched out. Like Anshassar, I draped my wings across my back and crossed my claws in front of me, content to watch the drama play out in the sky. Selis Anekh was the sun, Khamet and Amok the moons. They pulled no skyboats, they served no god. They were dragons, gods in their own right, and now I took my place among them, Goddess of the Nahr. I would watch the river forever.

And I did.

***

It seems so long ago that I laid my eggs. Like my mother, I hollowed out a depression in the sand for the nest. Not so deep, however, and under a river palm for shade. I remember 4 eggs and 4 hatchlings. Three blue and a green. No silver, no gold, and for that I was glad. They hatched, and they lived. They wrestled and they thrived, and I taught them to fish in waters, to harvest pic-bugs and scorpioch eggs, to watch for sobethi lurking in the reeds. As they matured, they left the nesting grounds for mates and lives and legends of their own.

I didn't miss them.

The reeds did not harass me in my station as river watcher. I think they knew I was there to protect them, and they rowed quietly as I reclined on the bank, wings folded, claws crossed. Some bowed, some touched their hearts. Often, they brought gifts of meat and dried fruit and cakes, and sometimes they would sacrifice an uru or sand buck and request a prayer be answered or a petition heard. I never answered prayers, but I did eat well.

Along with the offerings, reeds often brought gifts of jewels, gold, and carvings along with their paprush prayers, and they would leave them between my claws. At night, other reeds would slip in to steal the things left for me. I didn't mind. I had become a Market of Give and Take of my very own.

During those early years, I never let a Remoan warship back onto the Nahr. Each one that tried, I turned to cinder. I think, because of this, I held the power of nations in my claws. It was a fitting revenge against the land that had caused so much strife, and it set Gifah apart as a nation defended by dragons.

Once a year, Shesset would visit, bringing a parade of viziers and ministers, generals and suitors. Eventually, she brought a son. She would kneel between my claws, from dawn to dusk, head bowed in silence. She did this for many years and I barely noticed as she got smaller, thinner, greyer. She told me that her people would begin building her per ahmet behind me. It was tall and beautiful and adjacent to the per ahmet of glass that I had made for my mother. But when her people began to measure me with their levels and their rods, I knew they intended to build a per ameht around me. I lashed my great tail, destroying the foundation and dissuading them of that notion. They moved it directly behind my reclining form. It took them years to complete it, and it was the largest per ameht ever constructed. To this day, I believe it still is. Then, they built a third and a fourth, and then a temple dedicated to Selis Anekh herself. Eventually, my mother's clearing became what is now called the Valley of the Queens.

A fitting tribute to all of us, I thought.

One year, Shesset did not come, but her son came in her place. Then later, another Ophar, and another. A city grew up around the Valley of the Queens. It was loud and busy as reeds came to visit the temple and the per ahmets and me. There were many boats, and then ships with tall sails and barges that carried armies. Chariots became carts, carts became wagons, wagons became engines. I think there were wars. Years became decades, but I didn't count them. Dragons are not good at counting.

By then, I rarely moved, not even to hunt. I was very large and covered in a thick layer of sand and so, under the blistering gaze of Selis Anekh, I eventually baked into stone. I remembered the statues along the river at Karadoum, and I wondered if the reeds thought I was not dragon but sculpture now. I had much time for thinking, and I finally understood Netjeh, how he slept his days away and why he dreamed his path to the Fields of Ever Spring.

The Wheel turned and I watched, until one day, Selis Anekh herself came to me.

"Come, dear daughter," she said. "I am tired of pulling the skyboat of Rath'nahr. Let us trade places. I will watch the river and you can carry the god. All the people will gaze up at you and cover their eyes and marvel."

I thought a long moment.

"I have no wish to carry the god," I say. "I am no chariot dragon, forced to do the bidding of the reeds. I have pulled a cart and shattered it on the stones of a per ahmet. I have harnessed my flame to create glass and I founded the Valley of the Queens. I have broken the Wheel of Elements and reforged it in my image. I am Goddess of the Nahr, so, while the river still flows under my claws, I will stay and protect the land of Gifah."

She left me then, satisfied, but she also left me thinking.

The Sand and the Storm made the mighty river Nahr...

But what did the mighty river Nahr truly make?

The Nameless Sea, wide and vast, vibrant and deep.

Perhaps one day, I will leave the Valley of the Queens and take to the Nahr once more. My wings will span his great banks, my shadow will bring the night. One dip of my talon will flood cities, one flap will bring storms. I will leave the mighty Nahr for the Nameless Sea and search out Ankh Horys, the great dragon titan of the sea, who leaves trenches in the oceans so deep that no light can reach, and no fish can live. I will search for Aphorys, dragon god of the beginning, and I will search for Orophys, dragon god of the end. And I will take my place among the legends of the world, and perhaps then, I will soar to the skies to find my mother, Selis Anekh. Then, I will free her from the chains of a god.

I flex my claws.

The stone cracks.

The sand begins to spill.

OTHER BOOKS
BY
H. LEIGHTON DICKSON

Dragon of Ash & Stars: The Autobiography of a Night
Dragon
Dragon of Sand & Storm: The Autobiography of a
Goddess

EMPIRE OF STEAM
Cold Stone & Ivy: The Ghost Club
Cold Stone & Ivy 2: The Crown Prince

RISE OF THE UPPER KINGDOM
To Journey in the Year of the Tiger
To Walk in the Way of Lions
Songs in the Year of the Cat
Snow in the Year of the Dragon
Swallowtail & Sword: The Scholar's Book of Story &
Song

Coming Soon
To Fall from the Roof of the World
Cold Stone & Ivy 3: The Seventh House

Ship of Spells

ABOUT THE AUTHOR

H. Leighton Dickson grew up in the wilds of the Canadian Shield, where her neighbours were wolves, moose, deer, and lynx. She studied Zoology at the University of Guelph and worked in the Edinburgh Zoological Gardens in Scotland, where she was chased by lions, wrestled deaf tigers and fed antibiotics to Polar Bears by baby bottle. She has been writing since she was thirteen and pencilled her way through university with the help of DC Comics. She has a small zoo of her own at home, including three dogs, three cats, three kids and one husband.

An award-winning indie author, Heather has written the Scifi/Asian fantasy Upper Kingdom series along with Gothic thriller series, COLD STONE & IVY as well as the Award Winning DRAGON OF ASH & STARS: The Autobiography of a Night Dragon. She is now repped by Desiree Wilson of the Bent Agency.She also writes for Bayview Magazine, speaks at writing conventions and is a photoshop wizard when it comes to book covers.

Come join the conversation at
http://www.hleightondickson.com
or on Social Media
Facebook at http://www.facebook.com/HLeightonDickson
Twitter at https://twitter.com/hdickson62
Instagram at https://www.instagram.com/hdickson62

DRAGON OF SAND & STORM

www.ingramcontent.com/pod-product-compliance
Lightning Source LLC
Chambersburg PA
CBHW072002110726
47910CB00005B/1628